"Clive Irving maintains a confident grasp of facts while using fiction to explore the wider implications of events. Mr. Irving conveys the full range of political and religious differences that existed in the Middle East. . . . A talented writer!"
*The New York Times Book Review*

---

"FIRST-RATE."
*San Francisco Chronicle*

---

"An enthralling novel about a pivotal period in the history of the Middle East, carefully documented and beautifully written."
Chaim Potok

---

"EERIE IN ITS TIMELINESS . . . RICH WITH

PLOT AND SUBPLOT!"

*USA Today*

---

"Clive Irving gives readers an entirely fresh perspective on current events in the Mideast. Irving brings to vivid, gripping life a panorama of characters whose conflicts were dramatic then and still have profound repercussions."
*W*

---

"GRACEFULLY WRITTEN . . . ENTERTAINING!"
*Publishers Weekly*

# PROMISE THE EARTH

## Clive Irving

BALLANTINE BOOKS • NEW YORK

To Mimi Irving
whose research, as well as stimulation
and support, has made this book possible.

Library of Congress Catalog Card Number: 82-47789

ISBN 0-345-29444-0

This edition published by arrangement with Harper & Row, Publishers, Inc.

Manufactured in the United States of America

First Ballantine Books Edition: November 1983

*Maps by George Colbert*

## AUTHOR'S CAVEAT

The characters of Aaron and Sarah Aaronsohn, Absalom
Feinberg, Vladimir Jabotinsky, David Hogarth, and T.E.
Lawrence have been drawn from their own and other accounts,
but they cohabit with fictional characters in fictional situations.
I have tried, nonetheless, not to misrepresent them or their
beliefs.

*A historical note and chronology appears at the end of this novel for the benefit of readers who wish to familiarize themselves with the political developments that enter into the story.*

A Lord, a prince of the west side of the world, shall win the Land of Promise, that is the Holy Land, and he shall cause Mass to be performed again under that dying tree and then the tree shall become green and bear both fruit and leaves.

—*The Book of Sir John Mandeville*
Fourteenth century

# The Middle East in 1914

CASPIAN
SEA

•Tehran

P E R S I A

•Kuwait

P E R S I A N   G U L F

•Riyadh

▒▒▒▒▒ *Boundary of Ottoman Empire*

0          200          400 Miles

0     200     400 Kilometers

# The Middle East After World War I

TURKISH REPUBLIC
(est. 1923 from remnant of Ottoman Empire)

Lake Van

CYPRUS

SYRIA
(French mandate 1920)

*MEDITERRANEAN SEA*

LEBANON
• Damascus

Euphrates

Tigris

Baghdad

Haifa
PALESTINE
Tel Aviv
Gaza

• Amman

Alexandria

Jerusalem

I R A Q
(British mandate 1920)

TRANS-
JORDAN
(British mandate 1920)

Suez Canal

• Cairo

Nile

SINAI

• Akaba

E G Y P T
(British protectorate until 1922)

H I J A Z
(under Hashemites until 1925)

SULTANATE OF NEJD
(Saudi Arabia after 1926)

RED SEA

• Medina

• Jidda    • Mecca

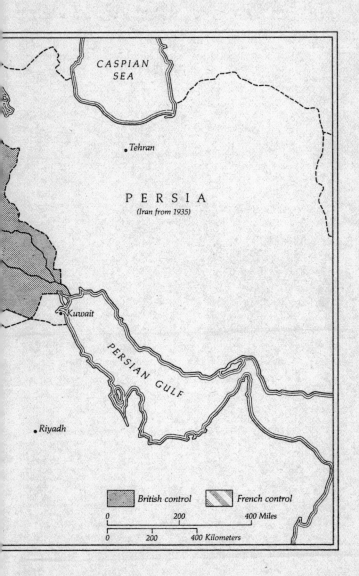

CASPIAN SEA

• Tehran

P E R S I A
(Iran from 1935)

• Kuwait

PERSIAN GULF

• Riyadh

British control     French control

0          200          400 Miles

0     200     400 Kilometers

# Part One

Part One

# 1

## Damascus ✳ April 1916

The weak seemed always to outnumber the strong; always the weak came in droves and the strong in platoons. This had been true for Asa Koblensky from the moment he had gained his first clear sense of his own place. Then it had been in Russia, with the fortunes of the Jews depending on the humor of the cossacks. Now, in Damascus, he quickly saw that the Syrian Arabs were another drove, a subject people with a broken spirit. He came to the city a fugitive, his senses narrowed to the needs of survival, but there seemed no escape from subjection. Here the Turk was master. It seemed the same under any sun.

And yet, even in flight, he was distracted by a contradiction: something endured. He began to realize that it was the city itself. Damascus mocked his European idea of age; for the first time he saw deep age, the real antiquity that was beyond clear human record. Damascus had outspanned the earth's prevailing gods; a city long before Christ and long before Mohammed, whose followers made it the capital of an Arab empire that stretched from the Atlantic to India. The Turks might rule here now, but it was still an Arab city, no doubt of that. Muslim on the surface, Muslim for thirteen hundred years, but the domes, minarets, and cupolas were adornments, the superstructure and not the essence.

The essence was in the gardens, abundant watered gardens shaded by poplars and scented by flowers and fruits and spices. Behind, to the west, the air was cooled by the iced peaks of the Lebanon range. To the south and east, the air was simmered by deserts. But the oasis air was mischief to the senses, an enticement apart from the worlds around it. To come to it as Koblensky did, from the bitter winter steppes of Europe, was to walk tantalized to an edge of things: behind him was a discarded life; in front of him an indistinct strangeness.

Clive Irving

He was a fugitive from the European war. But that war had now reached even Damascus. Koblensky had recently witnessed the barbarism of the Turks in his flight through Armenia. Before that there had been little valor and no mercy in what he had seen of war in the army of imperial Russia. At twenty-three, he was a veteran of war; he knew all of its falsehoods, its empty ideals. Moreover, he had sensed in that war's mounting chaos a greater upheaval, the end of an order. So he had taken the chance and run, driven by a sudden and barely conscious impulse to leave the drove. At first careless and lucky, he was now as seasoned in survival as an animal of the forest.

But in the melting pot of Damascus there was a refuge of sorts, in the confusion of tongues—Arabic, Turkish, French, German—Koblensky could lose himself in the anonymity of the destitute. It had covered him so far and brought him to the terraced steps of the Damascus railway station; yet to his feral instinct the steps seemed like the threshold of a trap, too inviting, too empty of threat—and too close to his goal, Palestine.

He went up the steps slowly. Once inside the station, he was engulfed in the chaos peculiar to an occupying army claiming its priority, chaos with a random danger of its own. At any moment the capricious hand of military authority could intervene.

By ill luck, the hand chose to fall on Koblensky's shoulder, from behind. He had been in line for two hours, waiting to reach the ticket office. It was not so much a line as a frantic, anarchic serpent, kicking its tail in an effort to reach the grille before the only train left. There seemed a deliberately staged contest between the raising of steam in the locomotive and the processing of passengers, a contest that a good half of those in the line would lose. The man in front of Koblensky was an Arab peasant carrying a skeletal chicken in a wooden cage. His transaction at the grille was prolonged and punctuated by several harangues. Finally a door at the side of the grille opened, the chicken and cage disappeared through it, and the ticket was handed over.

Behind the grille, as Koblensky waited, the clerk was disputing possession of the chicken with a Turkish army private. When he eventually turned to face Koblensky he had lost his claim, to a higher sanction than his own. He looked at Koblensky's linen jacket and flannel shirt, then at Koblensky's face—in order of evaluation. Koblensky's first problem was language. He pushed his papers under the grille and said nothing. On top of the papers

4

was a ticket needing endorsement for the stage of the line between Damascus and Jerusalem. With the ticket were two sets of papers, one in Turkish and the other in English. The clerk was chewing hard on something. He moved the ticket to one side, looked at the Turkish papers, and spat on the floor. He moved from his stool, taking just this set of papers. Koblensky overheard a protracted conversation, apparently with the possessor of the chicken. The chicken was the only moving object left in Koblensky's vision. Preening itself in the cage, it managed miraculously to inflate its emaciated breast to the point, unwisely, of seeming wholesome.

The clerk returned, without looking at Koblensky. He ripped out the redundant portion of the ticket and searched among a battery of rubber stamps. The English papers lay with Koblensky's discolored portrait on top. Behind Koblensky there was a new commotion as several flat wagons were shunted to the end of the train. Each mechanical impact was followed by fretful cries in Arabic. Koblensky kept his eyes on the rubber stamp as it was inked crimson and then smudged onto the buff ticket. Feet scurried across the platform; attenuated coughs came from the locomotive. Half a second before the hand fell on his shoulder, Koblensky was aware of a pungent wave of musk. The hand had two gold rings that rucked his jacket. He was pulled around and to one side of the grille.

"You come, please."

Koblensky was surprised that so short a man was so strong—the arm that pulled him around was extended upward to reach his shoulder. It belonged to a Turkish officer. Koblensky picked up his carpetbag and, still in the grip of the Turk, went through the door that had swallowed the chicken.

"Here, please."

He was taken into a large office to one side of the ticket counter. The wall facing the platform had a fine-mesh screen which gave a view of most of the train. At the far end, in front of a blank whitewashed wall, was a heavy mahogany desk, a chair behind it and three before it. On the left-hand side, against another whitewashed wall, was a cot with one threadbare blanket. The private who had commandeered the chicken came behind Koblensky as he followed the officer to the desk. The officer directed Koblensky into one of the three chairs and lowered himself into the more capacious leather chair behind the desk. The gold on his fingers was repeated in his mouth.

"American?"

Koblensky nodded.

Only one of the officer's eyes was mobile. It looked Koblensky up and down, becoming dubious. The Turk was unfamiliar with Americans, therefore an American should *look* unfamiliar, but Koblensky did not. He had a drawn-in, weathered face—weathered in some hard northern place. The Turk knew that look; the face might almost have been a Tatar's, Asiatic. American? He unfolded the document on the desk.

"You travel from Van?"

Koblensky wondered why, so frequently in Turkey, authority went with deformity. The eye stopped moving over the paper and lifted to him again.

"This paper. Signature is Djevdet Bey."

"The governor general of Van."

"Yesssss. Governor general. Koblinskee . . . ?" The moving eye finally aligned itself with the static one. "Koblinskee . . . Russian name." He swiveled slightly in the chair, but the eye remained fixed on Koblensky. *"Russian."*

Somewhere behind Koblensky, the private shuffled his boots on concrete. The room had two competing odors; the officer's musk and, from some invisible source, urine.

The officer waited for his assertion to be answered. Through the door the chicken could be heard clearing its throat.

"Many Americans came from Russia."

"Parents? Your parents Russian?"

"They went to America twenty-five years ago. I was born there."

The officer looked down at the papers again. Without looking up, he said, "Why you in Van?"

"There is a hospital there." Koblensky nodded toward the papers. "It explains—Dr. Clarence Ussher. I took medical supplies there from Constantinople."

"You Jew." The rogue eye wandered over Koblensky. "You Jew."

"Yes." Koblensky was unblinking.

"This mission in Van. It Christian mission. Why Jew go?"

"Why not?"

The officer spoke in Turkish to the private, who had come closer to Koblensky from behind. The private picked up Koblensky's carpetbag. He ripped open the straps and emptied the contents on the floor: a pair of trousers, two more flannel

6

shirts, a towel, a toilet pouch, a pair of rough canvas shoes with worn rope soles, a small bottle of brandy, which broke on the floor and splashed over the shirts, and a silk scarf.

The officer got up and walked around the desk, surveying the mess. He seemed disappointed. He pointed to the toilet pouch and told the private to pick it up. It was of gray canvas overlapped with two leather laces. The officer pulled the laces free and opened the pouch, finding a half-used cake of rough soap and a small hairbrush. He dropped the soap on the floor and kicked it away, then held up the brush and pouch, one in each hand, close to Koblensky's face.

"This I see before. Is Russian. Russian *Army*."

Koblensky shrugged. "It came from the hospital. That is possible. The Russians were there."

The officer slowly lowered his left hand, holding the pouch, and then, with a flick of his right wrist, hit Koblensky across the face with the back of the hairbrush.

"You lie."

The lower left corner of Koblensky's lip was split and blood began to run down his chin. His hands clenched at the sides of the chair. The private had come up directly behind him.

The officer walked slowly back to resume his seat, putting the brush and pouch on his desk on either side of the papers, arranged like exhibits.

"Russian Jew," he said, nodding confirmation of his own opinion. "Why Russian Jew go Jerusalem? I want know that."

Beyond the long metal screen, the sounds of the locomotive were more imperative, the steam reaching pressure. The Turkish officer glanced away to the screen and then back to Koblensky, parting his thighs slightly. Nothing in the debris on the floor would have fitted him, least of all Koblensky's trousers, cut for a man of almost ascetic spareness. The private's eyes kept straying to the flannel shirts.

The blood had reached Koblensky's lapel. He said nothing and moved not a muscle.

The chicken beyond the door broke into an operatic pitch. The door opened. A man entered who was so tall that he had to stoop to clear the doorframe. He wore a white naval uniform and, reasserting his height, came full tilt toward the desk, brushing past the private and Koblensky and stepping over the mess.

"Captain Mahil!" he barked in precise English. "You are supposed to be supervising this train, yes?"

7

The Turk recoiled, his chair sliding into the wall. "Your car is ready, Captain," he said weakly.

"*Ready?* Yes, everything is ready—but for one thing. There is no drinking water on the entire train."

"No time boil it, Captain."

About to resume the verbal assault, the captain saw the brush and the pouch on the desk. As though suddenly aware of the room's composition, he turned and took in Koblensky. "What is happening here?"

The Turk stumbled through an explanation in English, ending with, "I think he not American."

Koblensky saw that the captain's insignia were German.

"A Jew?" The German picked up the papers from the desk and scrutinized them, then turned to Koblensky. "You have other papers to prove your identity?"

Koblensky nodded toward the open door. "The booking clerk has them, with my ticket."

The private was sent to retrieve them. The German was able to sit on a corner of the desk without his feet leaving the floor. He had a florid, patrician face and then, light hair cut short. His cap was in his hand. He repeated himself: "A Jew? With a Russian name?"

The private gave him the papers. He compared the poor photograph with the man sitting before him, the blood drying on his chin.

"These papers seem in order," said the German, after further contemplation. He turned to Koblensky. "I am Captain Wernher Brusse, of the battleship *Goeben*. I, too, am going to Palestine. You may join me in my car." He swung away from the desk and bent across it to the Turk. "He had nothing of value, I suppose? Fool. The Americans are not in the war and we must hope they never are. We will wait until you can boil some water. We cannot leave without it." He nodded toward the floor. "See that this man's possessions are returned to him."

No other word was offered in explanation. The Turk complied with gestures of supplication, the contrast in their heights making the exchange grotesque.

Koblensky was not greatly reassured by the change in his fortune. Captain Brusse's car was one of a number of ill-sorted wagons toward the train's rear, its wooden frame painted a dull gray. This exterior bleakness gave way inside to improvised grand luxe, as though the fittings and furnishings had been ransacked from elsewhere and made to fit as best they could. An elaborate gilt chandelier descended so far that Brusse had to walk around rather than beneath it. There were two padded couches, one along each side of the car, horsehair breaking from several ruptures in their velvet, and at one end a circular table with a top of marble delicately inlaid in a mosaic design. The four chairs, gilt again, were, like the table, screwed to the coarse boards of the floor. As Brusse led Koblensky into the saloon, a Turkish orderly in the galley was trying to light an oil stove while a Turkish soldier arrived with a kettle of water.

"Sit, please." Brusse indicated a couch. For several minutes he checked his bags and hectored the orderly, ignoring Koblensky. It was humid in the train; the sun had gone and beyond the canopy of the station it had started to rain. On the platform, the line still thrashed around the ticket office, hardly shorter. Through a small curtained window Koblensky saw the Turkish officer walking off with the chicken in the cage.

Returning to the saloon, Brusse began to unbutton his tight uniform jacket.

"So . . . ?" he said, without expression. "A Jew bound for Jerusalem. A pilgrimage, yes?"

Koblensky was more unsettled by this apparent samaritan than he had been by the Turk. "It is my first visit."

"You choose a strange time for it—in the middle of a war." His jacket now hanging loose, Brusse sat on the opposite couch, picking up a small red-covered book. "You see this?" He waved the book. "The most valuable book in Syria. The Baedeker guide. Every German officer has one. Every Turkish officer wants one. That was what the station commandant hoped to find in your bag, perhaps." For the first time, Brusse smiled, though not in a way to encourage Koblensky to feel easier. "Dr. Baedeker fortunately anticipates armies as well as travelers, serving war as well as the grand tour. Very thorough." He put the book beside him on the couch and his unfolding frame became slightly less formal. "You are fortunate, my young friend. I do not speak Turkish. I face an unpleasant journey. To find someone who speaks English, this was salvation in the wilderness. I want conversation—and civilization." His patrician nose sniffed the rank air. "In Syria, movement is ventilation, a slight relief. The train, perhaps, will soon stir itself."

When finally they did get under way, the reason for anchoring the furniture became clear. Even though the train seldom reached thirty miles an hour, the track was so poor that each seam of the car seemed about to pull apart. The pretensions of the chandelier were proved empty by the onset of dusk; there was no generator on the train and the orderly lit four acetylene lamps on wall brackets. In this erratic light they moved to the marble table for supper. With the freer talk between them, Koblensky had lost some of his uneasiness and Brusse some of his military formality, aided by a bottle of Moselle from a private cache.

"In this war," said Brusse, "we suffer an alliance of the incompatible." The train had slowed to a crawl in the darkness, but still shook. "You see—German trains, Turkish tracks. The Prussian and the Oriental." His fastidious table manners were at odds with the saloon's motion: his chin was bright with fat. "With the Turks, it is suddenly the end of the Middle Ages. They cannot adjust." He dabbed his chin dry with a napkin and gave up the effort of eating. "The once great Turks. For centuries the only real force in Asia. You know about them—how they began? They were the mercenaries. Hired by the caliph as palace guards. An old story: Who shall guard the guards? They chose their moment—and suddenly they had the Muslim Empire. The Arabs made the empire, but the Turks were their swords." Shouting over the din and flushed by the Moselle, Brusse said, "Look at them now: degenerate, barbaric . . . hopeless."

"What are you doing here?" said Koblensky.

"You are the one to answer that question, my friend, not I."

Koblensky realized his error. "Every Jew wants to see Palestine once."

Brusse relented a little. "Just so. More and more Jews, I think." He emptied the last of the wine into Koblensky's glass. "They talk of the Return. Is that your belief too?"

"These days, the Jew cannot be certain of anything except that he is a Jew."

"Whatever you are or are not, my friend, you are certainly a Jew." Brusse put his napkin on the table and looked steadily at Koblensky. "Your papers say you came from Van. I know what has been happening there—and in many other places. They are slaughtering the Christians, the Armenians. We have been trying to get reports, reliable reports. What can you tell me?"

"It happened before to the Armenians, but that time they resisted, they fought back. This time their priests pray to God— and lead them out to the slaughter. Most of the men are killed, many of the women and children. The younger women—the

Turks take those for themselves. Unless they convert, become Muslims, they are killed too."

Brusse looked at Koblensky as though puzzled, then quietly said, "You do not seem sympathetic."

"They should fight."

"That is a new note from a Jew."

For the first time, Koblensky was provoked beyond his self-restraint, beyond caution. "In Russia, the Jews fight."

"In Russia . . . ?" Brusse repeated the words slowly. "You seem young to know so much, to have traveled so far." The train had stopped. "Your English is good, but not the equal of your curiosity, I think."

Koblensky finished the Moselle, more uncomfortable now under Brusse's assessing eyes.

"English is not your first language," insisted Brusse.

Koblensky tried to move his chair back, forgetting that it was anchored. "More American than English." He smiled.

"Perhaps. America is doing strange things to the language—that is so. I learned my English in England; perhaps you can hear that? I have often wondered: Do we think in our first language or our second when we speak it?"

Nearest the window, Koblensky peered out, seeing nothing. "I wonder why we have stopped."

"It is useless to wonder." Brusse stood up. "It is a good time to try to sleep. You will be comfortable on one of these couches?" Brusse went to his bunk and the orderly cleared the table. The train remained where it was. In ten minutes they were both asleep.


When Koblensky awoke it was not because of movement but because of light, a weak gray light at the windows. The train was not moving. For a few seconds he could not place himself; the transition from sleep to consciousness had become the hardest part of his struggle to keep his nerve. Each night brought a gallery of horrors, horrors of recent substance. He had seen more death among the innocent than among the armed—pyres of the Armenian dead, death on an infamous scale. All across Turkey. To save his nerve he had made himself callous, but by night his mind was not under rein. Each night weakened him. The last of his drive had nearly gone in bringing him this far. Now, looking at the interior of the car, with its absurd furnishings, he reflected

11

on the latest improbable agent of his salvation, the sagacious German who had so nearly penetrated his guard and his secret. But then he had already lost faith in the laws of probability; nothing seemed probable or improbable anymore. What was reality? The car's incongruity was a kind of waking madness.

He climbed down from the train and touched earth, the flint-peppered earth of an embankment, where the track ran across a shallow depression. The rain had stopped, but the humid gray pall foreshortened all horizons. The ground on each side of the track had the desolation of a battlefield: what seemed once to have been orchards was now a crater-pocked waste, relieved by patches of bright wild desert flowers that had sprouted from severed tree roots and had been intensified in their bloom by the rain. These bursts of color in an otherwise monotone landscape were not consoling; they were like blood in the snow or the colors of Armenian peasant dresses stiff with blood along the roadsides.

It was more than a minute before he realized what was wrong: There was no locomotive at the head of the train. Brusse's Turkish orderly clambered down from the car, following Koblensky. Realizing the absence of the locomotive, he began shouting. Eventually Brusse, too, appeared, unshaven and only half dressed. The orderly found a Turkish sergeant with enough English to provide explanation: The locomotive had overrun a water stop; in order to reach the next, it had had to run light. The train was waiting for its return.

Brusse and Koblensky walked along the track to get exercise.

"Look," said Koblensky, indicating the track. In several places the rails had broken free of the wooden clamps, which had rotted with the combination of heat and rain. "These sleepers will give way anytime."

Brusse astride a rail, looked up slowly. "Sleepers?"

Koblensky pressed a foot on the powdering wood. "These."

Brusse nodded. "I understand." He turned to resume walking, but this time encircled Koblensky with an arm. "You have given yourself away, my young friend. You did not learn your English in America. In America these are called ties." Now his foot kicked at the wood. "Railroad ties. Only in England, for some reason I do not understand, are these called sleepers. Rail*way*, also. You see—two different languages."

Koblensky was propelled along in the German's grip.

"I think it would be best if you did not try to explain. I do not think I want to know." Brusse was talking into the air, not to Koblensky. "From the beginning, there was something about your use of English. . . ." He stopped, releasing Koblensky. He pointed to the cratered landscape. "This valley was once full of olive orchards. Everywhere, wherever the tracks run, they have taken the wood for the locomotives. Last night, why the train was going so slowly—that was not because of the condition of the track. The wood they burn is green, and wet."

He turned to walk back toward the train. "It takes fifteen years for an olive tree to bear its first crop. You can imagine what that will do to these people."

But Koblensky's mind was not on the plight of olive orchards; he cursed his own carelessness and was now even more uncertain of the German's attitude. This sudden changing of the subject was plainly meant to reassure him, but in effect he was Brusse's hostage.

They remained silent on the walk to Brusse's car. There was no sign of the locomotive.

Their breakfast was unleavened bread and goat's cheese, with Turkish coffee. Brusse, now in a fresh uniform, his hair lacquered, picked at the food. Koblensky, to whom this breakfast was superior to most he had recently seen, ate with a nervous intensity.

Breaking a long silence, Brusse said, "You have the appetite of a man who expects each meal to be his last."

Koblensky decided to end the deception. He could not, in the circumstances, do much else. He edged aside his plate and spoke with a calmness he did not feel. "I have deserted from the Russian Army. I was in a unit at Urmia, on the border of Persia and Turkey. I was very sick, too sick to leave when the army pulled back. Some American missionaries were giving sanctuary to the Armenians, and they took care of me. They passed me to other Americans at Van. When it seemed the Russian Army was coming back into Van, I got the Americans to make out the false papers you saw."

"A deserter?" Brusse sipped his coffee. "The penalty for that is death. On what grounds did you desert?"

"There is a lot of discontent in the army."

"Bolsheviks?"

"Many. Yes. But that was not my reason. For years I had thought of coming to Palestine. And I was halfway there—or so it seemed. I did not understand what was really happening. Months . . . it has taken months."

"And your English. Where did you learn that?"

"From an Englishwoman. An Englishwoman in Russia. My father was bailiff of a large estate, and the Englishwoman looked after the children there, and she taught us English. I was her favorite pupil."

Brusse smiled, apparently convinced. "You took a chance, with those papers. They were not so well done." He resumed his breakfast, readjusting the napkin at his neck.

Koblensky realized that Brusse was in some way relieved by having learned the truth, that he must have been as concerned as Koblensky about the deception and about the calling of a bluff.

"This is not a good time in Palestine," said Brusse, "for Jews, or for anyone. There are serious shortages of food. The Turks have taken what stocks there were. I have seen stores of sugar left out in the rain, washing away. They take the grain for the army, then spill it all over the ground, while the Arabs in Damascus riot for food."

There was a distant whistle of steam.

The approach of the locomotive made Brusse's manner more urgent. "You should take care, great care. The Jews who have remained in Palestine—there are still many of them—are expected to be loyal. I hope so. We depend on them. Whenever something seems to work, there is a Jew involved. Everybody uses the Jews."

The car shook with the impact of the locomotive, coupling too fast. The chandelier above them gyrated, shedding flakes of gilt on the floor.

For another two hours the train labored across a high plateau, traveling due south. Sitting by the window, Koblensky felt the journey take on a trancelike quality, the monotony of the landscape and the undulations of the train dulling his senses. Brusse had fallen asleep on the couch. Patches of sunlight appeared in the middle distance. The cloud cover was breaking up. The train crossed a low bridge over a wadi. Camels drank from the saffron-stained water, and on the far side by the track were a few mud-brick homes. Beyond them Koblensky saw a dozen or so black tents, the first view of Bedouins. This must be the fringe of Arabia. The tents spoke of places and a life strange to him. Alongside the track, they seemed indifferent to the jarring intrusion of the train. Perversely, he felt himself to be the anachronism here, not the Arabs among the tents. They had an affinity with this place, they inhabited it as naturally as an animal or even a rock. He was coming to "inhabit" a place, but what did that mean? To reclaim roots? What roots? For Koblensky, "inhabit" was a word free of theology. *Everybody uses the Jews*. Brusse's words ate into him and were the only text he needed to confirm his starkly expedient choice of Palestine. To renew himself as a Jew, he needed a foothold in a place where no one could make a superior claim to the Jew and where Jews could no longer turn away to another horizon. "Inhabit" meant having a presumptive claim to press, with the chance of success, the chance to prove the *will* of the Jews as a people, no more a drove.

The train began to brake again, the brakes catching unevenly and jerking the car, waking Brusse. He pulled out a watch.

"We must be at Deraa."

Koblensky felt the train switch tracks and saw out the window that they were at a junction. There were scores of flatbed trucks, some carrying ancient field guns.

"We should turn west here," said Brusse, stretching the sleep out of his body, pulling his tunic straight. "In theory, the parting of God and War. The line south is the pilgrims' railway to Medina. In peacetime it is the overland route for the hajj, the journey to Mecca. We Germans built the railway so that the Turkish sultan could claim to have the pilgrims' welfare close to his heart. But as you see"—Brusse paused to peer at the guns—"conveniently, it also carries armies when there is trouble in the desert. Now we have to reinforce the garrisons all along the line. It is hard, almost impossible, to defend—if they attack."

"Who would attack it?"

Brusse hesitated as though wary of the question's innocence. Then he said, "The line down to Medina runs through the territory of several Arab chieftains. They are all supposed to be loyal to the caliph, and therefore to Turkey." Brusse shrugged. "Loyalty. Loyalty in the desert is inclined to vary from day to day."

The train stopped. Koblensky felt that Brusse had held back from telling him more. Without the relief of air moving through the car, it was suddenly very hot. The last of the cloud was behind them and the town of Deraa, approaching noon, was sweltering. The locomotive took on water and wood fuel. Brusse

15

and Koblensky got down from the car and walked over two lines of track to the station buildings. There were several large groups of Turkish troops sitting or squatting alongside one of the tracks in the shade of a train. A Turkish officer appeared from an office and came toward Brusse, greeting him obsequiously in broken English. He took them to a squalid but cool room and gave them coffee from a hearth. Through a half-garbled explanation, it became clear that some change had been made to the route of their train—for, it was claimed, Brusse's own benefit. Brusse seemed unconvinced. Walking back to the train, he said, "It seems that you won't go to Jerusalem on this train. It is being diverted, but I do not understand where or why. I think it would be wise for you to remain with me until we find out."

This news had also reached the rear of their train, where confusion and dispute broke out. All civilians were being turned off, leaving only the troops. Koblensky knew his own security remained best in the hands of Brusse. As they climbed back into the car, the orderly called from the galley. He waved a new prize: a chicken, still flapping its wings. He drew a knife across the fowl's neck, splashing the floor with its blood and laughing wildly.

To dignify this sinewy meat, Brusse produced more Moselle. The train was now following the sun west, and by the time they had finished eating, the landscape was transformed. In place of the desert they ran alongside a river, the Yarmuk, and gradually descended through mountain ranges, on their right the heights of Golan. In the river valley it was cooler and in some fields small oxen pulled wooden plows, while in others the winter crops were sprouting. The olive orchards here had so far survived and were in blossom.

Watching Koblensky's expression, Brusse said, "These are the gates of Palestine, my friend. You have perhaps heard the phrase 'the desert and the sown'? This is the sown. In a short while you will see Galilee—on the right as we come around this final escarpment."

To his own surprise, and with mixed emotions, Koblensky was affected by the associations of the landscape. When they reached the lakeside it seemed disconcertingly close to the Victorian watercolor illustrations he recalled from English storybooks: the placid water, the triangular-sailed fishing boats, and brooding in the west, the mountains, shaded with a gathering storm, a Biblical parable of the idyll menaced by divine retribution. The train turned south again to run down the Jordan valley, which seemed a subtropical jungle, the river lined with huge reeds displaying plumes of white blossom. A line from the Old Testament came back to him: "Behold, he shall come like a lion from the pride of Jordan." Voices, incantations, indelible sounds were intruding from the past. "The pride of Jordan" and the Hebrew for "pride": *ga-on*. A confluence of different voices rising in this unsettling chorus.

And Brusse was saying, "Think of how many people have fought here, over this ground—the Egyptians, the Romans, the Greeks, the Arabs, the Mongols, the Crusaders. *Why here?*"

Koblensky struggled to suppress his voices. They weakened his secular fatalism. The train lurched away from the river, heading west again.

"And so to Armageddon," said Brusse.

Koblensky said, "Too many names."

Brusse laughed. "The Bible and Dr. Baedeker go hand in hand."

"The Bible makes bad history."

Brusse looked at Koblensky with a new curiosity. "That, from a Jew, sounds like heresy—or Bolshevism."

"It encourages superstitions."

"Ah—superstitions! Harmless enough, surely?"

"If you wait for miracles, you wait forever. No one is going to make the Red Sea part for us now."

"You are too unsentimental, my friend. Perhaps you underrate the importance of imagination."

"Imagination is a luxury, or a distraction."

"You will have a very bleak life if you think that."

Koblensky did not reply. Brusse had vaguely annoyed him, countering each of the younger man's assertions with his more open mind, as though to be so sure of oneself, to be so dogmatic, was to be immature. A bleak life was, in any case, something Koblensky had already adjusted to. He liked the German, but the crisp white uniforms, the urbanity that tried to surmount the surrounding squalor, the pedantry of habit, all seemed to Koblensky a muddle of values, a failure to adjust, a misplaced standing on dignity. He suspected that Brusse thought him a curiosity that he was reluctant to drop back into the water from which he had been fished—as long as the German remained amused.

The track was running between mountains again, with a smaller river, a tributary of the Jordan, to their left. The day's effort had been nearly too much for the locomotive; they were on a shallow gradient, slowed to little more than walking pace, with the pistons wheezing. Brusse retired for a siesta in his bunk, leaving Koblensky with his uneasy speculations. What was a German naval officer doing so far from his command, traveling on his own? Where were Brusse's loyalties? His disparagement of his Turkish allies, his evident alarm at the fate of the Armenians, his practiced aloofness, confused Koblensky. The train's exhaustion underlined his own. But at least he was in Palestine now.

The train passed a summit and began to pick up speed. Only when Brusse reappeared, hair again freshly plastered back, did Koblensky note the train's recovery and its outstripping of his own slackened pulse. Brusse was preparing for something, was groomed and rehearsed for it, and a trace nervous.

It was nearly dusk. The sky was different from any Koblensky had seen. The sun was out of sight, ahead of the train. Where its glow dissipated into a darkening blue, the mingled shades gave the sky extraordinary depth. Russian skies, northern skies, lost all their body as the day died; this sky had substance and instead of retreating from the night seemed to embrace it.

Slowly, almost distractedly, Brusse said, "The end of a day is always the worst time. That is when I am forced to realize how long it has been since I saw Germany, and my family. All these days lost." He brushed dust from the trousers he had just changed into. "I have a daughter—she must be about your age—and a son. My son is fighting in France. He writes very long letters to me, very long. They take so long to reach me I can never know if he is still alive as I read them." He seemed in some way to be balancing Koblensky's existence and survival with that of his son, perhaps even hoping for a transmutation. "The things he says in his letters are things I wish he could have said to my face, but I don't think, if I had been there, he could have. You understand that? The letters and the distance have made it possible for us to come closer. That is the strange thing, is it not?"

Koblensky nodded, aware that Brusse expected more of him, but he had nothing to say.

"Is your father still alive?" said Brusse.

"Yes."

18

"Do you miss him?"

The question seemed as misplaced as the chandelier swinging uselessly above them. Koblensky could not even be subjective with himself; he was armored against that as against so much else in the severance from his past. But he was too dependent on Brusse's humor to evade the question completely, so he shrugged and offered a dishonest banality. "Sometimes."

The orderly came in to light the lamps, releasing Koblensky from further difficulty.

"We're coming to Affula," said Brusse, all intimacy dropped. "Beyond here I don't yet know my destination. This train will not take you any further."

Out of a window Koblensky saw a road coming up from the south, swinging round to run parallel to the railroad. A carriage drawn by three mules was overtaking several groups of camels. Oil flames by the side of the road illuminated clusters of Arabs. The train passed over a switching point and began to vibrate; the single track was joined by another and then a third, all parallel. There were more flatbeds, this time laden with heavy equipment. Koblensky saw several large stacks of logs and then two other locomotives getting up steam. Beyond the railyards were mud-brick buildings and beyond them several larger, plastered structures that looked like supply depots. There must have been a generator too, because for the first time since Damascus there were overhead electric lights as they came into the station.

"For the moment, you will stay with me, please," said Brusse. "Leave your bag here, with my orderly." He led Koblensky down to the platform. There were signs in Arabic, French, and even English. One said BARBERSHOP. The waiting room and administrative buildings were all on one central platform. On the far side of the track was another train, much shorter than their own, four nondescript passenger cars and, between these and the locomotive, an astonishing anomaly: a European wagon-lit, painted dark blue with gold piping, elaborate silk curtains at the windows, ablaze inside with electric light. At one end of this car Turkish soldiers passed up provisions from a trolley—a whole lamb carcass, chickens, a large canister of milk, even canned fruit. At the other end of the car, a long Turkish carpet had been laid on the platform between the train and an office or vestibule. Two guards flanked this carpet. But from among these exotic impressions Koblensky singled out one that was inimitably familiar—the smell, transcending all others, of chicken soup.

19

Brusse led him toward the carpet. Until they saw Brusse approaching, the guards had a dilatory, tired stance. Seeing his crisp white uniform and authoritarian bearing, they came suddenly to a rigid but still deficient form of salute. Brusse ignored the salute and climbed into the train. Koblensky, tieless and in his last clean flannel shirt under the crumpled and stained linen jacket, felt the guards' scrutiny but avoided their eyes and followed Brusse up the steps. The smell of soup, even stronger, mingled with others: coffee being roasted, cigars. Lights were suddenly harsh, forcing him to blink. Before he could focus, he heard Brusse being greeted in French-accented English. He also felt people suddenly behind him, two more guards who had been at the door of the car.

Brusse was taking off his braided cap and Koblensky saw two enormous dark hands come around his waist, and sleeves as gilded with rank as Brusse's cap. A face appeared at each of Brusse's cheeks in turn, giving an elaborate French-style kiss. On the second kiss this face moved clear of Brusse's and eyes settled on Koblensky from over Brusse's shoulder. Koblensky was later to recall this moment, this apprehension, as intuitive: the man's character was imparted like a comprehensive diagram on his mind, not instantly understood but there permanently for reference. It was a Turkish face, but more European than Oriental, with white skin, heavy black waxed mustache and eyebrows, and eyes that were strangely feminine, long lashes over hazel. The man was completely bald, and under the electric light the head was pocked and veined.

Brusse disengaged himself. "General, I wanted you to meet this young man." He stepped aside, leaving the Turk to scrutinize the austere figure behind him.

The Turk was nearly as tall as Brusse, but much bulkier, though with a muscular weight gathered in his thighs—thighs, Koblensky suspected, of a horseman, probably one who rode without stirrups, as many Turks did to develop their balance. Koblensky became aware of other eyes on him, of several other Turkish officers at a table.

Brusse continued, "I found him in Damascus. There was a small problem with his papers." He looked from the Turk to Koblensky. "I was able to clear that up. It appears that he is American—an American Jew, coming to settle in Palestine."

Koblensky realized that Brusse had at that moment committed himself to the imposture.

The Turk rested a hand on each hip. "An American?" He paused, running his eyes over Koblensky. "A Jew?"

Brusse addressed Koblensky. "This is General Jemal Pasha. The commander of all forces in Syria."

# 2

## London ✳ April 1916

The rain was corrosive with soot, streaking the windows of the cab. Occasionally patches of color glistened on walls: war posters, strident with patriotism. But the city's mood was dour. In Mayfair, the few pedestrians were bent within their mackintoshes against the downpour. Coming here from Hampstead, the cab had passed from gentility to drabness, from drabness to squalor, from squalor to a brassy, commercial vulgarity, and now, finally, into these gilded streets.

The cab's speed gave Michael Bron decent cause to hold Tessa Stanbridge close to him; hers was the only fragrance in the air to counter the permeating fog. As they turned into Park Street she moved gently apart, adjusted her hat, and coughed. Her cough was a slight thing, deprecating the evening.

"Dinner afterwards," he said.

"We *could* have had dinner without stirring from my flat."

"I know. But I had to come."

"*Had* to?"

Motor cabs were still something of a novelty to their drivers. The vehicle braked too sharply and, planing on water, sideslipped to the curb. She was flung forward and he moved quickly to restrain her.

"*Really!*" she said, readjusting her hat.

Beyond the glass partition the driver was soaking wet. His goggled face turned, featureless, and mouthed apology which they could not hear.

A doorman stepped forward with an umbrella.

Bron stuck his head under the dripping canopy of the driver's compartment. "You should take more care. Far too fast for the conditions."

"She's a bit of an 'andful, sir."

"All the more reason to take care."

"Very sorry, sir."

Bron gave the man a coin.

To pass from the street into the house was to leave not only the oppressive night but also England and English style. One foot on the marble floors of the lobby and they were in a miniature Versailles. A Francophile taste had taken the small house and fashioned it, from the Savonnerie carpets to the Limoges enamel plaques on the walls. The smallness of the house—by Mayfair standards—made a discipline of its own. It was not overstuffed but, like a museum, had been discriminatingly arranged to cover its chosen epoch. Bron saw a kind of ownership here that was more secure than nationality; wealth on this scale represented a greater estate.

"Mr. Michael Bron and Miss Tessa Stanbridge." A footman in Empire livery, with powdered wig, had taken their card and ushered them into a crowded salon.

Few people turned to look at the newcomers, but their hostess broke away to receive them.

"Mr. Bron . . . and Miss . . . ?"

"Stanbridge."

"Lord Stanbridge's daughter?"

"Yes, Mrs. de Rothschild."

"Of course! My husband knows your father."

"Your husband is with the army in France, I believe?"

"Yes." Mrs. de Rothschild shrugged and talked to them both. "James felt, with all our French involvements, he should serve, but it drags on so. . . ."

She was hard to assess: very young, with a beauty as fine and as fragile as her porcelains, but Bron fancied there was a force of will in her too. After a little more small talk she left them and they fell under the predatory eye of a man Bron recognized. Sir Archie Ferris was what the Edwardians had called a "heavy swell." He carried his substantial gut as though it were a point of allure, and pressed it now toward Tessa Stanbridge, squinting over pince-nez. To Bron, Ferris personified the vice of a class he despised: self-assurance without merit; rank without endeavor; complacency without cause.

"Harry Stanbridge's gel, I believe?"

She said, "I didn't quite catch your name."

"Ferris. Sir Archibald. M.P." He was annoyed.

"Ferris? You lost Ilkley in the election, I thought."

23

"I have Bournemouth West now."

"Bournemouth West?" She smiled. "Much safer, I imagine."
His eyes hardened.

Bron reluctantly rescued him. "Have you met the guest of
honor yet, Sir Archibald?"

"Met him before." Sir Archie's gaze moved from Tessa. "In
Manchester, some years back. He seems to have come a long
way since then, a damned long way." The tone implied a kind
of social offense. "Now he's charmed the Rothschilds."

"Yes. He is said to be very persuasive," said Bron, catching
sight of a cluster in one corner. "That must be him, the small
man with a beard."

"That's right. Holding court." Sir Archie deftly took a glass
of sherry as a silver tray floated by at chest height.

"Dr. Weizmann?" said Tessa, following their gaze. "What is
he a doctor of, by the way?"

"Chemistry," said Sir Archie, his watch chain brushing her
hip. "Didn't get a professorship, though. Too much interested in
his other passion; made the university nervous."

"You mean Zionism?" she said.

Bron could distinguish Weizmann's voice, though without
clearly hearing what he was saying. About a dozen people stood
around him.

"They say he has a messianic quality," said Sir Archie,
draining the sherry. "I always suspect men like that."

"He has won converts in the government," said Bron. "Had
you heard that?"

Sir Archie grunted. "Apparently so. Very tricky, if you ask
me. I mean, the Zionist headquarters is in Berlin; they're being
run by German Jews. Raises all sorts of doubts."

"But Weizmann is Russian," said Bron.

"Yes," Sir Archie answered, undiverted. "Bolshevism is just
as bad." His eyes rolled craftily. "So . . . have you not thought
of enlisting yet, then, young man?"

Tessa put a gloved hand on Bron's arm. "His firm is anxious
to keep him."

"Ah, yes," said Sir Archie, with the lightest of innuendo.
"Essential to the war effort. That's it, isn't it? One hears that
quite a bit. Must make it hard for you to know your duty, so
many of your contemporaries going off now."

The room did seem depleted of Bron's generation; most of the
men were of middle age or older, and it was the young unescorted

women who emphasized the disparity. These women were being skillfully conditioned to become the most effective recruiting agents: the posters had them happily waving farewell to the legions of manhood. But Tessa was not one of these. Like Bron, she resisted jingoism. And now she bridled at Sir Archie's crude attempt at moral blackmail.

"I think I know my duty," said Bron. As soon as he uttered the words he knew how pompous they must have seemed, but pomposity was one way of avoiding the trap that had been set for him.

"Of course you do." Sir Archie looked from Bron to Tessa, and seeing her mood, he took on an ingratiating smile. "Of *course* you do, dear boy."

"*I* would like to take a closer look at Dr. Weizmann," said Tessa with militant firmness. She escaped the ensnaring bulk by stepping sideways, pulling Bron with her. While still in earshot, she said, "I don't know how you kept your temper."

Weizmann's audience was growing. Mrs. de Rothschild introduced people to him as they asked questions, and occasionally put one of her own. The subject, when Bron and Tessa joined them, was Russia.

A tiny woman in black crepe spoke with a thick accent: "Dr. Weizmann, are you not worried, with there being so many Russians amongst your number, that you might, inadvertently, become a Trojan horse for Bolshevism?"

Weizmann nodded. "I know that worries people. I think it would only worry people who are unaware what it is to be a Jew in Russia. The regime finds it convenient to blame us for all its afflictions, including Bolshevism."

Mrs. de Rothschild intervened. "But surely, are not some of the leading Bolsheviks Jews? Trotsky, for example?"

"Some Jews see it as a path for their liberation, but they are mistaken."

Weizmann had the ease of a man who had fielded such questions many times before. Looking at him more closely, Bron was aware of something more than smooth advocacy. The small, dapper figure, carrying in middle age the first signs of a paunch, his head already nearly bald, had a peculiar intensity—not attributable to any one feature, not imposed by eyes or voice, but there. Bron wondered whether it was force of intellect, or of character, or more than the sum total of those things. There was no hint of the overbearing zeal he had expected, the bugle of a preacher.

Another woman was speaking: "If that is your objective, that the Jews should have a national home, surely it would be better for us if it could be in a place that was already part of a secure country, perhaps part of the British Empire?"

"Not Egypt. We have been there before."

There was a ripple of laughter, but Weizmann seemed aloof from his own joke; it was a device to humor them, outside his soul. And of those watching him, it was only Tessa Stanbridge who saw this.

"Dr. Weizmann . . ." It was a courtly old man who now spoke. "What do you say to people, people like me, who have been well served by their adopted country, when we say we feel that Zionism may play into the hands of those—and they are many— those who say agitation for this Jewish state proves that we have divided loyalties? Do you understand me?"

Weizmann dipped his head and spoke gravely. "Yes—of course I understand. What I say is, those of us who come from countries like Russia are born and bred in an aspiration towards a new and better Jewish life, just as the Englishman leads a normal English life, but that Jewish life is not possible for us." He broke off and looked at his questioner, judging the reception. "That is as legitimate a feeling as your own, that you already have a full Jewish life and can be happy here."

"How long have you been in England?" said Mrs. de Rothschild.

"I came to Manchester in 1904."

"Well, *look* at you, Dr. Weizmann," she countered. "You have prospered here, you speak English better than many natives, you have a family here—yet you still speak of being Russian, of being on some uncompleted journey. Isn't that just a little ungrateful?"

There were many nodding heads.

Weizmann bowed slightly, a gesture both of concession and of resolution. "Mrs. de Rothschild, I will forever be grateful for what England has done for me. Jews all over the world trust England. That is why—*that* is why we hope England will see the advantage to her of having, in Palestine, a people and a society that will reflect her own values and feelings, in a part of the world where England wants—indeed, needs—stability and order, in her own interests."

26

"I see," said Mrs. de Rothschild, though it was evident that she was not quite persuaded. For her, social decorum came before further debate. She addressed the audience:

"Dr. Weizmann has with him from Manchester two friends, Mr. Israel Sieff and Mr. Simon Marks. He has asked me to say that they will take the addresses of anyone of you who is interested in knowing more of Zionism—and of course, in making financial contributions." She paused, turning to smile at Weizmann. "Dr. Weizmann has already ensured my own donation."

In this hermetic salon, glazed with taste and wealth, Weizmann, Tessa had perceived, was external, admitted by favor, knowingly transient, skillfully opportunistic. He had found and stirred a sense of obligation without making a disturbance. The bond was racial, but tenuous. To most in the room this would be just one more round of dues to be paid and consciences salved. He knew the limits of his privilege. And she wondered about Bron. He had felt drawn here, but was casual about it. Several steps behind him and apart from the dispersing cluster, her own Englishness framed in and isolated by the room's exotica, she was complete in herself, but wondered about Bron's affinity with his own tribe.

She reached out for him. "That man casts a spell."

"Yes—he does."

"He's clever."

"Yes."

"Imagine saying Jews all over the world trust England."

"What?"

"*Imagine* it. Can he possibly believe it?"

"No." Bron laughed nervously. "I suppose he can't." He steered her away, clear of Sir Archie. "At least, I hope he can't."

When they returned to her flat in a Georgian mansion in Hampstead, the concierge was enjoying her fourth glass of gin and lemon. She nodded through the partition. "Evenin', sir. Miss Stanbridge, ma'am." Her voice conveyed indifference to the predictable. The mansion was advertised to accommodate "young ladies of gentility." In fact, the concierge had long been generously bribed by all the occupants to avert her gaze from the contrary truth. All the women were noble enough to be discreet and experienced enough to be discriminating. By the standards of the building, Tessa's relationship with Michael Bron was remarkably enduring. Engagement seemed imminent, though too long imminent; there was disappointed expectation in the concierge's manner too. She did not know, and had not guessed, that her hope rested on the resolution of one of the most stubborn incompatibilities of background, between the elder son of Jacob Bron and the second daughter of Lord Stanbridge of Sewell, the Brons being descended from the Bronsinskis who had arrived in England at the time of William III and the Stanbridges being descended from Normans to whom the Church of Rome had commanded first allegiance then and ever after, at the cost of several heads.

It was a fancy of Bron's, and a wild one, that Tessa's body replicated perfectly the proportions of bone and flesh that those unremembered Norman women had borne across the channel. There were bodies like it on medieval tapestries, some even set into the stone of cathedrals. This Norman frame was indelicate from feet to waist, long thighs supporting generous hips and buttocks, but then seemed to taper to leanness, with a flat chest and narrow shoulders—as she stood before him now, the linen collapsed around her ankles, the arms extended, and between them only putative breasts, rounded more by the nipples' crowns than by flesh.

She was taller than he; she embraced him and pressed down on him, her hands gripping the lower half of his buttocks and, as he went into her, lifting her to tiptoe. Like this, with his head pressed hard into the pronounced bone at the base of her neck, she carried his weight with the front of her thighs and flexed gently, her muscles familiar with his, the compactness of his body contained within her embrace. His hands gripped her shoulders. She liked the overture to their lovemaking to be upright like this, always coming quickly to her first climax, long before he did. Her right hand broke his flesh, a smear of blood appearing on the nail of her index finger. When they broke apart she transferred the blood to his brow, like a tribal mark.

Her bedroom had a deep window with a clear view south over the city; the night sky was now in two contrasting tiers—a lower bank of fog and above it leaden rain, concealing the basin of the Thames. Nearer lights in the Hampstead streets were enfeebled by the mist. Because the room was not overlooked, the curtains were never closed. At times during the day and at others at night they had lain in her great oak-framed bed and looked from it to the sky, which was never free of the ribbons of smoke. The city seemed always to be growing, always engulfing more.

Her furnishings had a Victorian heaviness, and the ineradicable mustiness that went with it: the bed was on a dark Indian carpet, tassels at the edges worn flat; there were three chintz-covered armchairs, a small breakfast table, oak cabinets, an oak wardrobe, and some potted ferns. A fire burned in a black-leaded grate. Bron always felt that the bed's bulk was in some strange way promiscuous, too copious and too responsive to accommodate mere chastity. It must have borne other lovers. It was not a bed to die in.

In the light of the fire they lay with energy suspended, she with unwound hair across his chest, he with his left hand on her moistness. Looking at the ceiling, the shadow of a bedpost wavering there, she felt a tenseness in his body that had not been dispelled by the lovemaking.

"What is it?" she said quietly.

His hand moved to her waist and it was a minute before he answered. "The war. It's the war. The mindlessness of it. Do you remember the first battle in France? The French cavalry—their belief in élan? *Élan.* One wave after another goes down. And still the same damned élan. We're just as badly infected. I felt it tonight. It was like being in the ballroom of the *Titanic*—going, with enormous confidence, to disaster."

She rolled over on her side to look at him, pushing the thick black hair from his brow. "Some people would say it's treason to talk like that."

"Ferris, for one."

"Ferris is a fool. The terrible thing, to me, is that it's not only the fools. . . ."

"I know. Then there's Weizmann."

"What about Weizmann?"

"I'm not sure. A feeling—a feeling that he comes from something I don't know, something I can't feel, but I *should* feel. Things have happened to him."

"If he hadn't been a Jew, he would have been a Jesuit. He has the same look: the gatherer of souls."

Bron sighed. "And of guilt."

"Ah—guilt. I understand guilt. As a Catholic, I'm an expert on guilt."

One of her improprieties was, in private, to smoke cigarettes. She took one from a packet while he lit it for her. Every gesture she made with the cigarette seemed like a declaration of carnality. She inhaled and continued: "One of the risks of an upbringing like mine is that you come to see the devil as tangible a force as God—on terms of personal acquaintance, as it were." The nervous cough came again. When it passed, she said, "It seems to me, Michael, that you have a different problem. Weizmann wants you not merely to remember the past but actually to relive it."

"You could see the skill of his case tonight—about a Jewish Palestine as a dependable ally for the empire."

"It has to be Palestine?"

"He's always set his sights on that. Herzl, the real father of Zionism—Herzl was ready to accept the British idea of a new Israel in Uganda. It was Weizmann who stopped that. Herzl died resenting Weizmann for it."

"Uganda isn't awfully Biblical."

"That's the part I really don't trust, playing on the Old Testament. How relevant is that now? Uganda would have been perfectly viable."

"I think," she said, pointing the dwindling cigarette at him, "I think Dr. Weizmann knows absolutely what he is doing, the kind of mind he is dealing with here. If he gets at those evangelical Protestants in the cabinet—and I'll bet he does—he'll convince them of their opportunity to become the Christian patrons of the Deliverance—oh, my, yes!" She took a final deep draw on the cigarette. "Oh, yes, dear Michael. Your Dr. Weizmann knows his Bible and knows his British. Thank God—if you'll pardon the term—thank God he *isn't* a Jesuit. Then I would be in as much torment as you obviously are." She stubbed out the cigarette. "Tell me, where does your father stand in all this?"

"Totally opposed."

"To Weizmann?"

"To Zionism. He admits some regard for Weizmann. But he won't listen to the idea of a new Israel in Palestine. He blames the American Jews for encouraging the idea so far. He says if the American Jews had been there long enough to feel American, they wouldn't be drawn to it, but that since the Americans themselves are a nation of immigrants, romantic notions of this kind appeal to them."

"Those reservations were apparent tonight."

"Yes," he said, "and Weizmann knew it."

"But the Rothschilds have financed settlements in Palestine."

"That's Baron Edmond in France, and that's *not* Zionism. The Rothschilds are split over it."

Looking at Bron lying on her linen sheets, his olive skin against her paleness, she was aware of how much he represented his family's commitment to assimilation. The first Bron to have gone from Winchester to Oxford, he was more comfortably English than any before him—but he was still indelibly Jewish and now, after this one encounter, unsure of his allegiances. The irony was that their affair had cost her more than it had him in family relationships. The Stanbridges, while professing to abhor anti-Semitism, had an inflexibly Catholic view of any kind of mixed marriage, and the idea of Tessa bringing a Jew into the fold had proved the ultimate heresy. Bron's father, however, had slowly accepted that he might now be living in such irregular times that the marriage could be sanctioned. Bron's mother, more religiously orthodox, was less sanguine, especially on the principle that the children of a Gentile mother could not themselves be Jewish. Generation after generation, the Brons had built their position and their fortune in London, through a merchant bank. Inch by inch they had sought acceptance, and inch by inch they had gained it. Talk of the marriage had caused strains; it seemed now in abeyance. Tessa saw the intervention of Dr. Weizmann as another complication and, perhaps, another excuse.

At least she seemed to have talked the tension out of him. The smell of her—a virginal, carbolic one that clung to her, oddly neuter and bloodless—was part of what soothed him, like the care of a nurse. They made love again, mutually an act of consolation falling short of the commitment neither was yet able to make.

It was only when he was alone, walking to the Brons' Victorian mansion on Hampstead Hill, that he realized what it was that he had seen in Weizmann's eyes: a sense of *plight*.

To build the mansion on the hill had been both colonization and separation. The Brons' old house had been in a tenement row—four stories and servants in the attic floor—a colony of successful Jewish families: bankers, textile magnates, traders, shippers, jewelers—wealthy but not ostentatious. The street had provided a Jewish sense of community and an eclectic vigor, both of which were missing on the Hampstead heights. Bron remembered a lost pleasure: a bedroom too cold in which the bed became a sanctuary of his own warmth. He thought of the

Rothschild house. Perhaps the old Jewish aristocracy of Europe was more secure in its internationalism than those with more national ties could ever be; perhaps in his astute way Weizmann knew that too.

In the night a wind rose and swept away the fog. When Bron woke in the morning, the heath was a brilliant washed green; some trees were in leaf and some kites were up. Weather shaped his mood. It was that point of the fickle English April when winter was in retreat and he thought light might reach him again. It was always a matter of shading, not contrasts. The English concept—*his* English concept—of balance was derived from the climate. Its freedom from extremes, its uneventful temperance, set a norm of behavior against which to measure the extremes of other nations. Latin volatility, Teutonic frigidity, French romanticism, North American impetuosity—he thought of them as faults of climate as well as of character, the two probably inextricable, while the Englishman was blessed with this weaker light and embalming normalcy.

He chose tweeds, walking boots, and a cap. Dressed, he ate a large breakfast. Somewhere in the grounds was a congregation of dogs, his mother their focus. Jacob Bron had left early to call on a cabinet minister; war loans were being devised. A sister was practicing piano—too ambitiously.

On the heath, eddies of tobacco smoke from pipes. It was a weekend phenomenon, noticed before. The strange fruity smell set apart bourgeois Hampstead from lower points, where the tobacco was sour. Such agreeable sensations were another blessing of the wind that kept all the toxic plumes of the basin streaking to the east over the docks. The young boys straining with their kites were more often now in the charge of mothers than fathers. This thought hastened his step across the crown of the heath to the old white-boarded pub named after a highway robber, Jack Straw's Castle.

The small bar he liked was thinly populated. From beyond, through a refraction of mirrors and a filter of partitions, came the glimpse and sounds of the larger saloon. War infection there too: a hysterical trace in the laughter, and belligerent patriotism at the piano, and more khaki than before. The barmaid, knowing him, filled a pewter tankard with champagne.

He sat in a red leather banquette, alone. With half of the drink gone, he was thinking of Tessa, one recurrent image of her in a nun's habit, smoking a cigarette. Then, in a corner of his eye, this fantasy was displaced by something less distinct but surely familiar, seen in mirrors, a face in profile, a face slightly altered: the scrawny neck a little more muscular, the jawline more solid, and the cheeks fuller, but the nose still that of a Caesar, sharply cut. It might have been a trick of the mirrors, but the skin was no longer pallid; it seemed burnished. It was still a profile that seemed predatory—fastidiously predatory. Beneath the face was khaki and a bolt of scarlet on a lapel.

Bron found his pen, and taking a coaster, scribbled between the champagne stains. He went to the barmaid.

"There's a gentleman in the saloon bar—tall, with a staff officer's flashes on his uniform. Could you give this to him, please?"

"I know the one," said the girl.

Bron went back to his seat, sitting so that he was able to watch the door.

Within a minute the young officer came through, half a smile already composed, eyes ranging the room.

"Michael—dear chap!"

Bron rose. He put out a hand, but instead was embraced. He laughed. "Owen—it must be three years."

The embrace was held a few seconds longer, then the newcomer took a pace back, appraising him.

"Still short-arsed," he said. "Yes, it's all of three years. Well!"

Bron was conscious of being the more nervous of the two. "So . . . I see it's *Captain* Owen Kippax now."

"And you, dear chap—not taken the colors yet?"

"Not yet. What are you drinking?"

"Whatever you are. My word, how good to see you."

Bron ordered two tankards of champagne. Waiting for them, he said, "I thought you must still be in India."

"Only just got back. Still officially in the Indian Army, but had some business at the War House." He took the tankard. "Here's to us, then!"

There was something in the way they walked back to the banquette that registered not only familiarity but a sense of seasoned reciprocation. A stranger would have noticed it, and the barmaid did.

"Well," said Kippax, "what does a geologist do in a war?"

"What does an Oriental scholar do?"

"You answer first."

33

Bron wiped foam from his lip. "There's a shortage of certain minerals. My firm has to find new sources."

Kippax's uniform was not made for Kippax's habits of posture. Slumped against the red leather, he had stretched his left leg out along the seat but, constricted by the cut of the trousers, had to swivel back again. The movement was part of his explanation. "We only wear this thing for the War House. Otherwise it's strictly mufti."

"You were a political officer, I thought."

"Am. We still are, dear chap. Been in Simla a couple of years, with the odd journey into the hinterland."

"That's intelligence work . . .?"

"A bit of this, a bit of that." Kippax smiled to cover his discretion. "Very labyrinthine, our Indian arrangements." He sipped the champagne and judged himself able to say more. "But that's all over now. We're off to new pastures."

"France?"

"Not on your life." Kippax lowered his voice, though nobody was in earshot. "That's going to be a graveyard of theories, all these bloody senile generals. No. We're off to Cairo."

"*Cairo*?"

Suddenly, as he enjoyed Bron's surprise, Kippax began looking at him with a new contemplation. "Yes, Cairo. Tell me—are you opposed, in principle, to joining up? You always were a bit wet about war."

"How charmingly you put it." They had, Bron realized, completely regained their old rhythm of exchange. "Why do you ask?"

"Well . . ." Kippax shifted again and found a compromise between the self-determination of his limbs and the restrictions of the uniform. "Well . . . it so happens, running over things at the War House, we're a bit short of expertise; quite heavy on idiot routine, but short of expertise. One problem we have to think about quite a bit, since we can't move an army without it, is water. The maps in Cairo are quite hopeless on that kind of thing, no work done on it at all. We've a chap out there already, doing mapmaking, but he's an archaeologist. Pretty hot on Assyrian temples, but not much use when it comes to water. So . . ." The shorthand between them was enough.

"You want a diviner—a man with a stick."

"Come on, dear chap. You're a bloody geologist."

"You have to admit, on a quiet Saturday lunchtime in

34

Hampstead, it's a little much to take in—the idea of my dropping everything to wander around Egypt looking for wells.''

''There are some''—Kippax broke off to drain his tankard—''there are some who would say that if you *had* to answer the call, you could do worse. Following a camel's farts around the Sinai could be more congenial than leaving your guts in Flanders.''

''I don't think they would let me go that easily, at the office.''

''They're owned by Rothschilds, aren't they?''

''Yes.'' Only after he had answered did Bron begin to wonder how Kippax knew so much.

''Then there'll be no trouble fixing that.'' At moments of determination, Kippax's voice was more lyrical than emphatic—one of the few traces of Welsh temperament in the measured pace instilled by an education at Winchester.

''Sinai?'' said Bron.

Kippax smiled. ''That was careless of me.''

In the past, Bron had found himself consenting too readily to Kippax, because of the man's easy appeal, and he remembered how others at Winchester had been similarly charmed, even some of the most adamantine of the masters. The trouble was that Kippax seemed to know Bron better than he knew himself, and the gap of three years had not changed that. But at least Bron was no longer a novice in Kippax's hands; a novice would not see that Kippax was steel coated in languidness.

''I'm not sure it will be as simple as you imagine to have me released,'' said Bron.

''How about a stroll over the heath?'' said Kippax, getting up and tugging the hem of his tunic. No tailor had ever managed to hang a tunic or jacket on Kippax; some misalignment of neck and shoulders defeated even Savile Row. The army tunic had a collar in search of its owner, never quite finding him. Seeing this familiar dishevelment, Bron was silently amused, while openly glad to have renewed a friendship. Walking back under the flapping kites with Kippax at his side, he no longer seemed an object of inquiry. While they talked of India, Bron saw a change in his old friend, from the apprenticeship of Winchester and Oxford to the enjoyment of the political arts.

They stopped on a summit, under a cluster of beeches groaning in the wind.

''I would like to know,'' said Kippax, ''what is your reservation about service? Seriously.''

''You were the one who spoke of senile generals. What are

35

you driving at? I mean, you can't disparage one theater of war and extol another; that makes no sense.''

"I see. It's moral, is it, your opposition?"

"Moral?" Bron was self-deprecating, "I didn't say that. More a question of purpose. It was supposed to be over in weeks. This government . . . Asquith as prime minister . . . it seems hopeless to me."

"Well . . . yes." Kippax accepted Bron's gravity. "It's true, he's no warlord. And it *is* going to go on—years, I suspect. That's why, dear chap, you ought seriously to think about what I said, why you should come out to Egypt. We have a different kind of war there, something we can handle better."

They walked off to the road. Kippax wiped a boot clean of mud in the damp grass on the fringe. The slight extra weight he now carried had made his eyes recessive, even less easy for Bron to read. Still looking down at the boot, Kippax said, "You'll give it serious thought, then?"

"How long do I have?"

"Until Monday."

"That little?"

"Either you do or you don't. It's not a matter for prolonged speculation."

This tartness, Bron thought, must be a part of the custom of command. It annoyed him, but he nodded. "Monday, then. How do I reach you?"

"I'll reach you, dear chap."

Watching Kippax walk away down the hill to the High Street, Bron realized that for all the military cladding and increased self-assurance, there remained in Kippax's gait a discordantly epicene trace. Kippax had had his vulnerabilities at Winchester too.


Between the walk on the heath and Monday morning, Kippax caught a cold. Prone to hypochondria, he took several proprietary medicines—an odious syrup said to defend "the chest"; pills to clear the head; another pill for sinus—and barley water with honey to summon his reserves of resistance. The result was that, following a clerk up a waxed corridor of the Foreign Office, he was nauseous and less alert than he wanted to be. He was not in uniform. His mixed allegiances required discretion, and in the Foreign Office he could have passed for a young chancery officer home from an outstation that might have been

36

malarial, his cold—or its treatment—giving him a hint of fever under his tan and the badly cut gabardine suit suggesting an Oriental hand.

The clerk took him to an anteroom. He waited on a leather sofa, under the eye of an aged secretary. Kippax saw in the secretary the desiccated manner of a man who was his own exact opposite, a man indivisible from his desk, little more than an extension of the furniture, a man who had happily reduced his world to this one station. And the secretary, no doubt, saw Kippax as one more of the dissolute adventurers from distant posts, an undependable agent of the global vigilance that England exercised on behalf of civilization. Kippax enjoyed the thought of giving offense and sat languidly until a buzzer indicated that he should be allowed into the inner sanctum.

This room was so large that it seemed somehow to have altered the building's scale. It had three deep windows, two to the east, overlooking the Horse Guards' parade ground, and one to the north, overlooking the park. The southern wall was a casemented bookcase running from floor to ceiling, and the western wall was indented for a deep fireplace with a double mantel above it, and to one side of this, between the wall and the northern light, was the Chippendale desk of Sir Cedric Assay.

Once the secretary retreated and closed the door on them, all formality fell away. Sir Cedric's hauteur had lasted only as long as the door was open; in the next second he was stepping lightly around the desk and grasping Kippax's arms.

"You look poorly, Owen."

"Nothing, sir, really. A chill."

"Well," said Sir Cedric, with a commiserating squeeze, "we shall have to see that you are taken care of."

Sir Cedric was taller than Kippax but pear-shaped, his height more in the trunk than the legs. He was nearly bald and his complexion was an even, light coffee shade, the outward mark of an exotic inner nature. Sir Cedric's grandfather had fought with Wellington in the Peninsular Wars and married into a noble Valencian family. The Spanish blood had, in son and even more in grandson, given to the Assays the gift of political imagination, where previously they had been remarkable only for simple military belligerence. Sir Cedric was said to be the apotheosis of this change. Wherever regular diplomacy failed he was ready to be irregular. His hidden hand had been behind many coups, subtle or draconian—from the making of alliances with

37

African despots to the invention of the concentration camp during the Boer War. He was known also for an extensive network of contacts in Oxford colleges, where he found likely disciples, of whom one of the most promising in years had been Kippax. Of course, there were critics. One or two prudish members of Parliament whispered that Sir Cedric shared both the beliefs and the methods of Rasputin, that his recruitment procedure favored the unscrupulous, but the war and the accolade of a knighthood had stilled these voices.

Kippax felt that he was no longer in the Foreign Office but back at Oxford in happy intimacy with a don. The secretary beyond the door would have been scandalized to see this side of Sir Cedric, who with him was as cold and remote as a viceroy.

"I've taken some medicine, thank you," said Kippax, finally released from the clasp. He went to an armchair by the fire, wiping his brow with a square of blue silk.

Sir Cedric stood over him. "Well . . . don't overstrain yourself; a chill can be most weakening." He took out a pair of steel-rimmed spectacles to study a note. "You say this man would be reliable?"

"Absolutely."

"I wondered, at first, about your choice of a Jew. I see that you were at Winchester together. You were his . . . what should one say? His guide to Gentile manners, perhaps? It was generous of you. His family certainly seems to have put its roots down. And I do see the value to you out there in having an English Jew of this background."

"*Two* values, really," said Kippax, putting away the silk and looking up. "One, reassurance for the Egyptian Jews who suspect us of encouraging the Zionists. Two, having somebody who will know what is being said by the Jews of all persuasions."

Sir Cedric became sardonic. "There *is* an ostensible function for him too."

"Quite. We do actually, in point of fact, need some help there too, on water sources."

Sir Cedric put away the note and settled into the armchair opposite Kippax, leaning back with the air of a man well pleased with his own devices. "As for yourself, Owen, I have got the India Office finally to see the sense of letting you come over to us. I fear you were in danger of becoming one of their indispensable men." His voice and stomach rose and fell together. "There was an elegance to your work that was quite novel in India. They had a reputation for clumsiness—even worse, for leaving traces."

"I took the trouble to find the best man, then used him alone, each time."

"I was sorry to hear of his accident."

"Yes," said Kippax impassively. "A faulty fuse."

"Quite so." Sir Cedric was unaccustomed to finding a mind that worked so like his own. "Quite so."

"Dr. Weizmann?" The man in the raincoat could not see to whom he spoke.

"Yes."

"Jabotinsky. Vladimir Jabotinsky."

The front door opened. Weizmann took the offered hand in a long, fraternal grip, not releasing it until the door was closed. "I'm sorry. We are eating in the kitchen; I barely heard the bell." He spoke in Russian. Taking the raincoat, he added, "I wasn't sure you would come tonight. These days, the trains to Manchester are so disrupted by the war." He guided Jabotinsky into the kitchen. "My wife, Vera—Vera, this is Mr. Jabotinsky."

A small, dark-haired woman got up from the table.

Though both Russian, the two men had no features in common. Jabotinsky was clean-shaven and had two thick, arching brows that gave him the appearance of being permanently startled. He wore a pair of cheap rimless glasses hooked crudely at the ears. Though vigorous enough, to Weizmann he seemed to have something of a hunted look.

"I have heard much about you," said Weizmann.

"Too much . . .?"

Weizmann smiled. "They gave you a hard time in London."

Vera Weizmann gave Jabotinsky coffee and he gulped half of it before replying. "In Odessa I would have expected it. But in London . . . I *still* do not understand. In the East End they howled at me like dogs. I thought they would tear me to pieces."

"Yes." Weizmann waved his wife to sit with them. "The Russian Jews here think the same as your people in Odessa; raising a Jewish army to fight alongside the British is tantamount to fighting on behalf of the Czar. No Jew would want to lift a finger to help the Romanovs; one understands that."

Vera Weizmann nodded. "We have the same difficulty."

Weizmann said, "There is another problem. There are still so many Jews living under the Turks. If the Turks find Jews on the

39

other side . . . well, you know what they are doing to the Armenians.''

"Dr. Weizmann." Jabotinsky was suddenly fervent. "For years I have followed you: from the moment you opposed the Uganda scheme. I have not always agreed with you, that I admit. But I cannot understand these Jews here. Now we must seize our chance. The Turkish Empire will collapse. What follows then? The only way the British will take us seriously, and our rights to Palestine, is for Jews to make an army. That is the only reason I want to have Jews fight alongside the British. The British do not believe Jews can fight, that Jews will *ever* fight.''

Weizmann stretched a hand across the table. "Now I can understand why they denounced you in the synagogue at Odessa." But he was grave. "There are seventy-five thousand Jews still in Palestine. Every one of them is a hostage to the Turks.''

For a minute Jabotinsky was silent, his hand in Weizmann's grip. Then he said, "I understand that. But we must prove that the Jew is just as ready, and just as able, to fight for the liberation of Palestine as a Christian or an Arab.''

"For that we must choose our time," said Weizmann. "Timing is everything with the English. You must understand how the English see the world. And if you will permit me to say so, I have several years' advantage over you in that.''

Tessa Stanbridge knew even before Bron spoke; he had never been good at feigning a lightness he did not feel, and this was after all no bolt from the blue for her, but a long-closing trap. He held each arm a little clear of his hips, hands clenched. His tie seemed to have been knotted hurriedly, giving him a trace of adolescence.

"I know," she said.

"Who . . .?"

"No one. I just knew."

The rigid arms slackened.

She walked away from him, to the window. "How soon?"

"It's not what you think."

She half turned. "Not . . .?"

"Not France. Egypt."

"My God!" She half choked and half laughed. "Egypt!" She turned to face him fully. "You really couldn't run away any farther, could you?"

"*Run away?*" He took a step toward her, then stopped, chin suddenly tight. "Run away?"

"You're running away, with honor."

"From what?"

"From me. From us. From whatever it is that torments you so."

They took a step toward each other simultaneously, she collapsing on his shoulder, right hand pulling at his hair. "It's a way of solving your problem without deciding anything." She was momentarily tearful, gradually easing from his shoulder and moving the hand from his hair to his cheek. "You still don't realize"—she spoke stiffly with the effort to regain control of herself—"you still don't believe it doesn't matter, do you? *It doesn't matter that you're a Jew.* If it doesn't matter to me, why worry about anyone else?"

His hands went to her waist. "I know that."

"Then why . . . *why?*"

"Nothing is certain anymore. What will happen? I have to be sure."

"Where, suddenly, did you get this idea of Egypt?" She had steadied herself enough to become acerbic.

"Pure chance. I happened to meet someone I knew at Winchester. I think you know him too. Kippax."

"Owen Kippax? Yes, I remember Owen Kippax." She seemed dubious. "I didn't realize . . ."

"He was in India; now he's going to Cairo. They wanted a geologist."

She appeared not to have followed these last words. "Kippax? There was something involving him, at Oxford. . . . I don't quite remember."

"He was an Orientalist."

But this speculation left her. She collapsed on the bed, folding her legs beneath her, holding her head. "Michael. You don't *believe* in this war. Why are you going?"

"It's not the same, out there. There is something I can do."

"It's still the same war, for God's sake."

She seemed more pitiable than he could remember; the last reserves of her self-esteem had drained away, with her color. He sat beside her. "An interval might help."

"An *interval?*" Keeping her head bowed, she turned slightly to look him in the eye, speaking softly. "It won't help *me.*"

He, too, had collapsed within himself. The room was left only

41

with its own resonances, a vibration between a curtain and a window, a settling of ash in the fire. The light was failing.

She fell across his lap, and he put a hand to the nape of her neck, feeling the line of the spine. Her hair was elaborately fastened at the back with combs. In a while he moved the hand from her spine and gently detached the combs. Her hair fell unevenly to each side of her face as she was aroused.

Later, coming naked from the bathroom, she went to the window while he lay back in the bed. There was an immodesty to her movements in this state that he alone knew. With each shift of her body, walking, sitting, squatting, in this softened light, there was always another surface to discover. At the window she stood with her legs slightly apart, and the lobes of her buttocks creased slightly where they met her thighs. As she turned toward him with her left arm on her hip, the slight profile of a breast was held in outline, nipple translucent. Then she sat unselfconsciously with crossed legs beside him, the tightened pelvic muscles spreading her upper pubic hair into a dark plume. It was not a carnal excitement he felt but an aesthetic pleasure at these many arrangements of her grace, which were so natural and needless of shame. Freedom from shame was the essence of her beauty—and the rock of her character.

As he left her she said, evenly, with no trace of reproach, "Just remember, Michael—just *remember*, please—the days we spend apart are lost to us forever."

# 3

# *Affula, Palestine ✳ April 1916*

"An American Jew?" murmured Jemal Pasha again. Everyone within earshot had fallen silent. The only sounds in the wagon-lit came from wherever the kitchen was. Jemal's mustache had an uneven trim that partly obscured his upper lip. As he spoke again, the lip tautened. "Perhaps you know Mr. Henry Morgenthau? *He* is an American Jew."

Brusse interjected before Koblensky could answer: "The American ambassador in Constantinople."

Koblensky had again been saved. "I have not met him. I have heard of him."

"Of course," said Jemal enigmatically, looking from Koblensky to Brusse and then back again. "I was with Mr. Morgenthau recently. We understand each other very well. We do not want the United States involved in this war." Jemal finally took his hands from his hips and, speaking to Brusse, said, "We must make all our American friends welcome, Captain. I should be happy for your young friend to dine with us."

As they ate, Koblensky noticed an uneasiness between Brusse and Jemal, kept in check, he suspected, partly because of his own presence and partly because of the courtesies of a collaboration resting more on military expedience than on affinity. It emerged that Brusse had been sent to inspect the coastal defenses of Palestine: Jemal believed that the vulnerable and extensive Palestine littoral would be the target of an Anglo-French landing. Brusse's methodical questions annoyed the Turk.

The comforts of the train were so all-embracing, and in the darkness they so effectively excluded the outside world, that Koblensky s emed a witness to a meeting in some European locale, the kind of thing, he imagined, that happened in places like Saint Petersburg, Vienna, or Berlin—not in a ramshackle junction on the fringe of the plain of Armageddon. He had not eaten as well as this for as long as he could remember. Soup was followed by baked lamb on saffron-scented rice; the lamb by canned pears topped with a rose-water sorbet.

As Jemal offered cigars, he finally turned his attentions again to Koblensky, tired of Brusse's incessant questions. "So, my American friend. You want to give up the comforts of America for the life of Palestine? You have heard how dangerous it is here, but do you realize how hard it is to live here—and the war will make it much harder, for everybody."

Koblensky regretted taking a cigar, but had done so for the sake of suggesting an American worldliness. He struggled not to choke over it, answering between breaths. "I do not mind that, General. I am young. I believe there can be a future here."

"I hope," said Brusse to Jemal with overt sarcasm, "that your talk with Mr. Morgenthau will have persuaded you that the Jews will be more useful to us if they remain in Palestine than if they are driven to Egypt."

Jemal rested the cigar on the tablecloth, where it began to scorch its mark, and he signaled an orderly to bring more cognac. He ignored the smoldering cloth and didn't directly answer Brusse, but instead addressed Koblensky. "We have useful friends among the Jews here in Palestine, as I hope you will find. Then perhaps you will be able to write to your friends in America that the Jews are as well treated as anyone under the Turks." He finished the cognac in one gulp.

Koblensky had all the time wondered why it was that he had been allowed to be a party to their war plans, fearing it to be the carelessness of men who knew the witness would not survive to recount it later. Now he understood: Jemal wanted both to counter Brusse's thinly disguised moral superiority and to take advantage of an American ear that would serve his own ends. Koblensky's masquerade had become even more audacious and precarious.

Jemal spoke again. "There is one Jewish family I know who would be interested in a man like you. They would be proof to you of how well the Turk and the Jew can collaborate. They came originally from Rumania, but they have received generous financial support from your country."

Brusse nodded knowingly. "You mean the Aaronsohns?"

Jemal was surprised. "You have heard of them, Captain?"

"Of course. The tall, redheaded one . . ."

"Aaron Aaronsohn," supplied Jemal irritably.

"Yes. He came to us in Berlin for chemicals to use against locusts. I remember him; an impressive man, very impressive."

"Then you will see him again soon, I think," said Jemal. "Not only have we had these disastrous rains, but now the locusts again." He turned to Koblensky. "This man Aaronsohn knows more about wheat crops than anyone else in Palestine—than anyone else in Syria. He has saved us more than once from the locusts. Yes, I think you should see Aaron Aaronsohn. Perhaps he could use a young man like you. I can arrange it." The smell of burning cloth reminded Jemal of the cigar. He retrieved it and drew on it. "Yes," he said, "I can arrange it."

Brusse said, "Then he should stay on this train."

"Of course," said Jemal.

"We are going to Haifa," explained Brusse. "It is not far. We shall be there by morning. And then perhaps . . . ."

"Then you will truly be in Palestine," said Jemal smoothly. "Aaronsohn lives in a small town near there, Zichron Jaacov." His mood seemed to alter in a second. His pale skull was now mottled by the heat and the flush of the drink. "I have not seen your papers."

Koblensky was taken off guard, and looked uselessly to Brusse, who was expressionless. "I have them," said Koblensky, fumbling in his jacket and then putting the papers on the table.

Jemal took a second cigar and lit it before turning over the papers, stopping at the bottom sheet, then looking at Koblensky with a new interest. "Djevdet Bey? This is his signature?"

Koblensky nodded, aware that Brusse was tensing.

"Djevdet Bey . . . ." repeated Jemal slowly. "A very stupid man. What did you see of his actions in Van?"

The question seemed innocent enough, but Koblensky knew it was treacherous. "Only the casualties at the American mission hospital."

Jemal exhaled with a rattling sound. "Djevdet Bey has been careless." Jemal's hand still rested on Koblensky's papers like a gesture of confiscation, heightening Koblensky's sense of nakedness. "But the British are, of course, exaggerating everything." The mustache had a way of moving on its own after each sentence. "It is the Russians who are to blame. They subverted the Armenians. We Muslims can live side by side with the Christians, and the Jews, in other places. As you will see in Palestine. But it is the Russians who turn the Christians against the Muslims, for their own ends. Therefore, we had to make an example of some Armenians, the worst only, to show where their loyalties should really be.''

That Jemal was unknowingly addressing a Russian produced between Brusse and Koblensky a double-edged complicity: of disbelief at this account, and of a renewed sense of danger.

"Yes," said Jemal, looking at them both. "*Loyalty* is all we ask.''

Koblensky watched Jemal's hand finally move from the papers.

"When I explained it all to Mr. Morgenthau, he understood. We have no quarrel with the Jews." Jemal carefully folded Koblensky's papers as they had been when handed to him and handed them back.

Only then did Brusse take a cigar. Producing a small silver knife, he cut the cigar with surgical precision and sniffed at it. He managed in his movements to convey to Koblensky both his relief and his distaste for their host, not lighting the cigar until assured of its quality.

Koblensky was given a sleeping compartment to himself. Brusse and Jemal remained with their cigars in the saloon for business that Koblensky rightly guessed would increase the German's pressing of the Turk. The smell of the sleeper was balming: the veneers impregnated with years of rich associations, male and female, of perfumes and tobaccos as well as an inimitable epicurean sediment. Koblensky felt suddenly secure in exhaustion. There was a small porcelain basin and an oval mirror above it, the glass around its two retaining screws ringed with rust. The water was also rust-tinted. Koblensky splashed his face and took stock of himself in the mirror, looking for the ineradicable marks contracted in this year in which he had seldom been still long enough for such vanities. There was a light bluish stain to the skin under his eyes and the eyes themselves seemed to have become more sunken, molding his cheeks in a pronounced Slavic way. Under the weak bulb the skin of his forehead was jaundiced and pitted near the hairline. At each corner of his lower lip were new crease lines, which seemed to disappear when he closed his mouth and set his chin. His neck was gaunt. He pulled at each eye in turn, inspecting the raw redness. He realized that it would be difficult to place his age between twenty and thirty. But this face had left Russia.

He had been sleeping for nearly an hour before the train moved. Unlike the train from Damascus, this one seemed in expert hands. It pulled smoothly out of the station and within a minute Koblensky was asleep again, half-consciously registering the raised voices of Brusse and Jemal in the saloon. When he awoke, there was light at the window and the train was moving slowly and crossing switches. Looking out the small window, more a porthole, above the bunk, he saw what seemed like a hallucination—a curved shoreline and an ocean with the mat silver coating of dawn. The Mediterranean, at last. Like nothing else on this odyssey, sight of the Mediterranean renewed his will and broke his confinement. This sea lapped the Orient, Africa, and Europe, and for Koblensky the sight of it was like breaking through a wall.

By the time the train reached the station, he had washed and made of himself the best he could. He took his bag through to the saloon. Neither Brusse nor Jemal was yet out of his berth. From the left side of the saloon Koblensky looked up and saw the dominating outline of Mount Carmel, with the old town of Haifa in the foreground and newer streets straggling into the foothills. The light was different, given more clarity by the sea.

In a short while Brusse appeared, despite his drawn-out night looking impeccable. There was a new distance in his manner with Koblensky, silent notification that their conspiracy was over, the service performed, and that Koblensky must be the master of his own fate. On the platform another carpet was unrolled. A nervous-looking group assembled, some in uniform and some not, but all of them distinguished from others in the station by being generously nourished.

When Jemal came into the saloon there was already sweat on his brow, the sign of a man's having struggled into a corset. Jemal ignored Koblensky and stooped stiffly at the window to scrutinize the welcoming party. He sighed and turned to Brusse. "They seem to be expecting Caesar." He loosened his belt by one notch. "There is one of everything—a Christian, a Druse, a Greek Orthodox, a Bedouin, a town Arab, a Jew, and even a Baha'i. Caesar had a simpler world."

"Caesar was a pagan," said Brusse briskly. "That made *everything* much simpler." He glanced at Koblensky. "And what of our young friend?"

Absently, hardly looking at Koblensky, Jemal said, "He will be taken care of."

Koblensky was left on a divan, watching the two men disap-

47

pear into the sunlight, composing their faces in readiness to intimidate. A discordant band broke into a march of uncertain nationality.

"Come, please." One of Jemal's adjutants appeared at Koblensky's side. Brusse and Jemal had been swallowed in the ceremony as it progressed down the red carpet and into the station building. The adjutant took Koblensky across the tracks to an apparently deserted single-story structure and left him on a wooden bench in a room bare except for a pedestal desk, a chair, and a crudely colored portrait of Turkey's ruler, Enver Pasha. A single fly, swollen and frenetic, shared the airless space. The shirt Koblensky wore still smelled of the brandy spilled on it during the interrogation in Damascus. As he heard the train pull away and the band recede, it seemed that one confinement always followed another.

After ten minutes, the door opened. The sudden strong light at first obscured the newcomer's features. He was a short, corpulent man in a black suit and open-necked white shirt. His right hand extended to Koblensky, who could still not clearly see a face, though he detected a pungent perfume.

"Mr. Koblensky?"

The hand that met his was soft and yet its grip was strong. The face had the same paradox: a weak, fleshy jawline, hanging cheeks, but penetrating eyes.

"I am Meyer Malik." The grip on Koblensky's hand did not relax. "You came with Jemal Pasha?"

"On his train."

"They say you are American." The hand released Koblensky's, but Malik stood, short legs apart, in an attitude of wary inspection. "Why have you come here?"

Koblensky bent down to pick up the unraveling carpetbag. "It's the end of a long journey, and a long story."

"The end? You want to stay in Palestine?"

"That is what I have come for."

Malik's frame threw a shadow that exaggerated its bulk. The fly passed between the two men. With a slicing stroke Malik crushed it on the wall without taking his gaze from Koblensky. "Very few people, even Americans, come to Palestine in such comfort." Malik's sarcasm covered what began to bother him: the ragged and almost emaciated condition of Koblensky, which seemed at odds with the style of his arrival.

Understanding this, Koblensky nodded. "I was lucky. Very

lucky. It was the German who saved me, in Damascus, and through him I made the journey here.''

''Brusse?'' Malik rubbed his hands to remove the stain of the fly and moved to one side. ''As you say, you were indeed lucky.'' He pulled a starched white shirt cuff clear of his coat sleeve, a gesture of vanity almost absurd in this setting. ''You can explain the rest later. We should leave. Jemal might change his mind . . . once he sees the mess here.'' He led Koblensky through the station and into the street. As suddenly as seeing the curtain rise in a theater, Koblensky was in a different world, a world where all his senses were simultaneously assailed. The street was paved with rough stones, and was a tangle of people and animals—mules, several camels, some barefooted men, others in sandals; a cross-legged youth holding an earthenware flask above his head poured water into his mouth with one hand while the other rested on a crude wooden cage in which about a dozen chickens squawked. It was because he kept his eyes from the harsh light that Koblensky saw first this subtle distinction of rank by feet—the unshod, and the varying levels of the shod. There was a wave of contrasting smells, some foul, some sweet, some of spices, and he understood now why Malik preferred his own heavy perfume.

With a grip on Koblensky's arm, Malik steered him across the street and into a vaulted passage that led to a courtyard, well shaded, where there was a fragrance of tobacco and freshly ground coffee. They went through an open arch into a coffeehouse. Malik nodded to a group of white-bearded men sitting at the edge of a small dais. From their skullcaps Koblensky realized that they were Jews—surrounded, it seemed, by all manner of other races. To one side there was a charcoal fire over which several youths held small copper coffee vessels on the end of long handles.

Malik found a low table in a corner. Squatting next to Koblensky so that they both looked over the whole room, he said, ''You see, Mr. Koblensky, you are in the Orient now.''

A boy brought two small cups of coffee.

''I must warn you,'' said Malik, taking up his cup, ''the coffee is not what it was. Very little is. The war is ravaging Palestine.''

Indeed, the coffee was thin and bitter, with the grounds floating in it.

"Now," said Malik, "since we shall be here for a while, I think you should tell me about your journey."

Koblensky continued with the fiction of his American identity, giving so much detail of his journey that he hoped Malik would not have any further curiosity. And certainly, as Malik listened, he seemed to become less reserved.

They had been in the coffeehouse for more than two hours, with Koblensky talking for most of the time, when a boy came to Malik and spoke to him in Arabic.

"Time to go," said Malik, waving the boy away. He seemed to have a trace of smile on his lips, but the impression went as quickly as it came. "Your story is truly remarkable, Mr. Koblensky. Remarkable."

Malik led Koblensky through a succession of passages and alleys, always keeping in the shade, but he began to perspire heavily, dabbing his brow with a scented handkerchief. They came to a much broader street. To the left, once again Koblensky was able to see Carmel, and to the right, the medieval harbor. By the harbor several carriages were drawn up, all of them mule-drawn except for one at the end, drawn by two small horses. Malik led Koblensky to this carriage. Its driver sat under a canopy, while behind him, in the style of the old European diligence, was an enclosed compartment. The driver recognized Malik and stepped down.

Malik shook Koblensky's hand. "I am sure we shall meet again."

The driver opened the door. Koblensky threw his bag inside and steadied himself as his weight tilted the carriage. He was half inside, still watching his balance, when he realized that there was another occupant in the dark interior, a woman dressed austerely in black. She nodded a greeting.

"I am sorry," he said, retrieving his bag, which had settled at her feet. "I did not know . . . ."

She was amused. "That I realized," she said. "I am Sarah Aaronsohn. It seems you need a home."

Her words made Koblensky realize how much he must have looked like a stray animal. Settling into the seat opposite hers, he could see her more clearly. She had a round, open face and thick dark hair gathered at the back into a bun. This and the black clothes made her seem matronly, but she was, he saw, quite young.

"Yes," he said. "I have heard your name."

"Jemal Pasha?"

He nodded.

"He seemed to think you would be of use to us."

The carriage began to move.

"He mentioned Aaron Aaronsohn."

"My brother. My brother has done valuable work for the Turks."

"So it seemed."

"You find that strange?"

Koblensky was surprised that she suspected this; his tone had been neutral. He was careful. "No. I know nothing of Palestine."

"Yes," she said, still with a hint of suspicion, "it must seem very strange. I have another brother. He is in America now. Which part of America are you from, Mr. Koblensky?"

For some reason, against all his usual instincts, Koblensky spontaneously decided to discard his pretense. For long afterward he wondered why. They were passing through the Haifa city gate; he saw a Turkish checkpoint disappear, he felt the cooler air from the sea, he seemed to shed all caution. Most of all, the sheer fatigue of the deception could not meet this new challenge.

"I am not from America," he said.

"But I was told . . . ." Her intelligence was such that already she understood.

He gave her a guarded version of the truth.

Digesting it, she said, "You may come to miss Russia, for all its troubles. At least Russia is Europe. *This* is not Europe."

"Europe has killed as many Jews as anywhere else."

She considered this silently, as though it was too facile. Then she said, "You will find the Jews here bring with them too much from where they come from—they cannot leave behind their old nationalities. They bring too many European ways; they don't even change their way of dressing. This is Palestine. I hope you don't expect too much from it. You really have to be born here to understand it. It will never change, not really, while Europe changes all the time. This war will certainly change it. And Europe has the new ideas." From being wistful, she suddenly insisted, "Don't you believe in new ideas? The Bolsheviks . . . What if there is a revolution in Russia? What then? Wouldn't that be good for the Jews?"

"The Bolsheviks want the Jews to believe that. My father . . . You see, it serves the Bolsheviks to enlist anyone, the more the better, but if they ever win power they will need new enemies to replace the Czar. Sooner or later, the Jews will be the enemy again. Russia is Russia.''

"You must not expect any better here." He had in some way failed her expectations—failed some hope she had held out for herself beyond the present and beyond Palestine.

The road now ran directly south. Carmel on the left was giving way to a plain. Parallel to them on the right ran the single-rail track and beyond it a rocky coastline. She followed Koblensky's eyes as he looked out to a promontory and the ruins of a castle.

"It was a crusader castle," she said, recovering her grace. "Beyond it is Athlit, where my brother has his agricultural research station. That is one of the things that helps us here, with the Turks." She paused. "I realize now you must find it strange that Jews should help the Turks . . . after what you have seen of their work."

"As you said, I should not expect too much."

She looked at him with the patience of a sorely tested teacher. "When the war began, many Jews were driven out, to Egypt. The Turks gave as their reason the fact that few Jews have elected to become subjects of the Ottoman Empire. It seemed the persecution would spread. There were plenty of others ready to urge it."

"The Arabs?"

"Not *all* the Arabs. But many. And even some of the Christians, the Catholics. The more successful we have become here, the more enemies we have." She hesitated for a moment, distracted, and then seemed to concentrate her will on Koblensky. "We—my brother, the family—we used our influence with Jemal Pasha to have him see how inconvenient it would be if all the Jews left. Jemal can be as ruthless as the rest of them. But for the moment he has a use for us."

Though anxious to persuade him, she had, Koblensky saw, a kind of propriety that checked her feelings; even if he was not persuaded, she would not have become more heated. But then, as he looked at her, she settled her hands on her lap and appraised him as though wanting to begin the relationship afresh.

"It must be very difficult," she said, "after what you have been through, to trust anyone. And yet you told me the truth."

He didn't answer.

"You obviously did not tell Malik."

"No."

"Just as well."

"I thought so."

"You must continue to be careful."

She sounded maternal—and it annoyed him. There was probably no more than a few years in age between them. He had not been with a Jewish woman since he left his own family, over a year earlier. In her voice and face was an echo of something that deeply attracted him and yet from which he had needed to break free—an insistent bond that pursued him the more he sought independence. As though further to reassert this hold, the landscape, too, had suddenly gained a hint of the familiar; in place of the wild littoral there were now cultivated plots, eucalyptus and orange trees in orderly rows, and even the air had the scent of fruit instead of ocean and reminded him of Moldavia. There, at this time, the spring crops would already be in the markets.

"It is different up here," she said.

He nodded.

"I was born here. It grew with me. I remember these orchards being planted. And how bare it used to be."

"So you are a native—truly."

"Of what?" She shrugged. "I don't know."

Her admission of insecurity was closer to his own spirit than anything she had said before.

The orchards gave way to the first houses. The road had been graded; the houses had picket fences. The smaller and obviously the oldest were little more than the crude cabins he knew from Russia, but they were succeeded by more solid brick villas. He was surprised by the evident prosperity and maturity of the town. They turned off the main street and went a short way up a hill and then into a driveway. Here was an even larger house, the kind only a successful merchant could have built in Russia, not merely functional but affording flourishes of brick and wood. Several dogs came rushing to the carriage. Koblensky felt the scene was somehow anomalous, that it should have been in the suburb of a European city, not here on a Palestinian hill. This was certainly not "the Orient" any longer.

Koblensky climbed down from the carriage behind her. From her manner with the driver and then from the way she walked into the house, as if she was the center of it, he felt sure that there was no mother in this family. And that, thought Koblensky sardonically, was the most Jewish of instincts. Sarah Aaronsohn's matronliness had an element of resigned duty in it; he ought to have seen that before.

"Aaron is at the agricultural station," she said over her shoulder as she took him through the house. "He won't be back until evening. He knows nothing of your coming, but we are short of help at Athlit; I know you'll be welcome." They reached the kitchen. A small, florid-faced woman was presiding over a stove where several caldrons bubbled and gave off familiar smells. "If you're to be of any use to us, Mr. Koblensky, we shall have to build you up. Nesta here will take care of that." She spoke to the cook in Turkish, and then, leaving him at the kitchen table, said, "Many things are becoming scarce. The Turks have taken the flour and the sugar. There is little meat. But Nesta is very clever. The cabbage soup is what you need. . . ."

The food made him sleepy. The house seemed to be empty. He went into the garden. Two lawns were intersected by a flower bed and rosebushes. The farthest lawn ended in an olive grove. He took off his jacket and lay in the shade under a tree, and within minutes he was sound asleep.

The rigors of the past months had, in one afternoon, fallen away from him. The knack of waking at the slightest movement, the keenest of his senses for self-preservation, had also gone—or at least lapsed. A shadow was over his face and a voice talking to him before he stirred.

"So."

Koblensky pulled himself up, feeling stiff in the neck from lying against the tree.

"So . . . you are the mystery man."

The man was young, wearing wire-framed glasses, and he had an asymmetrical smile. He reached down, extending a hand. "I'm Feinberg—Absalom Feinberg. Welcome to Zichron Jaacov."

Koblensky took the hand and deliberately pulled on it to help himself up.

"I saw Sarah," said Feinberg. "She told me. She explained also about your change of nationality." He grinned reassuringly. "It's all right. The secret will stay in this house." He nodded toward the town. "There are people here who could not be trusted with that knowledge." He began walking back to the house. "In fact, there are people here who would like to see the Aaronsohns disappear without trace."

"Other Jews?"

Feinberg laughed. "Of course . . . but this is your first day in Palestine. There is a lot for you to understand. There will be time enough. You will be having dinner with us—with the family." He stopped, looking Koblensky over. "It is quite a family. You are lucky, very lucky." He began walking again. "Sarah has a younger sister, Rivka. We are to be married. I work with Aaron. We are a close group. It is better that way."

Understanding the implication, Koblensky said, "Sarah is a striking woman."

Feinberg stopped again, and became almost aggressive. "She holds this family together. Her mother is dead, and her father is very old. He hardly ever comes downstairs now." He paused, clearly deliberating, then added, "Sarah has a husband. In Constantinople." He turned and walked on. He was not a slight man, but he walked with a strange delicacy, head pitched slightly down.

*Sarah has a husband.* It was an odd statement, both calculated and ambiguous, thrust on Koblensky and then left hanging.

Evening closed on the house very suddenly, reinforcing its strange isolated atmosphere. The last of the family to appear was Aaron Aaronsohn. Koblensky could see no physical similarity between him and the sisters: he was tall, squarely built, with thick red hair. There was a reserve in his eyes as he shook Koblensky's hand. Sarah had, it seemed, already given a full account of how Koblensky had reached Palestine. The fact that he had not concealed his real identity from her seemed not yet to have dispelled Aaronsohn's caution; he was, Koblensky saw, a man who would take nothing on trust from others, even his sister. And it was Sarah, as the talk struggled through awkward silences over dinner, who seemed to want a more open acceptance of the newcomer. A delicate hierarchy was involved: Sarah, mistress of the house, deferred to her brother on everything beyond it, and yet was as intellectually agile as he. The younger sister, Rivka, dark and birdlike, was treated as still immature, although she seemed to Koblensky to be strong-willed, perhaps even rebellious. Feinberg had a nervous energy that seemed to need Aaronsohn to steady it.

Aaronsohn began to question Koblensky as though conducting an interrogation. "This Captain Brusse—did he say what he was doing on the train with Jemal?"

"They were checking the coastal defenses."

55

Aaronsohn looked from Koblensky to Feinberg. "I thought so."

Sarah said, "They must expect the British and French to attempt a landing."

Aaronsohn sighed, turning back to Koblensky. "If only they would. What did you make of him—Brusse?"

"Very professional."

"He's German," said Aaronsohn caustically.

"Strange partners, the Germans and the Turks," said Feinberg. "The Germans do their best. Brusse's battleship is really called the *Goeben*, but they've given it a new name, the *Sultan Yaruz Selim*! Fortunately, they can't turn Turks into Germans."

"You came through Affula on the train," said Aaronsohn. "Did you see equipment there?"

"Heavy machinery of some kind."

"Tunneling machinery, from Germany," said Aaronsohn, nodding. "It's been there for weeks. So it's not moved." He lapsed into thought, then said, "Mr. Koblensky, I think you should have some idea of what is happening here. Last year Jemal launched an attack across Sinai, towards the Suez Canal. It's what terrifies the British, that their route to India will be cut. The British are weak, not well led, and poorly equipped. Fortunately for them, Jemal's army was in a worse state. Ran out of ammunition and medical supplies. When the Germans in the field hospital opened their surgery, they found that all they had was gynecological instruments. The attack ran itself into the sand. Now they're planning another, but there are other worries. The Palestine coast is not well defended. Even worse, we've had another plague of locusts; it seems we'll lose the spring wheat. That's why Jemal confides in me. I am supposed to be the answer to the plague."

"In this town, you *are* the plague," said Feinberg.

Aaronsohn shrugged. "They are frightened."

Sarah burst out, "They are treacherous!"

"Our guest seems perplexed," said Feinberg, looking at Koblensky.

"I wonder," said Aaronsohn. "Can anybody from Russia be a stranger to this problem?"

Sarah said, "You should explain."

Aaronsohn hesitated, still judging Koblensky. "Very well," he said finally, more to humor Sarah than to accommodate Koblensky. "You see, Mr. Koblensky, I have several sins. I am a scientist. As it happens, a successful scientist. To the Orthodox Jews here, my sin is to be practical; to the socialists, my sin is to be prosperous—or hopelessly bourgeois, as they would no doubt say in your part of Russia.''

''We seem to assume,'' said Feinberg slowly and with mischievous pleasure, ''we seem to assume that Mr. Koblensky, by being Russian, must be a Bolshevik.''

Sarah, Aaronsohn, Feinberg, and Rivka all looked to Koblensky.

''I am not a Bolshevik,'' he said quietly. ''But I understand why many Jews in Russia are. They believe Bolshevism will destroy their oppressors.''

''You think so?'' Aaronsohn's tone changed. For the first time he was reflective. ''You know, the Bolsheviks call Zionism bourgeois utopianism.''

''My father and my brother are Bolsheviks *and* Zionists. I have choked on the labels.''

''Beliefs have to have labels,'' said Feinberg. ''And are you a Zionist?''

''I am a Jew.''

''Well . . .'' said Aaronsohn slowly, ''I agree that that is complicated enough.'' He smiled. ''We are still some way short of our utopia. But whatever it was that brought you to us, we can use you.''

Koblensky was given quarters at Athlit, a bare room with a cot, living and working with a handful of men, Jews and Arabs, who remained to care for the experimental crops. His feelings about the Aaronsohns were difficult to resolve. They were a family at bay with their pride. Koblensky thought they might have been wiser to appear less grand, but Aaron was indifferent to the animosities they aroused in Zichron Jaacov. Their dealings with the Turks troubled Koblensky more; Jemal had spoken of their ''collaboration,'' and the word seemed deserved. And yet there was uneasiness whenever Jemal or the Turks were discussed within Koblensky's hearing. Sensitivity or discretion? He did not know.

It was Feinberg who remained the most ambiguous member of the Aaronsohn family—orbital rather than central to it, circling, touching, withdrawing according to mood. A part of him was cosmopolitan and extroverted: at fifteen, Sarah told Koblensky, he had been sent to France to finish his education. A part of him was solitary and remained defiantly native: he had been born and raised in Palestine, taught the Koran by an Arab and the Bible by his mother's father. His affection for Rivka seemed more a matter of protocol than of any real passion, and once, too casually, he had told Koblensky that Sarah's absent husband was the shadow of an arranged marriage that had never worked. Koblensky wondered about Feinberg's feelings for Sarah, but she was as reserved toward her prospective brother-in-law as she was toward him; scruple was part of the iron in her.

But in the weeks that followed, his speculations about the Aaronsohn household were overtaken by a more concrete disillusionment. Koblensky had expected to find a harmony in the adversity, that Palestine would kindle a new kind of Jewish unity. Sarah had warned of European intransigence, of failures to adapt. But it was worse than that. There was the wide religious spectrum, always there, from Zionist anticlericalism to ultra-orthodoxy; there were imported political sects of equal diversity and radical social theories more idealistic than political. He had pursued a distant light and found the torches in the hands of a disputatious mob.

The first person to sense his disillusionment was Sarah. From the beginning he had been an unsettling visitation; she more than the others saw the intensity of his drive and, therefore, their failure to measure up to it. She had seen this before in newcomers, but Koblensky expected more and found less. Koblensky expected altogether too much. The more she watched him, the more she suspected that nothing would have been able to satisfy his dream of Palestine, that perhaps he intended nothing ever should. Attracted and yet wary, she tried to mediate with the dream on behalf of reality, joining him for horseback rides into the western foothills of Carmel.

At first, his conversation was perfunctory, his animal nature clearer than his social one. Then one morning, early enough to ride into the low sun, they reached a rocky plateau where they could turn and see back across the tilled land, the orchards, to their own settlement and then the Mediterranean beyond it. They tied the horses to the stump of a scrub oak and sat down, she folding her legs under her ankle-length riding skirt and leaning on the tree, he lying on his side looking away from her—a habit of his that annoyed her, of talking without eye contact. His continued gauntness, in spite of an unstinting appetite, was another irritating implication of the impossibility of satisfying him.

"Before, it would have been all crops, from here down to the coast," she said.

He murmured something indistinguishable.

"The Turks don't seem to understand: if we have no seeds, we have no crops."

Between the tilled fields were barren ones, like flaws in a fabric.

"It's sometimes hard to remember what Aaron has done for this country." She felt on the defensive without meaning to be. "Without him, there would be no grain worthy of the name. People forget, they forget what he has done for them."

"The Turks seem to know." One of his hands was cutting into the earth around the roots of a wild flower.

She avoided the provocation. "Perhaps I should tell you how it started. Aaron was walking up in these very hills, collecting specimens. He saw something he hadn't come across before, but there was something about it—something familiar. It was wheat. *Wild* wheat. The same wheat that was grown by Babylonians, the wheat that gave the Fertile Crescent its name. He had wondered about that for years, and it was growing here, without any irrigation, but it was nearly extinct. There was so little of it that he said there must have been about one chance in a million of his finding it. But he saw what its survival meant. If it could survive for all those centuries, then it must be so strong that with proper cultivation it would grow as a crop again."

Koblensky levered a stone from the ground and tried to pull out the wild flower. Running out of patience, he broke the taproot. Finally he looked up at her. "I don't understand him, your brother. He makes a discovery like that, and what does he do? *He takes it to his laboratory!* He puts it in a catalog. He reacts like a scientist. And yes—he grows it, he proves it can grow."

"What do you mean?"

"Another kind of man, a different kind of man, would have pulled that thing from the earth, he would have held it high, and he would have cried out: 'Look! Waiting for us! The wheat of Israel. Still here!' He would have seen its significance, its *political* significance. People are still saying: 'Palestine is a desert; it is no use trying to settle there.' And what does Aaron do about that? He works in his laboratory. He gets money from America. He plants the fields. But *who* is he really doing all this for? Who is eating the bread? Not the Americans who give him the money.

Not the men who planted the fields. The Turkish army is eating his grain. And what they don't take the locusts will."

She flushed, but when she spoke it was so quietly that he could hardly hear her. "I know how it looks to you. I have seen you watching us. I do not like being watched like that. . . . Do you think I don't understand how it must look to you? But what do you know of it, of us? What do you expect of us? You come from nowhere, with your half-told story, you come with this look in your face, but what have *you* really done? You have escaped from something, I see that, and you want us to do something to justify your escape. That is the mistake we make, isn't it? We can't help you *justify* what you did."

There was the slightest flicker of apology in his eyes as he watched her, but it was not voiced. "You do not like being watched?" He paused and looked at her as though the idea was novel. "That is all you do not like? You like things as they are here? As for justification, I need nobody else to justify what I do." He was still holding the severed flower, passing the petals under his nose. "Strange scent . . . it has a strange scent. You know, I do respect your brother. I respect him more than those who are sitting and waiting for Yahweh, or whatever divine salvation is expected. Wailing in Yiddish. I hate that sound. It follows me. They seem to think it is a natural condition, to suffer, and that sound is a part of it. Believe me, I do admire your brother. He could truly change this land. But it cannot be done his way, as a scientific work, regardless of who rules the country. It cannot be done in servitude under the Turks—or under anyone else. It has to be for *more* than that, *much* more. Don't *you* want more than that?"

To her surprise, he seemed to have dropped the note of reproach; he spoke with an earnestness that was new. "What do you want us to be—politicians?" she said.

He smiled. "No—not if you mean what I think you mean by that." He rolled over, speaking away from her again. "It needs something more, something that can make people rise above themselves. It has to be possible to make a people out of this rabble."

"A people?"

"The people we already are. The Jewish people."

Silent for a minute, they both stared down across the fields. Then she said, curious now rather than defensive, "What do you think can be done?"

He stood up, throwing aside the flower. "Coming here was the only choice I had. There will be many more like me. When you know you have nowhere else to go, then you know what has to be done."

They untethered the horses. She said, "You miss Russia—your family?"

"Not at all. They seem like people in a book you've read but will never open again."

"But that's terrible—very hard to believe, to understand."

He helped her up into the saddle. She saw that it was a gesture with no physical intimacy at all. He had withdrawn into himself again. He was no longer such a puzzle to her—but for all his candor, he had not drawn any closer.

And so it might have drifted on, no better than a wary and expedient partnership between Koblensky and the Aaronsohns, but for an episode that made it impossible to leave things as they had been. It began with the barking of a dog—a weak and intermittent barking like flashes from a failing lamp. Koblensky had stayed late at the Aaronsohn home, detained after dinner by Aaron to check their dwindling inventory of supplies for Athlit, and it was not until just before midnight that he left Zichron Jaacov on horseback. The barking came from the left of the road, where an orchard ended and an uncultivated hillside began. The remnant of a stable, its roof collapsed, was on the far side of the orchard, and the dog was somewhere there. Koblensky knew the stable was not what it seemed—otherwise the dog would not have alerted him. There was no moon, but the night had a flat clarity. Koblensky slipped off the horse and tethered it to a tree.

There was about a hundred yards between the road and the stable. A low, dilapidated wall divided the orchard and the hill. He crawled along the outside of the wall to within a few yards of the stable. No more sound came from the dog. Koblensky lay against the wall for several minutes, listening. From behind the stable, at the foot of the hill, there was a faint sound, a stone displaced. Although he was hunched double behind the wall, he was able precisely to judge the position of this movement, but he waited. There was a different sound, of something heavy being dragged slowly across rough ground. The line of this movement was parallel to the rear of the stable; once clear of the stable, its cause would be visible to him.

The first thing he saw was a shadowy, cloaked figure bent in

61

the strain of pulling; then a sack and a second figure, pushing the sack. Koblensky was about ten yards from them. He dug the tips of his riding boots into the earth and crouched like a sprinter on the block, pausing to judge the distance and the surface of the hill, and then he launched himself headlong at them, aiming at the figure in the rear. The person he hit collapsed under him, with a boot to the groin. The sack ruptured, spilling barley. Koblensky recovered to attack the second figure, but his right foot skated on the barley and he missed his balance. The second figure was much larger than the first and was already turning on him. Koblensky saw a flash of metal. He fell on his right side, right foot still grinding barley into the ground. He kicked his left leg up sharply and the boot met a knife at its tip, falling. The knife went spinning behind Koblensky's head. But the man fell heavily on him—a still formless figure enveloped in a cloak, smothering him and pressing him into the ground. Koblensky's right leg was twisted under him, a hand was on his throat, and then a knee went into his groin. The assailant was utterly silent, not even straining in his breathing. A second hand closed on Koblensky's throat. With his right leg useless, he tried to find force in his left. The breath was being squeezed from him, and blood was in his eyes. He pushed up, trying to slip free, and then he was sliding in the barley, taking his attacker with him.

For the first time there was a curse—a deep salival oath—as neither man could arrest the slide, and the uppermost was losing his balance, and his grip on Koblensky. There was an intake of breath more enraged than the oath. Given the chance, Koblensky rolled sideways, clear of the barley. His right arm hit something hard—the knife. The cloak rose above him in outline. Koblensky had the knife in his hand, but before he could wield it, the figure fell on him again, hands reclaiming his throat. Koblensky saw eyes, starkly delineated eyes closing on his, and an ejaculation of saliva stung his face. The great body overlapped him and the grip on his throat locked and again he began to black out. There was a sudden, sharp pain in his stomach. Where saliva had been spat at him something else came—a jet of blood. They remained locked together, but the grip on his throat had relaxed. Koblensky managed to roll free.

The man had fallen on the knife and it was the hilt that had pressed back into Koblensky's stomach; Koblensky had not even kept his grip on it. The two hands, freed from Koblensky's throat, were still contracted, but gripped only air.

Behind Koblensky there was a whimpering sound. The slighter figure was on its knees, but hunched forward as a supplicant. Both wore the cloaks of Arab fellahin.

Koblensky could move only slowly; his right leg dragged and the bruise in his stomach was still winding him. He hobbled to the kneeling figure and pulled off the top of the cloak. It was a boy, probably no more than ten years old, his face contorted in an unresolved blend of belligerence and terror. Koblensky was angry and contemptuous. The boy began to wail in Arabic, looking at the body behind Koblensky. The dead man was like the sack of barley, suddenly depleted in bulk. Koblensky left the boy and looked at the dead man's face; it had thick white brows and a closely cut white beard, now discolored by vomit and blood. There was a small indented scar over the left eye. It must once have been a formidable countenance; it was still set in a grimace of resentment. Koblensky realized that the man's blood was all over his own clothes and face. He limped back to the boy and pulled him off the ground, propelling him toward the stable.

The stable concealed a small store of barley and wheat from the Turkish harvest collector. There was a corner where a section of wooden floor could be moved to give access to a cellar. The Arabs had taken the trouble to replace this cover and sprinkle it with dirt. Behind the wall lay the dog, with its throat cut.

It was nearly dawn before Aaronsohn and Feinberg had finished helping Koblensky bury the body and remove all trace of the struggle. Sarah, who had gone to bed before Koblensky left, had not been awakened. When she came down, she found them and the boy in the kitchen.

"As soon as he gets back to his village, everyone will know about the grain," her brother was saying.

Koblensky sat with his boots off and his right leg strapped from ankle to knee.

Feinberg answered Aaronsohn: "*That* is not the problem. They know about it anyway, and the others. The problem is *who* it was."

At this point they all saw Sarah, standing at the door. Aaron told her what had happened.

"Abdul-Hadi?" she said, raw-faced without makeup. "You have managed to kill Abdul-Hadi?" The accusation was finally directed at Koblensky.

" 'Whoso sheddeth man's blood, by man shall his blood be

shed, for in the image of God made He man,' '' intoned Feinberg. ''The divine command given to Noah and his sons and, my dear Asa, a principle embraced with enthusiasm by the Arab. The circumstances don't count. That obligation is passed on from generation to generation, the blood feud.''

Koblensky moved the leg slightly and winced. ''I am expected to worry? He nearly killed me.''

''Abdul-Hadi,'' said Sarah, ''was one of the best friends we had among the Arabs.''

''A true friend,'' snapped Koblensky, ''who takes your barley.''

''They are starving in that village,'' she said, standing in her nightgown with feet firmly set, in the way she had of making her whole body stubborn.

It was Feinberg who matched her sharpness. ''Whose fault is that?'' he said. ''Nobody in the whole town wants to help them, and yet the town would not exist without them. When my family came here, there were two hundred Jews and one thousand Arabs, and soon we were the masters and they were the slaves. Did we expect it to continue? So that when there isn't enough food to go round we look after ourselves and expect them to go short?''

Aaron sighed. ''It's not the time now to argue about that. The boy has to go back.''

''He's terrified,'' said Sarah.

Koblensky looked up and, with a remorseless set to his face, spoke very softly. ''He's a thief. His father was an animal. This will warn them off. I want the boy to be terrified. *I want them all to be terrified.* They should be terrified of the Turks, and terrified of us. We will take care of ourselves.''

Sarah's face drained of color. She looked at her brother, who held his head in his hands, then at Feinberg, who was looking at Koblensky as though comprehending his nature for the first time—but not, it seemed, with dismay.

Nobody spoke until, after ten seconds or so, Feinberg became suddenly assertive. ''He thinks like Ha Shomer! *They* talk like this. Maybe *they* should take the boy back. We should send for Abba Laski.''

''Ha Shomer?'' said Koblensky.

''The Watchmen,'' said Aaron Aaronsohn. ''A private army— vigilantes. Until now we have never needed them.''

Feinberg took up the explanation. ''You talk of taking care of ourselves? About eight years ago, when the Bedouin began attacking settlements in Lower Galilee, a handful of young men made up a defense organization. For the first time. There are hundreds of them now, although since the war the Bedouin do not attack. You have only to murmur 'Ha Shomer' to these Arabs and they get wet between the legs.''

Sarah had walked out, taking Abdul-Hadi's son with her.

''I thought you were on the side of the underdog,'' said Koblensky.

''In Palestine we are all underdogs,'' Feinberg grinned. ''In this case, I am thinking about your skin.''

''I would like to meet these people,'' said Koblensky, trying to move his leg again. ''Ha Shomer? And if they take the boy back, I will go with them, in spite of this leg.'' He rubbed his thigh. ''I was lucky with Abdul-Hadi. That man had killed before. It was on his breath.''

Aaronsohn was silent, looking out the door and listening to Sarah, who was talking to the boy in Arabic. Almost absent-mindedly, he looked back at Koblensky, then said finally, ''I don't like involving outsiders. It will make things worse, antago-nize the rest of the town. But it does seem the only way. . . . Sarah doesn't understand, even now, that if the Turks encour-aged them, the fellahin would turn on us.''

Abba Laski was little more than five feet tall, but nearly as wide, and his great buttocks so overlapped the saddle on his horse that to speak of his ''seat'' in riding terms hardly described the way in which the horse was subjugated to the rider. On first catching sight of him, Koblensky was reminded of a Russian butcher he had once known and not, in any sense, of a warrior. But Abba Laski was the leader of a Ha Shomer squad. On closer scrutiny, Koblensky was further dismayed to see a layered chin and a skin as unseasoned as a baby's, a rabbinical pallor under a broad-brimmed leather hat.

To complete the image, Laski's voice was virginally high-pitched. He gazed down at Koblensky, standing on the steps of the Aaronsohn front porch, and piped, ''So . . . you are the assassin of Abdul-Hadi.'' His horse snorted and he remained in the saddle, as though waiting for an answer. ''Bad leg to show for it.''

''You're Laski?'' said Koblensky.

Laski's horse flicked its tail and puts its muzzle into Koblensky's

face. "It's all right," said Laski. "He always tastes a new
face." It was when Laski swung out of the saddle that Koblensky
saw speed contradicting bulk—he was on the ground before one
movement of the horse's tail, pushing the hat lower on his brow
and extending a hand.

"Yes. I'm Laski." In spite of the disparity in their heights,
Laski was in no way the weaker figure. Still holding Koblensky's
hand and still speaking in an airy, fluting way, he said, "Have
you killed before?"

"Yes," said Koblensky, complying with the insolence before
he realized it. "Yes . . ." The sentence faltered.

Laski's grin was not at all childlike. "But not so intimately?"

"I was lucky."

"Yes, you were. He was a murderous fellow."

The word "fellow" seemed derivative of another, more refined culture.

"And where is his son?" Laski left the horse eating a vine and
went up the steps with effortless, springy steps.

The Arab boy no longer seemed fragile. In regaining control
of himself he had become aloof, impassive, looking at Koblensky
with the eyes of a cat. Laski spoke to him briefly in Arabic, but
required no answer. Feinberg joined them. Koblensky saw that
Feinberg's casual cynicism disappeared in Laski's company. As
they took the boy outside, Feinberg picked up a rifle, but Laski
waved it away. "We don't need guns."

Laski took the boy on his own horse. The slight boy and the
rotund dwarf in his wide-brimmed hat looked as though they had
strayed from some circus procession. Koblensky and Feinberg
flanked them and they rode east toward the poorer land where
the fellahin village was out of sight in a valley. In the heat of the
morning, the air was as dry as the dust on the road.

The Arab village seemed sited to concentrate the heat rather
than disperse it. Mud-brick houses were built in crescent formation at the base of a hill facing a rough square, with other houses
forming a street from the square to meet the one access road.
They rode into the village past its well, a deep boring with only a
low rim of brick at its head, the bricks worn into narrow ruts by
the wear of the bucket ropes. Apart from a withered ass lying by
the well trying to lick its own tail, there was no movement. As
they reached the square, a child's cry came from one of the
houses at the base of the hill and then a few figures appeared in
doorways—older men and boys.

Laski let Abdul-Hadi's son slip down from the saddle. The boy stood barefooted a few paces from the horse, looking toward a house in the center of the crescent. A woman, visible only in outline, appeared and remained in the shadow of the door of the house. As the boy walked slowly across the square, the other men and boys came into the sun, gathering but leaving a gap for him. They turned from the boy to the three horsemen. Laski reached to a saddlebag and pulled out what seemed like a bundle of rags. As he threw it toward the men it unfolded, taking brief flight like a wraith, then collapsed in the dirt, rags again, with a patch of caked blood on it. Laski pointed to it, Abdul-Hadi's cloak, and began talking to them in Arabic. In Arabic his shrillness took on a force that it lacked in English. His audience closed ranks as the boy disappeared, like sheep seeking mutual shelter. The boy had not looked back, nor did he appear to have heard a word.

"They're so *abject*," said Feinberg, more in pity than in contempt.

Laski pulled his horse around to head back out of the village. In spite of his exertion, his face remained colorless. He looked at Feinberg. "Not like the Bedouin," he said.

They passed the well again. Laski directed Koblensky's attention to it. "Look. Just a hole in the ground. No winch, no mechanism."

"The women fetch the water," said Feinberg. "I tried, once, to do it myself. I couldn't lift the pot from the ground."

Laski laughed. "Did you know, Mr. Koblensky, that our friend here is known to the Arabs as Sheikh Salim? He tried very hard to prove that all Semitics are equal. He lived among them—yes, he tried to understand them. He knows the Koran by heart. But look at him—does he strike you as a sheikh?" Laski laughed again.

The note of derision annoyed Feinberg. His boot heels dug into the horse. "They have a culture."

But Laski was already bored with the game. He turned to Koblensky. "You haven't much to say."

"I have seen that kind of abjection before—in Jews."

Laski's hands, the only part of him that seemed weathered and matured, closed on the reins. "Yes."

They rode in silence until the village had disappeared behind them. At the crest of the path they could see Zichron Jaacov.

Laski stopped and the others followed suit. "Yours are new

eyes here, Koblensky," said Laski. "Perhaps you can see us better than we can see ourselves."

Koblensky looked at the shimmering rooftops and saw only the delusion of security. His senses had been on edge since Laski had materialized. Laski's performance in the Arab village had kindled an exhilaration that Koblensky hadn't known for months. So physically improbable, this man was the first he had found in Palestine who represented what he had been looking for: militant self-assertion. He answered Laski: "We are very weak here. The Turks know the value of divide and rule."

Laski nodded. "The real weakness is within ourselves. It is not inflicted by others. You want to know what it is, in a word? *Family.* Do you know what I mean? The Jewish family is a tyranny. The tyranny of the elders. From the first moment that we can breathe, it is drilled into us—from the first moment that the fat breast of the Jewish mother droops into our face and fixes itself in our mouths, pumping away whether we want it or not. For every drop of milk it gives, it wants blood in return—a lifetime of blood. A lifetime of debt repayment, for the privilege of coming into the family, the Jewish family that smothers you like the great breast." He stopped. "You think I am blaspheming?"

The words had poured out in a tirade, but Koblensky was not disputing them. "No—it's not blasphemy to me."

Feinberg murmured, "Abba, something terrible must have happened to you at your mother's breast."

"You!" Laski glowered at Feinberg. "*You* should know what I'm talking about. Family . . . consenting to whatever the elders want. Sarah . . . the arranged marriage. You pretend it's Rivka you want. But it was Sarah, wasn't it? Ever since you've been—" Laski caught Koblensky's surprise and stopped.

But Feinberg kept his composure and repeated his mocking tone. "How do you propose to wean this new Jew of yours—the one with no family?"

Laski stared ahead, setting his horse into movement again. "We are going to abolish the family as a social unit. If we are going to build a new nation here, we don't need to inherit that institution. We can start again—a collective settlement, the *kvutzah*. The children will live separately from their parents; they will be part of something bigger than the family; they will grow up in a community that will share everything. . . ."

"Aha," said Feinberg. "Utopianism again." Then his sarcasm seemed to relent. "I wish you luck, Abba. Given the choice of bringing down the Turk or the Jewish family, I would rather take on the Turk.''

"And you," said Laski to Koblensky. "What about you?"

"Survival comes first."

Quietly, Laski said, "What do you suggest we do about that?"

"What can we do, on our own, if the Turks turn against us? We will need outside help.''

"Outside help?"

"Sooner or later, the French, the British, or both, will drive out the Turks.''

"You think they—either of them—care about us?"

"They must be made to believe we support them."

Laski laughed in his trilling, metallic way. "*We?* Who do *we* speak for? Those rabbis of Zionism? Or the Challukkah? The socialists? *We?*"

"A start must be made. An attempt, at least." Koblensky was beginning to show exasperation.

Laski scowled and abruptly rode off in a gallop, ahead of Feinberg and Koblensky. Perhaps, mused Feinberg to himself, Koblensky and Laski were too alike to tolerate each other. The promise of such friction had a healing sweetness for him; it induced the silent reverie that best soothed his nature and that only the Arab poets seemed able to express. With their verses in his head, he rode alongside Koblensky into Zichron Jaacov.

To Koblensky's annoyance, Sarah seemed to regard the killing of Abdul-Hadi as having been gratuitous, almost a crime, and a crime in character with how she now perceived Koblensky. That this was unreasonable, that it had been done in self-defense, she was not ready to concede. The offense was made worse, in her eyes—it was compounded—by then involving Laski, whom she called "that sadistic eunuch," looking directly at Koblensky as she said it, implying that the two were accomplices in spirit.

Caught in this emotional cross fire, Aaron Aaronsohn seemed himself to be coming to a new resolve. The day after the ride to the village, he broke off from a routine conversation with Koblensky and seemed suddenly burdened. Then, in a more embracing tone, he said, "I think it is time you understood how I feel, how I *really* feel, about our Turkish masters." One hand fell on Koblensky's shoulder. "Here we are not like Meyer Malik. We make no profit from the Turks." Both men stood in the twilight of Aaronsohn's study. Somewhere in the house a

69

shutter began to rattle. "I have won Jemal's trust. As long as he trusts us, then there is something we can do. If he does not trust us, then there is nothing we can do."

Koblensky seemed still dubious.

"You think that is too passive of us?" With an effort, Aaronsohn became more emphatic. "It might seem like that, but there is much you do not know. You would be surprised—very surprised, I think—if you knew how close in our thinking we really are." He waved Koblensky to a seat. "Please."

Koblensky had the disturbing association that the banging of the shutter was like the beat of a drum through a graveyard during a requiem; he had never seen Aaronsohn so lugubrious.

"We have had to wait," said Aaronsohn, still standing. "Everything is at risk. I have not told the others, not even Sarah, of how I have come to see things. They will have to be told now. You see, like you, I have decided that our only hope is to get rid of the Turk for good. But of course, we cannot do that on our own, and there never would have been an opportunity to do it, but for this war. It is different now." He stopped, half hearing the shutter, then regained his concentration on Koblensky. "Sometime the British will have to come. From Egypt, across the Sinai. Not for a while, but they will have to come that way, in the end." He sat down, looking out the window, where the light was fast slipping away. "The British are an unknown quantity to me. I know the Germans. I know the French. But it is the British we have to turn to. So we must convince them, as best we can, that we can help them."

"Who can you trust?"

The question drew Aaronsohn's face from the window as though it were an impertinence. Koblensky could not see his expression because of the shadow, but the set of his shoulders was part of his response. Finally Aaronsohn said, "*Trust?* Why do I trust you? I do not know. How can I know that? Perhaps it is not you I trust—but your condition. You are not like us. You have far less to risk than we. For you, it must seem much simpler . . . but perhaps too simple, much too simple."

Koblensky was incapable of deference, but he could see the justice of what Aaronsohn had said, and he sat silently as though taking advice from a patriarch. Aaronsohn *was* the patriarch here.

After a long pause, Aaronsohn said, "Sarah says she thinks that you are very *Russian*." He smiled without humor. "By that I think she means you are unfathomable. I think that this is a new experience for her; she is normally a good judge of character. This is why, perhaps, she continues to take an interest in you. I—I am not so interested in puzzles. To know what it is you want—that is enough." Aaronsohn leaned closer to Koblensky. "For years we wanted nothing more than to do our work, to make our own lives here. Nothing more. Jews alongside Arabs, and Christians—and with the Turks. It seemed to work. It is not like that now. So . . . perhaps it surprises you, but I do know the Zionists. I have met them. I can tell you, Zionism has committee sickness. Those people have an idea of Palestine that is not mine, and it is the ones who do not know Palestine who talk most of Israel. *Israel* . . ."

"I am not a Zionist."

"And yet you talk of a Jewish *people?*"

Koblensky recalled the conversation with Sarah. "Yes. I believe that."

Aaronsohn stood up. "It will never be that simple. You ask who we can trust? We begin here, in this house, *my* house. We will have to depend on each other."

It was strange, thought Koblensky, that the dissension in the house had brought such a positive result: It had introduced a cold lick of reality. No one would be thankful for it, but no one could evade it.

"I will have to tell the others what I have told you," said Aaronsohn. "I cannot do less. You will stay for dinner? It is best done now."

The dinner began in a tense formality; Aaronsohn, at the head of the table, waited until each plate was in place, and then recapitulated his view.

Sarah was the first to break the silence that followed. "Why should the British help *us?* I do not see it."

Koblensky said, "We have something they need."

Aaronsohn tried to avert argument, and answered her gently. "If they come across the Sinai, they will meet the Turks at their strongest. They know that. They will find it difficult to know how the Turks are deployed, what their strength is, their reserves. . . ."

"And *we* are to tell them *that?*" said Feinberg, looking from Aaronsohn to Koblensky. "It is fantastic, reckless! How can *we* become *spies?* And how do we know what we would get in return? Of course, of course—I realize why it is that Asa would

71

like to do this. He would like the British conveniently to open the gates of Israel, and the Jews to take advantage of that. Or rather, the Zionists."

Koblensky checked his first impulse and, with restraint, said, "You do not have to be a Zionist to want our freedom."

"But *you* want more than that—don't you?" interposed Sarah, before Feinberg could answer. "Of course we want our freedom. And our dignity. There is not much dignity in living here now. But you want more. You talk of the Jewish people—but that means a Jewish state. *You want it all!*"

Feinberg nodded and, almost shouting, cried out, "You ask too much. You make us into a special case. We are *not* your special case. *We are not the only persecuted people!* The Arabs are as persecuted as we! Why should *we* claim to be peculiar? We do that, and it only helps the people who all the time say we *are* peculiar—don't you see that? The more *Jewish* this struggle against the Turks becomes, the more *selfish* it is, the less it is going to find support. Don't you understand?"

"You forget," said Koblensky sharply, "you forget we *are* peculiar. We are stateless."

Feinberg bridled. "Yes—we are. But why must it be a *Jewish* state? Why must we go back? It is not nationalism I oppose—it's *racial* nationalism."

Even before Feinberg finished, Sarah was nodding her head, and she said fervently, "*Exactly*. What gives us the right *here* to dominate the others?"

Aaronsohn intervened, looking exasperated. "To me, we don't have to argue about it. It doesn't arise. In our circumstances, it is wishful thinking. Here in Zichron, we cannot even agree on how to live as Jews."

There was an uneasy interval, and then Sarah, sounding more conciliatory, said, "At least we should do something more than we have, something more than talk. We cannot go on as we have. I am tired of it."

"Perhaps you cannot agree with me," said Koblensky, responding to her tone. "But for now, if we cannot be sure of our friends, we can be sure of our enemies."

Aaronsohn nodded. "We will never want for enemies."

Sarah said, "And some of them are Jews."

"Malik?" said Koblensky.

"Not only Malik," said Sarah. "Why do you think Malik is always coming here, in that grand carriage of his? He knows the

72

rest of this town. He doesn't have to worry about them. But he is never quite sure of us.''

"That, at least, is a compliment to us," said Feinberg.

"He is the most dangerous—because he knows Jemal," said Aaronsohn.

"And because he is envious of your standing with Jemal," said Sarah.

"So," Aaronsohn nodded. "In any event, there will never be many of us. A few more, outside this room. Lishansky, Belkind—men like that."

Sarah thought: There is little warmth in this room. The only heat had been in the argument that had aroused them, but at the same time had shown the space between each of them. Even between Aaron and herself: at times like this he was more father than brother. Feinberg and Koblensky had no meeting ground that she could see. Feinberg—volatile, romantic, melancholic, impulsive. And Koblensky—what was it in his voice? *We can be sure of our enemies.* The voice was Koblensky's and yet not his: the eternal, watchful, cynical, obdurate voice of a collective experience. Unlike Feinberg, there was no self-pity in Koblensky, and very little, if any, pity for anyone else. She heard the shutter; it summoned her as from a distance. "You hear that?" she said, into the trucelike silence of the table.

Aaronsohn listened, and then seemed alarmed. "The wind."

"Surely," said Sarah, "it is too early for it, too early in the year . . .?"

"Sometimes it comes early." Aaronsohn strained to hear beyond the shutter to the rising wind itself. "That would be one burden too many." He got up and went to the window, looking out at the trees. "It *is* coming from the southeast." He turned back into the room, ashen. Seeing that Koblensky was perplexed, he said. "The scirocco. It comes here from across a thousand miles of desert. It burns the air out of your lungs. It incinerates the crops."

Sarah said, "It shouldn't be here until September."

Aaronsohn looked out the window again and then said, "By dawn it won't be possible to go into the fields." The loose shutter had picked up its beat, becoming less funereal and more manic. "So," he said, "we shall have little else to do except conspire. If we are going to do the work of spies, we should think about how to reach the British."

\*     \*     \*

73

By dawn, the temperature was one hundred and nine in the shade; by noon it was one hundred and twenty-five. Life had drained from the land. To the east it was impossible to see beyond a quarter of a mile. The wind ate into the soil. The scirocco was formed in some far corner of Arabia by a combustion of air and heat, and then continued to regenerate itself as it came headlong across the desert. When it hit Palestine it brought the kind of catastrophe that Biblical legends were made of. It was a full week before the tail of the wind passed out to sea and the scirocco spent itself in the Mediterranean. As with a beach after a storm, so with this landscape: contours seemed changed, horizons rearranged, paths and landmarks obliterated. An ocher dust coated everything.

Koblensky went with Aaronsohn to judge the damage. Aaronsohn squatted, with his right hand breaking the crust of the ground to find a root in what had once been a wheat field. He found something little more than shriveled straw, put it in his left palm and rubbed it. It broke into dust.

"We lost about a third of the crop to the locusts," he said, dispassionately precise as though lecturing a student in his laboratory. "What was left then was stunted, it had short stalks, but it would have been sufficient. The stalks are as important to us as the wheat itself. They are used for winter fodder. So you see"—the dust tipped from his palm back into the earth—"in one stroke we lose the grain *and* the fodder."

Aaronsohn dusted off his palm and stood up. "Whatever happens in the war, there will be famine here. The sooner the British come, the better." He looked away toward the cliffs. "You know there is not a single coastal defense battery between Gaza and Beirut?" He nodded to the promontory at Athlit. "Smugglers came in and out of here without any trouble. We could have a system of getting messages out to a warship; it would be possible. Someone will have to try to get through the lines at Gaza, and then across Sinai to Cairo, to put this plan to the British." He rested a hand on Koblensky's shoulder. "If anyone could do it, it would be you."

Traces of the wind remained: spirals of dust came and went fitfully, lifting debris from the storm and then dropping it in the new desert. Hawks circled with wings motionless in funnels of hot air. There was nothing to draw them to the ground.

# 4

## Cairo ✳ May 1916

"Cairo! Ah, Cairo! So lax—so *very* lax!"

As he spoke, Kippax inhaled the morning air as though it were a narcotic. He had slept in a cot on a small balcony, two floors up from a narrow street, and now he stood, still in his nightshirt, looking from the balcony back into the room, where Bron was inert on another cot. There certainly was a flavor in the air, though for Bron is was not a stimulant; the air to him was still part of an enveloping alienness, as layered with unidentified scents as with sounds—and not all the scents were fragrant.

"The most *delinquent* city in the world!" Kippax leaned against the frame of the balcony door, in profile. "Didn't you feel that, just coming through the streets last night?"

Bron raised himself drowsily from the pillow. "Seemed like Babel to me."

"Yes, of course—but what a mixture!" Kippax came into the room. "Every race you can imagine; must always have been like it. *Ungovernable*. Therefore, ideally suited to British care." He came to rest on a sofa. "Where's that bloody orderly?"

It struck Bron that the nightshirt was the only garment that had ever successfully draped Kippax; it made him seem graceful in a catlike way. He was less English and, puzzlingly, more himself.

They were in a nameless street several blocks east of the Nile, in a building that had once been a French officers' mess and had now been appropriated by the British Army, with three flats on this floor in which officers were billeted, quarters below for orderlies and batmen, and a small mess hall. French decor persisted in pink plaster and baroque mirrors, and French plumbing with the absence of pedestal toilets; for the first time Bron had had to squat on foot pads, using unfamiliar muscles.

Kippax's enthusiasm left Bron numb; only when the orderly

appeared with their breakfast tray did he begin to revive, and then it was due to the sight and smell of something familiar: fried eggs and bacon, toast and marmalade.

They were both dressed in their tropical khakis, showing rank but no regiment. The other occupants of the billet were wearing regimental flashes and seemed instinctively to keep their distance, half knowing and half curious. All anyone yet knew was that Kippax and Bron were assigned to a new bureaucratic growth in the Grand Continental Hotel, and that morning were pampered enough to have a staff car collect them, though it was a journey of less than a quarter mile.

Kippax had fallen silent during the ride, but as they were led up a short side staircase, he said, "Don't go on appearances."

They seemed to follow a strong smell of coffee, first into a narrow room containing little more than two empty desks, and then into a huge, high-ceilinged ballroom hung with heavy chandeliers. One wall was lined with chairs covered in plush velvet; the opposite wall was punctuated by three large French windows which led to a deep balcony. Two-thirds down its length, the ballroom was divided by Chinese screens. Kippax and Bron stopped at the brink of the larger section of the room. Spread across the floor was a map, at least eighteen feet square. Gazing down at it was a man in a white naval officer's uniform. He seemed unaware of their arrival, although their steps had echoed across the room. Kippax coughed theatrically.

"It's all right, Owen. I know you're there." The man unfolded his arms and stroked a small goatee beard, then turned toward them. "And this is our water diviner, I take it?"

The naval officer was without his cap and Bron could not tell his rank from the rings on his sleeves. He was half inclined to salute until he saw Kippax's right hand make a restraining gesture.

"Yes," said Kippax. "This is Michael Bron. Michael, this is Professor—I'm sorry—Commander Hogarth." He began walking around the map. "Must get used to these ranks. Yours is very illustrious, David."

Hogarth laughed. "I only put on the bloody thing if I'm dealing with the generals. They treat one very disdainfully unless they see appropriate plumage. A matter of appearing to be professional." As he extended a hand to greet Kippax, his arms were revealed as unusually long, giving him an apelike reach. "My dear Owen, we've missed you. Things are coming to the boil.'' He looked beyond Kippax to Bron. ''And *you* come with high endorsement, young man. Welcome. As you can see from the map, it's very much a patchwork job.''

They looked down at the map. It was in three colors, mostly a thin watercolor brown for desert, darker brown for hills and mountains in relief, an occasional red line for a track or road, and isolated patches of green. ''Sinai?'' said Kippax.

''Sinai,'' confirmed Hogarth, as though burdened. ''The map sections were sent out without numbers or labels. Nobody knew how to put the thing together, not a clue. Then I found Lawrence. *Behold:* In one night there was a map of Sinai, plus his own amendments.''

''Where *is* Lawrence?'' said Kippax.

''Wish I knew.'' Hogarth shrugged. ''Disappeared in a westerly direction; said something about making contact with an agent of the Senussi. His parting shot was: 'Don't think the Sinai is an obstacle. It looks far worse than it is.' '' Hogarth turned to Bron. ''It's going to be your first headache. We have to be sure of the wells.''

''Surely we're not dispatching an army across it yet?'' said Kippax.

''We'd better talk,'' said Hogarth. ''Follow me.''

They went to the other side of the Chinese screens. Two long sofas faced each other, with a low wicker table between. Hogarth pulled a tasseled cord and a bell rang sharply.

An Indian orderly in naval whites appeared.

''Coffee—and then keep everybody out,'' said Hogarth.

The coffee was Turkish. Hogarth hunched forward on one sofa, Kippax and Bron faced him on the other. Bron saw the mannerisms of tutor and pupil, knowing that that was the origin of the relationship between Hogarth and Kippax. Hogarth had been the mentor of a generation of Oxford Orientalists, and Bron was intrigued to see how this once obscure specialty was being put to military use.

Hogarth spoke with crisp authority. ''As you know, the Turk has made one attempt already to come across Sinai to Suez. It was wide open, but for some reason they seemed to run out of steam. They will almost surely try again. They have been emboldened by our disaster at Gallipoli.''

Kippax murmured, ''Yes; another exercise in cannon fodder.''

Hogarth's voice suddenly sharpened. ''That's easy hindsight. The landings at Gallipoli were a bold idea. God knows, we've made no ground in France. We need bold ideas. It might well have succeeded.'' The sharpness dissipated with a sigh. ''Leadership—it's a question of leadership. Gallipoli was mismanaged, dreadfully mismanaged. It's been bad for morale. A loss of nerve . . .'' He stopped again, as though remembering military discretion, then chose to remain candid. ''We need to substitute brain for brute force, since brute force seems not to achieve anything.''

''It would be novel if it did,'' said Kippax.

Bron had a feeling that this tone struck an off-note with Hogarth, that perhaps Kippax was too familiar too soon.

''I think we require some more coffee, gentlemen,'' said Hogarth, more formally. ''There is much I have to explain—about why you are here, about the peculiarities of Cairo.'' He looked from Kippax to Bron. ''No doubt you were hoping for explanation. It's a singularly picaresque city, Cairo. And in a way, therefore, sympathetic to our business.''

During the following hour Hogarth spoke without pause, and Bron now understood his academic reputation.

As they left, Bron looked again at the sprawling map of the Sinai and saw the careful notations in a spidery hand. ''Who is Lawrence?'' he asked Kippax.

''Lawrence? Ah, Lawrence.'' The switch from the querulous to the contemplative was another trick of Kippax's. ''Lawrence is very assiduously preparing himself to become an enigma.''

''I see,'' said Bron, lingering at the map as Kippax began to walk away. ''There's nothing enigmatic about his maps. Damned good.''

Kippax grunted—and impatiently waited.

The map, Bron sensed, was too tangible an achievement by a rival. But a rival in what?

Hogarth's sardonic rehearsal of the work ahead of them had relied too easily on innuendoes—innuendoes that Kippax grasped better than Bron. It was not done to offend Bron so much as from a habit of intercourse in which Bron was still the novice.

The two desks in the anteroom were, it turned out, to be theirs. There were three oval mirrors in gilt frames on one wall and the room had a too-sweet smell. At the far end was another door, with panels of inlaid pink baize. Beyond it, as Bron suspected, was the rest of the original room, a vast one with a marble floor and walls covered in the pink baize. To the left were three marble washbasins, with faucets fashioned in Babylonian

style from brass capped with ivory. In the center of the far wall
were three cubicles, each with an enormous porcelain pedestal
toilet. Framed above them was a crudely lacquered portrait of
George V and Queen Mary.

Coming in behind Bron, Kippax trilled, "My God—the throne
room!"

"The plumbing on which rests an empire."

"Yes. Can you imagine?" Kippax caught his reflection multi-
plied three times in the mirrors above the basins and unconsciously tugged at the rear hem of his tunic. "Can you *imagine*
the night of the High Commissioner's Ball—all the secrets that
must have spilled out between these walls?"

"Running a war from the powder room. It's a practical joke."

"Look," said Kippax impatiently. "You won't understand
what this is all about in one morning." He leaned against one of
the washbasins, trying a tap. Yellow water came from the lips of
an ivory asp. "Cairo is a center of causes. There are those who
dream of Egyptian independence. There are those who want
something larger: Arab independence and an Arab kingdom.
There are Turks who dream of Ottoman rule over the whole of
Arabia. There are Turks who want to restore the rule of the
Turkish sultan over Islam. There are Turks who want to cast off
Islam altogether and have a secular state. There are Greeks here
dreaming of Smyrna, and Italians of the conquest of North Africa,
and the French, who want Syria. There are those who do not
dream at all but are quietly at work creating dissatisfaction, and
those who are simply drawing good pay selling information and
expect to draw even better. There are ears outside every room
and sometimes in the room." He rubbed his hands in the yellow
water.

"I'm beginning to see what I've walked into."

"No," said Kippax, turning from the basin. "No, you can't.
Not yet."

Bron came to feel more in Kippax's care than he wanted,
more adrift in unknown waters than he had expected. He was
surprised that Kippax slipped so easily into this setting; sometimes,
in the evening, Kippax would look out to the sky, a dust-filtered
orange flare at the horizon and a progressively deeper turquoise
above, as it filled with the cries of the city's muezzins and when
all voices seemed cast to the sky, and Kippax was at ease with
the fervid, ascending prayers. As much at ease as if it were the
tumult of a Latin mass. Bron remembered earlier speculation on

Kippax's vocation. For a while he had seemed drawn to the
church, though not so much from the discovery in himself of
piety as from a calculation that ecclesiastical power would suit
his taste. To have chosen instead this very different path might
seem—to someone who knew Kippax less well than Bron—the
most unlikely alternative. But Bron saw a consistency: Kippax's
ambition had always needed the focus of duty; whether duty
drawn to a theological or a secular attraction did not really matter,
as long as the duty enabled Kippax to assign his scruples to some
authority greater than himself and more abstract than mortal. If
the Army had supplanted the Church, it had to be the greater
power. But this power also had to have its human agents. With
Kippax the Winchester prefect, it had been the masters who were
that, beneath the greater authority of the headmaster. At Oxford
it must have been Hogarth. But if Hogarth, tutor and mentor,
was now only an intervening hand, what represented the absolute
allegiance? King? Nation? Or some other warp of duty, a new
abstraction? Through the fetid Cairo summer he watched Kippax
at close quarters, and the more Kippax seemed at ease, the more
Bron felt compromised in some way he did not understand.

"A Jew, sir."

"A Jew?"

"From Palestine, sir." The lieutenant's voice kept a professional neutrality.

The colonel sighed, and looked hard at the lieutenant. "From
Palestine, you say?"

"Yes, sir."

"From, but not of, I imagine." The colonel looked at a
docket identifying the visitor. "The name sounds Russian. The
worst kind."

"Looks it, sir."

"Don't know why they keep sending these people to us."
Overdressed for the heat, the colonel pulled futilely at his tunic
belt, sighed again, and pushed the docket to one side. "Bring
him in."

The man who entered wore a suit that was too large at the
shoulders and too tight at the waist; the lieutenant recognized the
hand of a Cairo tailor, probably in the bazaar. Despite these
faults, the man was unselfconscious, physically superior to his
raggedness. There was an unmistakably Asiatic cast to his face,
prominent cheekbones and elongated narrow eyes. The lieutenant

waved him to a seat at the colonel's desk, and himself sat at the other side of the desk. The colonel did not rise and waited for the visitor to settle, looking him over with obvious reservation.

"Koblensky?" said the colonel, finally.

Koblensky nodded, fixing the colonel with resolute gray eyes.

"Russian?"

Koblensky nodded again, and the colonel had an uncomfortable feeling of their roles being reversed—that it was he, not Koblensky, who was receiving the more detailed scrutiny.

"But you came from Jerusalem?" The colonel's voice sought to reassert his primacy.

"No. From the north, from Athlit." Koblensky's English was oddly expressionless, as though read from a book by a child unsure of its meaning.

"You came through the Turkish lines at Gaza?"

"At night."

The colonel broke the eye contact first, looking down again at the docket, hesitating. "You were taken to the refugee camp at Alexandria?"

"I am not a refugee."

The lieutenant intervened, speaking quietly: "You were interrogated by Alexandria Intelligence; they decided you should come here. They couldn't make up their minds about you."

"I gave them all the details; I do not think they believed me. They wanted to know about Russia. I am not here with a message from Russia, but from Palestine."

Koblensky's tone would have been insubordinate in a soldier, but the man's intensity offered a more complex challenge than sheer rank was able to cope with. The colonel hesitated, slightly unnerved, and then said, "We don't know who the hell you are. All sorts of people are coming through my door these days. Alexandria is full of Jews from Palestine. I want to know why you were picked out."

"I represent a group of people; we can give you information, military information, about the Turkish positions in Palestine."

"Spying?" The colonel appeared to find the word distasteful, perhaps even the idea.

"Why should you want to help us?" said the lieutenant, while the colonel seemed still dismayed. The lieutenant left his chair and paced behind Koblensky, as though conducting the interrogation of a suspect. "There has been precious little help from you

81

before. The Jews in Palestine seem to be of two kinds. Either they run from the Turks, claiming persecution, or they collaborate.''

Koblensky looked up at the lieutenant. ''That is true. But not everyone is like that. Some of us can see that the Turkish Empire is coming to an end.''

''Oh, I understand,'' said the colonel. ''You want to change sides, is that it?''

Koblensky shifted slightly in the chair, tensing. But when he spoke, the tone was still loud, though constrained. ''To get to Palestine from Russia, I came through Turkey. You know what has been happening in Turkey? To the Armenians? Thousands, hundreds of thousands of them? A massacre. It is called a Holy War.''

''Yes. Well . . . of course, they are a barbaric race, the Turks. . . . How many of you are there who feel this way?''

''A small group. It cannot be any bigger, but it is big enough.''

The colonel tired of the problem. ''This kind of thing is not really my cup of tea. We're military intelligence, not espionage.'' He turned to the lieutenant. ''Mellors. Do we have somebody who could look into this? It's a bit irregular.''

''Hogarth, perhaps, sir.''

''Hogarth? You mean that bunch at the Arab Bureau?''

''They do run a bit of espionage, sir.''

''Odd lot.'' The colonel slowly connected this oddness with the problem seated before him. ''Good thought, Mellors. Look, Koblensky, I'll have to refer you to these other chaps. More their line.'' He tugged again at his belt. ''Mellors here will arrange it. Good day.''

Mellors took Koblensky to another office and made a phone call.

From afar, Koblensky had thought of the British as a race of merchants. His knowledge of English history was sketchy, but— given the coloring added by the nanny—he had reckoned that such an empire must have been founded on mercantile cunning. Sitting here in a corner while the arid-voiced lieutenant spoke on the phone, he watched their faceless military bureaucracy at flood tide. He simply could not see, if this was the hub of their military machine, how such men had built an empire. There had been drilled conformity in the Russian Army, but that was an extension of despotism, and despotism at least transmitted a charge of energy, which this system did not.

Mellors addressed him as though he were a clinical specimen, of interest but to be kept at arms' length. "Here, I'll make out another docket for you, old chap. See the sergeant at the gate; he'll get you taken over to the Grand Continental Hotel. That's where you have to go. The chappies at the Arab Bureau."

At the hotel, Koblensky presented his new docket to a young corporal at the reception desk. "Aha," said the corporal lightly. "Been expecting you. I'm afraid the commander isn't here at the moment. I'm sending you to Captain Lawrence. Hold on a jiffy, and we'll get you taken up there."

Puzzling over the measure of "a jiffy," Koblensky undid the neck button of his shirt. He was already beginning to perspire.

Captain Lawrence's quarters were not so much an office as a salon: a long room blessed with two balconies and therefore more air. Along the inside wall ran several trestle tables covered with maps and littered with books. The wall above the tables, covered in an Edwardian flock paper, had been pinned with random items: circulars, notes, photographs, more maps. Koblensky noticed that few of the books seemed to be of a military nature. The room was otherwise furnished with several deep leather armchairs and at the far end another trestle, behind which Captain Lawrence remained seated, scribbling on a pad and barely looking up as Koblensky advanced.

"Sit down, won't you?" He nodded to a plain wooden chair by the desk and carried on making notes for a few seconds while Koblensky settled himself. Beneath the trestle Koblensky saw what seemed slender adolescent legs, bare knees under khaki shorts, but the body above the trestle was that of an older man and the head was larger still, as though the three portions of the man had grown at different speeds. Lawrence's hair, fair and fine-textured, was worn longer than Koblensky had seen in his progress through the army so far, and his officer's tunic lacked the belts common to others.

Lawrence stopped writing but didn't raise his head fully; he looked at Koblensky almost shyly. "You've had an interesting journey."

"I do not make much progress."

The curtness seemed to dislodge Lawrence. He moved back in the chair and folded his hands across his chest. Still not looking directly at Koblensky, he said, "I can understand your feeling that." Then he simply fell silent.

Koblensky didn't speak either.

Finally, Lawrence, gazing down at his hands, said, "I think

you had better begin at the beginning. Say, with General Tchournazoukov.''

"I told them about that, at Alexandria."

"I know. I want to hear it for myself. Only a summary."

Straining to be patient, Koblensky began his account. "We were ordered to pull out of Urmia January second. I was in the hospital of the American Presbyterian Mission with typhus."

"Why not in the Russian military hospital?"

"The Americans had the medicines."

"The general was ready to leave you there?"

"The general was not aware of my existence. The brigade major, yes. He was happy to leave me there."

"You were suspected of being a Bolshevik agent?"

"Who was not?" Koblensky sensed a flicker of amusement in Lawrence's face. He continued: "I was too ill to be moved. I think they thought I would die. Miss Platt, Miss Mary Platt, the American missionary, she thought so too. As soon as the Russians left, while I was still too ill to know, they took in ten thousand refugees, Armenian and Nestorian Christians from the villages around Urmia. The Kurds were just waiting for the army to go, then they would do the Turks' work for them."

"Yes. With the Kurds it's not a question of religion, just the habit of killing."

"It was a month before I recovered. There were many sick: dysentery, measles, scarlet fever—and fear. By February nearly a thousand had died. They had no medicines left, little fuel, not enough clothes. There were vermin. There was nothing I could do. Except make one less mouth to feed. It seemed the best thing, to go west through Turkey, to make for Damascus, and then Palestine." Koblensky paused and shook his head. "I didn't know."

"The Jihad? The Holy War?"

"I did not know what that meant."

"It means genocide." For the first time, and then only for a moment, Lawrence looked directly at Koblensky. "I am sure you understand what genocide is. When faith becomes blind faith, goes demented, it is a terrible thing; there is nothing holy in it. Alas, Islam has that germ in it. In this case, the poor Armenians are the infidels. The Turks imagine they prove their faith by butchery. But that won't wash with the desert Arabs. Constantinople isn't Mecca. . . ." He stopped, suddenly withholding himself. His eyes fell to his notes again. "Now . . .

Aleppo, Damascus, Jerusalem, and Cairo. Mr. Koblensky, you seem to have exhausted several lives already.''

"I have been lucky.''

"What people call luck is often a matter of intelligence. You were a sergeant in the Russian Army. You look young for such a rank. These times, everything speeds up so. We shall be old men too soon; youth dies so quickly in the fire.''

Lawrence's whole body seemed cramped in some kind of reservation. He let slip a thought, half a thought, and then held back. Koblensky had the sense of tempting Lawrence into more than the customary questions.

"The problem is,'' said Lawrence more directly, "the problem is to have you *trusted*.'' His eyes were back on Koblensky, this time stripped of reflection. "Are you Zionists?''

"Very few Jews in Palestine know what Zionism is. Most of those who do will not support it.''

"Are you Zionists?''

Koblensky saw that he would have to satisfy the new tone of interrogation. "I do not like these isms. I believe in Jewish freedom.''

"You should take care. Zionism makes many people here nervous.''

"We are Jews. Surely, that is enough.''

"Yes.'' The challenge was over. "It is to me.''

They talked for another hour, but Lawrence did not stray again from his professional agenda. He checked and rechecked Koblensky's information against maps, and when finally he seemed satisfied, he said, "You've been a great help. I'm convinced you and your people could be invaluable to us. Of course, that decision isn't mine, and I have to keep you out of the path of the dimwits. It may seem odd to you, but Naval Intelligence are by far the cleverest bunch, a wholly different kind of mind. Fortunately, my chief, Hogarth, wears that color. If we could get you back up there by sea, could you get ashore?''

"It is rocky at Athlit, but the rocks give good cover.''

"Yes. . . .'' Lawrence's memory seemed to be searching for something. "I feel the propitiousness of this must not be lost; there are so many who disparage the Jews without knowing their past. 'Walk about Zion and go round about her . . . and tell the owners thereof, mark well her bulwarks, set up her houses.' You might well take that as your text, Mr. Koblensky.''

85

Biblical rhetoric made little impression on Koblensky. He smiled obligingly, but said simply, "I want to begin."

"Yes. Of course you do. It's a big game, and at last one worth playing."

It sounded too flippant.

"I was thinking of the strategy," said Lawrence, catching Koblensky's reaction. "It's a huge thing, this war, with almost no limits. Look, don't expect miracles. It's going to take time. We'll have to get you around a bit, to prepare the ground. Have you seen any of your own people, here in Cairo?"

"The Egyptian Jews? No."

"Then we must put that right. You know, I think I can see how you became a sergeant so swiftly. Things here are a bit slacker. You'd best get used to it—if you want to win friends."

Koblensky had been quartered in a camp on the edge of the city. Within a day Lawrence had him in a room at the Grand Continental—a small room smelling of the kitchen somewhere below, but a room with a window, nonetheless, and through the window he watched the British come and go. There seemed no contact with a war, any war at all, here. The inertia was difficult to understand. The British Empire's jugular ran up the Red Sea and through Suez. He kept thinking of Lawrence's image: *It's a big game, and at last one worth playing.* Cairo, it seemed, was a place where games were played and everyone wore fancy dress of one kind or another. Koblensky had the one suit, and three shirts.

He heard nothing more from Lawrence for two days, and then an invitation arrived. It was formal, a gold-rimmed card with copperplate script, a gap left where his name—"Mr. Asa Koblensky"—had been written with a pen in a flowing hand. It came from the home of Sir Victor Harari Pasha. Koblensky was invited to dinner that evening. The style of the card did not match the style of his suit. He didn't much care.

The Hararis were Sephardic Jews; the knighthood marked Sir Victor's family as having successfully transferred its allegiances from French to British rule. Other Sephardim were valued as civil administrators in Egypt. Now, borne by Mercedes-Benz from the hotel to a sprawling villa, Koblensky wondered what use they had in mind for him. The chauffeur was a Syrian Arab; Koblensky already knew the dialect. The chauffeur regarded his suit with open distaste.

Sir Victor, however, was undismayed—forewarned, perhaps. Sir Victor was tall, slightly bent, with an extraordinarily white skin. His English was without accent. He clasped Koblensky's hand as though reluctant to let it go. Before he spoke, his head nodded gently several times and a strand of his dark hair fell over one eye.

"Mr. Koblensky . . . you are most welcome in my house. Most welcome. Captain Lawrence has told me your story. Most remarkable, most remarkable . . ." Finally he let go the hand. "Please, won't you come this way." Without waiting for Koblensky to speak, he ushered him through the lobby to a large salon with a fountain and pool at the center, under a high dome. It was the coolest place Koblensky had found in Cairo, cool enough for Sir Victor and another guest to be wearing starched white shirts and white ties without discomfort. To one side of the other man, on a sofa, sat two women. One was directly introduced to him as Lady Harari; the other, much younger, as Esther Mosseri. And the man as Professor Leo Solomon.

With the coolness of the salon went a softness of light; lamps burned around the base of the dome and were reflected in the pool. Lady Harari, like her husband, was very pale; Esther Mosseri had skin which in this light looked like chamois. Her beauty disturbed Koblensky as he was introduced to Solomon. She, in turn, was watching him. In the formal luxury of the villa, his accent was as much at variance with the setting as his dress.

The professor was saying: ". . . and we get so few reliable accounts of what life is like in Palestine nowadays."

Collecting his concentration, Koblensky said, "Life under the Turks is never pleasant." He was still aware of Esther Mosseri's eyes on him, unsure of the tone of her appraisal.

"We," said Sir Victor, his head still nodding, "we have been most anxious about our fellow Jews."

Koblensky held his patience. He held it much longer, well into the dinner, until he realized where the conversation was leading. By then he had had four glasses of hock, two of red wine, and was now drinking port in exclusively male company. His head was clear, only his tolerance was diminished.

Receiving the decanter of port and pouring it with fussy precision, Sir Victor said, "I'm told the land has been transformed where it has been scientifically farmed."

Koblensky said, "We are near famine."

The professor said, "In any case, the place could never be self-sufficient, surely?"

"It depends on how many people it has to support."

"And how many do you think?" said Sir Victor.

"Half a million—to begin with."

"Half a million!" The professor gasped. "That would be politically impossible."

Sir Victor, similarly disconcerted, said, "Refugees, you mean?"

"Settlers."

"But," said Sir Victor, nodding again, "what of the Arabs? They could not accept that."

"What have they done with the land?"

"The Arabs have different values," said the professor, focused now and patronizing.

"Is starvation one of their values?"

Sir Victor tried conciliation, though reluctantly: "If the change came gradually, perhaps—perhaps you might carry the Arabs with you. The more intelligent Palestinian Arab can be quite a sophisticated fellow."

"Gradually?" Koblensky drained his port. "How gradually?"

"Twenty years?" said Sir Victor.

"And how many of our people are going to die while they wait, in places like Russia?"

The professor said, "What matters is not only the speed but the manner. One thinks of some lines from Aeschylus as being rather the core of the thing: 'A man *comes* to his country when he has never been banished, for he simply comes without any misfortune implied, but an exile both *comes* and *returns*.' " The professor leaned back, happy.

Koblensky said, "This is not academic, not poetry. It is life and death. We have a chance now to get British support. The strategy gives them the morality."

The professor was puzzled.

Sir Victor said, "I think I follow you. You mean if we prove to be the most dependable subjects?"

"Subjects?" Koblensky flushed.

"Surely . . ." Sir Victor faltered.

"That may be the case in Egypt."

Now it was the professor who flushed. "But we cannot antagonize the British. You see, Mr. Koblensky, it is all very well to formulate these Zionist ideas in Russia. You don't understand how much damage they do—it plays into the hands of anti-Semites. That kind of aggression bears out their fears.''

"Aggression?" Koblensky laughed. "*What* aggression? All over the world it is the Jew who turns his cheek.''

Koblensky embodied ideas that the other two men had previously known only from an impersonal distance. But Sir Victor could not face conflict without applying balm. He reached for the decanter again and said, "You must understand, Mr. Koblensky, that we have lived with the Arabs for centuries. We have remained Jews. They remain Arabs. Nothing can change that. We do have an accommodation, however, and it works in spite of everything. We are not inconsiderable; there are many thousands of us here in Egypt and elsewhere. But we are vulnerable." He poured the wine and looked at Koblensky, his head quite still now.

Koblensky caressed his glass in his hand and settled to a more even temper before replying. "I see that. But things will change."

"Yes. . . . I fear they will," said the professor ambiguously.

"The strategy gives them the morality?" repeated Sir Victor. "There is certainly truth in that."

The contention was allowed to pass. Koblensky had suddenly seen the fragility of their world. He had seen it first in their eyes, then as the universe they had woven around themselves—not only the grandiose villas and the British modulations of habit but the limit they set for their wills. His anger was contradictory, dismissive and yet protective. He feared them as a corruption of himself, despised them but accepted them, and would use them.

For a moment he was alone, the present dissolved in the wine: Screams in Kishinev. An Englishwoman's voice. A child's wonder lost so early. Sir Victor's shirt breast was flecked with port. Small gestures were magnified. The professor's breathing had gravel in it. *Asa, where are you?* said the English voice in the cellar.

As they left the dining room he heard the women laughing somewhere. He watched Sir Victor's cigar smoke rise in the convection of air over the pool, misting the web of light. The chauffeur, obsequious when in Sir Victor's vision, relapsed to character beyond it. At the hotel, Koblensky let himself out of the car.

"Koblensky? Asa Koblensky?"

A tall young man in a crumpled white linen suit intercepted him in the lobby, still folding a newspaper he had been reading.

"My name is Kippax, Owen Kippax. I'm with Commander Hogarth's office." He extended a hand. "I wonder, do you think we could slip away to a quiet table in the courtyard?"

Koblensky's head was only just clearing of the wine. The thought of coffee was appealing. He nodded. "Of course." Kippax's step was light and fast, leaving Koblensky several paces behind as they came out into the night. The sky was a parody of the postcard Orient: a thin sickle of a moon and to one side a dun-tipped mosque. Kippax was already pulling a chair out for him.

"Yes—d'you see, the commander's asked me to take an interest in you."

"An interest?" said Koblensky.

"Get things moving. There are problems, though; you won't mind answering a few questions? . . . No? Good. Small things, really. I've read your statement at Alexandria, and Lawrence told me about his conversation with you."

"Yes," said Koblensky. He couldn't come to any kind of judgment about this man.

"I'm interested in the Turkish Army in Palestine. Were there many of their Arab units there?"

"At first, a few. But then they were all moved north. Just a few interpreters left. The Turks don't trust the Arabs."

"Quite so. Did you ever hear speak of a subversive group amongst the Arab officers, the Young Arab party?"

Koblensky shook his head.

"No? The Turks are very worried about it." Kippax saw the waiter approaching with the coffeepot. He stretched himself back in the chair, putting his hands behind his head. They waited for the waiter to go. "As I understand it, these Arabs are looking for restoration of Arab sovereignty. . . ."

"Sovereignty?" Koblensky laughed. "To which king?"

Kippax seemed suddenly annoyed. "It's very important to us, that they turn from the sultan and follow Hussein of Mecca. That, apparently, is where they *are* turning."

"And the British want that?"

Kippax became cautious. "And the French, of course."

"Ah, of course, the French." Koblensky was careful in his tone. "They have their claims, too."

"The problem is," Kippax said, now with some assertion, "that if we give any open assistance to you, and these Arab interests were to learn of it, they would become rather concerned about our intentions."

"You think we are Zionists?"

Kippax drained the coffee and looked away to the sky. "It doesn't matter to me what you are, quite frankly. Just as long as this is seen strictly in terms of a part of our military intelligence, and not as the beginning of something else."

Kippax's speech had gone from the languid to the emphatic, with other emphases between, as though he was used to playing his voice like an instrument in order to set moods; Lawrence's voice, in contrast, had been almost devoid of expression and yet invested with character. Koblensky understood the point being made.

He said, "What is your phrase—looking a gift horse in the mouth?"

"As long as we're agreed." What was it about Koblensky? Kippax looked at the implacable face, the steady eyes. Something made him uneasy. It wasn't that he was a Jew; in fact, he didn't resemble any Jew he had known. He was oddly aloof, as though never plagued by emotions of any sort. Too much of the peasant. You never saw that in the English Jew; Kippax was sure Bron would dislike it as much as he. But the face lingered in the night.

Koblensky slept late and awoke with a head clear enough to review the encounters so far. He had a feeling that he was in some way on trial, that each meeting introduced a different kind of test. There was soon another: Taking breakfast on the same terrace where he had sat with Kippax the night before, a shadow fell across his face.

"Hello."

It was the young woman from the dinner at Sir Victor's, Esther Mosseri. She was in a white dress and her dark face was shaded by a wide-brimmed hat.

He nodded.

"May I . . .?" She went to take the empty chair opposite him.

He nodded again.

Several pairs of eyes from adjacent tables followed her. She put her elbows on the table, pressed her hands together and rested her chin on them.

"You're a man of few words, Mr. Koblensky."

# Clive Irving

Realizing his apparent churlishness, yet not actually withdrawing it, he said, "I am surprised."

"I imagine you are." It was difficult, with the shading, to know her expression. "I came on the off chance that I might see you." She looked at the toast on the table. "It's a little late for breakfast."

"I had a long night."

She moved her arms from the table and arranged her hands in her lap, in one gesture becoming less coquettish. "We didn't really get a chance to talk last night."

"Mmm."

"Afterwards, the professor seemed distressed."

"He did?"

"Agitated, on the way home."

"On the way home?"

"He was my escort."

"I see."

She pulled one hand from her lap and adjusted the hair that fell behind an ear. "*Do* you? I work in his department at the university."

She was beginning to feel irritated by his apparent lack of interest.

"Archaeology?"

This was a marginal advance. She nodded. "Coptic."

"You don't look like an archaeologist."

Was this a trace of humor? "What should an archaeologist look like?"

Finally, half a smile. "Like someone who lives in the past."

"I don't know whether to take that as a compliment or an insult." She settled the stray hand on the table. "We cannot escape the past."

This one sentence composed her features with more gravity, and—in spite of himself—won Koblensky's sympathy. Blatantly, he examined her in more detail. He had noticed the night before how her lower lip was much thicker than the upper; it gave her a sullen look that was not matched in her eyes. "No," he said, "we cannot." His eyes settled on hers, waiting for explanation.

"I wondered—have you seen the pyramids yet?"

"No."

"May I take you? I have a car."

92

He finished his coffee. "I would like that."

She drove a Renault as though immune to the anarchy around her.

"You're surprised that I'm able to drive?"

"It is unusual."

"My family live in Alexandria. It couldn't have happened *there*. But here . . . well, it was quite easy. You see, there are many things a woman cannot do here, even the Christian and Jewish women. For example, I cannot go on archaeological expeditions. That would be unthinkable. In the university there are problems too. But they have not yet made any rules about cars. I think the problem never occurred to them."

Soon, in the distance to their right, he saw the first group of pyramids, given dimension even this far off by the sharp division of light and shadow. In spite of their size and peculiarity, they appeared to be natural outcroppings and not, as he had expected, grossly implanted. He said this to her.

Slowing the car, she looked at him. "That's strange. I thought I was the only one who felt that. Most people think they are so obviously man-made, but I can't see that. I mean, I *know* they are, but there are some things where human intervention seems incidental rather than decisive, as though just arranging things by someone else's will. Do you understand what I mean?"

"Yes. I know what you mean." But concurrence of feeling did not put him at ease. She perplexed him. Her voice was so molded by an English education that it seemed at odds with her features, which were classically Semitic—and it seemed at odds, too, with her eyes, in which he saw another nature seeking expression. As she stopped the car she took off her hat to remove the headscarf she had tied over her hair while driving. The black hair fell to her shoulders.

There were still, despite the war, tourists here. But because Esther Mosseri was known to the curator, they were able to wander separately. Standing a third of the way up from the base of a pyramid, looking east toward the Nile, they had both reached that point of reflection when the presence of the past overwhelms the sense of the present. She sat down, and looked up at him from under the brim of the hat. His left leg was flexing, the toe pressed into the stone, a restless gesture. His jawline was dark with beard. The line of his head from the back of the neck to the crown was angular, a series of planes rather than curves, the short hair crudely cut in the same alignments.

"How old are you?" she said suddenly.

He didn't look down. The left foot settled, his weight shifting from one leg to the other. "Twenty-three."

"You seem older."

"How were these things built?"

She looked away from him, her right index figure running lightly along the surface of the stone. "We don't know."

"By slaves."

"All empires are built on slavery of one kind or another," she said, looking up at him again.

"How long has your family lived here?"

Ignoring the implication, she said, "The family left Spain in fourteen ninety-two—the time of the great expulsion."

"Fourteen ninety-two?" Somehow the precision of the reply seemed funny.

"They ended up in Damascus, and two centuries later, here."

"So long, with the Arabs?"

"Even longer. When the Arabs overran Spain, in the eighth century, the Sephardim were their administrators."

"Yes. Always the tools."

She became ominously quiet, the finger scratching more deeply into the stone, her head turned down again.

"I'm sorry," he said.

"You don't understand," she said, straining to keep control.

"I do understand," he said, the conciliatory tone already gone. "What I understand is simple. Until you have a nation you cannot have a people."

She took the hand away from the stone and laid it across her lap, the fingers tinged ocher. "I have lived here, in Egypt, for nearly thirty years. I was brought up to believe in loyalty— loyalty to the country of adoption. We are still Jews. We are still good Jews. Your views do not make you a better Jew—just a more arrogant one."

He hadn't realized her age before; she looked younger—except, as he looked down now at the hand in the folds of the dress, it alone seemed that much his senior. "It's going to change," he said. "Don't you see that? It's all going to change. It cannot last."

"There have been upheavals before."

"Not like this." He sat beside her, not touching, and looking out over the plain. Below them, three American matrons arranged themselves on camels for a portrait, while a fourth, aligning a camera on a tripod, giggled.

Quietly, more composed, she said, "You see, I do love this country."

He turned and looked at her steadily. "That is dangerous. It is not your country to love."

# 5

## *Northwest Arabia* ✳ *October 1916*

From a quarter of a mile away it looked like a strand of thin smoke detached from its source and blown downwind across the wadi from west to east, altering in outline with the caprice of the wind. The boy, sitting in the lee of a tamarisk bush and watching the cloud, knew that it had a life of its own and was not smoke but a swarm of red locusts, drifting passively until carried to some vegetation, which would be stripped bare in five minutes. The boy was grateful that they were so far off.

He watched a hundred or so sheep that were feeding from patches of recently sprouted grass—their first taste of grass for a month. They looked more like goats than sheep. Their coats of fine, wiry jet-black hair could not conceal how gaunt they were; to survive in such a place, animals and men alike were bred with frugal appetites. The boy, though fifteen years old, was slight and seemed to have been almost swallowed by his black cloak as he huddled under the tamarisk. Only a keen and knowing eye would have seen significance in the cloak; instead of coarse goats' hair, it was of camel hair. An even keener eye might have seen in the boy's profile another hint of quality in the fineness of his nose, a fineness already more of the man than of the boy, as though the nose had come to maturity ahead of the rest of his face. The dark stubble on his chin was not yet thick enough to be shaped into the beard that would have completed the force of his profile. His mouth had not hardened and his lips were blistered from days in this bitter wind. The darkness of the beard to come was foreshadowed by the density of eyebrows that almost met across the bridge of his nose and gave an extraordinary depth to his hazel eyes, eyes that seemed simultaneously to be serene and alert, eyes that moved around the wadi and occasionally to the empty yellow sky.

The boy knew that emptiness was the greatest of the desert's many deceptions and that the sky, like the desert, was inhabited by things evanescent and elusive, which were felt before they were seen. Even the yellow haze was a furtive trick, making the dawn an uncertain guide to the cast of the day, a sun suppressed by an atmospheric change that the boy enjoyed as a kind of suspense. How the day would resolve itself would determine whether he remained here with the fresh grass or turned the flock south within safe reach of shelter.

A single gray shrike came out of cover and rose from the eastern fringe of the wadi, beating into the wind as it climbed. The yellow flare was weakening as the bird gained height, and the boy, following its flight, knew that the sky would darken from the west and seal off the sun. A white stallion, little larger than a pony, was grazing on the fringe of the sheep. The boy gave a thin, fluting whistle through his teeth. The horse raised its head from the grass and shook its mane, turning toward the boy. For a few seconds it tuned its senses to the world above the grass, its ears bending back in the wind, and then it cantered over to the boy, who swung a camel bag over its back. With the movement of the horse the sheep had stopped feeding. One began a staccato, assertive call and others picked up the same note, their snouts rising out of the grass. The uniform black of the sheep's coats was suddenly broken by the white of their heads, and as they drew closer together the flock became a strange two-toned mass, fluid and ragged at the edges. One ewe was left apart, her hind legs spread, as she urinated noisily.

The boy climbed onto the horse's bare back, pulling up his cloak so that his thin legs could grip the flanks, which lacked stirrups. Without a command, the horse broke into a gentle trot and circled the sheep from a distance of twenty or thirty yards. The flock began to follow its own trail back to the southern end of the wadi. The shrike, high above them, had hit a stronger wind and was being driven back to the east. There was now an insipid gray light that took away all contrast from the landscape and enclosed it from one wall of the wadi to the other. The boy led the sheep down a dry watercourse. The wind pressed one side of his headkerchief hard against his cheek and he held his head slightly to the right to shelter his face. The horse and the boy, though both fighting the wind, had a grace that was indivisible.

At about the same moment that the boy had called the horse in

97

the wadi, his father had watched a rider approach his village, outlined in the last band of the yellow haze to the east. For the keenness of his sight the father was sometimes called the Hawk, and this sense had not diminished with age. While the rider was still a good distance from the village, the Hawk, whose real name was Mugbil Ibn 'Abbas, had discerned the peculiarity of the man's headdress. The Bedouin headkerchiefs were secured by a ropelike band; this rider's head was different in outline. A red and white checkered cloth was bound to his brow by a narrow turban, just above the ears. Some people thought that from a distance this turban gave the aura of a halo. Mugbil Ibn 'Abbas was not so deceived. He stiffened and turned away. Walking along the top of a battlemented wall, he stepped onto the roof of a house where two other men stood.

"It is as we thought," he said.

The two other men nodded but waited for their headman to speak again.

"We shall listen, that is all," he said, and then climbed down a ladder from the roof into a communal courtyard.

To reach the village walls the rider had to pass through oasis gardens which, even in winter, had a feeling of lushness. There were palm trees, a delicate variety of tamarisk that looked like cypress, fig trees, and vines. This fertility was in contrast to the severity of the land around it. To the north and to the south were great lava fields, blackened and pitted. To the east and west were rolling downs of light, flinty gravel. A few wadis, like the one where Ibn 'Abbas's son had taken the sheep, gave a sparse relief only when rains revived the vestigial rivers. The oasis served travelers with the nerve to navigate from Damascus or Amman in the north to the Arabian interior. It was also on the fringe of the simmering struggle for the mastery of Arabia among three dominant tribes: The Hashemites of Mecca to the southwest; the followers of Ibn Rashid in Hail to the east; and Ibn Saud's Wahhabis from Riyadh in the remote southeast.

The survival of the village depended on avoiding an open alliance with any of the disputing powers. No resident authority was claimed here; it was too far from anywhere to be important. But Ibn 'Abbas was of the Shammar tribe and he knew that other factions in that tribe had already given their allegiance to Ibn Saud. "Given" was a generous term. Ibn Saud had persuasive enforcers, who were called the Ikhwan. It was one of the Ikhwan who now rode through the village gate.

Mugbil Ibn 'Abbas was a good deal taller than his son Khalid, though just as spare. Under him the village had enjoyed an unusually long period of peace and had been able to repair the ravages of earlier tribal struggles. There were only a score of plain mud-brick houses within the walls, of which the headman's was little larger than the rest. To withstand the desert wind, each house faced an interior courtyard. Despite the fortune of its oasis, the village was barely self-sufficient, with little to sell beyond its own consumption. The flock of sheep in Khalid's charge was its prime asset. The village was indifferent not only to the Arab monarchs but, like other remote settlements, to the demands of the faith. Ibn 'Abbas, though not a vain man, was seen as a more tangible provider than Allah.

But the Ikhwan were Allah's messengers, seeking out all with less severe piety than their own. This particular messenger did not appeal to Ibn 'Abbas in the flesh any more than in the spirit. Even in the cold wind he carried the odor of the devoutly unwashed, and his cloak was stained with more than the soil of travel. His hair fell to his shoulders in a knotted tangle—but paradoxically, his mustache was precisely cut to the line of his upper lip, the only part of him that was groomed.

Ibn 'Abbas was obliged to observe the courtesies of desert life. He received the man in his coffee room, the *kahwah*, and gave him a place by the hearth in the center of the room. There was no chimney and the only ventilation was through two small square holes near the roof; the tamarisk burned with little smoke. The heat heightened the visitor's body stench and Ibn 'Abbas kept a pace farther away than was the custom. There was a rude arrogance in the man, as though he was preoccupied with higher things. This arrogance was more marked when, having produced a letter addressed to Ibn 'Abbas, he found that Ibn 'Abbas was illiterate and had to wait for a scribe to read it aloud.

Squatting by the hearth, Ibn 'Abbas darkened in mood by the second. The scribe managed to keep his diction neutral, though he, too, was outraged as he read:

" 'In the Name of the Most Merciful God.

" 'From Faisal al-Dawish to Mugbil Ibn 'Abbas.

" 'Peace be upon him who shall follow the true direction. We solicit peace for you all, male and female.

" 'He who comes to us will enjoy the safety of his property and his family and will really resign himself to God and should be protected by the Sultan Ibn Bijad and the Ikhwan and you, O

# Clive Irving

Mugbil Ibn 'Abbas, if you come to Islam, you will take your camels and your flocks and be in the safety of God. Peace will be with the Shammar.' ''

The scribe put down the letter and subsided into a tense silence. Ibn 'Abbas took up his coffee and slowly sipped it. The Ikhwan messenger stared fixedly at them.

Eventually, with quiet asperity, Ibn 'Abbas said, "How far have you ridden with this?"

The messenger was evasive. "From the camp of Faisal al-Dawish."

Ibn 'Abbas glowered. "I have heard that you are camped outside the walls of Hail."

For the first time the messenger seemed uncomfortable, surprised by Ibn 'Abbas's knowledge. "It is not the season to take Hail."

Ibn 'Abbas poured himself more coffee. "To take Hail? You would assault the palace of Ibn Rashid?"

"All infidels will be swept aside."

Ibn 'Abbas smiled grimly: here, in its essence, was the real message of the Ikhwan's letter to him. "Infidels?" he said. The wind outside had increased and was beginning to blow the fumes of the fire back into the room. "Surely it is true that Ibn Rashid's God is but the one God we all know."

"He is godless who does not live by the Book." The statement was impersonal, as if delivered by rote.

Ibn 'Abbas waved away a strand of smoke in a gesture that managed also to imply a disdain of dogma. "I have heard what you mean by living by the Book. In this letter you offer peace to the Shammar. It is a strange peace. It requires us to leave our villages for what you call your *hujar*, which are not villages as we know them, and where people must live as you live."

"Only Ikhwan can live in the *hujar*."

"And to become an Ikhwan . . .?"

"You must live by the laws of the Prophet."

"But we can be good Muslims and not be Ikhwan?"

The messenger's mustache flexed superciliously. "Are you good Muslims?"

"We know God." Ibn 'Abbas heard himself speak as though listening to a stranger.

The messenger sneered. "Without a mosque? You know God without a mosque? I see no mosque in this village."

100

"A prayer mat and the sky are enough—according to the Book."

The messenger had the face of a scavenger. He looked around the room, bare though it was, as if offended by its comforts. "Ibn Rashid claims your village is his," he said finally.

"The village is *ours*," blurted Ibn 'Abbas, all patience gone.

The messenger's eyes completed a survey of the palm-thatched roof and returned insolently to Ibn 'Abbas. "The letter is clear," he said. "What am I to tell Faisal al-Dawish?"

Abandoning etiquette, Ibn 'Abbas rose from the hearth while the messenger was still seated. "We thank Faisal al-Dawish and the Sultan Ibn Bijad for their declaration of peace to us and we pray with them that peace will join us under God."

The messenger remained on the ground, looking up at Ibn 'Abbas. The hem of his crusted cloak had moved up his calf, revealing a woolen sock sewn to leather slippers. Ibn 'Abbas knew that the leather slipper was part of the Ikhwan battledress. Slowly the messenger uncrossed his legs and stood up. Without another word, he went into the courtyard to his horse.

The scribe stood behind Ibn 'Abbas as they watched the small children of the village cluster at the heels of the messenger. The scribe, too, had seen the significance of the slippers. He said, "He has not bothered to water the horse."

Ibn 'Abbas nodded. "I would like to know how many they are."

"They do not come from God. They are dogs."

In the courtyard the wind billowed the light cloaks of the children as they watched the messenger mount and ride out through the gate in the wall. The sky had now the heaviness of ink, with several low streaks of white like the vapor over boiling water. There were distant echoes of an electrical storm; Ibn 'Abbas remembered his son and the sheep.

In fact, Khalid was already in sight of the village, though a dust cloud obscured all but the watchtowers at the four corners of the wall. The sheep behind him had packed themselves as closely together as they could. Still inclining his head away from the wind, the boy failed to see the rider coming out from a line of tamarisks until he was nearly upon him. Against the poor light, rider and horse combined in silhouette, the rider's cloak flared by his speed and the turbaned head like that of a bird's rising from half-extended wings. The boy had no chance to see a face, but felt danger. The sheep veered from the horse's path, momentarily losing their order and squealing. In the boy's mind the danger took metaphorical wing. The rider was a familiar omen. This was not an act of imagination: the boy had no mundane sense of metaphor. All such images were supernatural, and most of them punitive. The metamorphosis of horseman into bird was holy wrath come flashing by, a text in flight. The boy's immediate world was narrow but concrete; anything alien had also to be supernatural—a visitation. The danger carried a thrill, the promise of a divine disturbance of some kind; the storm about to break was a disturbance too, but it was far from novel.

By the time he reached the village wall the wind had gone. He pulled his horse to one side of the gate and the sheep tumbled through and found their way to their enclosure. Khalid followed them.

Ibn 'Abbas waited for the boy in his courtyard. Other men had joined the scribe in the *kahwah* and were drinking coffee and beginning to sound agitated.

"You wasted no time," said Ibn 'Abbas as Khalid slipped down from his horse.

"It was a pity," said the boy. "There was good grass."

"Did you see anyone else out there?"

"Only a rider coming from here."

"No tracks?"

The boy was surprised by his father's concern. "Only those of dogs," he said. Tethering the horse, he turned again and looked more carefully at his father. "Who was the rider?"

Ibn 'Abbas did not by habit offer intimacy to his son, but now he put a hand on his shoulder, having seen in the boy's eyes a trace of himself. "You must come and sit with us while we talk of it." He looked away to the east. "The rider is in the path of the storm, wherever he is." The streaks of white had gone from the sky and the darker clouds were lower. The boy went ahead of his father into the house.

The men talked for nearly two hours. The boy saw that his father held back from imposing a judgment while the others quarreled; it was often like this, because his father's authority was that of a partriarch who preferred to have all dissent aired before he looked for the common ground. By this means Ibn 'Abbas was never thought of as partisan in any dispute, but this was a more heated exchange than the boy had seen before and his father needed to be more assertive than usual.

The boy had heard of the Ikhwan and understood the argument.

Ibn 'Abbas reasoned that if they had been singled out for a written edict, then the Ikhwan would be unlikely to leave it at that. Nobody could know, he pointed out, whether the next Ikhwan visitation would be a handful of men or an army. Part of the village's income depended on its convenience for travelers between Syria and the interior, and if it became another Ikhwan settlement it would soon be avoided like the plague. The best course, he argued, was to make a gesture of more rigorous religious observance without embracing the regime of the Ikhwan. He spoke of Ibn Saud: "a great warrior, a man without fear. The Ikhwan say they carry the sword for Ibn Saud yet Ibn Saud manages to be pious without being of the Ikhwan himself. Whatever Ibn Bijad may ask, we will follow the example of Ibn Saud." This idea seemed to calm the others.

As they dispersed to their own houses, Ibn 'Abbas was left alone with his son. He nodded to Khalid to sit by the hearth while he remained himself in almost total shadow. There was a long silence as the father scrutinized the boy. The hand on Khalid's shoulder in the courtyard had seemed almost furtive, and they seemed unable to come any closer.

The boy put more tamarisk twigs on the fire and stared into the flames. He could hear his father's strained intake of breath before he spoke.

"The storm will be gone by morning," said Ibn 'Abbas. "By sunrise I want you to be ready to take the flock back to the grass. Stay there for as long as there is food; work farther north if you can. After this storm, the water will lie by the black rocks."

Behind his father's directions Khalid heard a new fatigue somewhere at the core of the voice, the effort he had known before only in old men's throats. He peered into the shadow, trying better to understand, but the firelight was too fickle. He was expected to obey with no more curiosity than anyone else when directed by the headman, but he wanted to *be* curious now because of the strangeness of his father's voice.

Ibn 'Abbas felt this curiosity in his son but could not satisfy it. There was an unbreachable space between them, induced not so much by rigid tribal custom nor even an explicit disappointment, for Khalid was manly enough, but by inimical natures. From an early age the boy had acquired a serenity that was very close to sanctity. It set him apart in the village and hastened his choice as shepherd, for he seemed to relish the solitary life.

Ibn 'Abbas's prediction was right. The storm fluctuated in

103

strength for the rest of the day, threw down one final rage, and then petered out during the night. The result was the kind of dawn that made the desert beguiling. All malevolence seemed to have been purged from it. The light advancing before the sun clarified the horizon with a primal crimson. No matter how frequently he saw it, the boy always felt in these aftermath dawns the force of nature's renewal, the world really *was* made over again with each day. He had an adolescent's disregard of the past, both recent and distant, and he led the sheep out without once looking back to the village.

The calm of the day lulled the village. Some of the men who only the day before had been among the most agitated now forgot both the agitation and its cause and talked of greyhounds and game. The women carrying water through the palm groves sang lightly and enticingly and further distracted the men from serious work. One or two desultory searches were made to the east, looking for traces of the Ikhwan, but the storm had erased all tracks. By evening most of the men lay with their wives and were then as ready as children for sleep. Ibn 'Abbas thought restlessly of his son and found peace only an hour before dawn.

It was not such a pure dawn as the last; there was dew and a ground mist in the gardens. The smallest birds, larks and wheatears, rose out of the mist in the first weak light and came skittishly over the village walls, where they woke a man posted in a tower. Still lethargic, he pulled his cloak tighter about him. This movement proved fatal. A spear went between his shoulder blades and clear through his rib cage. All along the wall between the towers, turbaned men appeared silently. The walls were seven feet high, easily scaled by rope. The climbers leaped into the still-muddy ground on the other side. A score or more were in the main courtyard within a minute. They carried an assortment of weapons: spears, knives, and bamboo staffs. The mud seemed to make them more fearsome. Irritated by the villagers' slumber, they formed a crescent and cried out:

> "The Winds of Paradise are blowing!
> Where are You, Who seek it?"

First, a few dogs barked feebly; then more birds stirred into the air; and finally, the village was aroused. Simultaneous with the cry, a dozen camels, each bearing two or three men, came at a gallop through the village gate. These reinforcements spilled into the advance party just as Ibn 'Abbas appeared. One glance at the intruders stilled him; it fulfilled his expectation and so resolved his fate. While the other men were incoherent in panic, he already knew that panic was the last self-deception. This fatalistic calm marked him out. He stood implanted with his feet slightly apart, scanning the invaders for a leader.

The camel-borne Ikhwan were still dismounting when another camel appeared, bearing only one man. The others were pulled aside so that he could ride through to confront Ibn 'Abbas. He was the only one of them carrying a rifle; across his breast was a bandolier of ammunition, more a mark of rank than armament. The rifle hung on a strap from his left shoulder. His left arm held the reins and in his right hand he brandished a thick staff. His dress was as slovenly as that of the rest, but his powerful bearing left no doubt of his command.

The babble from both sides stopped, leaving only the noise of the dogs, until this, too, settled like the dust.

The leader said, "The merciful Sultan Ibn Bijad offered the hand of peace and the protection of God, but you, Mugbil Ibn 'Abbas, have turned against God to the ways of the infidel."

Ibn 'Abbas was unflinching. "We are all brothers under God; we are all Arabs."

"Brothers under God?" The Ikhwan leader's eyes flared. "You are more devout with sport than with faith. As we gave up our prayers at first light, your village slept. Not one man here has unfurled his prayer mat, and you speak of brothers under God. What God do you know, you with your superstitions and your charms? You who call yourself Arabs but do not live like Arabs?" His eyes moved from Ibn 'Abbas to the cowering men behind him, and then to the houses behind them. "We solicited peace for you all, male and female, and yet your lives continue to blaspheme and to turn aside the merciful sultan who serves only God and the imams. I, Ibn 'Aqil, will purge the land of all unbelievers and cleanse the land befouled by them. *Aywallah.*"

"*Aywallah!*" cried his warriors.

The dogs renewed their yelping.

Ibn 'Aqil moved his camel forward to where Ibn 'Abbas stood. He raised the staff and brought it down with enormous force on Ibn 'Abbas, but missed his skull and smashed his right shoulder. Without a cry, Ibn 'Abbas collapsed into the dirt. Ibn 'Aqil pulled up the camel and raised the staff again, but this time in a gesture indicating silence, just as the men in his own ranks were lunging forward to the rest of the village men. "We shall bring these dogs for one last meeting with their God!" He leveled the staff at the village men. "Now we shall see how you pray with the last breath in your bodies." The staff swept the air again as a command. "*Take them,* every man and boy child."

In the dirt, Ibn 'Abbas was still conscious though riven with pain. Blood seemed to be pressing behind his eyes and he saw only through a film of scarlet. The sole coherent sensation was of the pounding of the earth. Slowly he became aware that he was being dragged by his feet through the dirt. His cloak rode up his legs. He survived now in a world diminished to elementary sensations. Pain obliterated the last concern for his body and his mind felt removed: a separate thing. His head had twisted again and the scarlet filter was clearing into a precise, narrowly rectangular field of sharp blue as though viewed through a visor. This blue lacked one dimension, depth. He could not be sure whether it was infinite or shallow. The blue transfixed what was left of his being. When his head was severed, his face retained in death this repose, disgusting his executioner, Ibn 'Aqil, who imagined it to be an insolently peaceful mask. Maddened by this thought, Ibn 'Aqil led his men in savage mutilations of the men and boys still prostrated in prayer.

The roofs of the village houses, interwoven with palm branches and leaves between rough beams of tamarisk under a top crust of mud brick, were brittle-dry on the inside even though water still lay above. The Ikhwan had no trouble firing the houses, and once the beams burned, the roofs collapsed soon after. A thick, rust-colored smoke billowed and blew across the palm gardens.

The women and girls went unmolested into a fig orchard; Ibn 'Aqil condoned looting because the Ikhwan always donated their spoils to their mosque, but he was a severe enforcer of chastity when raiding. Some of his men, seeing the agility of the younger women in flight, were checked more by the certainty of punishment than by religious scruple. It was seeing the women cluster like sheep among the fig trees that reminded the man who had been the original messenger of the boy shepherd. Entering the village just as Ibn 'Aqil was ordering the incineration of the corpses, he approached his leader deferentially.

"Master, they have many sheep, but they are not here."

"You know where they might be?"

"The shepherd boy is the son of Ibn 'Abbas."

Ibn 'Aqil turned from the pyre and looked out across the gardens. "Then he cannot be too far."

"The sheep would fetch a good price."

"And the boy is like the father."

The destruction of Ibn 'Abbas's village was now seen to be incomplete. One boy, and even the sheep, might have seemed a minor oversight in the circumstances, but not to the Ikhwan; terror lost its point if it seemed negligent. There was another reckoning, too, in the calculations of Ibn 'Aqil. As long as the Ikhwan's main opponent, Ibn Rashid, survived in his citadel at Hail, the loyalty of this distant but crucial region would remain uncertain. Punitive expeditions had to continue, and gave to Ibn 'Aqil's men a momentum he did not want lost. And so the focus of the purge now became one elusive boy.

There were still two hours before nightfall. Ibn 'Aqil ordered his best tracker to determine the boy's direction; the tracker, having found the sheep's droppings, was back in an hour. The boy had gone northwest toward the *harra,* a wilderness of black lava beds. It would be a simple pursuit of no urgency. They camped in the ruins of the village and went to sleep to the plaintive wailing of women.

The boy watched a buzzard, almost motionless above him, riding an upcurrent with only the splayed tips of its wings flexing, its head hooked in vigil. The boy wished he were the bird: He wanted to see the land as a whole, particularly to know its limit. He knew there was a limit to it, but he had never seen an expanse of water in his life. He thought of the desert as bounded not by seas but by a great encircling river, for he had heard stories of the two great rivers, the Tigris and the Euphrates, and could conceive of no more decisive limit than these. Rivers that could end one world and begin another. There were rivers under the desert, and as a small child he had believed that if you dived deeply enough into a well you could find them. This belief had nearly killed him and he smiled grimly at the recollection of it.

He knew his direction from the black rocks of the *harra* around him; their north face was always covered with lichen. His route was northwest, passing through a succession of shallow craters, climbing easy gradients out of one and then dipping down into another. On this, the end of the second day, he found a patch of camel pasture and the sheep did not want to move from it. Behind him was the risen lip of a crater. The next crater was some way ahead, beyond the pasture. On the left, to the west, the land rose to a steep defile. To the east were more ridges of black rock. He unrolled the stitched goatskins that served as both tent and blanket for him, ate a bowl of date molasses, and went to sleep, knowing from the way the sheep had pressed together that it was going to be a severely cold night.

He woke—he had no way of telling the hour because it was pitch dark in the tent—with a chill that had nothing to do with the temperature of the air. It was the shock of a dream, but the dream itself had gone in the waking, leaving only sharply alerted instincts. His first struggle was to give these order. He was close enough to childhood to be ashamed of the delirium and close enough to manhood to trust his senses. The tent was claustrophobic. He crawled out. The air cut clarity into his head, as it had clarified the heavens. The only cause he could imagine for the alarm of the dream was the *ghazu,* the professional raiders of the desert. He knew how helpless he would be against them; he had been in skirmishes with them, but Ibn 'Abbas and his men had beaten them off. He began to trust the instinct of the dream, to treat it as a supernatural warning. Alone in this wilderness, he was too easy a target. The *ghazu* would have no mercy. He slept no more, and as soon as the eastern horizon lightened he had the sheep moving again.

Instead of continuing northwest, he turned half back on his tracks, making roughly southwest out of the *harra,* toward the mountains. It was harder, even more unforgiving land, but the sheep had already eaten well enough to go for days, perhaps a week, on nothing more than sparse, stunted bushes. His point in taking this route was precisely its unsuitability for grazing—the last place anyone would expect to find sheep. Wells were scarce and the terrain hard on camels and tricky even for horses. The one flaw in his plan was that nothing could mask the sheep droppings. He hoped to find a wadi retaining enough water so that he could drive the sheep along it long enough to confuse pursuit. But the first wadi he reached had little more than a mantle of mud and this embossed every movement. It was not until nearly midday when, coming to the top of a ridge, he saw below a belt of fresh grass at least two miles long and, beyond it, a wide and shallow watercourse. He allowed the sheep to pause in the grass for half an hour, while he ate dates, and then, much to their distaste, drove them into the water against the light current, cranking his route even more acutely southwesterly. He knew the expectation would be for a shepherd to go downstream with the current.

The water was ice cold. To drive the sheep he had to ride in frequent passes on either flank. The horse, too, became difficult to manage. Only after three hours of struggle in the numbing water was he satisfied that he had done all he could to conceal his tracks. He let the sheep come out of the water in a shallow gulley where a gravel bank had replaced the mud flats, and led them into a flinty gradient going directly west, in the track of the declining sun.

Ibn 'Aqil's party had left their own tribal lands three months earlier. They had covered, in an erratic course, more than a thousand miles, most of it through the two great interior deserts of the Dahna and the Nafud. They had ridden through extremes of heat and cold, through sandstorms and through driving rain. There were fifty of them, ranging in age from ten to seventy. Ibn 'Aqil did not like the meager glory to be had from fitful raiding, little better than the lawless life of the *ghazu*. It was the large movements, with upwards of twenty thousand men in the field, that met his ambitions. Then the divine mission of the Ikhwan was borne on an irresistible tide behind the streaming green and white war banner, and given that sight, no one should have been in any doubt that the whole of Arabia would succumb. Ibn 'Aqil loved the mystery of the Ikhwan: the mystery that could make the desert seem empty one minute and line the horizon with warriors the next, an army that could materialize and disappear at will. All the years of tribal delinquency, of bending to corrupt men like Ibn Rashid, with his Turkish paymasters, were now to be swept away. And was not Ibn 'Aqil, who had killed thirty men in one day, already beginning to be spoken of in the same breath as the two greatest generals of the Ikhwan, Faisal al-Dawish and Sultan Ibn Bijad? Surveying the preparation of his camel and the unsated eyes of his men, Ibn 'Aqil was furious that one boy should require such illustrious pursuit.

Following the boy's track across the gravel downs was simple enough, but the *harra* was a different matter. It was a harsh and unfamiliar surface for the camels, and the men disliked the feeling of being enclosed by the craters and the unremitting blackness of the place. This was, they agreed, where God had delivered a punishment of his own by loosing fire fierce enough to make rock boil. In this fearful place they were able to confirm the terror of the power they ultimately served, but they were anxious to be gone from it. There was no option, though, but to make camp there, because the camels needed rest.

The sun failed to shine through clear in the morning. The men bowed to Mecca with renewed urgency, believing themselves to have been cursed in the night by choosing this site for rest. Even as they pressed into their mats they could feel a wind so close to the ground that it carried flakes of frost. Only the rock was impermeable; everything else—thistle, lichen, camels, and men— was shriveled by this blast, and without light of any brilliance, everything had the cast of gray that overcame the dead. Ibn 'Aqil had never before heard the glaze of frost rupture and come spitting at his feet like blown grit.

Beyond the eastern rim of the crater where there should have been sky, Ibn 'Aqil saw that the darkest gray was a moving, coiled cloud of rising, not falling, currents—and that the surface wind was the suction of this advancing cloud. He had seen many sandstorms before, but this one was darkened by the malign landscape.

Not all the tents were down before the storm struck them. The camels, squatting on freezing rock, turned their haunches to the wind, but their eyes bulged in terror, and the men trying to shelter in the lee of the camels, grasped at flying tags and ropes, worsening the animals' panic. Men and camels went slithering into crevices and serrated stone tore at their flesh. Insecurely lashed tents unfurled and took off, disappearing in seconds. The storm had fueled itself from the gravel desert to the east of the *harra*, holding the debris in its vortex. When it hit the bare black rock, gravel showered down on them viciously. A man who lost his grip on a camel rope was spun into a boulder and before he could avert his face the gravel had filled his mouth and ripped his eyes. The hide of the camels was blistered within seconds and other men, shaken loose, were knocked senseless and lay with their cloaks being torn to shreds. Ibn 'Aqil wedged himself between a rock and the necks of two camels, but even there his mouth became raw as the air was sucked out of him.

The intensity of the storm, its coiled concentration, lessened its duration. Its swath was no more than a quarter of a mile wide and passed in minutes. It left an awful stillness. At first, the men who could move were too petrified to do so. It was the camels, less damaged but more frenetic, who first rose. Though some of them did not; their legs were broken.

110

Ibn 'Aqil made a quick tally of the cost. Six camels would not move again. One man was blinded; one of the older men had a head wound and was in a coma; there were several broken arms, one broken leg, and almost every man had lesions and raw lungs. Tents were lost and supplies ravaged. In the flat calm, the demonic presence seemed reaffirmed. Not even a sudden, warming shaft of sun could remove this feeling. The *harra* had broken Ibn 'Aqil's squadron as no other adversary could have. His rage was a constrained, deliberating one. There could be no question of continuing the pursuit in the same way. He directed the man who had been his messenger to Ibn 'Abbas's village, and who was now limping badly, to consolidate the remnants of the force and take them back into more hospitable territory. He, as obliged by honor and leadership, selected three men, including the best tracker, and took three of the strongest camels, to continue the pursuit.

The tracker's task had become far more difficult; the storm had erased most of the traces he looked for, including the sheep's droppings. It was as if the earth had been peeled like a skin. At first, the tracker assumed that the boy had continued along the main trail of the *harra*, used by all travelers. They followed this course through several more craters and then came into the interval of camel pasture.

The tracker led his camel around the edges of the trail, sending the two other men, who shared a camel, farther afield to survey from a hillock. The tracker stopped and squatted on the rock, squinting along it and then rubbing a forefinger into a crevice and sniffing it. He called to Ibn 'Aqil: "The sheep were here—for a night."

Ibn 'Aqil nodded. "It should not be long."

The tracker climbed back onto his camel and recalled the scouts, who had seen nothing. Ibn 'Aqil rode behind the tracker and ahead of the two scouts. In the wake of the storm the sky had only slowly cleared. By late afternoon they had left the pastureland and were back between weathered black boulders. Several times the tracker descended from his camel and groped around at the perimeter of the trail. Finally, with the sun already half obscured by haze, he looked up at Ibn 'Aqil with perplexity.

"There is no trace of sheep, master."

"Can you be certain?"

The tracker looked around him helplessly. "It is not easy,

111

master. These rocks cannot tell me anything." He paused and tried to assume more confidence. "It is my feeling, master, that he has left the trail."

Ibn 'Aqil had an expression of lethal tranquillity. He looked from the scout across the rocks to the alien skyline. A pair of shrikes flapped nonchalantly overhead. "He has won himself another night, this shepherd," he said softly. "We can go no farther today."

The boy had seen the sandstorm early from his vantage point in the lower reaches of the western escarpment. Even before he saw it he felt it in the fugitive movement of air and the aberrant dawn. Above him, no more than a quarter of a mile, was a patch of scrub oak and, as far as he could judge, a spill of boulders that might mark a ravine. Normally the terrain would have been easy for the climb, but the sheep disliked the ice and kept splaying their hind legs as he drove them. By the time he reached the trees, the wind was helping to propel them. The boulders were in a strange, almost deliberate formation, like the stunted pillars of some great imperial gate that had been reduced by vandals or invasion. The gradient fell away sharply into a gully running across his route. This gulley, invisible during the climb, widened out to his left before rising in a far steeper wall of layered limestone. At the base of the wall were several caves, and the boy made for the largest of them, with the sheep spilling down into the gulley behind him. When the storm reached them, its main force was deflected by the lip of the eastern wall. A partial vacuum, created as the yellowing coil of the storm raged above, sucked air from the caves. Not all the sheep had followed the boy into the cave; some balked and were edged out of the way, and others went off at tangents. Many of these were hurled kicking across the gulley into the sheer wall. The boy and his horse reached a roughly domed gallery from where they could barely see light at all. The tumult of wind paralyzed the sheep, and the boy looked out over a sea of bulging eyes. Some of the sheep wedged in the cave entrance were suddenly plucked out and smashed into the limestone with the others. Then the pressure in the cave's atmosphere reversed and a blast of sand rushed into the gallery, making the horse rear and temporarily blinding the boy. He cowered against the freezing wall of the cave for what seemed like an age, until more light began to filter through the haze.

When he was able to stand again and gulp for cleaner air, the scene was bizarre. In their panic the sheep had become wedged in the neck of the cave, creating a logjam that would not break. The entire top surface of their black coats was stained yellow by the blast of powdered limestone. When the jam suddenly broke, the foremost sheep were hurled crazily into the gulley and the smaller were trampled by the larger.

Outside, the boy found at least half the flock either with smashed skulls or lame. The survivors had re-formed themselves into a bickering, apprehensive cluster. The energy for flight had been knocked out of the boy. He saw no point in running anymore. The gulley was a haven. What was left of the flock needed to be rested and calmed, and there was little he could do with the others except leave them to the vultures and ravens—once they, too, recovered their nerve. In a contented lassitude, the boy sat by one of the pillars and watched the color return to the sky.

That evening he baked the leg of one of his own sheep in a hearth formed by limestone rocks making the three sides of a square. The meat was poor and sinewy, but he ate voraciously and then slept, dreamlessly, in the mouth of the cave.

Unusually, he slept through the sunrise and was wakened by the sound of birds. Two vultures were picking their way through the carcass of a ewe. But the boy heard the piping of smaller birds too. Focusing blearily, he thought the earth had changed color in the night; in place of the limestone was an intermittent red crust. It was this that engaged the larks and wheatears. Their beaks stabbed away, discarding fragments with flicks of the head. The floor of the gulley was covered with the bodies of thousands of red locusts. The frost had been so severe that it had frozen them to death as—the boy supposed—they drifted down from a swarm passing over the gulley. The brittle snapping of the locusts' shells was like small-arms fire, heard from a distance. The vultures continued their own single-minded scavenging. The boy found the odorless death of the locusts more nauseating than the stench of the crudely gutted ewe. The gulley had suddenly become inhospitable.

Once he left the place he began to feel that perhaps his elaborate maneuver had been pointless, induced by ungrounded superstition. The storm, for all its terrors, seemed to have removed the sense of being pursued. Perhaps what had infected him was no more than anticipation of the storm itself. He forgot the way his father had urgently arranged his flight. The reduced flock was easier to handle, the weather was tolerable, and he turned his back on the disagreeable highlands to make for the more familiar ground between the *harra* and the village.

Feeling more sportsman than shepherd, he sought a place where the sheep could graze for days and where he could enjoy his horse. On the edge of a gravel plain tufted with *ghada* and *yerta* bushes, well concealed in a quirky horseshoe depression, was a small spring in a clump of palm bushes which he had used before. The water hole was minute—barely three feet wide and no more than two feet deep, but it never overflowed and always replenished itself. The water was sweet and good, its wholesomeness assured by the insects swimming in it; dead insects were an infallible sign of brackish water.

He pitched his small tent in the palm grove and made another crude hearth. All he lacked was meat. Coming here, he had seen gazelle tracks and droppings. He found evidence of their lair after an hour, in an outcrop of rocks. Disturbing them, he speared a female through the neck as they broke cover.

He made his way back to his camp, the carcass lying behind him across the rump of the horse. Soon he saw the outline of his flock at the tip of the depression that concealed the palm grove. They were stretched out in a satiated, inert line under the noon-time sun. The pleasures of the present were complete and expunged the past. Leaving the sheep where they were, he canted down to the well, took a long drink of the water, and then began skinning and gutting the gazelle. When he was finished, it was still warm enough in the shelter of the palm bushes for him to repair the exhaustion of the hunt with sleep.

Later, chilled suddenly by shadow, his arm stirred, but settled again lazily across his cheek as he dug his face deeper into the goatskin blanket.

Standing silently over him, Ibn 'Aqil was not moved by the sleeper's air of angelic innocence. The three other men stood behind him. All four were too wearied by pursuit to feel any exhilaration now in having settled on their quarry. They had not recovered his trail for days; his diversion to the highlands had defeated the tracker and they had combed the *harra* with mounting frustration and intensifying venom. They were retracing their route south, resigned to defeat, when suddenly one of the scouts spotted the line of sheep. Now, coming upon the comforts of the boy's refuge, their mood was, if anything, even more incensed.

They saw the precisely quartered meat of the gazelle and the hearth laid in readiness.

Ibn 'Aqil directed a travel-hardened foot at the boy's back.

Knocked into abrupt consciousness, he gazed up and saw only a looming silhouette against the pale light.

"Dog!" spat Ibn 'Aqil, aiming another kick, this time into the boy's groin. "Son of a godless dog!"

# 6

## Cairo ✳ October 1916

Kippax was not susceptible to hallucinations, but the Nile played tricks with him. Looking down into the churned amber wash of the boat, he felt that the evening light in the water reflected phantoms of a bygone glory; the Nile was Cairo's link with all the rich superstitions of Africa and Egypt's own immutable bloodstream, but it was also the blood of a catastrophe. In one blow, Mohammed's Arabs had wiped out all living trace of ancient Egypt, the pharaohs left only as the vast and brooding effigies in sandstone cliffs. Why had that desert faith been such an overpowering force? The river had no answer.

At the boat's stern, a group of young English officers watched the island of Gazira recede to the north. Three spinsterish European women were succumbing to the enchantments of their Egyptian guide. A single French officer, in the shade on the port deck, had eaten too well and was dozing. At the bow, under a canopy, a dozen or more people sat in deck chairs, some looking upriver and some to the banks on each side. Amidships there was a small saloon, made too hot by the poorly ventilated engine room below, but the bar was here. To one side of the bar, where there was a breeze, a woman sat alone. She wore a black linen dress and, sipping a lime juice, looked demure.

Kippax wiped his brow with a crimson handkerchief pulled from his breast pocket, picked up his panama hat from a seat, and went into the saloon. He nodded to Esther Mosseri, and she nodded in return without looking any less demure. He went through the ritual of requesting permission to join her, though the barman's attention was elsewhere—until he was summoned by Kippax, whose voice had to strain to rise above the sound of the engine. Waiting for the drink, he put his hat on the empty

116

chair beside him and looked across the table. "The river enables one to breathe," he said.

This pomposity was typical of his awkwardness with her. Had she known less about him, she would have dismissed him as yet another floundering young consul, but his reputation had preceded him and she made no such error. "Is that the reason why we always meet on the boat?"

"It's a precaution."

His gin arrived and he was impulsive in drinking it, having to cough lightly before speaking again. "Well . . . what did you make of him?"

"Koblensky is his real name, and he did come from Palestine; we know that from our people in Alexandria." She smiled. "*Our* people in Alexandria, not your people."

"Mmm." Kippax had already drained the gin, and signaled for another. "Another lime juice—or something stronger?"

"I don't drink anything stronger." Her tone was gently reproving. She waited for his second gin to be delivered, then said, "There is no record of him as a Zionist, but then that is almost impossible to be sure of. He *could* be a Turkish agent, but I don't think so—I really don't think so. There is something about him I haven't seen before: more than self-reliance, more than independence . . . a kind of solitariness."

"I see he's made an impression."

"He's the coldest man I have ever met."

"*Really?*" Kippax moved from slyness to amused curiosity. "I daresay that is distressing for you. Well, I'm afraid you must persevere. I want him watched."

"Aren't you making too much of it?"

"Can't take any chances. The man came out of nowhere. Some people are inclined to take him seriously, so if you wouldn't mind . . ." Kippax's smile was both mechanical and coercive. It was a face, Esther Mosseri thought, that was in a hurry to age.

She knew enough of the British not to be deceived by their apparent casualness; everything they did, however deadly, had always to be given the facade of amateurism. The Turkish, German, Italian, and Russian agents in Cairo were too easily betrayed by their earnestness of purpose. Compared with them, Kippax looked superficially a hopeless misfit, dropping his hat as they left the saloon, then misplacing it on his head, seeming to any onlooker a timorous suitor mismanaging an assignation.

But she had seen in that mottled face not ineptitude but a chameleon gift, and something else—a total absence of feeling.

She recalled the rehearsed gentility of their first encounter, at the home of another enigmatic figure in the British hierarchy, called the "Oriental Secretary" (there was a dark wit in this title). A lithographed card in French and Arabic had invited her to the secretary's "Wednesday Tea." Kippax had called to collect her from the museum. Decorous conversation had been made over the tea, followed by Bach played by a trio of European women. Everyone had then left except herself, Kippax, and the host. By then only an ancient Egyptian cylinder converted into a lamp shed light on the meeting—and, filtered through alabaster, gave the two Englishmen a waxen, jaundiced pallor. Speaking with the delicacy of a man whose soul was still possessed by Bach, the Oriental Secretary explained that, as she probably realized, Cairo was infested with secret societies and that one of her colleagues at the museum was suspected of involvement. All they wanted, he said, was for her to flirt a little and find out what she could—"without courting risks." Her own integrity was so admired, her "referees" so distinguished, that they would be deeply in her debt. Part of this debt could be dispensed in the form of a private bank account (it was Kippax who was left to introduce this vulgarity).

It had never been so much as hinted, but she knew what the real pressure on her was: that the Jewish minority should demonstrate its loyalty. In the event, this first assignment was futile. Only days after she was given it, the young man at the museum had disappeared. Kippax was annoyed, but said it was just bad luck. And then Koblensky had appeared.

Seeking a breeze, Kippax had slipped away under the canvas at the bow and melted into the tourists. The French officer, waking, saw Esther Mosseri alone, adjusting her hair as she watched a felucca, one of the Nile sailboats, glide past them on the port side. The outline of her body in the shade disturbed the Frenchman—she was eerily close to being a tangible companion of the circle of courtesans who had enticed him in his dreams. As her left arm moved the hair around her neck, half the lobe of a breast moved under the linen with it. The heat of Cairo was said to deaden lust, but the Frenchman had found it otherwise. He was transfixed by this one movement of hers. She turned away from the river and caught his eye. Her face assumed a ferocity of denial that cowed the Frenchman before he could move. She walked away feeling disagreeable. He was too banal for her, and Kippax too arcane. But she wanted a man. Had the Frenchman seen that? To ask the question undermined her self-esteem.

She walked as though curbing her impulse, in flight but not flying. When the boat docked on the east bank, she stepped ashore looking as chaste as a matron. Driving the Renault seemed to release her frustration and her mood became detached, more calmly reflective. She drove south, cut away from the river past the main mosque of old Cairo and to the surviving Christian enclave around the fortress of Qasr al-Sham. She drew into the gardens at the back of Saint George's Church and stopped the car where, in the same eyeline, she could see the church's dome and the mosque's minarets, a deceptive image of religious harmony. Islam had overrun Qasr al-Sham in the seventh century, but the Coptic Christians had survived alongside the Arabs because they had shared the Muslim contempt for ancient Egypt as a godless aberration. Ironically, it was the Copts who were the pure-blooded descendants of the pharaohs and still thought of themselves as the *real* Egyptians, aloof from the mingling of Arab and Egyptian blood that had come with Islam. Race, religion, and nationality—these were the incendiary ground on which the mosques, churches, and synagogues rested, and they made the conflict that so often tortured her.

The Oriental Secretary was now interesting himself in the Coptic reclamation. The small Coptic Museum behind the church, where she worked and where she now went, had acquired a dome from its British patron. Whether or not this was a disinterested act of amateur scholarship or something more devious she could not decide. But it was here, between miniature marble columns and under carved beams and ceilngs, that a fragment of the lost civilization was reappearing. The floor of the small room in which she worked was of inlaid marble cut more than a thousand years before.

With these treasures came a peculiar scent. No incense burned and no oils were used, but the copper, bronze and silver, the woods, wool and linen, the alabaster, marble and mud-brick, breathed into the air a concentrated and sensuous fragrance. Especially as now, after dusk, this dark congregation of artifacts conjured the presence of the hands that had shaped them and the eyes that had conceived them. She knew she was among spirits that were nearly tangible—indeed, "tangible" was less than they were, because this was a sense beyond the physical. She heard their hymns and chants and knew the pulse of their faith as intimately as if she lived in that ancient Cairo before Mohammed's horsemen bore down on it. And through their agency she heard her own people too. The tribes of Israel had given their monotheism to Christians and Muslims alike. Fancifully she imagined a continuity rather than a wrangling of gods. And then, earthbound, she knew better.

The light in her room was a mingling of one vellum-shaded lamp and the lattice-filtered light that moved with the moon across one wall. She worked on her notes without noticing time; many nights poring over documents in this light had begun to give her mild myopia, and she did not notice how her head had acquired the incline of scholarship.

A slippered tread crossed the marble. A draft lifted a corner of her manuscript, and only in reaching to replace it did she realize that the door was open.

Professor Leo Solomon had stopped midway between the door and her desk.

"What time is it?" she said, not yet able to focus on him.

"Eleven. I waited an hour."

"I'm sorry." She moved the manuscript to her left and saw him more sharply. "You know how I forget. . . ."

The hesitancy in his step had gone as he went to the desk and put his right hand on her face, lifting it to his. "I know." But he was not commiserating with her so much as chastising. He bent down and kissed her. His lips were thin and dry and seemed to want nourishment from hers. He made her tongue meet his and the taste of her caused him to tremble. Breaking the kiss and pulling away, he said, "You work too hard."

The hours at the desk had sublimated her frustrations from the boat, but not even his inept kiss had stirred her again. She smiled impertinently. "You should be used to waiting."

"It's too late for the restaurant."

"I wasn't thinking of food."

Her forwardness always injured his sense of propriety. Standing at the other side of the desk was—for a moment—not her lover but her professor. The imbalance of dignity and appetite made him absurd, as it had the first time she saw it four years before. His neck had a nervous tic that moved his shirt collar.

She stood up, smoothing the linen over her hips with a downward brush of her palms. "The restaurant would only have delayed us."

Solomon had the leanness of a man who seemed slowly to be ingesting himself. His suit hung as though trapping pockets of air; as she took him by the waist the jacket collapsed until her hands hit bone. Her voluptuousness and his emaciation mated like active and passive movements of a lock and his was the passive. Her hand slipped inside his jacket, past his waistband to his left buttock.

She said, "I don't think I can wait. Why not here?"

"Here?" But there was more recoil in the word than in his movements. "In this room?"

"Why not?"

"It's the museum!"

She laughed. "It's not sacred."

"But . . . ." His voice trailed off as she pulled the jacket from his back.

"Come along," she said, as though to a child. "No one will ever know." The idea had been spontaneous; once voiced, it was there to be done.

The door of her office screened them from the ecclesiastical vestments and vessels, but they both felt the excitement of violation. "Here," she said, turning so that he could unbutton the dress. The perforations of light from the moon now fell partly on the wall and, distended, across the blue velvet of an ottoman. Discarding the dress, she sat on the ottoman and pulled off her underclothes. One patch of light fell on a breast, turning the skin from chamois to burnished metal.

Solomon had only traces of hair over each ear, but these were still dark, while the spool of hair on his concave chest was white. His arms had no biceps and his buttocks were puckered, the pelvic bones clear under drawn skin. When she had first seen him like this, she wondered whether such a frame could sustain the effort of making love, but she had discovered that all his vigor was concentrated in his genitals—he drove into her rapaciously, a satyr sprung from an academic gown.

Knitted on the ottoman, they suggested two textures: one a mortal white and the other a mythical bronze, in the way that an ancient frieze would distinguish good from evil by a bias in form. She raised her knees as she opened herself to him and his semblance of frailty once again fell away. The proximity of desk, door, and museum aroused him; the scent of the place was in the ottoman and seemed to be drawn out by their exertions. With so little weight in him, she was able to lift as he thrust down, balancing his aggression with her own.

Once he was spent, she laid her head on his stomach. His veins and pores were magnified into a kind of landscape in miniature; the roots of his pubic hair could be seen as individually as plantings. His subsiding penis was ridged where the contracting veins were still knotted. Fascinated, she ran a forefinger over this surface until the skin tightened and the veins thickened and the penis excreted one lubricious teardrop, with which she anointed afresh its risen head.

A change in the light woke her. The moon had gone. One of her arms was stiff under her. She turned over sideways and rubbed the hand on the velvet to bring feeling back to it, still slumberous. Under the light of the desk lamp she saw Solomon. He was dressed and sitting in an oddly stiff way, with his chin resting on the tips of both hands. He watched her sit up, the unbridled hair fall over one shoulder.

In a muscular illusion she felt that he was still inside her, and then the contraction passed. She remembered, though uncertain whether it was before or during sleep, that for a moment her carnal companion had been not Solomon but Asa Koblensky. Solomon's baleful face had flickered out of focus and been supplanted by Koblensky's. Koblensky was not much more substantial in body than Solomon, but this fleeting impersonation had engulfed her. Happy in the deceit, she looked at Solomon and then knew that he was changed in mood. She remembered how she had left the manuscript on the desk and saw that it had been moved, replaced by something else.

He watched her eyes move from him to the desk, to the paper, and then back to the desk under the lamp. "When did you know Mazhar?" he said. "How long?" One of his hands floated from the other to the desk and picked up a photograph, not turning it to her but holding it under the vellum shade.

"At Oxford."

"Aha!" he said softly and disbelievingly. He saw the shift in her from drowsiness to alarm. In other circumstances she might have managed to dissimulate, but her nakedness made her vulnerable. She tensed in a way he found erotic.

"He taught Arabic there," she said, getting up.

"I know." He flicked the photograph over and put it face

122

down on the desk. "I did not know, however, that you knew him. You have never mentioned him—*not once.*"

She was pulling on a girdle, face away from him. "Why did you go through my papers?" she said.

"Naturally I was interested in what has so taken up your time. Your cataloging of the icons is impressively thorough, the notes faultless." He waited for her to finish dressing.

More composed, she came to the light, reaching for the photograph. He let her hand touch it and then his own clamped down on hers. "The picture means too much to you."

"Let me *have* it!"

"Point proven." He relaxed his grip so that she could take it. "I found the letter too," he said.

"Damn you!" she said, groping around the desktop as though blinded.

"What I want to know—what I need to know—is how far you shared his views, and whether you still do."

"He's dead."

"You persist in telling me only what I already know. I'm touched that you are so tremulous. I hope you know exactly how he died—*exactly*. Because if you are keeping the company of such fanatics, perhaps you don't understand how they work. He was given the great honor of martyrdom, although he didn't appreciate that that *was* the arrangement. He believed that he had been chosen simply as the assassin. But assassination is a dangerous trade. Who shall assassinate the assassin? After all, it would be too dangerous to have him caught alive."

She had slumped on the ottoman, head in hands.

Not relenting, he continued: "So your young friend Mazhar organizes an ambush, in Constantinople. The idea being that if you remove a figurehead you decapitate a regime. For an Oxford-educated man, that is surprisingly gullible. However, he manages to empty two rounds of ammunition within three yards of the khedive and only wound him slightly. Before he can so much as turn to run, Mazhar himself is cut down. By whom? By the committee that hired him—by the people you appear to be involved with."

"He was true to his convictions. He—" She broke off and became defiant instead of contrite. "What do *you* understand? What do you *stand* for?"

A humorless smile came to his face. "Stand for—or against?" He sighed. "How can *we* stand against anything? You know how vulnerable we are—how very vulnerable. How can *we* be involved in Egyptian nationalism—even if it was not in the hands of scoundrels like the Committee for Union and Progress?''

''*We* are Egyptians too.''

''*We* are Jews.'' The sentiment stirred a memory. ''That young hothead at dinner the other night—Koblensky. Let them try, if they like, to set themselves against the world in Palestine; let them try. They will come to their senses. But that's one thing. *This* is quite another.'' He got up from the desk. ''How very esoteric of you: You show your great independence of mind by becoming a scholar of Christian antiquity; you accept assimilation as we have always done; and then you take an Arab lover and lose your head to this chimera of nationalism—not even Jewish nationalism, but Egyptian!''

She tried to rearrange her hair, pulling at it in an effort to dissipate some of her anger. It was an anger that was turning lethal.

He went to the door and then turned. ''It was said at the time that Mazhar had lost his heart to a Jewess and his head to Sheikh Shawish. The loss of sanity seems to have been conjugal.'' His shirt collar rose as the nervous tic returned. ''Your British paymasters would be rather alarmed to know of this connection.'' He went out through the museum, leaving her by the desk.

Koblensky had been introduced to the British Army's ''per diem'' allowance, with arrears, by a quartermaster sergeant who had no idea who had authorized it, or why, but had the name on his list. This inference of adoption was not much, but aware of his threadbare wardrobe, Koblensky found an Armenian tailor who cut him a suit in cream linen that was the best he had ever worn. He bought sandals and three cotton shirts and felt less conspicuous and less diligent simultaneously.

Captain Lawrence invited him to a polo match between an army team and that representing the international community. Koblensky knew that field sports and Lawrence were not natural partners. But it took time to get to his motive: Lawrence talked of polo's evolution as a game in Persia and India, which in turn digressed to a reflection on the importance of the horse in history. He was still talking as they found deck chairs in a corner of the grounds, not bothering to acknowledge anyone or even the progress of the game. Then, half disappearing into the chair's slack canvas, he looked at Koblensky as though remembering something.

"You don't mind, I hope—this sort of thing?" he said.

In an opposite corner of the field, the polo horses were being lashed into conflict. Koblensky was reminded of cossack styles in riding. "I wonder," he said, "how all these officers can play and watch polo instead of fighting the Turks."

"That kind of speculation is not encouraged," said Lawrence. "Look, I came here so we could talk—that is, what might appear to be idle talk." He looked around him. "This is the home of idle talk."

Koblensky aped British manners by leaning back in the chair with hands linked behind his head. Three horsemen maneuvered near them, a British subaltern cornered by two opponents. The subaltern's pith helmet overpowered his narrow head and his face seemed to have been set in a permanent petulance. As one of the other men, a muscular Indian, wheeled to reach the ball, the subaltern aimed his stick at a leg of the Indian's horse. The horse keeled over and the subaltern gave a war cry and hit the ball, while the second opponent could only gape in horror. Nobody in the crowd around them saw any exception in this and Lawrence was not even looking. Speaking under the din, he said, "I would like to know more about the people who sent you, what their aims might be after the war." He checked himself to make sure Koblensky had heard. "You don't mind?"

This diffidence, Koblensky knew, was part of a skilled purpose. Koblensky had nothing to lose by being frank with Lawrence. Something had to make these people move. He said, "I can't speak for all the Jews of Palestine." He stopped and then added wryly, "It would be a fool who did—and a liar. We are a minority, a small minority. For different reasons, many others will not commit themselves. As for what will happen after the war . . . well, that does not seem to be in our hands. But I will tell you what I think matters. There is an idea that Palestine cannot support even as many people as it already has: Jews, Arabs—no more of any."

"You think the Arabs waste the land?"

"Their traditions are different. We believe, if we introduce modern farming, Palestine can support a much larger population."

"But can the Jews prosper without antagonizing the Arabs?"

"Nobody prospers now."

"You want the chance to prove this. That means a lot more

Jewish settlements. You see the point? By enlisting your help now, we shall obligate ourselves to much more. You have a strong political interest in the future of Palestine. A sentimental interest too."

Koblensky nodded.

"We are also obligated to the Arabs." Lawrence spoke almost in a whisper when subjective. "It's not good to see two sides of questions when you have officially to follow one."

"Is that why we came here?"

"Be careful with Kippax," said Lawrence, still subdued. "There are claws under his fur."

Koblensky frowned, as though squinting in the sun.

Under a tide of bellicose shouting, Lawrence murmured, "People think the Jew enjoys a disproportionate degree of success— *wherever* he is. A strange prejudice." The thought preoccupied him as he stood up and he looked over Koblensky impersonally as if Koblensky himself embodied the riddle.

The game reached its halfway interval. Other spectators made for the drinks in the pavilion. Lawrence and Koblensky walked back to their car, where the army driver was asleep. Koblensky had never been with anyone who so misfitted his surroundings. Lawrence made no adjustment to conform to either the social or the professional conventions of army life in Cairo. Behind them the polo field held the sounds of a tribe happily continuing its ritual. It was not Lawrence's tribe; in confiding in Koblensky, he was like one iconoclast on the loose with another, as yet with only alienation in common, not sure that there was any stronger tie to make. *Claws under his fur?* He would remember that.

Although he had made little money in his life, Professor Leo Solomon had managed to keep up appearances. Living, outwardly at least, as a bachelor, he had few obligations and spent carefully. Fifteen years earlier, he had arranged a small land purchase near the river with a modest bribe to a French official. This plot became his sole material indulgence. He designed a small pavilion in the seventeenth-century Persian style and built it parsimoniously of limestone and mud brick with two Egyptian artisans. It was octagonal in plan. In the center was a small fountain, surrounded by galleries. The outer wall was really a series of archways with lattice screens. There was an upper-level gallery overlooking the pool, and the whole was crowned with a mud-brick dome. Solomon had designed a small Persian garden to surround it. The overall effect was of opulence in miniature.

Few people—one of them being Esther Mosseri—knew that like a true Persian pavilion, this one had its secret pleasures. The most private of its galleries had a sunken marble bath large enough for a dozen people. There were only five people in it the first time Esther Mosseri saw it, which was the first time she had obliged her mentor. The small hashish parties were as fastidiously decadent as the building itself.

There were four people in the bath on this evening: Solomon, Esther Mosseri, another professor, specializing in the court of Rameses II, and an older Egyptian woman, a retired prostitute who now lived among the relics of Rameses II. It was the evening after the argument in the Coptic Museum. Solomon had been surprised that Esther Mosseri had arrived, but the Thursday quartet was a fixture and she seemed eager to preserve it. He had an impression that she wanted to drown her sorrows—indeed, she came with her own supply of hashish, already with an oddly glazed stare.

Solomon liked to take his opiates through a hubble-bubble. He sat cross-legged at the edge of the pool, drawing on the pipe. The other man lay in a postcoital trance, half in the water and half out of it. The pavilion was embraced in a languid mist of perfumes, oils, and hashish, rising slowly in the air under the dome. Esther Mosseri was on her stomach alongside Solomon, apparently reaching a level of detached bliss. The other woman sat dipping her toes in the water; she was of Amazonian proportions, skin tanned like hide, with unusually long and muscular thighs and small, sharply tipped breasts. No one had spoken for some time; they had, it seemed, removed themselves from each other. Solomon had a trickle of saliva from the left corner of his lip to the chin. The gurgling of the hubble-bubble came unevenly. His head began to sway from side to side in the same uneven rhythm and his eyes were no longer able to focus on Esther Mosseri's oiled buttocks, although his penis enjoyed an independent life.

The other man pulled himself up and rested his head on his knees. Less detached, his friend began playfully kicking water into his face. Esther Mosseri half turned, lazily taking in the metronomic Solomon and then lifting her head slightly to smile at the others. Solomon was unaware of her movement. She rose to a squatting position and shook water from her hair. Still

Solomon seemed oblivious. Slowly she stood and then pulled the hair clear of her face, gathering it at the back of her neck and flexing on her toes at the same time. She stepped behind Solomon. His head was still swaying, but the mouthpiece of the hubble-bubble had fallen free. She raised her right foot and put it between his shoulder blades, resting it there as his head sagged slowly to his chest. With the foot she pushed harder and there was no resistance in him. He toppled over into the pool, the hubble-bubble hissing as it rolled away on the marble.

Solomon's head and trunk floated, face upward. He had a beatific smile. The Amazonian woman stepped into the pool and got behind Solomon, picking him out of the water by lifting his arms. She stood him up, his head still on his chest, and then she pulled him down between her thighs into the water and straddled him, pressing him to the floor of the pool.

Esther Mosseri stood at the edge of the steps, hands on hips, watching the familiar skeletal body disappear in the distortions of light and water, taking on a new grotesqueness. Bubbles rose from the body as they had from the hubble-bubble, only fitfully, and then dwindled and stopped. A few rose petals, displaced by the movement in the water, reassembled as a cluster over the body. The other man had remained exactly where he had been, head rested on knees, looking at Esther Mosseri and feeling himself aroused. The Amazonian distracted him, beckoning for help. The two of them lifted Solomon up the steps.

Esther Mosseri picked up the hubble-bubble and carefully reassembled it.

"It tallies," said Hogarth, putting aside the manila file and rubbing his nose reflectively. "In fact, where he knows more than we already knew, we extrapolate and it is all consistent, as a picture, and not a little useful." He looked from the top of his desk to Kippax. "The Turkish Fourth Army gathered sixty thousand camels for the Sinai attack. Only five thousand survive. Water buffaloes have become their principal means of transport. There don't seem to be more than fifty motor vehicles south of Damascus. They've taken all the pumping engines from the Jaffa orange gardens. What d'you suppose that's all about?"

"They must be laying down a water pipeline somewhere else." Kippax answered absentmindedly, thinking of something else at the same time. "So you think this Koblensky is sound, that there might be something in this spy network of his?"

"The head of Naval Intelligence is *very* keen." There was still reservation in Hogarth's voice. "Captain Hall—you know him? Not entirely objective, I suspect. The Jews have got at him in London. I wonder, do they imagine the Jews, of all people, will ever be united? From London, perhaps, it may seem so. From here, I fancy otherwise."

Kippax nodded. "I have a clear impression that our friends among the Sephardim take a poor view of the Koblensky type of Jew."

"And where does our young friend Bron stand on this?"

"Michael? Michael is sound enough. Still a little bemused, perhaps, but that's all."

"Bemused?" Hogarth rubbed his nose again. "His work is quite thorough—that is, the *routine* work. I wonder, could he take on more . . . something rather more *subtle?* Is he ready for that?"

"Just what did you have in mind?"

Hogarth fiddled with papers. "He may have to take on some of your own duties."

"Mine?"

"Do you remember Captain Shakespear?"

"He was killed a few months ago."

"I think the desert turned his head, poor chap. Love of desert—the worst of loves, they say."

Kippax nodded, but without evident sympathy.

"In any event, we knew precious little about that part of Arabia until Shakespear penetrated it. And we know too little still. It seems permanently to be at war, though not, at least, with us."

"Yes. Shakespear made the mistake of taking sides."

"As far as I can see, there's not much to choose between them, two primitive tribal despots."

"Ibn Rashid and Ibn Saud?"

"What do you know about them?"

"Lawrence says Ibn Rashid is just a bandit and he judges Ibn Saud to be a passing force."

"Everywhere you look, Lawrence has his own favorites. One sometimes wonders . . ."

"Don't ask me to explain Lawrence."

Hogarth shook his head. "Who can? *Who* can?" He was between conjecture and paternalism. "You know, I rather think Lawrence would like to follow Shakespear's path. Which brings

129

me back to my point. . . .'' Hogarth referred to a sheet of paper. "There was only this one eyewitness report of Shakespear's death, and that is somewhat hysterical—from his Indian cook. Shakespear had—imprudently—ridden into battle with Ibn Saud. According to this, he was at first wounded and then shot in the back. When the cook found him, everything had been stripped from him. There are more unwholesome details; these people really are *savages*. Yet Ibn Saud claims great piety for himself, and his cause. The thing is, Owen''—Hogarth looked up from the paper—''we need to pick up where poor Shakespear left off. We need to be sure that Ibn Saud is our man.''

"*Our* man?"

"That he will comply, toe our line. He should be made to understand that there is only one Mecca and we have room for only one king of Mecca. We did not make Hussein the grand sharif, but we are bound to keep him there if we are to rally the Arabs behind us against the Turks. According to Shakespear, Saud has little time for Hussein. It appears that to these Arabs of the interior, the ruling family is too conspicuously decadent. Saud clearly considers the entire Hashemite tribe unfit to have care of the holy of holies. It's all the usual Arab stuff—invoking a test of religious zeal to cover what is no more holy than irredentism. We don't want Saud undermining Hussein, just as he becomes our rallying point. Saud had better grasp that.''

"You want to send me?"

"It's a request, not an order. I don't need to tell you how dangerous it could be—not only the tribes, but the terrain, the heat. . . .''

"I would have to get to Riyadh, Ibn Saud's fortress."

"Think it over."

"That won't make it any easier. I'll do it—of course."

Hogarth seemed still to be dubious. "You do realize the distances involved? A map gives you no idea; indeed, the maps are useless."

"I could save time, and distance, if I could take a boat down the Red Sea and around up into the gulf, to Kuwait. Then it would be overland to the Nejd, about four hundred miles."

"You anticipate me."

Kippax smiled. "I don't share Lawrence's view of Ibn Saud. He won't go away. As for the heat, the worst will be over by the time I could reach there."

Hogarth frowned. "You don't seem sufficiently intimidated by this journey."

"Intimidated? I have made such a journey many times—in my mind. One cannot get to the core of their religion without knowing the desert. After all, it came *from* the desert."

"This isn't a spiritual mission. It's political."

"In the desert, gold takes care of politics."

Hogarth was irritated. "From you, I would have hoped for something a little more elegant."

"Yes. And with me gone, you want Bron to lose some of his political virginity?"

"I thought we might ask him simply to keep an eye on Koblensky—Jew to Jew. My misgivings on Koblensky are, as it happens, greatly eased."

"And the woman—Mosseri?"

"I think we can rest her, for the moment. You have doubts?"

"Nothing concrete. A feeling."

"She was not my choice, as you know. However, Sir Victor Harari has always been a loyal servant of ours, and he vouches for her. I think by nature these Egyptian Jews have the subtlety and sagacity that one is glad to have on one's own side."

"Quite."

"Bron should not be told about her; see that there is nothing in the papers he might come across. Fancy some luncheon? You will need to build up your strength."

To Koblensky, history as a whole, history as a subject for leisured study, was a luxury confined to people whose lives had been unmolested by it, and ancient history even more so. His ignorance of history was not something he felt obliged to apologize for, but in certain circumstances it put him at a disadvantage. He remembered an afternoon lying on the ramparts of the crusader castle at Athlit with Sarah Aaronsohn. She had told him how Saladin had broken the Christian armies, how Saladin remained as the beacon of Arab generalship, and of Arab tolerance. His interest had flickered. Now another woman tried to draw him to history. But Esther Mosseri was not, like Sarah Aaronsohn, talking from the sidelines. She seemed almost to embody her subject.

"The French and the British take the best things, back to their own museums." She led him through a gallery of the Egyptian Museum, a hand lightly touching his elbow. "I think, if they were able to do it, they would dismantle a pyramid. Do you know, the British took an entire obelisk, Cleopatra's Needle, from the banks of the Nile, and shipped it in a specially built boat back to London?''

She spoke possessively; her long eyelashes moved in protest. When she said "to do it," the plain English words were enriched in a way that her English education had failed to suppress. She stopped at the corner of a glass case, but looked at Koblensky and not the artifacts. "You are not bored by this?"

"No," he said.

"I like your new suit."

His right foot moved in the sandal, betraying embarrassment.

"There is something here *much* more interesting. Not many people know about it. Especially not the British.'' For a second she assessed him, and then took his elbow more firmly and led him past the remaining glass cases without a glance, to a door marked "Private" in English, French, and Arabic at the far end of the gallery. She let go his arm and found a key in her purse and they slipped through the door.

They were in what seemed to be a storeroom. Shelves were stacked with shards, haphazardly sorted. On the floor were several large carboys of dark blue glass encased in straw, with wax seals on the corks. There was a motley collection of smaller glass containers, some containing clear liquid and others different-colored powders. But what most struck Koblensky was the smell. It was like nothing he had known before, a combination of mustiness and acridity as well as a suggestion of perfume. The room had only a small skylight; otherwise it was windowless. The beam of light focused by the skylight was dense with suspended particles that came sharply to life when the door opened and then closed, like some disturbed spirit. While his eyes adjusted to the change in light, she was putting another key in a further door. This door was wooden, but its edges had been rimmed with strips of copper to make a seal, work that he could see had been crudely improvised. As she opened this door, the intensity of the peculiar smell increased, hitting him in a wave as he followed her.

This inner room was in darkness relieved only by what light still came from the open door. She groped for a second in a corner and then the flame of a candle grew inside a bell jar. She gestured to him to close the door. The air in the room—or what passed for air—was sharply dry. Closing the door, he was, for a few seconds, sightless. Then he followed the light in her hand and came to her side by a casket on a trestle. The casket was little more than boxwood braced with more copper strips applied by the same crude hand as the door seal. She held the light a little away from her face. It exaggerated the thickness of her lower lip. She nodded down to the casket, her left hand coming again to his elbow.

At first the form in the casket was featureless and its contours only vaguely human. Then, as she lowered the light a little more, he could see the outline of trunk, arms, and head. Even the outline, though, was oddly lacking in substance, like the clustered particles in the outer room. The chest had collapsed, rib cage and all, into a concave amalgam of uneven flakes of pale gray plaster with a few traces of some kind of fiber. Koblensky's perception of this form assembled in a few seconds of mingled revulsion and fascination. Only one thing seemed securely tangible: a coil of gold thread around the semblance of a throat. Above this ring the head was only slightly more definitive than the rest—a skull under a gossamer layer of the same gray plaster. Even the teeth had fallen away, except for a few tenuous stumps. The essence of the enveloping smell was in this body.

Distractedly Koblensky saw her wrist holding the light. The completeness of her wrist was suddenly something he wanted to grasp to dismiss the obscenity below. The light wavered as she began to speak, not in the whisper that he anticipated but in a natural, fiducial way. "It's about two thousand five hundred years old, a minor princess. We can tell that from the thickness of the gold. That's the way they measured rank. At first, when they acquired the techniques for preserving corpses, that, too, was a measure of privilege. It was very expensive. Later, much later, everybody made some attempt at it. Death was a far more important event for celebration than birth."

Still not able to equal her strength of voice, he said, "It is grotesque. Not just this, this *thing* itself. The wish to be immortal. *That* is grotesque."

"You have to understand their world. The ba, the soul of the dead, was lost unless the body was in a condition to preserve the ka—the ka was their concept of the spark of life."

"Wanting immortality—that is the greatest vanity, and the most useless."

She heard the quiet, faltering outrage in his voice. She looked down again into the casket. "According to Herodotus, the treat-

ment took seventy days. They kept the organs separately, pre-
served in jars. The body, as you can see, was dehydrated.''

The impersonality of her voice irritated him. ''If there is such
a thing as a life force . . . what did they call it?''

''The ka.''

''If there is, whatever name you give it, a soul or a ka, it
doesn't wither and decay like our organs. It goes in an instant. I
know. When a man dies it has gone. In a second. Whatever it
is.''

''How many times have you seen someone die?''

''Too often.''

She fell silent, moving the light a little, eyes wandering over
the body.

His irritation persisted. ''When people believe in life after
death, our religions are no better than these pagans'. If people
believe in paradise they make too little of life. We should live
knowing what death is. That way we live more.''

''That is your philosophy?''

He didn't answer. His face was too far away from the light for
her to see his expression. ''I understand that,'' she said, becoming consciously more interested. ''I'm beginning to understand
*you*.''

In a final gesture of disgust, he turned away from the casket,
becoming virtually invisible to her. ''One life is a very small
thing, an atom. But sometimes it can make a difference. And if
it does not . . . it will never be noticed. It is not much to risk,
even if it is all we have. We should give all we have, without
thinking that it is any more than it is. *That* is why I hate this
thing—for its useless vanity. What can dust do? What did this
woman do? Religion is vanity. And fear.''

She moved the light away, trying to find him. ''You must
have worried the rabbis,'' she said, straining to pick out his
face.

''It depended on the rabbi. Some of them were not so bad.
People need them.''

''What do *you* need?''

''I have very few needs.''

She held the light to his face, saying nothing, but unable to
decide whether his arrogance was a strength or a weakness.
There seemed not a weak line in his face; it was cut in too
austere a mold and would probably never be any fleshier than it

was now. She moved the light toward the door. "Come on. We need a change of air."

In the storeroom, holding back, she said, "It is a secret, all this. You realize that? If the British knew about it they would take it."

"Of course." He put a hand on her shoulder. "I am pleased that you let me in on your secret."

"Yes," she said, carefully not enhancing the intimacy of his gesture. "Yes, you *should* be. You know, it was an accident. They were working in a tomb; they thought it was empty. One of many that have been robbed. They found a hollow wall; behind it was another, smaller tomb. Very little in it, but this one mummy, and the wrappings had been damaged. By the Persians, we suspect. Anyway, once the air had reached it, its future state was uncertain, so we—the professor involved and a small group of us—we decided to smuggle it back here, remove the wrappings, and try to preserve it long enough to learn something. . . ."

There was a light tapping at the outer door.

She looked nervous. "Please—get behind the door," she whispered.

By the time she opened the door she was more composed, and opened it as though in irritation at being disturbed.

"What is it?"

Koblensky heard a tremulous young man's voice. "It's Professor Solomon. His body has been found—in the Nile. Drowned."

From his vantage point, Koblensky was struck by the fact that nothing in her body conveyed surprise.

# 7

## *Arabia ✣ October 1916*

Ibn 'Aqil hesitated before kicking the boy again, not from mercy but because he wanted to leave him coherent enough to be questioned. The boy had drawn his knees up to his chest in the spasm of pain. He made no effort to protect himself and looked at Ibn 'Aqil with tearful but obdurate eyes. His refusal to wail or plead helped Ibn 'Aqil to restrain himself; the boy's expression had an impudence that, in the circumstances, invited respect. Ibn 'Aqil drew back his foot and waited for the boy to get his breath.

The boy, without knowing Ibn 'Aqil's identity, was in no doubt of his authority. Ibn 'Aqil was in the garments of the Ikhwan and the Ikhwan, to the best of the boy's understanding, were agents of the wrath of God, the kicks the first impact of that wrath. The puzzle was not the identity of his punisher but the cause of his offense. Ibn 'Aqil fulfilled the boy's expectation of what an agent of God should look like. It was—though Ibn 'Aqil had failed to see it—*respect* that gave the boy his impudence and apparent valor. Ibn 'Aqil must be, he reasoned, if not the Cloaked One, well acquainted with the Cloaked One. And so, when the boy at last found his breath, he said, "Are you the Cloaked One?"

Ibn 'Aqil was disconcerted—a man who had chased a fox and found a lamb. He stepped forward again and peered at the boy. "What did you say?"

"Are you the Cloaked One?"

One of the men behind Ibn 'Aqil began to laugh, but was checked by a wave of Ibn 'Aqil's hand. "What do you know of the Cloaked One?"

The boy sat up. " 'You that are wrapped in your vestment, arise and give warning. . . .' "

Ibn 'Aqil's face had ceased to have the fury of the thwarted. He faltered. "You know the words of the Book?"

The boy began dimly to perceive his advantage. He still had an acute pain from his loins to his stomach, but he clasped his hands around his knees and struggled for composure. Ibn 'Aqil bent like an arrested shadow over him. At first slowly and then with increasing assurance, the boy recited:

" 'Some of us are righteous, while others are not. We follow different ways. We know we cannot escape on earth from Allah, nor can we elude His grasp by flight. When we heard His guidance we believed in Him: he that believes in his Lord shall never be wronged or harmed. . . .' " The boy had spoken staring ahead; now he looked up at Ibn 'Aqil again and said, "It is written, the Jinn."

The other three men had closed around Ibn 'Aqil, gaping down at the boy.

"You know more of the Book?" said Ibn 'Aqil.

The boy nodded. "I know all the Book."

"*All* the Book? But you do not read. Nobody in your village could read. You are all ignorant—*juhl.*" He spat out the pejorative.

"I learned every word."

"Learned . . . how?"

"My grandfather was Sayyed Ibn 'Abbas. He was a holy man; he had kissed the stone. My grandfather had the whole of the Book in his head, and he gave it to me."

"You know the *whole* Koran?"

"Everything is there—it is all a man needs to know."

This was too much for Ibn 'Aqil. He laughed thinly. "A man?"

Given the license, the other men laughed too.

But the boy said, without reserve, "I am man enough."

"And also *holy?*" sneered Ibn 'Aqil.

"No. Not holy. That must come."

"You speak with your grandfather's voice, not your father's," said Ibn 'Aqil.

"My father is a good man, but not a holy one."

"He is holy now," said Ibn 'Aqil with a coarse laugh, echoed by the others. But he was uncomfortable with his own humor, aware of a disturbing quality in the boy—who had already gone far to remove the grounds for killing him. Ibn 'Aqil's three companions would not normally have shown such restraint, but the boy's performance had checked them too, obliging their

137

swords to hesitate before the sacred litany. They might still overcome this hesitancy, but Ibn 'Aqil did not want to risk the responsibility—or trust to their silence if the boy was killed.

The boy understood the meaning of their humor. He tilted his head slightly, the better to judge Ibn 'Aqil's face, seeing its wood-grained skin and broken teeth. Under the mustache, the mouth in laughter revealed more of his age than any other part of him. It was a humor of limited patience, as ready to kill as to kick. His father was surely dead, the boy knew; no true messenger of God could have spared him.

"Stand up!" said Ibn 'Aqil.

The pain had subsided and the boy rose from his knees without fear. His smallness surprised the men.

Ibn 'Aqil bent forward and gripped the boy's cloak at its hem, and the shirt beneath it, and raised them.

"At least he is circumcised." Ibn 'Aqil kept the garments raised. "There were men in your village, and boys, who were unclean, infidels in their bodies . . . and you speak of your grandfather being a holy man."

The boy was unflinching. "My grandfather told me of the teaching of 'Abd-al-Wahhab." Ibn 'Aqil stiffened, and the reflex let the boy's cloak fall from his hand. The boy closed his legs, a boyish gesture of modesty. "He said that his was the only pure faith, the only teaching true to the Book. But he said that many of our forefathers had forsaken these teachings and even forgotten 'Abd-al-Wahhab. My father would laugh at my grandfather. He said the world was changing. The caravans came from Damascus, and even from the ends of the earth beyond Damascus. They came from the land of the great rivers, and the people there had not heard of 'Abd-al-Wahhab. My father told my grandfather: 'Look, are these travelers not worldly men, and do they not prosper? What prosperity has 'Abd-al-Wahhab brought you?' My father would say that our village was poor, too poor to be the work of God. My grandfather was angry and they had many disputes, but most of the men agreed with my father." The boy saw a new stillness in his audience. He continued, "My grandfather told me that one day the strength of 'Abd-al-Wahhab would be seen, that my father would learn the error of his ways. He said that a new king had appeared from a distant desert and that the flame of 'Abd-al-Wahhab was burning again. He said he would not live to see this king reach our village, but that I should expect it. Are you from that king?"

Ibn 'Aqil said slowly, "You will leave this place. You will not go back to your village. The village has been purged. You will ride with us. We will see how well you know the teaching of 'Abd-al-Wahhab, and you will see how you must live by what is written—and how we deal with unbelievers."

The boy persisted: "Are you the soldiers of the great king?"

Ibn 'Aqil snapped, "We are the Ikhwan." He put a firm hand on the boy's left shoulder, gripping through the cloth. "The creed of the Ikhwan is written in the Book. You should remember it. . . ." He brought his face close to the boy's and rasped out the words, half chant and half instruction:

"Cling all of you to the rope of God
    and do not separate and
Remember God's blessings, for you were enemies
    and he joined your hearts together
And you became, by the grace of God, brothers."

Still gripping the boy, he kissed him on each cheek and the tip of the nose. His eyes, yellow and red-veined, fixed on the boy's. "We are the brothers. There is no bond greater. There is no family. There is no village. There is no tribe. The brotherhood is, by the grace of God, the only path to Paradise. *Do you understand?*"

"Yes—I understand. It is in the blood."

"In the blood?" Ibn 'Aqil was impressed. He pulled himself upright and the grip on the boy's shoulder relaxed. "Yes—it is in the blood." He noticed that the other three men had acquired a grudging respect for the boy. "We shall rejoin Faisal al-Dawish, and he shall see the face of our new brother." He looked up out of the palm grove to the grazing sheep. "We shall sell the sheep in the Nafud. We have no time for flocks or possessions, or the vices of the town. You shall sell the horse too, and take camel with another until you are man enough to ride alone." The sourness of Ibn 'Aqil's breath lingered in the boy's senses. He began to see that living with the holy and filthy Ikhwan would require a coarser manhood than he had known.

Over the next days the familiar landscape slipped away from the boy. They went south into the Nafud, the desert he had never seen. He did not know it bisected a quarter of Arabia. But he was conscious of a different world, and conscious too that the farther south they went, the more contented Ibn 'Aqil seemed. The featureless red sand had no relief until they saw a single pinnacle of rock, higher than the buzzards flew, which proved to be Ibn 'Aqil's objective. The Ikhwan guide and scouts were impatient with the tardiness of the sheep. The boy had driven them as hard as he dared, but they didn't like the coarse sand and had to go for two days without water.

At the rock they met the remainder of Ibn 'Aqil's original party, now repaired from the ravages of the storm. There was discussion about the sheep. This encumbrance prevented the speed needed for raiding, but Ibn 'Aqil wanted the money the flock would fetch. After an argument at the coffee hearth, he made a virtue of the problem. The Ikhwan never attacked a town or village without first sending in a spy; that had been the role of the letter bearer at Ibn 'Abbas's village. Why not, proposed Ibn 'Aqil, send the boy into a village to sell the sheep? Then the boy could be truly tested as a spy; they would get the money for the sheep, and then they would take whatever was left in the raid. The boy was fetched from where he sat with his horse. He was told that if he went for only half a day along the trail to the south, he would find a small oasis, and he was told what to do.

The boy listened to Ibn 'Aqil with an expression of due reverence. He could feel the bridled energy of the party. He was honored, he said, to be their agent. And as he knelt with them in the prayer of first light, he began for the first time in his life to know the intoxication of a divine mission.

What the boy had not foreseen was his own peril. When he came into the village he aroused suspicion, and when he announced his purpose the village shepherd was called, The shepherd was an old man for his craft. He limped around the flock, looking at fetlocks and tapping heads, but his greatest skepticism was reserved for the boy. The shepherd pushed his staff at the boy, poking him in the chest. He wanted the name of the boy's father, and the names of all the men of his village. This harangue attracted more men. The boy found himself enclosed in a circle of bickering, attention passing from him to the shepherd and then back to him.

"He says his village was destroyed in a storm and that they must sell their sheep," shouted the shepherd.

"There was a storm," murmured an onlooker.

"But why does his father not sell the sheep?" said the shepherd, losing his voice and his patience at the same time.

The boy guessed that many of the men were ready to dispense with the formality of a sale, and would simply take the sheep.

But an elder of the village intervened. He said, "The boy has brought the sheep this far. That is proof enough that he is his father's shepherd. There is no law greater than the law that rules the ownership of sheep, for we all know the penalty for stealing sheep, which is the habit of those who have no honor and no village. How could such a boy have stolen the sheep? Is he not to be praised for doing honor to his father and bringing the sheep to us?" The man paused and waited for challenge, but none came. He looked from the boy to the sheep. "They are good sheep, and the boy should have a good price."

The shepherd muttered inaudibly. The rest of the men conceded to the elder. The boy realized that the dispute over the sheep had supplanted any suspicion that he might have another purpose there. The elder invited him to his house and insisted he stay the night. In the morning a sum in gold coins was counted out and put into a pouch of camel hide, and he left the village unmolested. But the hospitality failed to deflect his sense of duty. He had noted an absence of younger men in the village, that its wall was in poor repair, and that the gold was kept in the house of the elder. He had also seen that not even the rudiments of the faith were practiced there.

Ibn 'Aqil absorbed these details with the kind of satisfaction that mutely vindicated his choice of target. He needed to return to Faisal al-Dawish with more than he yet had. The party had been marauding now for nearly a month. The boy had been the cause of a lengthy diversion and the storm had seemed the devil's work. Now he sensed that retribution was at hand. He complimented the boy on his vigilance and took the gold with what was, to the boy, a strangely chaste gesture, conveying none of the avarice that the boy had always seen when gold appeared.

He put the pouch aside and put a hand on the boy's shoulder. "I have chosen the time. You must learn how we choose our time. Sometimes we appear with the sun, that is *al-Sabah;* sometimes when the sun is at its highest, *al-Ghara,* but that is best with the whole army; sometimes it is *al-Ruhah,* when the sun is sinking. But for this village we shall strike according to *al-Hijad,* in darkness. This is difficult, but you have given us eyes in advance."

They did not move until midnight, and they came within sight of the village in two hours. A waning moon gave the village a dull gunmetal hue, casting long shadows. The party divided into two parts. Twenty or so men left their camels tethered and went to the village wall. The remainder stayed on their camels and formed a column. Ibn 'Aqil led this column and put the boy on the camel with him.

No night guard had been posted at the gate. Two men scaled the wall easily, and noiselessly removed the wooden beam securing the gate. The gate scraped across the dirt as they swung it open, but nothing, not even a dog, stirred.

Ibn 'Aqil kicked his camel into motion and cried out:

> "I am a Knight of Unity,
> Brother of He who obeys God.
> Show your head, O enemy!"

The column charged through the gate and on through the village, uttering warnings of the winds of paradise and their power. The boy clung easily to the camel and joined the cries. At first, the onrush of men and camels was unimpeded; they weaved between houses and completed a circuit before a few men appeared. So great was the cacophony of the Ikhwan's cries that the boy could not hear the voices of the stirring village. He was waving his own lance in the air and already becoming hoarse. Two dogs ran out from an alley across the path of the camels and narrowly avoided being trampled; their yelping was the first response the boy was aware of. The houses swam past him in the blur of dust and colorless light. Ibn 'Aqil brought the column to the main courtyard of the village, where the boy said the elder's house was. As his camel wheeled into the courtyard, the boy saw half a dozen men appear, at first paralyzed by the sight of the camels and then dispersing in confusion.

Ibn 'Aqil set his camel after one of these men and, still yards from him, threw his lance. The man continued to run even as the lance passed through his body. He went headlong into a wall.

The boy saw that Ibn 'Aqil's plan was being fulfilled: As soon as the men realized the size of the camel column, they made for the gate in blind panic. Running through the gate, they were cut down by the second contingent.

Now the camel column divided and began a systematic sweep of the alleys. A few women appeared, but Ibn 'Aqil ignored them. He saw an older man limping and headed the camel at him; the boy recognized the limping man as the shepherd. Ibn 'Aqil deftly pulled the camel abreast of the man and cut down at him with his sword. The force of the blow sent the man spinning and as he spun a limb detached itself. The boy saw the arm fly into the dirt, the hand still in the gesture of futile deflection. This object so obsessed the boy that to follow it he twisted around on the camel. The movement unbalanced him and he found himself flying over the camel's rump. He ended up in the dirt several yards from where the shepherd was crawling and screaming. The boy only narrowly missed being trampled by the following camels.

His own lance had gone in the fall. He got to his feet as the last of the camels went by. The dust of the charge was chest high about him and it wasn't until it cleared that he realized the shepherd had crawled and settled at his feet. All the tumult of the attack seemed a long way off, though it was concentrated barely thirty yards away. The whimpering at his feet overwhelmed the boy's consciousness. The exhilaration of the charge had gone and he was paralyzed by the sight of the dismembered shepherd. The man recognized him. His whimpering stopped and he peered up at the boy with the manic concentration of sudden shock. His remaining arm rose and gripped the boy's cloak just above his right knee. A bubble of blood and saliva came from between the man's parting lips and, in a film as delicate as a fly's wing, expanded with a gust of breath behind it and then atomized, spraying the boy's cloak. Behind the breath was a sound like a cock's rising note in the dawn. The boy wanted to disavow his identity: It was the fact of having been recognized that distressed him more than the blood. Nothing as refined as guilt occurred to him; he could not define his offense. He surrendered to a wild surge of self-absolving anger, directed first at the obscenity of the hand clawing at his cloak. He kicked sharply into the man's chest. Another eruption of blood came from the man's mouth as he pitched backward. The remaining hand went with him.

The boy felt more through his foot than his mind. The kicking foot had felt as if it were going into a reed basket, at first resilient and then brittle. Something had snapped; he looked down and saw that the foot was bloody. The thong of his sandal had given way and his toes were spattered. It was the foot that bloodied the boy; it had killed the man. As he comprehended this, the boy also became aware of something moving behind him. He reacted too slowly and had only half turned when a bamboo staff broke across his left shoulder, but the movement had been enough to save his head.

The pain of the blow and the poor light confused the boy's sight. He could not distinguish substance from shadow; both came at him. The staff descended again, but the boy threw himself to one side and the assailant went clear by him, unbalanced by missing the blow. Now the boy saw more clearly. A small but broad-cloaked figure skidded through the dust and wheeled to attack him again. This time the boy regained the initiative and danced nimbly backward, confusing the attack. The broken sandal had come off and his right heel hit something hard in the dirt: his lance. He took another pace back and in one movement found the lance and got behind it in a low crouching position, with its hilt on his right hip. His assailant appeared not to see the lance and came with staff flailing in a light, feline jump. All the boy's strength was behind the lance. His assailant was impaled, though the billowing cloak made it impossible to see where. There was a strange, attenuated sigh and the cloak became lifeless.

The boy left the lance in the body and bent over it, pulling at the cloak. A face—a smooth, silver-gray face—stared at him. It was a woman. In the baleful light she had the composure of stone. Whatever animus had driven her had left no mark; in the instant of death it had gone and the boy was spared acquaintance with it. The revelation of an unequal struggle was an injury to his honor. With no stronger outrage than that, he bent down to cover the face.

From above him a voice said, "Those who wear silk are damned."

The boy had not heard Ibn 'Aqil return. He looked up at the silhouetted figure, uncertain of its reaction. "I did not know it was a woman."

"She is in silk."

"I did not know. . . ."

"Silk is the beguiler of men. There is no paradise for those who wear silk."

"She attacked me."

Ibn 'Aqil disregarded the remark. He looked away to the other corpse. "These men are as you said. None will see the dawn." He brought his camel to its knees so that the boy could remount. "We have not finished yet."

The pursuit and herding of the surviving men and boys was

completed efficiently. Again and again, individual screams added to the tally. The boy remained with Ibn 'Aqil as, from the camel, he supervised the slaughter. The boy was more aware of the low pain in his shoulder from the woman's first blow than of the meaning of what he saw. He had never been squeamish and he accepted the inevitability of the killing as a natural and prescribed force. He knew there was a difference between quartering a gazelle and spearing a man, but it was not so much an emotional or a moral difference as a technical one.

Ibn 'Aqil rode for five days across the eastern fingers of the Nafud, skirting the besieged enemy Ibn Rashid at Hail and giving the boy an increasing sense of the immensity of Arabia. Parallel, to the south, he saw the majestic Jebbel Shammar, violet-tipped peaks; beyond them, he imagined, might be the ends of the earth. Finally they turned southeast and reached the tip of the Dahna desert. Here, coming suddenly over the brow of a vast U-shaped depression, the boy saw something he would never forget: Against the sand, which the morning sun had tinted a crystalline ocher, was a pattern of black tents, looking to the boy like rows of teeth set in glinting gums. There seemed to be hundreds of tents, over two thousand men, and nearly as many camels. Coffee was brewing over many hearths; each hearth was the center of a unit of men.

Ibn 'Aqil led his party through the camp to a dominant tent that had been pitched to the east of the well—the well that had determined the campsite. Outside this tent a dozen men were in conclave around the hearth. Ibn 'Aqil halted his party at the well. Even as he lowered his camel to the ground, the boy behind him saw in Ibn 'Aqil's arrangement of his cloak and body something novel: humility. Ibn 'Aqil went alone across the dirt toward the hearth, his cloak skirts gathered up clear of his ankles, his head subtly bent. The others of the party around the boy were devotedly incurious: they busied themselves watering the camels and one of them, seeing the boy's rooted gaze at the tent, hissed a warning at him. The men jabbered like adolescents, and laughed with false confidence. They knew, though they left it for the boy to guess, that Ibn 'Aqil was making his accounting to Faisal al-Dawish and that this was a collective due, assessed not simply on bounty but on the not so easily proved reclamation (or dispatch) of souls. Once the boy grasped the cause of the men's strained humor, he fell in with it. They retold individual accounts of the sacking of their last target and then, carelessly, one of them mentioned the fate of the boy's own village.

Beyond knowing his father's fate, the boy had never asked about or discussed that attack. The men hesitated, but the boy insisted on knowing every detail, and soon they were competing for the most lurid version. The boy listened with apparent simpleminded fatalism. The men already regarded him as a curiosity, but one that had a vaguely abstracted quality, and they were not surprised now to see in his attentive eyes no more trace of contact than had they been describing the conquests of Omar. All of them became so engrossed that they failed to see Ibn 'Aqil's return. He came with a discernibly lighter step. Good-naturedly he stirred them from their tales and directed them to where they were to pitch their tents and to resume their place in the main force. Then he took the boy aside.

"Our master, Faisal al-Dawish, the great and the dutiful, has a holy man, one of the *ulema,* in his tent. He has ordered that I bring you to the tent after nightfall, that you shall show your knowledge of the Book." Ibn 'Aqil's face broke uneasily into a smile. "Our master has not heard of such knowledge in one so young. You must show him." The smile had already dissolved. "There is no greater learning than that of the *ulema.*"

Without a trace of being intimidated, the boy said, "Who are these *ulema*?"

"They are the keepers of the word, and the teachers."

"Of the Prophet's word?"

Ibn 'Aqil stopped abruptly and turned on the boy. "Of the Lord's word. The Prophet only carried the word. The Prophet was no more than any man in the face of Allah."

The reprimand reduced the boy to a confused silence. This was contrary to his grandfather's instruction. Without Mohammed, the word would not have had a voice.

He was left in no doubt of the Ikhwan's zeal for the word when the noon prayers were called. The men turned to the southwest and began with a cry that reverberated around the camp and then rose into the sky:

"It is You Whom we adore,
And You from Whom we seek help!"

The prayers were led not by Faisal al-Dawish but by the tallest man in the camp, a man whose height seemed to give greater depth to his voice, the chants arcing from him. Since the prayer leader was behind him, the boy did not see him clearly until they were finished, and then he saw only the man's towering back as he returned to Faisal al-Dawish's hearth. So this was the *ulema*. The boy was more curious than awed.

In the afternoon, a listlessness overcame the camp. Ibn 'Aqil's party replenished their supplies of dates, flour, and water, the only provisions they carried. Their next target required a massed attack, and a new supply of rifles had arrived. Some of these were given to Ibn 'Aqil's party, and the men treated them with jealous fastidiousness.

The boy was being shown the mechanism of a Lee Enfield when the fringe of the camp became animated. Coming over the horizon into the depression was a small column of camels, at its head a green and white banner.

The man showing the boy the rifle nodded to the column. "We shall know soon where we go. These are the orders from Riyadh. That is the banner of the King Abdul Aziz, King Saud."

Riyadh was a living myth to the boy, the capital that Ibn Saud had reclaimed for his family with only a token army, the first humbling of Ibn Rashid and the wellspring of all the legends that were filling the boy's head and energized all those around him. So the approaching camels were giving substance to legend, and in standing to see them, the boy was touched at last by awe.

After dusk the campfires illuminated the faces of men playing with rumor. No one had yet had word of their orders, but there was plenty of speculation. The one attested fact was that the camel column was more distinguished than they had expected. It was led by Abdullah Ibn Jiluwi, a power in the land second only to Ibn Saud. But the boy noticed that some of Ibn 'Aqil's men were disrespectful. One of them whispered, "Ibn Jiluwi is a milk drinker." Others were more discreet, advising that his presence meant direct instructions from Ibn Saud. Still others met this with a cynical interpretation: that Ibn Jiluwi was sent to make sure that no booty was held back. His column was seen to have empty baggage camels. Ibn 'Aqil remained silent. It was known (confided a camelmaster to the boy) that Ibn 'Aqil and Ibn Jiluwi were as fond of each other as a viper for a goat—though the man would not say which was which.

Faisal al-Dawish was obliged to provide the visitor with a feast. The smell of baked lamb came as an affront to the austere diet of the rest of the camp. They knew that to have offered less to the king's emissary would have been an insult, but it reminded them that the habits of Riyadh were not as abstemious as those of the Ikhwan settlements.

When the feast was finished, one of Faisal al-Dawish's lieutenants came to fetch Ibn 'Aqil and the boy. Away from their fire, in the short interval between the tents, the night was already sharply cold. But the boy knew that he was shivering for other reasons.

Faisal al-Dawish was at the center of a dozen men, flanked on one side by Ibn Jiluwi and on the other by the *ulema*. The *ulema*'s eyes immediately fixed on the boy.

"This is the boy—Khalid Ibn 'Abbas, master." Ibn 'Aqil pulled the boy to his side and pressed him rudely down.

Faisal al-Dawish whispered something to Ibn Jiluwi, whose aversion to Ibn 'Aqil was transparent. "It is said that you carry the whole of the Book in your head. You shall recite to us. Which of the Book do you choose?"

The boy saw that the *ulema* was looking at him with skepticism. He answered firmly: "In the Name of Allah, the Compassionate, the Merciful . . . I will recite That Which Is Coming."

The boy saw no skepticism in Ibn Jiluwi's eyes, and felt encouragement. On his knees before them, he recited with a lilting, expressive tenor: " 'When that which is coming comes, and no soul shall then deny its coming, some shall be abased and others exalted. . . .' " As he went on, the verses became more rhetorical and he entered fully into their spirit, at turns reverential, at times vigorous, and at times plaintive. There was a faint, amused stirring when he cried out: " 'Behold the semen you discharge—did you create it, or we?' " but a glance from the *ulema* froze all impiety. The boy's breast filled and rose with a culminating fervor as he cried to the darkened shrouds of the tent: " '. . . if he is an erring disbeliever his welcome will be scalding water and he will burn in Hell. This is the unalterable truth. *Praise then the name of your Lord, the Supreme One'!*"

Silence brought the boy to awareness of his impact. The *ulema* no longer had any trace of doubt. Faisal al-Dawish, his face yellow in the dancing flame, had the reserve of a man who was unsure of the others' reactions. But Ibn Jiluwi was unrestrained. He did not stand on dignity. He said, *"Salaam, alaykum,"* a greeting usually reserved for dignitaries. "You touch my heart." He narrowed his focus to Ibn 'Aqil, who was still standing equivocally behind the boy. "Where did you find this angel among boys?"

Ibn 'Aqil moved his weight from one foot to another. "On my campaign. He comes from a village of unbelievers."

"Of unbelievers?" Ibn Jiluwi became openly derisive. "Then how is he so equipped with holiness?"

Ibn 'Aqil mumbled an explanation.

"A strange story," said Ibn Jiluwi. "Of course, all the unbelievers have been put to the sword?"

"Of course," said Ibn 'Aqil indignantly.

"Of course," repeated Ibn Jiluwi, turning slowly to the neighboring ear of Faisal al-Dawish but speaking audibly. "This boy has a quick mind."

"He is illiterate," interrupted Ibn 'Aqil, but realized the breach of etiquette and addressed Faisal al-Dawish. "I am sorry, master, but the boy is illiterate."

For the first time, the *ulema* spoke. "Does he ride with you?"

"He is a good fighter," said Ibn 'Aqil, not judging the *ulema*'s meaning.

"One boy does not make a difference to an army," said the *ulema*, "but one boy like this is a rare thing. We must value rarity when we see it." He turned to Faisal al-Dawish. "The boy should be taken in the care of teachers. What he has now is impressive, but it is not knowledge. Let him know what learning is. He must understand the meaning of this gift he has."

Faisal al-Dawish nodded. "It is a gift. It is our sacred duty to nourish it."

Ibn Jiluwi said, "His gift is the power of the ear, not the mind. All our words have been passed down in this way. Illiteracy is no shame. It preserves the memory." He looked at the boy across the flames. "Learning destroys memory."

"But we should take the boy?" said the *ulema* cautiously, impatient with Ibn Jiluwi's urban philosophizing, but aware of his authority.

"Yes—take him," confirmed Ibn Jiluwi in an almost slumberous tone, "take him, and make him learned in all the sacred words, and in all the sacred laws. And when you have done that, we shall take him and give him knowledge of the world—but first make safe his knowledge of God. Without that, the world may take him." He looked from the boy to Ibn 'Aqil. "We have need of skills beyond the sword. This boy will soon be a man."

# 8

## *Kuwait ❈ December 1916*

It was galling to get to this desert behind another. Captain Shakespear, Kippax's forerunner, had been a maverick, ignoring orders, choosing sides, falling to a kind of heroic madness. But Shakespear had left maps, recording bearings, altitudes, temperatures. Kippax had made copies of Shakespear's maps, resenting them too. The world was running out of uncharted places, that was the sad truth. Romances were still spun around the "dark continent" and the corrupting, pagan places, but the sad truth was that almost anywhere worth finding had already been found; he had been born too late. So Kippax's enthusiasm for this desert began with no romantic impulse; it was an act of calculation. He knew enough of Arabia to see what Shakespear had seen but wasted: the chance of alliance with an underrated force, perhaps the making of a career.

In Kuwait, the political agent had said, "Shakespear was a little touched, if you ask me. It happens to people, apparently. Quite lost his judgment."

"And his life," said Kippax.

"Yes. Turned out he was four hundred pounds in arrears. The books were in a bloody mess here, I can tell you."

Kuwait, and that fool, were behind him now. There was no sun. The sky was an inert gray blanket. His caravan had been efficiently assembled and equipped for the wet season. There were eighteen camels—a dozen for baggage and six of the *dhahuls*, the prized female riding camels. Kippax was advised to wear a thick goatskin robe, but his camel had been the first to see through this charade. As he mounted, she kept her head tilted sideways, one eye on him. But within a minute of rising she seemed reassured. The next doubt was Kippax's name. The three tribal guides curled the word in their throats and offered the resulting noise with amusement. To simplify things they settled on "El Khibeg." Kippax was more concerned with tuning his ear to their dialects, noting the difference in each one. Because they had to cross the lands of the Sbei, the Mutair, and the Ajman, a guide had been drawn from each of them. As well as the guides there were herdsmen, a boy in charge of six sheep, and an older youth, Nawaf, deputed as Kippax's personal servant, who had come from Riyadh, their destination.

From Kuwait their route ran west and then southwest, funneled between a great valley, the Al Batin, on the west, and the Al Mussanah ridge on the east. Beyond that lay the red desert of the Nafud, but they would turn southeast, away from it, for the last leg to Riyadh. The advantage of winter was that they could travel by day; even then the journey could take as much as a month.

At first it went well, in spite of cold nights and squalls of harsh rain during the day. In fact, each day stealthily educated and broadened Kippax's understanding of the desert. Within a week, the arduous and unsanitary life had both hardened and attracted him. Stripped of almost every customary thing, he learned how much was dispensable. He became less and less a curiosity to his companions. His classic Arabic began to bend with their inflections and to cease the simple mechanical functions of language, to serve feelings and experience. The fellowship of the caravan had the manliness expected of it, and yet within it Kippax saw something else, a subtle, almost secret bond quite unlike the masculinity of the Aryan world. It was like the land. It, too, was hardness itself and yet it stirred him as no meadow ever had.

This mood was broken only by chance. Early one afternoon they came upon another caravan in camp. It was in a sheltered depression where the rain had brought bushes into flower. Kippax's Mutair guide recognized his own tribe—indeed, one of its loftiest families, cousins of Faisal al-Dawish. The choice of camp was puzzling. The caravan would not normally be at rest at this place and at this time. Etiquette required elaborate greetings; eventually the Mutair guide came to Kippax with a tall, solemn man.

"El Khibeg, they ask for your help."

The tall man was introduced as Sheikh Hamud. With a mixture of dignity and desperation, the sheikh explained that the caravan was carrying his sister, the Princess Zein, to Kuwait.

151

The princess had had "ill fortune" and was being taken in search of doctors, but had now become too ill to move.

Kippax had meager resources: quinine, chloroform, seltzer, kaolin, yeast and salt tablets, dressings and iodine, cough syrup, and little else. His only medical training had been elementary, at the hands of the army. He said, "If I could see the princess, perhaps I will know if there is anything I can do."

There were delicate problems yet to be overcome. When women traveled in a caravan, they were as segregated as when they were in their homes, and for an outsider even to glimpse them would normally have been a serious trespass. Hamud led the way to a tent. He stooped to a sealed flap and whispered through black goatskin. There was a sequence of relayed consultations, the sound of several women's voices, hoarse and high-pitched. Hamud turned back to Kippax. "In a short time, we return."

Whatever the preparations, they took several minutes. Finally Hamud gestured Kippax through the flap. The tent was larger than it seemed from the outside. There were several partitions. The first section contained two rolled mattresses and a small rug and smelled of incense; the second, to the right, was much darker and had an odd, acrid smell. Kippax was led into it by a woman whose face he never saw but who seemed more venerable than any of the men. There was a litter in the corner, covered in a lamb's skin. As his eyes adjusted he saw, in the litter, a small huddled shape.

The old woman stepped back to let Kippax get closer. The smell was stronger now. He turned to the woman and asked for light. She did not answer, but disappeared. Kippax knelt by the litter. He picked out a face—or rather, a pair of eyes—passively, almost lifelessly, still. The whites of the eyes, as was the custom, had been painted blue with antimony, but the color had become as glazed as if on clay. Kippax touched the girl's head. It was hot with fever.

The woman came back with an oil lamp.

Kippax said, "How long has she been like this?"

Muffled by her veil, the woman said, "For six days." She pulled back the lamb's skin. The girl wore a white shroud to her neck. Under her left breast the shroud was soiled with pus. The woman raised the girl's legs and pulled up the shroud over her body to uncover the wound.

As far as Kippax could tell, the girl was only just past puberty. Her skin was white and drawn tightly over the pelvic bones, veins standing out on her upper thighs. The wound was at her waist, swollen reddish blue and clumsily dressed.

There was a problem of vocabulary. The old woman was reluctant to explain. Kippax persisted, and finally established the trouble had begun months earlier, as some kind of growth. At first, said the woman, they thought it a bruise. Then the girl complained of discomfort, and the swelling had grown and become sore. Finally the woman disclosed that the tribal doctor had decided to lance and drain it, two weeks earlier. This— Kippax gathered without surprise—had been done with a knife, after which the wound had been simply bound with cloth.

No sound came from the litter, but the girl had been watching the two of them through the conversation. Kippax turned and put his hand on her brow again. He felt abjectly unqualified to deal with her. Yet he knew that if something was not done she would be dead, probably within the day. The fateful step had been the lancing. Whether the growth was malignant or not, it was the knife wound that had turned septic and her blood was probably now pumping poison through her, the cause of the fever.

Somewhere beyond this section of the tent was another. Kippax became conscious of other women, catching their scent. The heresy of a stranger admitted to the harem, and now allowed to witness nakedness, was subsumed by an invisible but powerful willing of life back into this pale and failing girl; he was the focus of this feeling, and even the old woman now had no reservation left toward him. He dreaded this trust, and knew that all it rested on was his peculiarity, not his ability.

He remembered that one of his guides had a short knife like a Scottish dirk, carried at the waist in a leather pouch. As he went to get his medicine kit, he asked that this knife be heated in the embers of the coffee hearth, and be brought to him when the blade was too hot to touch.

The old woman sat back in the shadows while Kippax arranged the oil lamp to hang over his head above the litter. He had no surgical spirit. He did have whisky, and he soaked cotton wool with it and cleaned the wound as best he could. There was a call from outside and the old woman went out and returned with the knife, a cloth wrapped around its hilt. He asked the woman to remain with him, and soaked a cloth in chloroform. Still the girl watched them without making a sound. Kippax explained how to press the cloth to the girl's face and to hold it there. He put more whisky on the wound and on the skin around it. The stench of the whisky overcame the stench of the pus. He dipped the knife into the whisky and waited for the chloroform to have its effect. On his knees, he put his left hand on the girl's left wrist and then, straining to see under the poor light, slowly cut a first incision around the wound. The girl's flesh parted like paper.

The circle he inscribed was about an inch and a half across. The lancing cut had been an inch wide. So far there was little new bleeding and he swabbed the wound with cotton wool, preparing his own nerve for the next cut, trying to keep his right hand steady. The old woman watched him from behind her veil; the girl was unconscious. Kippax cut into flesh as he would have done to separate the meat of a grapefruit from its skin, in a slanted circular motion. The knife was very sharp and there was little resistance. With his left hand he stemmed the bleeding, and then cut again, about half an inch deep. There was something hard there, like a very small ball of fat. With one more cut it came free, almost perfectly round and blood-veined. There was more bleeding now, and he swabbed for several minutes. He dabbed iodine around the wound, and poured it onto a thick dressing and bandaged the dressing in place, cleaning the surrounding skin with whisky.

The operation had taken barely ten minutes, but it had seemed an age. The old woman had been motionless. The girl remained inert. He told the woman to remove the chloroform-soaked cloth while he felt the girl's pulse. It was very weak. He diluted some whisky with quinine water and poured it into a small flask. He made three more dressings and left the iodine with them. He told the woman to give the girl a sip of the whisky solution when she came round and then every two hours, and told her to re-dress the wound each morning. There was nothing more he could do.

Outside the tent, Hamud listened gravely to Kippax's advice not to move for at least three days, but there was no question of whether the girl had been saved: The magic was assumed done. Kippax knew he was obliged not to leave without eating with them, and so they were not able to continue the journey until the following dawn. By then he had confirmed an earlier suspicion: Most of the Mutairs' rifles were Turkish. Hamud's own bodyguard were a fearsome bunch, with plaited hair and bandoliers of ammunition over coarse cloaks.

Nawaf, Kippax's attendant, seemed relieved to be gone. Riding abreast of Kippax, he called in his girlish voice, "El

Khibeg, they have killed many men for the king. They kill the unbelievers.''

"For the king?"

"They are of the brothers—the Ikhwan.''

In Cairo, Kippax had read intermittent sketchy reports of the Ikhwan, usually described as Saud's religious enforcers, but no European, not even Shakespear, had seen them at close quarters. So after all, the delay had been of historic value. "I have heard of the Ikhwan," he said, with more calmness than Nawaf thought wise.

The deeper they were into the desert, the more composed Kippax seemed. This was not the sand sea of Victorian imagination. Its true nature and power was the casting off of all harmony. This desert had immense diversity. Gravel, mud, sandstone, lava, granite, mud baked smooth as glass, fine-grained sand, salt-tinged sand, quicksand—the earth splintered into every conceivable manner of defile, escarpment, gorge, wadi, plateau, every conceivable rupture of harmony. And it was not barren. Having crossed a formidable barrier, an escarpment called the Tuwaik, they came suddenly on abundant cultivation. There were date palms, wheat fields, well-irrigated pastures, and two walled towns.

To this oasis Ibn Saud had sent a personal escort, six horsemen to go with them to Riyadh, now less than a week away. Nawaf embraced the horsemen; Kippax knew he was now under the care of a power that in this territory was absolute. That night, to avoid the risk of heresy, he emptied his last two bottles of whisky into the sand and prepared to present himself in a more ascetic guise. That night also, as his men sat with the newcomers around the fire, the delicate membrane of desert kinship was more clear to him. He now had a full beard, a hardened body, and skin burnished by wind and sun—but he was still the alien, though far less the apprentice.

Riyadh, when he first saw it, was an unprepossessing walled city at the center of another oasis. The absence of a grand design, the simple and random mud-brick buildings and the rough streets, suggested a significant modesty. In 1901, the young Ibn Saud had recaptured his tribe's capital from Ibn Rashid with a force of only forty men. Though it had risen mightily since then, nothing advertised the resurgent clan—except, perhaps, the absence of grandiosity. Kippax felt that impersonation was over. He discarded the desert robes and substituted an unmarked khaki drill uniform and pith helmet, but left the beard, because it had firmed up his face.

In Riyadh he was kept waiting for a day, while an audience with the king was confirmed. The next morning, he was taken to the palace, through an outer and an inner courtyard and then, leaving the camels, into a galleried building and to a large whitewashed room where three men waited: in the center, inches taller than the others, was Ibn Saud, and two of his brothers, Saad and Abdullah. As well as being unusually tall for an Arab—over six feet—Ibn Saud was thickly built; although his robes concealed his real girth, Kippax sensed a body of immense stamina. His headcloth was plain white, those of his brothers checkered. Under their dark robes they wore fine embroidered shirts.

After the ritual greetings, Ibn Saud waved Kippax to the rich carpet on the floor before him.

"El Khibeg," said Ibn Saud, "We hear you are not only the messenger from the Great Government, but a doctor."

"What has become of the princess?"

Ibn Saud smiled. "Faisal al-Dawish will be forever in your debt."

Servants entered, with tea, coffee, and sweets. The room had less a ceremonial than a workmanlike feeling, as though it might well be the place where campaigns were planned. There were several long, low wooden boxes against the wall and in one corner a pile of papers.

In spite of his strength, when Ibn Saud was sitting there was an uncommon delicacy about him. His hands were fine, with slender uncoarsened fingers, and his speech, like his movements, was measured, almost lethargic. For fifteen minutes or so he restated his understanding of the alliance reached with the British, ensuring that Kippax confirmed each detail as he came to it, and showing a more literal grasp of diplomatic language than Kippax found comfortable. The he came to his point:

"I know of the wisdom and strength of the Great Government, El Khibeg. I can see into the future. I can see what will happen when the Turks have gone. This is why, for so long, I have told the Great Government of my support. This is not simple for me. We are a pious people, and you are the infidels, the infidels of the Book. Can we share the same world as the infidels?" The heavy lids of his eyes closed, a mannerism of punctuation. "I have to face God, and I have to face the realities."

The two brothers nodded.

"El Khibeg, the Great Government has now made an alliance with the sharif of Mecca. I know this family, the Hashemites. They are not of the desert, they live a different life, and they have been softened. Do not expect too much of them."

Kippax leaned forward. "They have the Turks in their land."

Ibn Saud took a sip of tea and then his voice hardened: "They take your gold, but have they yet defeated one Turkish garrison?"

"They are preparing."

"For five thousand pounds a month you have received far more than preparation from me." Ibn Saud's eyes betrayed no mood. "El Khibeg, I am greatly honored that you have come so far to see me. I do not want your journey to have been wasted."

"We must be assured that you will support the Arab revolt." Listening to his own words as he spoke, Kippax comprehended the real dissonance in the room. Not simply the dissonance of translating Foreign Office phrases into Arabic, not even the wariness of each side for the other, the real dissonance was in the fabric of the place, in the wrenching of the Middle Ages into a twentieth-century intrigue, in the step being taken over a threshold that would lead God knows where. But Kippax was not the catalyst. It was this thirty-six-year-old Bedouin prince, who had somehow married the gifts of elemental survival with political imagination. Ibn Saud saw well beyond Kippax, and it did not unnerve Kippax so much as awe him.

For several minutes, from one of the courtyards outside, there had been the stirrings of some kind of assembly. Now Ibn Saud turned to his brothers and then back to Kippax. "For the moment, we should leave our conversation." He got to his feet. "You must come with us now; you will see some of our ways."

He explained that each morning when he was in Riyadh he conducted the *majlis*, a form of audience and people's court where subjects could bring their problems, their disputes, their petitions. Kippax would find that despite Ibn Saud's mushrooming dominion, the *majlis* remained the means of unpretentious contact between the prince and his people; though patriarch and warlord, he affected humility here. On this morning there was a motley line of appellants and accusers, breaking now and then into high-pitched dispute. Throughout it all Ibn Saud patiently listened and judged. Kippax noted the presence and occasional interventions of the learned clerics, the austere *ulema*, who were consulted on Koranic laws. Here, for once, Ibn Saud had to defer to higher authority. Kippax suspected that Ibn Saud's dispassionate calm concealed a muscular impatience, as though a leash were kept on him which only just held.

There was going to be no swift result to their negotiations, Kippax knew that. Though any explicit complaint or direct confrontation was anathema to the Arab way of dealing with a problem like this, it was clear enough that Ibn Saud already knew the ambiguity of the British arrangement with him. The Saudi spies were the most effective in the desert, and Ibn Saud's contempt for the ruler of Mecca was based on something more substantial than tribal enmity. The more Kippax saw of the court of Riyadh, the more he studied the coherence of its government, the more he perceived his problem: What had been arbitrarily decided at desks in London and Cairo took little account of the force rising in this oasis.

The cumulative frustrations of a week spent between *majlis,* prayers, and administration erupted early one morning without notice. Ibn Saud called a hunting party, and invited Kippax to join it. Assembled with military precision, there was a squadron of fast camels; a pack of the desert greyhounds, the salukis; trained hawks, and a file of baggage camels.

As soon as Ibn Saud was beyond the city walls, the burdens of government fell away from him. His camel setting the pace, the king with his great nose and beard seemed to Kippax in profile like the prow of a man-of-war driven under full sail. Encouraged by earthy cries, he swept them out through the oasis and over an escarpment until the horizons had the uncertainty of pulsing heat and there was nothing of softness left. In an arena like this the prey lived clandestine lives, driven by the sun into caves, under bushes, under rocks. The hunters brought out their hawks, and as the salukis scented the game, the hawks went in for the kill. Cats, wolves, foxes, and hares broke from their lairs and were pinned by the birds. His right hand clad in his leather falconer's glove, Ibn Saud directed the killing as he would have in a battle, watching the coordination of hound and hawk, taking the camels at speed, gown flowing in the wind.

By evening there was enough fresh meat for a full-scale feast. Kippax had cast off his army khaki and was back in the Arab robes. He had cut loose from more than a uniform: It seemed that all his detached academic preparation had now been consummated in the experience of the desert. The Bedouin riddles, the Koranic verses, the singing poetry, were set free from the page and were alive in the great tent over the coffee fires. He was intoxicated by his temperance.

The sun did not appear in the morning. It was unseasonably cool, and there were signs of rain. The rapid change of weather brought also a change in Ibn Saud. The élan of the hunt was gone and in its place came political concerns. Messages had arrived from the capital. Kippax was summoned.

Ibn Saud was seated in the tent he used for the *majlis*. He waved Kippax to the carpet before him.

"El Khibeg, you know where our Prophet was born?"

"Medina."

"It is sacred ground. Medina and Mecca, these are the first cities of Allah. It is a matter of shame to us that these places are still under the control of the Turks. In Medina now there are many Turkish soldiers, with many guns. In the place of our Prophet's tomb."

Kippax nodded.

"I have heard that the Great Government has asked the sharif to attack Medina. The sharif selected for this honor his son Abdullah. Abdullah, like us, is a man for sport. He enjoys his hunting. But he does not like hunting anything larger than a hare. This Abdullah will take your gold, but he will not free Medina."

Kippax did not dispute the point.

"You should know the sharif's mind, El Khibeg. He has already waited one year. He is not sure, even now, who will win, and therefore who should have his support. He was hoping that if he saw the Great Government at the throat of the Turk, he could make a separate peace with the Germans. This is the way he chooses his friends."

Kippax knew this to be true. And he had, over several nights, thought through his own tactics. He nodded. "Tell me, how many sons does the sharif have?"

Ibn Saud's face lifted slightly, his eyelids raised. Was Kippax learning the Arab habit of riddles? "There are four princes."

Kippax moved away from the carpet to the sand. He pulled out his baton and began drawing lines with it, large enough so that Ibn Saud and his brother Saad could see the diagram from where they sat. He traced the deformed triangle of Arabia, then the smaller triangle of Sinai, then crudely the sprawling, less defined shape of Syria and Mesopotamia. Finally, above these, he marked out Turkey. The men on the fringe of the tent were all

159

now craning to watch this inexplicable ritual, believing that perhaps Kippax had lost his mind. But Ibn Saud's eyes were steady on the lines in the sand.

Kippax stood up, with the map between him and the carpet. Slowly, with his right foot, he smudged the loop that was Turkey.

"When Turkey is broken, when she is no longer to be reckoned with, there is much space to fill." He pointed with the baton. "Cities. Baghdad. Damascus. Aleppo. Jerusalem. Mecca. Medina. Jidda." On each name he indented the sand. Then he marked off the Red Sea and the Suez Canal. "The Great Government is concerned only about the safety of its communications, principally the canal." He turned the baton again to Jidda. "Who controls Jidda can control the canal." He stepped over and jabbed at Palestine, Syria, and Mesopotamia. "Four princes? Three, really. The fourth is too young." He looked enigmatically at Ibn Saud. "Three princes to go where? And wherever they go, they leave the old man in Jidda." He stood now in the spot where figuratively was Riyadh, and his left foot pushed sideways, cutting a trough in the sand toward Jidda. "In time, the moment will come."

Ibn Saud sat perfectly still looking from the sand to the gowned figure of Kippax, his face too bland to be judged.

"El Khibeg, *Maktub*."

The literal translation was "It is written," but the word had an exquisite subtlety that Ibn Saud and Kippax shared without need of translation.

The obligations of the *majlis* were not escaped in the desert. Three of Ibn Saud's son's—Turki, Saud, and Faisal—had been brought from Riyadh to join the hunt. On the way their escort had met a shepherd; the shepherd had caught a youth in the act of carrying off a sheep he had killed. It was a capital crime, and required Ibn Saud's judgment. The shepherd, the youth, and the king's sons were now ushered into the tent, and Kippax was motioned to sit alongside Ibn Saud and Saad while the case was heard.

As the shepherd told his story, the youth was kept bound, on his knees before the great carpet. The shepherd's recital was melodramatic, with eyes popping and arms waving. The youth seemed extraordinarily tranquil. His eyes ran along the line of princes and settled on Kippax as the oddity. He leered.

The shepherd's case was conclusive. The youth was not called upon to speak. Ibn Saud cited a passage of the Koran and offered the youth's soul to Allah. The youth's hands were unbound and he pressed forward, his head touching the carpet, and uttered his prayers.

Three tall black Sudanese guards came from the wings of the tent. Two of them picked up the youth and moved him across the sand to an open space. The third, plumper than the others and with a ragged headgear that fell over one half of his face, drew a long curved sword.

The youth was given a large shallow copper bowl. He held it to his chest, half stooped, and looked across the sand to the *majlis* tent, saw Kippax again and smiled. The Sudanese at his left side pushed his head further forward so that he was bent double, with his neck on the rim of the bowl. Ibn Saud nodded. The sword fell.

Kippax, from the moment the youth smiled at him, felt a warm surge of blood to his head and was transfixed. There was one clean stroke and the head lay in the bowl, and the bowl was still gripped in the youth's lap. Then the decapitated corpse sank slowly sideways into the sand. The two flanking Sudanese threw a black sack over the remains, pulling the ceremonial bowl clear. There was a sweet smell of death.

Kippax felt insulated from the surroundings, and for a second thought he had lost his hearing, so profound was his separateness. The trance was punctured by the excited talking of Ibn Saud's sons.

Ibn Saud turned to Kippax. "El Khibeg, does the Great Government deal with sheep stealing in the same way?"

"At one time," he acknowledged, realizing that it was in fact less than a hundred years since rustlers had been hanged. "But our laws have changed."

"Changed?" Ibn Saud frowned. "Laws cannot change. They are in the Book." He paused. "You must explain your Book to me, El Khibeg." He got up and looked at the leaden sky. "We will not hunt today. We should return to the city."

As he stood up, Kippax became aware that he had an erection.

Before they reached Riyadh, the rain was driving at them; Kippax thought of the last traces of his map dissolving in the sand.

Before they reached the city gate, as though seeing an apparition suddenly through rain, the royal party came upon a camp—

black tents grouped to one side of the trail, flaps closed to the wind, horses and camels huddled and still. No men were visible.

Nawaf whispered to Kippax. "Ikhwan, El Khibeg—they are Ikhwan."

The sullen tents gave Kippax the impression of unseen sentinels, and a strong sense of being watched without knowing by whom. The king's men gave barely a glance toward the tents, but the column seemed to close up and quicken its pace to the gate. The blackness of the tents was intensified by the rain, conveying an oppression greater than the storm.

Inside the citadel, Ibn Saud's men were noticeably subdued; the spoils of the hunt were spirited away, and when Kippax was summoned the next morning to the palace, there was an air of abstemiousness that was new to him, like a cleansing accomplished overnight. It was still raining. In the innermost rooms of the palace, it was cold enough to chill Kippax in his khakis. He had not been told what to expect, except that there was a formal audience of some kind.

Ibn Saud was flanked again by the brothers Saad and Abdullah. Once Kippax was ushered in, the four of them were left alone; this had not happened before.

Ibn Saud waited for Kippax to settle on the carpet, then said, "El Khibeg . . . I have been thinking of your laws that change. This we do not understand." He looked from Kippax to his brothers and back again to Kippax. "There is too much we do not understand, of the things beyond our country—the ways of the Great Government, and of the other governments that we have never seen. It is a weakness that we do not understand these things." He sighed, though not with any appearance of resignation or modesty. "Perhaps it is too late for us, myself and my brothers, to begin to learn so much." The brothers nodded gravely. "El Khibeg, you can help us."

The distance between Kippax and the monarch, several yards of carpet, was, in the silence of the sanctum, paradoxically intimate. Kippax said, "Of course, I am at your service, Your Majesty." He wondered how far this avowal had transgressed his diplomatic protocols; he did not care.

"We have learned men in Riyadh, El Khibeg. They are our constant guides to the will of God. The *ulema* are men of great wisdom."

All this was intoned without a flicker of insincerity, yet Kippax knew by some instinct that he was being drawn into a test of his subtlety—not the subtlety of Whitehall, but an even more intricate balancing of interests and propriety. He waited with as much impassivity as he could muster.

"By the grace of God, my kingdom is already a large one. We come to the ends of what we know, but we cannot stop. We are called to continue our path and there are things a king must know . . . things not of sacred learning . . . things that the *ulema*, for all their wisdom, cannot tell me. There must be in the future—sometime in the future, when I cannot tell—there must be among us, among our sons, those who have traveled beyond Arabia, who will visit the lands of the Great Government, who will learn of the world where there is no desert. My own sons, perhaps, will see these things."

There was an unstated wistfulness in this passage. Ibn Saud the hunter, Ibn Saud the warrior, Ibn Saud the man who had outrun the salukis on his camel, who had discarded his own city like a too heavy mantle, was in some way now chastened by thoughts of a future which would curtail his sport, a future for which he had little appetite, but a future he knew to be irreversible. Kippax would have liked to commiserate. He knew as well as Ibn Saud, probably better, how rudely Arabia would be disturbed; his own presence in this chamber was the onset of such a disturbance.

"Yes, El Khibeg, when the time comes that my own sons should need this learning . . . But it is not yet." Ibn Saud looked once more from brother to brother, then said, "My sons cannot be the first. It is wise that strange food should be tasted first by others. It has happened that one of the noblest of my chieftains, Ibn Jiluwi, has come here with a story that has greatly interested me. My Ikhwan warriors came upon a boy, the son of the headman of a village—a village of unbelievers purged by the Ikhwan. This boy was saved, he was spared, because he was found to have an uncommon gift. He knows every word of the Koran. An ignorant boy, he cannot read, he knows nothing of the world—and yet, El Khibeg, he knows by memory the whole of the Book. Ibn Jiluwi has delivered this boy to the *ulema*, so that he shall know the true piety. He will be in the care of the holy men until he knows the true meaning of his gift."

Kippax had to strain to follow the deft nuances of Ibn Saud's Arabic; the king's face gave no help as to his meaning.

"This is what has come to me. With a boy of such unshakable piety, we can then allow him to taste the ways and the learning of your world, send him to your teachers."

"If your majesty wishes, the Great Government would be happy to take such a boy into its care, to advise on his education, to show him our culture."

"When that time comes, El Khibeg, I will send a message to you. You are an honored man among us, El Khibeg."

Kippax extended his own ritual of courtesies, eulogizing Ibn Saud as the magnificent servant of Allah, and left the chamber. In this far and meager place he had found a man who would, he was now convinced, have been equally dominant in the most urbane courts of Europe. And yet Ibn Saud was cursed by his own vision. The desert warlord was riding headlong into collapsing world order, and he knew it with a visceral certainty—knew it better than many a Foreign Office clerk schooled in the permanence of maps. Kippax was shedding his own complacencies, too, with each day.

For the journey back to Kuwait he wanted a less cumbersome caravan; he was that much more the chameleon in the desert. He replaced weaker camels, cut down the baggage, and planned the days between wells. It was too hot now to travel by day; most of the journey would be by night.

On the night before they were due to leave, he went to take his formal leave of Ibn Saud. What Kippax had been sent to get he had got: the assurance that while the British offensive into Palestine was planned and carried out, Ibn Saud would harass the Turks in the east, and not renew the quarrel with Hussein. But there was now a complicity between them that might, Kippax hoped, outlive these contingencies.

At the end of the evening, Ibn Saud drew Kippax aside.

"El Khibeg, the boy Nawaf, he has pleased you?"

"In every respect."

"Then you must retain him."

"Keep him?"

The difference in translation between "retain" and "keep" nonplussed Ibn Saud for a moment, then he explained. "He will return with you to Kuwait. Whenever you come to us, he can be at your calling."

Aware that such slavery was normal, Kippax was not shocked. Indeed, to have thought of it as slavery would have insulted the intention; it was an unanticipated gift, and a substantial one— though also perhaps a precaution, since Nawaf would no doubt report everything seen and heard.

"I do not know how to repay you."

"You have no debts here, El Khibeg."

Each day of the return journey brought unremitting heat. Kippax was glad they were traveling lighter. There were occasional problems with water, but he was training himself to go longer without it. During the day they took shade where they could find it, but it was often scant. He had not bathed for two weeks and his clothes were badly soiled. They came finally to ample wells and he decided to allow a pause for laundering and his own toilet. He had bad saddle sores and was aware of his body's odors. The ablutions had been primitive and his bowels loose.

Nawaf had been watching him with concern, without venturing comment. Now, sent for hot water for the canvas bath, he became as solicitous as he could.

The night was blessedly cool. As Nawaf brought the boiled water in pans to the tent, his passage left a wake of steam. Kippax's sores burned in the water, but he lay back and sponged himself as best he could. Nawaf insisted on boiling more water, and in a second soaking, Kippax began to recover his spirit.

The water carrying over, Nawaf came into the tent. He brought a small skin holding liquid. "El Khibeg—please take this in the water." He handed the skin to Kippax. It contained an oil scented with some desert herbs.

"Here—pour it over me."

Nawaf poured some first into Kippax's hair, then more down his back, and began to massage it into his skin.

Kippax stretched out in the canvas and allowed himself to be anointed again. The oil had a warming, emollient effect. He caught Nawaf's hand and held it lightly, then directed it with more precision. Nawaf smiled and complied, then stepped behind Kippax.

When he came back he was naked. Kippax, for the first time, realized that the boy had been gelded, which explained the falsetto of his voice. By desert standards the wound had been expertly treated, and there was only the lightest of scars. Kippax climbed from the canvas.

Later that night he recalled the inept and furtive sodomy of Winchester. Nawaf's finesse and suppleness had taken him far beyond that apprenticeship.

# 9

## *Cairo* ✳ *November 1916*

Bron had known of Koblensky long before Hogarth had passed on the file on him; Kippax had mentioned him and Bron felt that Kippax was subtly warning him off. Subtly? Subtlety in Kippax was a many-surfaced thing; at Winchester, Kippax had helped Bron around genteel prejudices against Jews, and the army had its own variants. Koblensky, Kippax implied, might provoke the worst of those attitudes in some people, so Koblensky was best steered clear of. Thinking of it again, Bron could not remember the warning being as specific as that, but that was the sense of it. With Kippax gone—gone with a strange relish to a wasteland— Bron had now to embrace the pariah. Hogarth, edging his way to candor, had said, "Perhaps you can judge this fellow the best, with all the benefits of your own background," and then added, "Of course, he's not a type you will be familiar with."

Bron's study of the Koblensky file had revealed more about the interrogators than about the young Russian; their skepticism did not, he saw, rest exclusively on military prudence. The first interrogator in Alexandria had written of "a typically Russian obtuseness, an impression of shiftiness, a possibly fraudulent story and lack of military bearing." The first examiner in Cairo had noted an "overweening arrogance," and even Lawrence, in his initial report, spoke of "some strength of purpose that he does not altogether wish to articulate." Lawrence, though, had more thoroughly tested Koblensky's background than the others and had been able to verify it in important respects. Kippax's contributions were different: Bron knew Kippax well enough to see that Koblensky must have taxed his patience.

Bron's first personal impression of Koblensky, when later the Russian was ushered into the former powder room, was contrary to the bias of the file. Koblensky was in a neatly pressed linen

167

suit; only his sandals suggested the "lack of military bearing."
But Bron was still careful to keep his distance. He nodded
Koblensky to a seat by his desk and did not attempt to shake
hands. Koblensky had a pucker of amusement at the corner of
his mouth.

"It is a bit like a high-class brothel," conceded Bron.

"I would not know about that."

"Quite." Bron smiled uncertainly. "Well, we've kept you
kicking your heels for long enough."

Bron seemed the least self-assured of all the officers Koblensky
had met, and he was puzzled. "Yes. Things do not move swiftly
here."

"It must be frustrating." Koblensky didn't *look* very contagious.
"At any rate, I'm happy to say that we can put all the delays
behind us. I've been asked to get down to some specific planning,
for you and your people in Palestine. No more politics."

"War is politics."

A Russian after all, thought Bron. "Well," he said, "let's not
worry about that."

As the briefing progressed, Koblensky saw Bron's competence
but also that his manner was more rehearsed than natural; his
courtesy could not conceal this, and in fact emphasized it.

"All that remains, then," said Bron, "is the navy's arrangement.
I'm afraid there's no way of letting your people know in advance
when you are coming." He stood up, but kept both hands firmly
on the desk. "That's all, then—until we get you off to Alexandria.
In the meantime, you've plenty of preparing to do. I should
make the most of your last days in Cairo, if I were you."

The phrase seemed unfortunate to Koblensky. He didn't like
the studied lack of hand contact. "Yes," he said, gathering up
his notes, "but I think Cairo has already seen enough of me."

This was the first abrasive note from Koblensky, and when he
had left, Bron sat down feeling unaccountably troubled. It was
nothing professional, only . . . and then he realized that Koblensky
had given him a glance of sympathy.

There was nothing euphoric for Koblensky in the moment of
decision; by now the Aaronsohns must have thought he had
vanished without a trace. Attempts had been made to contact
them, but all had failed. The news from Palestine was of continued hardships and more Turkish military activity. The paralysis
of the British must be as bewildering to the Aaronsohns as it was

frustrating for him. There was only one adieu he was tempted to make in Cairo; the temptation sprang from a rare ambivalence. Esther Mosseri was always companionable, but with her he felt too much under inspection, a specimen being added to a collection. And then there was the affair of Solomon's death. It had become something of a scandal, said to be no simple drowning, and hushed up without explanation. Solomon had been given a respectable funeral by the Sephardic community, but that had not buried the rumors. The regality of the Sephardim annoyed Koblensky and he enjoyed their discomfort. It was a redeeming virtue of Esther that she also enjoyed it, so he went in search of her again, to the Coptic Museum.

At first, he watched her without her knowing. He saw her come from her office to answer a question from a Frenchwoman. He hadn't realized that she was fluent in French. She was unselfconsciously impressive, even adopting the French way of using her hands. This image of cosmopolitan poise reinforced Koblensky's sense of being an outsider, and he was half inclined to turn away without going to her. But then she saw him. Without neglecting her client, she gave a clandestine hand signal toward her office. Koblensky stood by the door instead of going in.

Returning, she pretended to treat him as another student. "I have the paper for you," she said, steering him through the door and closing it behind him before she changed her manner and smiled. "You shouldn't come without warning. The walls have eyes."

"You are difficult to find."

"I saw you at the funeral." She walked toward the ottoman. "Why did you go?"

"To remind myself I am a Jew."

She arranged herself demurely on the ottoman, looking up at him. "Oh, *you're* Jewish, there's no doubt about it. Why *did* you go?" Despite the fact that he was standing over her, he felt unassertive. "It was that simple."

"Very few things are that simple, these days." She smiled again. "I'm sorry; I've been on edge. It is nice to see you . . . of course."

He looked around the office. "You work here?"

"When I can."

He lost interest in the details and turned back to her. "Will you eat with me tonight?"

169

She seemed unprepared for this.

"Will you?"

"I have a better idea. You haven't really seen much of our nightlife, I fancy. We can go to a special place I know."

She collected him later from the hotel, leaving her Renault there and taking a cab to the old city. They had to walk the final few hundred yards through a congestion of people, animals, and carts. Koblensky felt conspicuous as Western dress disappeared. Esther Mosseri was wrapped in a cloak distinguishable from those of other women around them only by its gauze-textured fineness. The alley had the twilight vapors of bodies, perfumes, spices, and sewage. In this light Koblensky was conscious of eyes, imagining more searching in them than was really there, but in the tangled animation it was only eyes that seemed to have identity. She led him through an archway and into a courtyard. Bales of cotton were stacked along one wall and a camel reclined alongside them. The courtyard was soiled like a stable floor. In one corner, steps led down to a curtained door. She took Koblensky through the curtain. The fetid squalor of the courtyard was replaced by an atmosphere of austere coolness. They were in a vestibule that also formed a gallery overlooking a long rectangular basement. All the walls were whitewashed. The only color in the place was provided by some worn but exquisite tribal rugs on the stone floors.

They were received by a man dressed in what seemed a parody of a Western majordomo's uniform. His trousers, Koblensky recognized, were Turkish army officer pattern, but he had slippers on his feet. Over a coarse cotton shirt he wore a black serge jacket with red piping, more reminiscent of a railroad than an army. Around his ample girth was a maroon silk cummerbund. Somehow the man conquered the absurdity of his costume with his bearing. His face was finely patrician, white-skinned, with blunted nose and a Mongol cast to the cheekbones.

"Miss Mosseri . . ." He spoke with a bedroom voice.

Koblensky's eyes had only just adjusted to the poor light. Three men were in a corner of the vestibule, smoking from hubble-bubbles. Only parts of the basement were clear, and there, on plain tables, lamps burned. The host was nodding to Koblensky. ". . . and welcome, sir."

He led them down to the basement and to a table against a wall. Koblensky was now able to see a curtained wooden dais in the center of the floor to their left, where three men played muted music: a drummer, a horn player, and a fiddler.

"You see," she said, her right hand settling on his left, "there are no tourists here—and no soldiers."

As far as Koblensky could make out, the other people were predominantly Egyptian and mostly male. There were a few other women and some men who were Levantine in dress—and one jet-black man in saffron robes, extremely tall, with two Egyptian women. Nobody appeared to be taking notice of anyone else, which in Koblensky's experience of Cairo was unique. Some of the Egyptians were already lost in the solitary reverie of the hubble-bubble.

The exclusion of the world above them gave Koblensky unaccustomed ease. The music, an uncertain pastiche of East and West, reminded him of hybrid Russian entertainments. The food, a succession of small dishes of rice, mashed corn, spiced meats, and fruits, was the best he had had in Cairo.

When the meal was finished, she said, "Would you like to try the hubble-bubble?"

He shook his head. "Not tonight."

Her hand engaged his again. "You should sometime."

The music lost its restraint. The drummer, previously confined to a smothered skin, began striking brass. The horn player increased decibels and narrowed tone to evoke an ascending pain. The fiddler became frenziedly melancholic. From a curtain beneath the dais a dancer appeared. She was small and fleshy, her only sign of abstinence a pinched waist. A light layered skirt hung from her waist to her ankles, leaving the stomach bare. Her breasts were swathed in silk gathered at the back of her neck. She carried a tambourine in her right hand and her left hand was heavy with rings. Her face was veiled by silk squares attached to a headband. Her appeal, Koblensky realized, rested too much on the dimness of the light.

The music was as suggestive as she was coy. Its energy outstripped hers. She did several circuits of the tables, passing with short, seemingly overburdened steps. Then she went to the middle of the floor beneath a weak spotlight. The drummer marked a more torpid beat and she threw off the veil. Remaining on the same spot, her body began to move differently; no longer trying to simulate a waltz, she swiveled her hips in preparation for a belly dance. Her legs came slightly apart, the layers of skirt divided to give a glimpse of porcine knees and calves. But her heaviness was no longer a restraint. She shed all compromise with the bastard music and imported choreography and danced with an intensity that was neither promiscuous nor elegant, but erotic in a completely self-absorbed way. The movements were solitary in a masturbatory sense, impossible of participation. And oddest of all, even the girl's face seemed aloof from all feeling.

In seeing the dancer's paradoxical chastity, Koblensky was made more conscious of Esther Mosseri's overt carnality. Although nothing in her behavior had been importunate, her former careful reserve had gradually melted away. In the last two hours a physical attraction had anticipated anything that might be said between them. She had led it, in the clasp of a hand or the brush of a thigh, and he had not resisted.

Her hand fell on his again. "Will you excuse me? I'll be back in a minute."

The last movement of the belly dance was a head bowed to breast in mock shame. The applause was uneven, more spirited from the African in saffron than anyone else. As conversation resumed, Koblensky saw Esther returning. At the foot of the steps from the vestibule she hesitated, looking uncertainly into shadows. A youngish man in Egyptian dress stepped halfway from the shadows and spoke to her. She frowned and then tilted her head back slightly in the way Koblensky had seen when she answered the Frenchwoman in the museum. Several men moved between Koblensky and this scene and when they had gone she was already returning to the table.

"Well," she said, standing before him, "shall we go?"

In the courtyard, the coolness of the night lessened the odors. She slipped her arm into his. "We can walk from here. My flat is very near."

She lived in a building that housed a Greek shipping merchant's office. A Victorian shell had been given a facade of new yellow brick, with a large mahogany-framed window featuring an impeccably made model of one of the P & O line's steamships that linked India to Britain. To reach her flat, they had to pass through an outer office arranged with desks for the shipping clerks. A second door led to the stairs, and when they reached the top, the original period of the building reasserted itself. Her flat was one large balconied room and two smaller rooms.

"Usually, I sleep on the balcony," she said.

He could see a mosquito net over a low divan.

"It isn't overlooked," she said, "except by the sky." She

looked at him calmly. "Do you like making love under the stars?" She put a hand to his jacket to unbutton it. "But I imagine it is some since you had the opportunity."

While her hands were still on the button, he took hold of her face, with his thumbs gripping under the chin, forceful but not hurting. "I can do that myself."

"Yes," she said, without intimidation. "I hope you can." She drew away and took out the pin that gathered her cloak at the left shoulder. "I'm sure you can." The cloak had only lightly suggested her body. It was cut in a bias and was wrapped in several layers. As they disengaged, the gauze was semitransparent, a delicate shade of peach. The final layer provided a partial modesty. There was a deeper color where it clung to the nipples and a larger opacity below her waist, until she stepped from the collapsing material and, without looking at him, gathered it up and walked away to the divan.

Koblensky was again aware of her being older than he: the figure that was full when dressed was in places slightly too full when not. As he watched her open the mosquito net, he saw that her buttocks had lost tautness and her thighs were broad and ductile. She turned to see him coming to her. "Not everything about you is undernourished, I see," she said, and laughed with a discordant girlish note.

He was gauche and self-conscious in his movements. She guided him with subtlety, but even then he had an economy of action that was not far short of being perfunctory. It was not a night, as she had hoped, of imaginative lovemaking. She held herself back from innovation and did nothing to embarrass his rawness of experience. Even though he could be maladroit, he had an energy that rose above sheer animal power—but, as yet, little refinement in its uses. The real force in him, the force that attracted her, was a concentration of life. She understood better the drive in him now, and wished—she knew futilely—that she could help him to become more polished; that would be something, no doubt, that he associated with weakness. She lay awake looking at the body that had been so easily satisfied and felt a pang of recollection for her own distant innocence.

Giving him coffee in the morning, she saw that he had already consigned the night to an incident free of obligation. She guessed that from the perspective of his background she appeared frivolously modern. That look had come over his face the moment he saw her take the wheel of the Renault. The asceticism of the unworldly, she thought, needed occasional confirmation of its superiority.

He paced about the room with the coffee. It was only just after dawn. A dog yelped somewhere below.

"You are leaving Cairo soon," she said, without question.

"Yes." He was still looking down into the street. "I have been here long enough."

"You will return to Palestine?"

He sipped the coffee again, and then turned back into the room and looked at her as though from a far greater distance. "In the museum, when they told you of Solomon's death, you were not surprised."

She was sitting at a table with her coffee. Her hand closed on the cup as though wanting warmth from it, and she hesitated while adjusting to the change of mood. "No—it wasn't a surprise."

He waited for elaboration, but she took her time, refilling her cup.

"He had been keeping strange company. . . . I heard stories; at first I didn't believe them. But you know how it is in Cairo: There are many things said that seem fantastic and some of them are always true. Well, I don't know a lot about it, but he had been smoking a lot of hashish; he owed people money." She shrugged and settled her eyes calmly on Koblensky. "It was something like that."

Koblensky of the night was not the Koblensky of the day. He put the cup on the table, tucked his shirt inside his waistband, picked up his jacket, and stood over her militantly. In his eyes she saw a precariously withheld violence. Her only suggestion of recoil was muscular, revealing a minor flaw where the cheek pulled too tightly at one corner of her mouth. She felt him regain control. He had not swallowed her story and she knew it. Why was it such a test of her? What did it matter to him?

Koblensky did not explain. He left without another word, feeling unattached to the night and to her, but knowing what a dissembler she was, and resenting having been patronized by her lies.

"Longitude 30.001; latitude 31.34."

As he called the reading, the corporal shaded his eyes from the nearly overhead sun.

Bron stood a few paces away, shaded only by his pith helmet. To the south and north of him, two fingers of a limestone ridge enclosed a plain. To the east, these fingers converged into a ridge that was itself the edge of a desert plateau. Where Bron stood, the plain had gently ascended from the west. The corporal had calculated that they were twelve hundred feet above sea level.

"It's extraordinary," said Bron, running his boot through thick, springy grass. The grass was like a skin blemish—an unnatural coloring amid the even dun of the arid plain. The green ran in an irregularly contoured patch extending four or five hundred feet at its widest point. Bron had found it purely by chance while scanning the ridge through binoculars. He and the corporal had driven their Ford to it across untracked ground.

Interspersed through the grass were small flowering bushes. Bron bent down and broke off a thorny stem. "Look at this, Baxter—as fresh as if it were irrigated."

The corporal put his notebook on the Ford's hood. "Rum thing, sir."

"You know, Baxter, it's a pity we can't get our hands on an airplane. I fancy if we got up there, we might see a pattern to this."

"A pattern?"

"I'm not sure, but with the glasses I thought I saw a series of depressions that were too regular to be accidental—over there, to the north. That would mark an ancient underground canal. They existed, you know. Can't risk the car on this terrain, though, and I can't pick out anything more with the glasses from here. Under here—somewhere—there must be a hell of a force of water." He looked east up to the plateau. "We'd get a better picture from up there, but we'd need a proper party for that. Had enough of this heat for now, Baxter. We'd better head back."

The Ford reached the city well before sundown.

After Kippax left for Riyadh, Bron had moved from their original billet to a wing of the hotel, cleared of tourists for the army's needs. As the Ford pulled under the palms in the car pool at the back of the hotel, a private came seeking Bron. There was a hint of impudence in his face. He had something in his hand.

"A lady asked me to give you this, sir."

"What is it?"

"A glove, sir." He held out a white kid glove.

Irritable and not able to see clearly, Bron was short. "A glove?"

"The lady insisted, sir."

175

Baxter had come from behind the Ford to watch.

Bron took the glove with one hand and wiped his eyes with the back of the other. He hesitated and then sniffed it. He looked beyond the private to the hotel. "Where is the lady?" he said quietly.

"In the lobby, sir."

Bron folded the glove in his hand, almost crushing it in a gesture of concealment, and went into the hotel. His uniform was soiled and his bare head streaked with dust, scorched brown to just below the hairline and then white where covered by the pith helmet. All the other men in the lobby were groomed and laundered for the evening, but Bron was unmindful of his condition. He looked around the lobby searchingly but without result. He was walking to the desk when someone behind him called.

"Hello, Michael."

Tessa Stanbridge was two or three paces behind him, and having apprehended him, she stood still as he turned.

"How—*how* did you get here?" He was suddenly aware of his appearance.

Her head was slightly inclined in an expression of constrained intimacy. "They still advertise Nile cruises for the winter. . . . You don't seem pleased."

"It—it's so completely unexpected."

"That *should* increase the pleasure."

They were within earshot of several officers at the desk and a group of men and women at a table, all of whom seemed suddenly to be watching. Bron glared at the men at the desk, who insolently kept looking on. He went to her and took her arm, guiding her with almost exaggerated formality across the lobby to a vacant table.

"I must say, Michael," she said as she sat down, "looking at these people here I was getting quite a new impression of the sacrifice you made by going off to war, but you do seem a little less pristine than they. In fact, you look uncommonly handsome with a coating of desert."

"You look marvelous, Tessa. I'm sorry, it *is* a very welcome surprise, although that rather understates it, if anything." He sat down and turned to wave for a waiter. "I realize it doesn't seem much like a theater of war, not in here."

They both fell self-consciously silent, until Bron ordered tea.

He settled himself and looked at her with concentration, seeing for the first time signs of strain. "Are you—are you all right?"

"It was a difficult trip, despite what they say in the advertisements." She folded her hands across her lap. "Michael—what *is* going on here?"

Bron was sardonic. "Staff work. I think it's called staff work."

"Michael . . ." It was her innately purposeful look. "Do you have any idea of what it's like in France? Ghastly. Thousands of lives being thrown away every day to gain a few feet of Flanders mud."

He nodded and said, rather defensively, "We have had our catastrophes here too."

"Gallipoli?" She looked around the lobby. "They seem to have got over it rather well."

"Why *have* you come?"

"Is pursuit an unladylike quality?" She poured the tea.

"How long are you to be here?"

"I have nowhere else to go."


Corporal Baxter had lost his normal stoicism. As the arrogant sergeant he had just delivered to the hotel was taken off by an orderly, Baxter removed his cap and ran his hand through the short crop of his hair in a movement of exasperation.

The private who had delivered Tessa's glove saw Baxter's distress. "He looked a real jumped-up Tartar. Fresh from London, I bet."

Baxter shook his head, but he was beginning to calm down. "That's right. Name's Jabotinsky."

"Jabotinsky? A four-by-two? Another bloody Yid?"

Baxter was reluctant to share the vocabulary. "From the War Office. Especially to see Lieutenant Bron."

"You know what they say about these Jews in the army? When they are ordered to attack, they signal back, 'No advance without security.' "

Baxter looked at the private with a new caution and walked away.

Jabotinsky had rejected the orderly's offer of help with his bag. He appeared at the door of Bron's boudoir with the bag still in his left hand as he saluted with his right. Bron came round from behind his desk and instead of returning the salute, put out his hand. "That's all right, Sergeant. We'll drop the formalities."

He kept his grip on Jabotinsky's hand. "*Very* pleased to see you. Your reputation has preceded you. . . . I had a note from Lord Rothschild."

Jabotinsky finally put the bag on the floor. "That was good of him," he said. He took off his service cap.

"Sit down, please. You've had a long journey. You could have rested up first."

But Jabotinsky's energy answered the question. Even sitting in the chair he retained his martinet manner, and he looked over the desk expectantly while Bron resumed his own seat and unconsciously tidied a pile of papers.

"Yes. Lord Rothschild gives an account of your academic interests. Garibaldi's Italy, for example."

"That's not entirely academic," said Jabotinsky with a hint of impatience. "How to make a nation from a squabbling rabble."

"Quite." Bron was suddenly aware of advancing beyond his intentions. He fingered the papers again. "Well, we should get down to this business. You will have read the reports on Koblensky?"

"I want to meet him."

Bron reasserted himself. "Of course; he's waiting. But first I wanted to make sure of our understanding about this. There are no political overtones to the scheme; it's a purely military exercise. You appreciate how sensitive this is?"

Jabotinsky, for the first time since he came into the office, seemed to hesitate. He regarded Bron afresh. "I don't know what Lord Rothschild said to you, but there is a better *understanding* of Zionism in Whitehall than before, and of course an anxiety to free Jews from the tyranny."

Bron adopted the manner of a man hoping that his desk would amplify his authority; he squared up behind it and said, "All the same, we want no suggestion that we are supporting partisans. One whiff of that kind of thing and, I can assure you, the general staff will lose interest."

"Naturally," said Jabotinsky, a little too readily. "Naturally. You obviously know how the general staff thinks."

"Yes." Bron stopped, seeing that Jabotinsky was inferring more than was at first evident. Aware of the risk of seeming pompous, he continued in a more quietly insistent tone: "My understanding is very clear, and I have to ensure that yours is also." But Bron already knew that he faced a man who was naturally incautious. Even when Jabotinsky was motionless he conveyed the impression of incipient action. "So, Sergeant, it's time I introduced you to this young man. I think you and he will understand each other perfectly." Although Bron had deliberately reiterated Jabotinsky's rank, he felt that the disparity in their positions actually gave Jabotinsky the advantage. As they walked silently down the corridor, Bron sensed that he was taking a prophet to a disciple.

Koblensky had reverted to old ways. His trousers looked as though they had been slept in for at least a week and his once crisp shirt hung in wrinkles over his waistband. He had several days' growth of beard and—the ultimate nonconformity—he was barefoot. Everything had become secondary to preparing for his mission.

As Bron introduced Jabotinsky, he could hardly conceal his disapproval of Koblensky's appearance. Jabotinsky, however, was unperturbed. He not only shook Koblensky's hand but kissed him on each cheek—a cultural aberration that Bron had long since forgotten. Bron was left standing to one side while Jabotinsky broke the embrace and said, "Shalom! *Shalom!*"

Bron had never seen Koblensky so reduced to intimacy.

Koblensky said, "I heard of you in Odessa, two years ago."

Jabotinsky shrugged. "So . . . too many people talk in Odessa!" He laughed.

"Yes—particularly the rabbis," said Koblensky.

Jabotinsky laughed more raucously. "*Particularly* the rabbis!" He then seemed to remember Bron, and took in the room. A trestle table was covered with maps and sheaves of notes. "You seem to have a lot on your mind."

Koblensky nodded. He glanced almost impersonally at Bron. "I don't know how much time I have got . . . before I leave. I want to be ready."

"Well," said Bron, "I think I should leave you two to talk. If you need any help . . ."

"I'm fine," said Koblensky briskly. "Thank you."

Closing the door on them, Bron paused, hand on the handle, frowning; and then, feeling some indistinct misgiving, he left them.

Koblensky waited to be sure the door was closed, then he said, "The first time I met him, I didn't know he was a Jew."

Jabotinsky went to the trestle, looking at the maps. "There are many like him in London." He picked up a map. "I didn't realize you had such detail."

"It may be out of date now. I've been delayed here for months."

"At first, so I hear, they wanted nothing to do with this scheme. They smelled Zionism." Jabotinsky loosened the neck of his tunic and sat on a corner of the trestle. "They prefer to deal with Arabs. When they see a Bedouin they think they see the pure soul of the Arab, unadulterated. It doesn't matter that he's a primitive. He's pure-blooded, racially intact. That impresses them. Take Kipling, who fell for it in India. He has a line: 'the *real* native, not the hybrid, university-trained mule.' Can you see their problem, when it comes to Jews? Where can they pigeonhole us? Where do we belong? Where is our racial purity and innocence? We have one foot in their world and one in this. It annoys and also frightens them."

"You're wearing their uniform."

"I'm becoming expert at that." Jabotinsky smiled grimly. "That's why I was anxious to see you before you leave for Palestine. I am not merely a sergeant; I am a political army in my own right."

"Political?"

"That word seems to terrify our lieutenant." Jabotinsky eased himself from the trestle and went to the window, looking down on the assembled staff cars and the milling, bored soldiers. "You know, we did get them to use a Jewish unit at Gallipoli. The Zion Mule Corps. We had to accept that servile position, but we surprised them; they saw that Jews *will* fight. But it scared them too. They've disbanded the Mule Corps." He came away from the window and confronted Koblensky with intensity. "Why this scheme of yours is so important to us is that when the British invade Palestine, I want Jews to be a part of that army. If you people can win their trust, that makes it much easier for me."

"A Trojan horse?"

Jabotinsky smiled. "*Exactly.*"

"I *think* I'm ready." Tessa Stanbridge stood before a full-length rattan-framed mirror. She wore a severely plain white silk gown that emphasized her flat chest and fell chastely to her ankles. A single red rose was pinned at her left shoulder. Standing behind her, Michael Bron was worried that the white gown underlined the pallor of her neck and face. He smiled. "Yes. You'll do."

Already they could hear the string quartet playing below them in the ballroom. Bron was in tropical dress uniform, with a tightly starched wing collar and shirt breast. His hair was heavily brilliantined and his skin seemed to have been steamed to a florid moistness.

"You *do* look uncomfortable," she said, pecking him on a cheek in a way that parodied gentility.

"Hogarth is fortunate. The navy uniform is less of a straitjacket."

"He's a deep one." She was pulling on elbow-length gloves.

"Hogarth?" Bron tugged at his collar without relief. "When you get to know him, he's all right."

As he took her arm she pushed it down again and stopped him. She looked at him solemnly. "You're sure . . . you're absolutely sure now?" He nodded and she abandoned the pretense of formality, taking his head between her gloved hands and kissing him fully on the mouth. Then, stepping back, she said, "It would be difficult, I suppose, living in sin here. It's not Hampstead."

"No—it is not Hampstead." He pulled out a handkerchief and wiped the lipstick from his face as she took a mirror from her purse to make her own repairs. He said, "We don't have to wait long for the marriage."

She laughed. "No. That's certainly true. It's funny. No synagogue will take you and Rome certainly won't take me. I should be used to being a pariah, I suppose."

The banality of Strauss overlapped the babble of varied tongues as they walked into the ballroom. Seeing them arrive, the bandmaster, a corpulent Grenadier, abruptly changed tempo from Strauss to a regimental march. On this cue, the babble died away and was superseded by applause. Bron and Tessa looked on a coalescing crescent of faces, few of whom were familiar to her. Bron walked her around the line, making the introductions. He forgot the discomforts of the uniform. To his surprise, he felt completely at ease.

"It looks peaceful enough from here." The Royal Navy lieutenant's binoculars picked out the distinct promontory even though there was no moon. He increased the magnification and settled on the part of the cliff where the vestige of the crusaders' ramparts seemed an outcrop of the rock. "This is the place."

Koblensky nodded. "The creek runs just below."

They were half a mile offshore. The frigate wallowed in a light swell. Its boilers were damped and the men on deck walked carefully to avoid making a noise. The lieutenant and Koblensky

181

were on the starboard fringe of the bridge. The lieutenant lowered his glasses. He had a light brown beard, what the navy
called a "full set," and he spoke with a gentle West Country
brogue. "I've always wanted to see Palestine. Jerusalem, of
course. And Nazareth and Bethlehem. It's a funny thing, how
this little strip of land runs through our history." He grinned
self-consciously. "And yours, of course." The lieutenant, in
two days' acquaintance, had come to like Koblensky, in spite of
his laconic manner. "Well, we'd better get you off."

There were two hours more of darkness. The line between
ocean and shore was only a slight shift in shades of indigo. The
stillness exaggerated two sounds, the constrained power of the
frigate's engines and, more distantly, the meeting of tide and
rock. Koblensky looked at the impersonal blankness, his thoughts
with Sarah Aaronsohn and the house at Zichron Jaacov, on a hill
that was just discernible through the binoculars. He had been
away for nearly three months—so long that their faces had
become imprecise. He remembered voices better: Aaron Aaronsohn's methodical instructions, Sarah's wistfulness. Had they
despaired of seeing him again? He knew that the famine in
Palestine was worse than Aaronsohn had foreseen.

Leaning by the davits, the lieutenant directed the lowering of a
boat. Even the oiled winches made a disconcerting scraping
noise that must have carried to the shore. The boat settled into
the water with only a small disturbance. The two sailors who
were taking Koblensky inshore climbed down.

Koblensky picked up a waterproof sack and strapped it to his
chest with the lieutenant's aid.

The lieutenant said quietly, "All set, then?"

The weight of clothes and the bulk of the sack seemed to make
Koblensky suddenly fragile. He knew the lieutenant was looking
at him as at a man he would never see again. "Thank you,
Lieutenant." They shook hands and Koblensky climbed with
surprising agility down the swaying rope ladder.

# 10

## *Northwest Palestine ✳ April 1917*

A wet Mediterranean wind blew unstintingly across the coastal marshes. A train moved slowly south down the single track. The engine, pulling a load greater than it was designed for, and burning wood instead of coal, had difficulty getting traction on the soaked rails. The engineer had to keep leaning from his cab to check the track ahead; he and the fireman were both under-nourished Syrians whose loyalty had to be ensured by the gun car hitched behind the engine. Made negligent by the rain, the Turkish gunners had closed all their observation hatches and were playing cards. The train crossed a small trestle bridge and then had slightly easier going on a gently descending gradient.

A quarter of a mile to the east, on a bluff giving a partial view of the track below, two figures lay covered by dark oilskin raincoats. One of them scanned with binoculars a stretch of still-empty track.

"It's difficult to see; the rain is getting worse," said Koblensky, taking the glasses from his face and trying to wipe the lenses with a cuff.

"It must be nearly there. I can hear it clearly," said Sarah Aaronsohn. Her voice was hoarse.

Koblensky put the glasses to his face again and tried adjusting the focus, but the rain curtailed his view. He could hear that the train had picked up speed: The weight of the wagons and the debility of the track began to create a sound like distant artillery fire. As he located the dim outline of the locomotive, he saw one flare of light from the cab. He moved the glasses down and to the left, trying to keep pace with the two driving wheels, but the image in the glasses had no clarity and all he saw was a dark mass shrouded in smoke, steam, and rain. Sound was a better guide than vision.

For a moment the beat on the tracks settled into a steady rhythm as the gradient leveled out. Then there was a series of resonant impacts as the locomotive jumped the track and began slicing through ties. The abrupt deceleration telescoped the rest of the train and the gun car was the first to go askew of the line. The locomotive's boiler erupted in a plume of steam that sent a high-pitched scream echoing through the foothills, a scalding sound that transcended all the others and persisted like an imbecilic siren long after the wreck had settled.

Neither Koblensky nor Sarah moved or spoke. They listened as mechanical distress was overtaken by the human; at first, there were a few isolated cries and then, gradually, a mixture of plaintive calls and confused commands. The locomotive remained upright, but at a tangent to the track and embedded in flint ballast, as much out of its element as a beached boat. The gun car was compressed, crushed between the locomotive and a flatbed carrying a tarpaulin-draped howitzer. The howitzer had shot forward clear of the flatbed and swept the top of the gun car from its chassis, decapitating two gunners and trapping three more. It was from the gun car that—as Koblensky now established—the most urgent commands were heard. The rest of the train—five covered cars, two more flatbeds, and a troop car at the rear—had left the tracks but seemed relatively unscathed.

Picking out the mortal cries from the others, Sarah finally said, "I didn't realize it would be so bad."

"They were going too fast."

She was not deceived; even if the results were more catastrophic than planned for, Koblensky was not dismayed. She pulled herself up to a kneeling position, drawing her oilskin more tightly around her. Her thick black hair had been matted into the form of a skullcap, which emphasized the pallor of her face. Silently she looked down toward the wreck with a feeling of nausea. All she revealed to Koblensky was a kind of fatalistic resignation—which he was apt to misinterpret as a fragile form of courage. She wondered whether Koblensky would ever be troubled by a dialogue with himself. Looking at him now, she doubted it. But the force of Koblensky's will had become a necessity of life, and whether it was congenial or not did not matter, because little else was congenial or could be.

Aaron had left Palestine. He had gone before Koblensky was landed by the warship. Hearing nothing from Cairo, he had hatched a deception. He convinced Jemal Pasha that to feed

Palestine the locusts must be eradicated, and that the solution lay only in German laboratories. Jemal had sanctioned an overland trip to Berlin, but Aaronsohn's real objective was London.

The winter was as punitive as Aaronsohn had warned it would be. There was famine in many of the Arab areas and food was hard to come by in the towns. The Jews had lost the income from the Jaffa oranges. Typhus, cholera, and dysentery ravaged both the civilian and the military populations. But despite everything, most of the Jews in Zichron Jaacov looked askance at the Aaronsohns because of the suspicion that they were active sympathizers with the Turks' enemies. The worse the strains of war became, the more the Aaronsohn home took on the atmosphere of siege.

As Sarah and Koblensky went back to their horses, she wrestled with the ambivalence of her feelings for him: the reassurance his determination provided, countered by the hostility he aroused. He had become slightly more tactful about the passivity of other Jews, but only from her tuition, and she knew how much it really went against his grain. His continued immaturity lay now in one thing: not being able to distinguish between his severe demands on himself and responsibility for the demands he made on others; his own disregard for danger was not so easily expected of others. Did he expect it of her? She had gone reluctantly with him on this mission, she had helped lever apart the joint in the rail and clawed ballast from the railbed. It was infuriating to know that Koblensky believed she relished the risk as much as he did. Sitting there astride his horse as they turned up the hill, he manifested this conceit, and she felt compromised by him.

By the time they sat down to supper that night, the extent of the wreck was the talk of the town. Although it had seemed like an accident, the suspicions of Zichron Jaacov were already turning heads toward the Aaronsohn enclave. Feinberg, whose position in the community was that of an uneasy bridge between the watchers and the watched, arrived at the table knowing already what was being said, and as a result, in fragile humor.

The table bore evidence of the frugality that they had been reduced to. Feinberg took a bowl of soup from Sarah and sniffed at it. The liquid was a grayish color and had a skein of fat on the surface, in which had settled some coarse chunks of an even grayer meat and shreds of green. "We seem to have eaten off this goat for some time," he said grimly.

"We're lucky," she said, in a deliberately peremptory voice.

"I'm not sure we are," said Feinberg, stirring the soup warily. "And even if we are, our luck may be running out."

"What do you mean?"

Koblensky followed her question by looking sharply at Feinberg. But Feinberg took his time. He sipped the soup with an exaggerated frown, swallowed, and then said, "The train: It has shocked a lot of people in the town." He deliberately took another sip of the soup and then, making clear the direction of his innuendo, said, "I thought it was supposed to be done without killing anyone. It was not a pleasant way for them to die."

Koblensky put down his spoon with belligerence. "*Pleasant* way to die?" he repeated. "There are no pleasant ways to die. At least it was quick. They never knew what was happening."

"From what I hear, there are same gruesome injuries—legs lost, even worse. . . ."

But Koblensky was not apologetic. "You should get used to it. It is war."

Feinberg made to answer, but was overtaken by Sarah. She had been standing to serve the soup, but now she sat down in a way that implied both exhaustion and impatience with them both. She was looking at Koblensky. "*Must* you keep killing?"

Koblensky's arrogance with Feinberg moderated when he turned to her; something akin to affection had weakened it.

Feinberg took advantage of this hesitancy. "He's a soldier, Sarah. A Russian soldier. Killing is a vocation; he has to shame us with it."

Incensed that Feinberg was trying to appropriate her allegiance, Koblensky answered Sarah, not him, with the cutting accusation, "You were there!"

But Feinberg intercepted him again, raising his own voice: "You do not understand! She doesn't *enjoy* it. She was there because if she wasn't it would be somebody else! Perhaps me." He laughed caustically. "Yes—perhaps me. Somebody she could not trust not to learn to enjoy it, like you. One professional killer is enough." He looked to Sarah with too much possession.

Koblensky looked at her too, but disbelievingly.

She found herself unreasonably trying not to disappoint either of them. She let the aggression of the raised voices dissipate itself in the echoes of the desolate house. Then, speaking quietly to Koblensky, she said, "I know these things have to be done.

There may be no choice. But this, today—it was not what I expected."

Feinberg, with a little more composure, said, "I don't mind the espionage. That was what we *all* agreed to; that's the risk we're all taking, and that's what Aaron wanted. But this kind of thing is far too dangerous; it's too conspicuous; it provokes reprisals."

Koblensky sighed impatiently. "I agree. I agree that it could be dangerous. But this was an exception. Everything worked for us. First, you know the line is in bad condition. Second, the weather. There have been landslips before. With this rain they will not know whether the track was broken by the ballast being washed away or whether it was deliberate." He became sarcastic. "And since they have no experience of anyone trying to wreck their trains until now, there is no reason to suppose that they expect it."

"Sometimes—sometimes I think you are waging a private war," said Feinberg, sipping his soup again.

"Private war?" Koblensky exploded. "It's a *real* war. We are fighting for our survival *as Jews!*"

"Everybody wants to survive," said Feinberg, sensing the advantage of remaining cool. "It's a question of how."

Koblensky was even more enraged. He waved his spoon wildly around. "Look at this house—just *look* at it! There are scores of others like it here. You built this complacent, soft life for yourselves and you forgot, if you ever knew, how the majority of Jews live." He put the spoon down ominously and pushed the bowl of soup at Feinberg. "You began by making a joke of this soup. This would be a banquet in many homes I know, and I am not even talking about war. It would be good for you to know what an empty belly feels like—it would be *very* good." He glowered at both Feinberg and Sarah.

But Sarah was far from intimidated. She had tensed and now she squared herself at him, but spoke with a cold control. "How dare you sit in this house and moralize about it? Yes, it is a big house—and there are many others like it. I'm glad there are. That should tell you something. There was *nothing* here before my parents came, *nothing*. We are the roots of this country, of everything. We made everything. My father, Absalom's father. We know how to build. You know only how to destroy." The last sentence was an impulse driven by her fury and she regretted it the moment it was spoken.

Koblensky checked himself at last, then after a tense silence he bowed toward her in mock injury, and said with uncharacteristic gentleness, "It is because you built it that you must fight for it. *That* is what makes the rest of them here so shameful."

"Shame again!" said Feinberg. "You always fall back on that."

But Sarah had no more tolerance for taking sides. She pushed back a strand of hair that had been dislodged in agitation. "We have to remember how dangerous it is to be alone," she said.

"Yes," said Koblensky, still moderately. "I know that. But there is nothing here except us that makes me believe that we will ever live to see Israel."

"Israel" was not a word that any of them felt easy with; it had an archaic connotation that usually confined it to Orthodox litanies. Sarah was surprised to hear it cross Koblensky's lips with such naturalness. Inexplicably it frightened her, like a childhood taboo.

It silenced Feinberg too.

Koblensky saw that the dispute had shifted the ground between them, irretrievably. He had the uncomfortable feeling of understanding more than he wanted to. Each of them had seen more of the other and liked it little. But the differences had to come out; their suppression would have been worse.

They finished the soup in silence. Koblensky helped Sarah clear the table. Feinberg seemed to have absented himself mentally from the room; he had edged his chair clear of the table and sat with one leg crossed over the other in a languid, dreamy pose that suggested the feline side of his nature. Koblensky followed Sarah into the kitchen. He felt her sense of isolation: as well as Aaron, her sister Rivka had left for Europe and Nesta, the cook, was too ill to work. Sarah ran the house and what was left of work on the estate. For the first time since the argument, Koblensky spoke.

"How is your father?"

She was rolling up her sleeves over boiling water and did not look him in the face. "The winter is always the worst time. Each year I don't think he is going to come through." She shook her head resignedly. "But each year he does. This time, of course, it is harder. The diet is so poor, he is getting weaker."

Ephraim, her widower father, lived as a semi-invalid, most of the time in his bedroom. Koblensky knew that it was really her father whom Sarah feared would be most exposed to the dangers of the life they were leading, though he knew nothing of it.

"How much do you remember of his first farm?" asked Koblensky, preparing to wipe the dishes as she passed them.

She looked at him with undeceived intelligence, knowing that this was a grudging concession to the force of what she had said. "It's very clear in my head," she said. "I remember believing as a child that this country was one big garden, because that was how it looked, if you had seen nothing else. I used to sit on the hill and think: This must be the most beautiful place in the world. But I could see only to the next hill. It *was* beautiful. The orchards were young, everything was so neat, laid out like a pattern. When I was older, and began to ride, and could go beyond the next hill—then I saw what it must have been like before they came. There was a line; the pattern ended like a carpet on bare boards. He never said anything about how hard it must have been. But you know how hard it can be now, how hard Aaron has worked. And yet to have started with nothing . . ."

There was no injury left in her voice, but Koblensky wanted somehow to retract his attack on the house and, by imputation, the family. He didn't know how.

It was she who had the greater generosity, and spoke first. "I'm sorry about what I said—about your only knowing how to destroy. It was wrong of me. I know I can't really *feel* as you do." She looked at him gravely, with candor. "We haven't seen the things you've seen. We ought to be strong without going through that kind of experience, but you can't get that kind of strength from your imagination. It's something, I suppose, like a wound that you can't forget. I can see it in you, sometimes it frightens me, but that's not your fault."

"You have great strength—yes, strength," he said, observing her physical reserve. "You have already done more than I should have expected."

"You mustn't be hard on Absalom," she said, turning to stack away the china. "He's very loyal."

Koblensky faintly resented this defense, but said, with little conviction, "I know. He's very clever, and very useful."

She caught the trace of insincerity, but said simply, "Yes, he *is* very clever." She was too relieved to have pacified him to call his bluff on that point.

In the truth of the night Koblensky restlessly tried to see the cause of his outburst—or if not the cause, at least its object. It seemed uncomfortably close to the shallow antibourgeois slogans of Russia, a chorus he had never joined. This connected with an image, of a great house with yellow light in every window, of people cosseted by the house and by that light, while outside there was a driving snow—but the people had no faces and the house had no location. The image had the feel of childhood, a grievance without secure anchorage. Why had it surfaced now, and why had he let it lacerate the one person in this place whom he esteemed? Was it now more than esteem—was that why he had done it? He struggled to kill the question with sleep.

He left the house in the morning before anyone else was stirring and rode north toward Haifa, keeping clear of the roads. The storm had left a tail of high, streaked cloud and so much mud on the bridle paths that his going was slow. With the horse tiring, he rested on the lee of a hill at a derelict shepherd's cabin that he and Sarah had used as a rendezvous on reconnaissance missions. In the past month they had, on British request, tracked the laying of new telephone lines and noted where they connected. To their astonishment, they found that although the Turks had good connections between Damascus, Haifa, and Jerusalem, there was no link to the coastal lookouts, which were still so thinly spread that it was clear the Turks had no belief in an Allied landing.

He pulled a slab of dry rock from inside the shelter and used it as a stool, sitting with his hands behind his head and his back against the flint wall, while his horse nosed around in a futile search for anything green. Thinking of his British patrons, he wondered if they would ever come. His reports had tried to prove how haphazard were the Turkish defenses, and how much dissension existed between the Turks and the Germans. He knew enough of the minds in Cairo to realize that this information would be greeted with skepticism, since the British appeared to believe that military competence was common to all armies, like the rules of a club—evidence of their own failings notwithstanding. He recalled Lawrence's apartness from this clannishness and wondered whether *he* was ever taken seriously—and what was the point of having Lawrence in an army to which he was so alien. The British, he reflected, didn't burn their heretics; they found a niche for them that made them both useful and harmless. The Russians would never have that kind of composure.

He became aware of a distant droning, like a car laboring up a hill. It came from somewhere in the west. It was not a car, but an aircraft. He picked it out: It was cruising in a wide arc that would bring it overhead. A minute later, it banked over him and he saw its dark green color and the German crosses, even the outline of the pilot's head. Koblensky realized he must be the only sign of life on the hill, but the plane lost its curiosity and descended west, toward the coast. He wondered if its appearance had anything to do with the wrecked train; it was the first military plane he had seen here. The only previous aircraft he had seen had been British, in Egypt. It worried him. Their own scouting would be made more dangerous. The British would have to be told. He was disturbed, too, by a different sense of intrusion—by the sound of onrushing change.

He was diverted by another movement, on the Haifa road half a mile below him. A black carriage was coming south, and he recognized it as Meyer Malik's, distinguishable as one of the few carriages still able to have not one but two horses; even the oldest horses were now being bought avidly for their meat. Malik's visits to Zichron Jaacov had become those of a consul, the eyes and ears of the Turkish satrap. In the town Malik had grown in acceptance. Their relative immunity to Turkish deprivations was known to be due to his influence. This simply proved—as the rabbi himself proclaimed—how wise they were in showing their allegiance to the Turks.

Something in the way Malik bore himself when he came to the Aaronsohn home was ominous, an ill-concealed competitiveness. As long as Aaron Aaronsohn was there, Malik's access to Jemal Pasha had been checkmated, but with Aaron gone, there was a double-edged danger: They no longer knew Jemal's mind, and Malik came unchallenged as Jemal's delegate. Koblensky tried to ride back to the village ahead of Malik, but the mud slowed the horse and he arrived to find the carriage already at the door.

Uninvited, Malik had chosen the chair once used by Aaron. Sarah was bringing him coffee when Koblensky appeared. There was no sign of Feinberg.

Malik seemed annoyed by Koblensky's intervention; he was on the point of requesting privacy, but Sarah was too quick for him. She said, without a trace of anxiety, "I'm sure Asa will be interested in this. . . . Asa, Mr. Malik has some news of Aaron."

Koblensky admired her calm; there had been no word of Aaron since his departure.

Malik glowered at him, but then forced himself to courtesy as he looked to Sarah. "Yes—although it is something of a puzzle. As you know, Jemal arranged his travel to Berlin, where he was to contract for some chemical supplies. He took the train from

191

Constantinople to Berlin, and everything seems to have gone according to plan. Then he announced that he had to go to Copenhagen.''

''Copenhagen?'' said Sarah.

''You, too, are surprised?''

''It wasn't in his original plans,'' she said, but then thoughtfully added, ''Of course, he may not have found what he wanted in Berlin, and he has been to Denmark before on business.''

''Really?'' said Malik. ''Well, that doesn't answer the puzzle. It seems that in Copenhagen he didn't find what he was looking for, either. He caught a ship to New York.''

''*New York?*'' This time Sarah's surprise was authentic.

''Definitely. We had it confirmed from Berlin.''

To Koblensky the ''we'' was further incrimination. He interceded. ''His brother Alexander is in America. He has probably gone there for help with the chemicals.''

''You think so?'' said Malik, openly dubious. ''It is a long way to go. Jemal finds it very strange. After all, this journey was sanctioned by him, and he did not expect it to become so ambitious. Of course, America is *still* a neutral power. They have not been tricked into supporting the British and the French, though I hear that many American Jews are clamoring for that. That would be a disaster for us, if they prevailed.'' Malik drained his coffee noisily and looked expectantly at Sarah.

She said, ''I'm sure Jemal understands that Aaron's concern is for the crops. He would go to the ends of the earth for our sakes.''

''The ends of the earth . . .'' repeated Malik, slowly, as though it were the key to something. ''Your coffee is still the best in Zichron Jaacov. People complain, of course, about the many shortages. But we profit from the trust placed in us, otherwise things would be much more unpleasant.'' He watched her refill his cup. ''I had hoped that perhaps you had heard yourself from your brother.''

''No—this is the first I knew. But the war makes communication so difficult—unless, of course, you can use the military channels.''

Koblensky enjoyed this subtle sarcasm.

''Well,'' said Malik doubtfully, ''if you do hear from him, I want to know. It would help to clear Jemal's mind.''

Koblensky and Sarah knew well enough that Malik would

know of any communication before they did, since all mail was intercepted and opened by censors in each city it passed through.

Casually, after sipping from the refilled cup, Malik said, "It is very distressing about the railway accident. Very distressing. Jemal himself is to lead the inquiry." He finished the sentence with an alert glance at Koblensky.

"It wasn't surprising," said Koblensky. "There have been other accidents. The track is poorly maintained."

"You take an interest in railways?" said Malik.

"I came here on the railway," said Koblensky unblinkingly.

"Yes. I know that. I thought in America it was known as the rail *road*."

"I have been away a long time."

"So you have—a *long* time. Long enough to pick up our habits. I imagine you are a very useful man to have around." He glanced to Sarah, and sipped the coffee.

Koblensky was cursing his own slackness.

Sarah said, "He wanted to go back to America, but we persuaded him to stay."

Koblensky was astounded by this invention. It was several minutes before he saw its ingenuity.

Malik smirked. "Really? I thought, Mr. Koblensky, you were dedicated to the Promised Land."

"He wanted to see his family again," said Sarah, improvising with dedication.

"Then it is a truly noble sacrifice you make by remaining with us, Mr. Koblensky. Nothing is more sacred to the Jew than his family. Perhaps you can persuade them to join you here—once the war is over."

"Perhaps," said Koblensky, gaining the nerve to sustain the fiction. Malik had, it seemed, completely forgotten the semantic slip.

But Malik frowned. "It is a pity, I think, that you do not mix more with the people of the town—you, Mr. Koblensky, as well as the others in this house. There is a feeling that you have become outsiders in some way, that you prefer isolation. At a time like this, it is unfortunate. We must all be seen to be a community."

"Who says this?" said Sarah combatively.

But Malik would not answer. He put down his cup and rubbed the already glinting toe of a shoe against his trouser leg. "Just consider what I have said," he said. "It is good advice. I think you need good advice—without your brother here."

Koblensky was incensed but checked himself. The vain gesture of Malik's foot emphasized the man's offensive prosperity. But it was futile to feel murderous toward him; Sarah was the vulnerable one—Sarah, who had been quick-witted enough to cover up for him, Sarah, who had much more to lose than he. Forcing himself to civility, he accepted Malik's handshake as he left, but recalling its grip took care to lock Malik's fingers in his own and held them a second or two longer than was needed. Malik's eyes were expressionless, as though the hand were no part of him.

With him gone, Sarah unburdened her perplexity. "Do you think it's true—about Copenhagen?"

"I don't think he invented it. Yes, I think so. I think it's true."

"Why?"

"It's the nearest place to Berlin where it's possible to get a neutral ship."

"But New York?"

"I do not understand that. Did he ever say anything about going to America?"

"I don't think so—no, I'm *sure* of it."

"You were clever—and I was not."

She smiled hesitantly. "He's no fool."

"No, he is not. But what holds him back?"

"Holds him back?"

"He plays with me. Like a cat—waiting. Why?"

"How much do you think he knows?"

"What does he know—and what does he suspect? That's his game with us, leaving us to guess. I see what he has been doing, here in the town. He makes sure that we do not win any of them over. Not that there is a chance of that."

"I despise him." She seemed to lose her composure, fatigued by maintaining the pretense of confidence, and slumped into a chair, looking up at Koblensky with uncharacteristic passivity. "Are we risking too much?"

Koblensky wanted to embrace her, in a surge of kinship, stronger than the embrace of a brother for a sister but innocent of sexuality. As before, he was paralyzed by the propriety that she imposed in this house, and on all of them, like a governess in unruly company. This constraint, he felt, made him clumsy in handling himself. "We have to trust ourselves. That is the biggest risk."

"Are you worried about Absalom?"

"No . . ." He tried harder to convince her. "No, he is loyal. He is not suited to acting alone, but I think he accepts that. What I meant was, there are—how many of us now? A dozen. It would be dangerous to bring in more. With some of them it goes to their heads, they enjoy it too much, they see it as a game. That can make them careless; they would like to boast about it."

"I know." Then she sighed and smiled in a way that perceptibly broke through her reserve. After all, he saw, the dispute of the previous evening had drawn them a little closer in their understanding of each other.

It put him in a rare good humor, which extended to indulging Feinberg when he gave their parlous work a poetic flourish by proposing as their password the acronym NILI—from the Hebrew for "The eternal one of Israel will not lie"—and they became the NILI group to their British masters. Koblensky suspected that Feinberg's nomination of "Israel" was a placatory acceptance of Koblensky's commitment. The histrionic and the poetic cohabited uneasily in Feinberg's nature.

Their appointments with the Royal Navy were troublesome. The navy was unable to guarantee arriving off Athlit on a specific night, let alone hour. British cooperation seemed halfhearted, like their attacks on the Turkish lines, which never so much as dented the force Jemal positioned to meet them. As the winter storms receded, it should have been easier for the ships to be punctual during the moonless phases of the months, but things did not improve. It meant successive nights of vigil on the cliffs, with the constant risk of being discovered by a Turkish patrol.

Perversely, the next frigate arrived on a night when Koblensky had almost called off the watch because of the roughness of the sea. He was sleeping in the shelter of a wall of the crusader castle when Joseph Lishansky, one of the NILI's most zealous recruits, came to wake him. Lishansky had spotted a light but not the ship.

Koblensky moved clear of the wall and was brought tartly back to alertness by the force of the wind. "Are you sure? They have never come in weather like this."

"It was the usual signal, repeated."

"Let me see." Koblensky took the binoculars, hunching his

shoulders in the cold. There were whitecaps on the sea and the horizon was barely discernible; rain came in squalls. His skepticism grew, but then he suddenly picked out the flashes. "You're right. They are crazy, these people." He went back behind the wall and found their own signal lamp. Struggling against the wind, he turned up the flame and clanked the shutter. After a pause he saw the acknowledgment. "Come on. They will be blown here in this sea."

When they reached the pebble beach in the inlet, the sea was making such a din that they had to shout. As well as the surf sucking up the gravel, there were rocks beyond the inlet, where the breakers were bright with foam. They strained to see any sign of the tender which had to navigate a narrow channel between the rocks in order to reach the inlet, and once there, had to hold off about twenty yards short of the beach to avoid being grounded. Even in a calm sea it was a tricky maneuver; tonight it was courting disaster.

When they did see the boat, they could hear no engine and it seemed to be a phantom carried playfully on the whim of the surf, but at the crucial moment it gained a will of its own and came precariously swinging through the rocks and lurching into the inlet, bringing its stern around as it came, the propeller churning up foam as the skipper used it as a brake against the surf. The anchor went over the bow but at first dragged uselessly in the loose gravel beneath. The boat was in danger of being brought broadside onto the beach, listing and rolling, but with hardly anything to spare, the anchor caught and the boat jerked back into stability.

They had to wade and then swim to the port side. They got through the surf, but the surface of the water was an abrasive compound of spray and the smaller pieces of gravel, and as they dipped their heads into the water their faces were seared raw. A rope net was lowered for them. As he pulled himself out of the water, Koblensky was fighting for breath, his eyes unseeing. A strong hand closed on his uppermost wrist and pulled him up the rope and over the edge of the boat as though hauling in a broken fish. He lay on the deck looking up at a bearlike figure who seemed to be wearing several layers of sweaters but no oilskin. The sailor grinned at him. "You nearly copped it in there, mate."

Too winded to speak, Koblensky remembered Lishansky. He twisted round just in time to see him plucked from the rope by another sailor, to collapse onto the deck. The sailors waited for them to recover, making no more attempt to revive them but exchanging glances implying how unimpressed they were with their catch. They stepped aside to make way for an officer who was more rigorously clothed than they were, in an oilskin storm coat with tightly drawn hood. The officer peered down at Koblensky. "Are they alive?" he said in a drawl.

Anger brought back voice to Koblensky. "You—you chose the worst night." He levered himself off the deck with an elbow and felt reluctance in every joint of his body.

"We don't *choose*, old chap," said the officer, reaching down and helping Koblensky to stand. "We come here when we can. We would have been here three nights ago, but we were warned of a Turkish submarine in these waters." There was a polite rebuke in his tone.

Koblensky shook gravel out of his hair and spat salt from his mouth. "A submarine?"

"We'd better get some rum inside the pair of you, otherwise you'll never make it back." The officer led them down into a shallow cabin that afforded scant shelter. The boat was slewing round on the anchor and beginning to roll. Lishansky stumbled and sank onto a bench.

The officer handed Koblensky a flask. "A dose of that will put the lead back in your pencil." Looking at Koblensky more closely, he was astounded at what he saw. The only visible flesh was his hands and his face, emerging from layers of what looked like crude swathing with rubber waders and coat, the body too insubstantial for the clothes. Then he saw Koblensky's feet—strapped in a kind of leather gauntlet that left the toes bare. Water was coursing from under the waders and the toes were contracted in cold. The officer was torn between contempt for what seemed to be amateur bravado, and respect for their determination. He had never really been clear about these missions, which put his frigate at more risk than they seemed to justify, and if this was really the face of Jewish resistance, he didn't give it much of a chance. He watched Koblensky gulp down the rum, and then said, "Ordinarily we would have given up, in this sea. But we have something that seems to be important. Cairo was most insistent."

Trauma had drawn Koblensky's skin to a jade tautness across his cheekbones, accentuating his Mongol appearance. The rum warmed him but made him nauseous at the same time. Speaking was an effort. His teeth wanted to remain clenched; his whole jaw was on the verge of locking. He managed to grunt, "Important?"

The officer took the flask and gave it to Lishansky, who was still paralyzed on the bench; he could not conceal the dubiety in which he held the pair of them. While they had to grip the woodwork to remain steady, he balanced easily on his sea legs in spite of the roll and went forward to his quarters. He came back carrying two large waterproof pouches, each about the size of a knapsack.

"They are sealed," he said. "They were sealed in Cairo and you had better keep it that way until you get home and dry."

Koblensky took a pouch and put one strap around his neck and the other around his waist, as Lishansky revived himself to do likewise. It fitted like a life jacket, but its weight suggested the reverse. Koblensky tried to look confident, bracing himself as he tightened the straps, but he was having great difficulty in holding down his nausea.

The sailor who was at the wheel shouted, "I don't think she'll hold much longer, sir. We're beginning to drag."

The officer gave Koblensky and Lishansky one final, pitying look. "At least you'll have the sea with you," he said, taking them back to the rope at the stern.

As soon as he hit the water again, Koblensky vomited. The weight of the pouch pulled him down, and although he kicked out, he no longer had any self-determination left. He was swept like a piece of debris into the shore, given the chance of only one gulp of air before the surf somersaulted him into the shingle. The sea had cut the pebbles into a steep bank that was depleted and replenished with each pulse. He hit the bank first with the back of his head and then the rest of his body was pushed under and sucked out again. On the third attempt he managed to go in face down and threw himself, clawing at the pebbles, over the brink of the bank. He felt the sea give him up.

Inert in every muscle of his body, he rolled over onto the beach. He was in the same kind of paralysis that he had known before only in a recurrent pursuit dream, in which his leaden body failed to respond to command. He lay with one side of his face against the pebbles, his back to the sea, and retched. It was more than two minutes before he remembered Lishansky. As he knelt and then pulled himself up, he felt a cascade of small gravel run down his back between the ripped clothing and his skin. The din of the sea had dulled all his other senses and he stared uselessly into the spray. Then, too confused to be sure of his priorities, he checked the pouch. The waist strap had given way and it must have been the movement of the pouch that had forced him under the water. He pulled the neck strap over his head, and freed of the weight of the pouch, was better able to kick life back into himself. The pouch was intact.

Lishansky lurched out of the dimness to his right, in what seemed a kind of drunken ecstasy. He tottered up to Koblensky, looking him in the face as though unsure of his identity, and then collapsed. Koblensky had a delayed sensation of pungent breath and then realized that Lishansky must have emptied the flask of rum and completed the swim to the beach in a stupor. There was something to be said for it, thought Koblensky, whose body was sharply conscious of its injury.

Had two other NILI agents not arrived to relieve the watch, Koblensky would not have got Lishansky beyond the foot of the cliffs. He was on the brink of collapse himself when they found him, and was put over the back of a mule, like a wet sack, for the journey back to the station at Athlit. Lishansky did not regain sobriety for twelve hours, but then appeared unharmed except for facial lesions. By then Koblensky had a severe fever.

Sarah nursed him through three days in which, several times, he rambled incoherently and the fever reached a malarial intensity. The NILI doctor—the only medical man they could trust was an obstetrician—seemed both pessimistic and useless.

"He's so *wasted*," said the doctor, pressing a hand to the scarlet brow. "He has no reserves—and even if he had, this degree of pneumonia would overcome them."

Sarah was as calmly practical as she could manage, but she, too, looked at Koblensky's sunken eyes, bruised face, and thinly masked ribs and saw how narrow the gap between life and death was. It was now, she knew, a matter of the spirit, and that was too intangible a thing for her to trust in.

"What do you know about his history?" asked the doctor, more curious about her concern for Koblensky than about Koblensky himself.

She looked at the doctor unhelpfully.

"His medical history, I mean."

"Why?"

"There's a color in his eyes, a look to him. I've seen that look before. He's had typhus."

"Is that why he's so weak?"

199

"The typhus was fairly recent." The doctor reluctantly conceded that Sarah would not be forthcoming. "And fairly severe. The blood is the problem. It's not helping."

"What about the new drugs from Cairo?"

"Fine—if it was a headache he had."

She didn't appreciate the cynical levity, and turned aside from the doctor to resume her seat by the bed, openly dismissive of the doctor and moving her will to Koblensky.

The room had been improvised hastily as a clinic. In one corner, stacked on the floor, remained a pile of Aaron's notebooks, some with leaf and plant pressings in them. The room still smelled like an agronomist's laboratory. Perhaps if it had had the sterilized impersonality of a hospital room she would more easily have accepted the doctor's prognosis; as it was, her own spirit was subtly reinforced by the evidence around her of nature's diversity and resilience. As the light faded at the end of the third day, she checked Koblensky's temperature and saw that he still had a high fever, and was apparently comatose. She made herself a rough bed on an old chaise longue; this sagging, curlicued relic had, she remembered, come with the family on their original migration from Rumania. She could recall its various lives. In one memory, her own eyeline was only a little higher than her father's waist as he fed her cherries; she saw the moist red tips of his fingers as he pitted the fruit. She remembered Aaron, from a different eyeline, his boots planted firmly apart as they always were when he declaimed his visions of his Palestine of wheat fields. The vigor of this memory was acutely in contrast to the fragile, almost concave outline of Koblensky's body in the bed. There were more than the two of them in the room now, she knew. There were the restless associations of the past, not spirits or ghosts but vocal companions in her head. She pulled the blanket more tightly to her and went to sleep facing the bed where Koblensky lay.

# 11

## *Cairo ✳ May 1917*

The chants were led by a priest in a gilded miter, supported by a dozen choristers in white silk surplices, but there was no liturgical book, nor any musical instrument except a pair of brass hand cymbals to punctuate the verses. Rome, thought Kippax, Rome stewed dry and mixed with the Magi. The chants were at least fifteen hundred years old, uttered alternately in ancient Pharaonic, Greek, and Arabic. This was too archaic, the voice of an obsolete faith, an encrusted faith long ago overwhelmed by Mohammed's austerity. And yet the past was never neatly severed. This voice had echoes. The "roofed" religions—Judaism, Christianity—had traces of it, but so also did Islam in the unroofed cries of the mosque. There was a thread. Islam was the knotting of many threads, the last of the great faiths to break from the desert, and to his mind the most powerful of them. He had seen now where that faith had been hardened, and understood it better.

So, as he listened to this curious relic of a religion, it served an expedient purpose: Under the roof of the Coptic temple of Abu Sarga, between bare stone walls, Michael Bron the wayward Jew and Tessa Stanbridge the lapsed Catholic had found a priest free enough of dogma to marry them (and to welcome a handsome donation). Tessa, in a severely plain gray suit, was as close to spiritual calm as Kippax had ever seen her. Bron, in his staff officer's finery, seemed bemused.

It was Kippax, with Esther Mosseri's help, who had stage-managed the wedding and Kippax who was best man, a role unknown in the Coptic form of ceremony, which they had, nonetheless, incorporated.

Four tapers burned by the altar. The congregation sat on stone flags, in extreme discomfort. Among them were Hogarth, Sir Victor and Lady Harari, Esther Mosseri and her academic accom-

201

plice who specialized in Rameses II, and Vladimir Jabotinsky. Christians, Jews, and Muslims were seldom, if ever, under the same sacred roof; Kippax had scored a social and theological coup. Hogarth murmured that the event might be promoted as an example of how the British administration encouraged religious tolerance. It was a fine joke, but it was gratuitous. For all its oddity, the service achieved a dignity that even Kippax could not mock. And Kippax was not so glib as to believe that this awkwardly perched congregation in any way represented the Cairo beyond the walls.

Incense lay over the crypt in a fine mist, turned the palest of ambers in a single shaft of light from a skylight in the dome. Bride and groom, though European in dress, seemed through this mist to be bathed in an Oriental spell. The voices died and the cymbals alone upheld the mood and paced the step for the procession from the altar, the mitered priest leading the choristers, then Bron and Tessa, then Kippax and the congregation. Tessa, head slightly bent, found Bron's hand and squeezed it. Kippax saw this movement and thought it too swiftly possessive. The back of her neck, below where the hair was drawn up into a bun, was still white where hats and veils had held her modesty from the Egyptian sun.

Outside, an Armenian photographer disappeared under a black hood to frame the group.

Hogarth moved to Kippax's ear. "Most engrossing . . . the New Testament *con brio*."

"Certainly different."

"But is it legitimate?"

"In whose eyes?"

Hogarth prepared his expression for the camera, but still answered, in a hiss. "Do you suppose God has a preference?"

"I thought you were thinking of the registrar."

Hogarth froze for the photograph.

When it was taken, Kippax continued: "The papers *look* very impressive; even embossed, in gold."

"These days, that's something." Hogarth looked around him, beyond the dispersing group, to the rooftops of old Cairo. "One misses the mellow spires."

Kippax wondered if Hogarth was wearying of the place—or the game.

A well-nourished fly circled them and then settled audaciously on the peak of Kippax's cap. But his attention had moved elsewhere. Esther Mosseri was walking to her Renault with her male escort. There was a quirk in the man's gait, a weakness in the left leg. Despite this impediment, and although their bodies did not touch, Kippax had the impression of an intimacy between them.

Hogarth reclaimed his attention. "Owen, I think I may put in only a very brief appearance at the reception. You don't think they'll mind?"

"I doubt they'll notice. They do seem unusually *soppy*. After all, it's not as if they have had to endure a long abstinence."

Hogarth primly disliked this tone. "Well, then, let's get the car."

Through the rattling glass of a side window, Hogarth pointed to Jabotinsky, with the Hararis in the remaining group of guests. "That man Jabotinsky. Have you read the stuff he's sending to London?"

"Yes."

"He has the same characteristics as a locomotive; given a head of steam, he thunders down the line, absolutely glued to the rails, and nothing can divert him."

"Unfortunately, he's finding encouragement."

"Yes—I've seen that too." Hogarth slumped back into the warm leather. "Why must these Jews *push* so?"

Even in the late afternoon the heat inside the Mercedes-Benz was stifling. Because of the dust, the side windows could be opened only slightly, and since they were traveling east, the sun burned through the small rear window. Tessa Bron, as she had now been for several hours, had shed the gray suit after the reception for as light a cotton dress as was decent, but Michael Bron was still in a uniform tunic. The road to the east of the Nile was rudimentary. It seemed that they were heading into a void, with coarsely bushed dun stretching on each side and ahead. Then, at first as a small rupture of the horizon, they saw green—poplars and tamarisks, not in a naturally random outcrop as at an oasis, but regimented into a screen several trees deep. Only when the car passed the first poplars were they able to glimpse the house, built of a dull pink stone that absorbed enough of the evening light to have the luster of a moistened rose. Their journey ended at a white marble portico set on a graveled forecourt.

The house had the proportions of an Italian villa, but the ravishments of the architecture were overtaken by the scents of the garden—a quartered garden, each quarter outlined in flowering bushes and bisected by shallow irrigation channels. The sound of water coursing on stone provided the most calculated extravagance; all around this sculpted and manicured paradise was, for mile after unremitting mile, a desert.

Tessa stood in the shade of the portico while slippered servants took valises from the car. When the car pulled away, she took Bron's arm and said, "You'll have to convince me that this is not a dream."

His right hand settled over the fingers crooked at his left elbow. "I thought it might be a mirage." He clicked a heel into the white marble. "It *seems* real enough." He looked up. Set into the ceiling of the portico was a circular mosaic, studs of lapis lazuli mixed with larger tiles of yellow and café-au-lait. His hand tightened on hers. "I had no idea it would be like *this*."

"It's the most profligate thing I've ever seen," she said. One of the servants, a midget Egyptian wearing, as they all did, the headgear of the *amma*, a soft fez wrapped in a silk turban, and what appeared to Tessa to be the white linen livery of the P & O shipping line, held open the cedar-paneled main door. At the wings of the doorway, the night lamps had already been lit, burning acetylene.

Tessa's life had already given her a dark and driving intransigence when such plums were offered, as they had been, and this seemed perhaps the ultimate in the testing of that virtue. But it *was* her honeymoon, albeit an after-the-event formality, and she knew that Bron was more susceptible to luxury than she. So she broke from his arm and, disguising the satirical impulse, spun across the marble lobby with petticoat rising, in the final steps of an imagined gavotte, to the music of strings absent in the frescoed gallery above. In this tenuous make-believe she enraptured the gaping servants.

She was to realize that the sense of sexual initiation expected of a honeymoon, counterfeit in their case, was recoverable as a fantasy. The bedroom was at the rear of the villa, central to the gardens, where lamps burned over the cut-stone channels. The whole place, in this supernatural bluish light, seemed to have become detached from the desert, from the earth, and to be floating like an aberrant jewel in some cosmic limbo. The servants evaporated into their quarters and left the lovers beyond all eyes. The bed was a resilient plateau of orange satin set above white marble. Apart from three Isfahan rugs and two enormous

Ming vases flanking the terrace windows, the bedroom was clear of decoration.

She thought of the bed as a sacrificial podium. Their lovemaking acquired the precision of a tableau, each separate movement like a choreography of limbs and interlocked surfaces. The wanton quality that she had in London now seemed discarded and in its stead was a pure ardor free of all inhibition. Bron realized that for once, even the antivoice that shadowed her had been put briefly to rest. Her face in sleep as he looked down on it relapsed to what he had never seen before: infantile peace.

But morning returned the senses to anchor. The gardens appeared terrestrial again, and Tessa had a glint of her old gravity. She stood in outline on the terrace, while Bron remained lethargic on the bed. It was in the first hour after dawn, when the light had clarity but not yet depth. Her body moved in a way that he thought too stoic. She spoke without glancing back into the room. "I don't mind—I most *surely* don't mind—living like this for a week. I couldn't bear it for a minute longer."

"It was good of the Hararis to arrange it."

"Yes—it was. Do you know there are *pigeons* here? Just listen. How did they do it?"

"They sank an artesian well—at God knows what expense."

She half turned from the terrace, head tilting up as she spoke. "I think that's what I find so offensive. The sheer *whim* . . . all put down here against the force of nature. It's a demonstration, again, that if you have enough money you may alter anything, even desert, to your convenience. I really think that's gross."

"I think you're superb, quite superb."

She frowned. "Michael, you mustn't appeal to my vanity like that. Not now. Not ever."

"But—"

"I'm *very* happy. Very. I feel . . . well, I feel we have severed ourselves from what was expected of us, each of us. We can begin, not only a marriage, but life, *on our terms.* Even in such a place as this. Its very absurdity lifts us free of the past. Don't *you* feel that way?"

"I have to feel able to tell you what I feel about you."

"Of course—of course you do. I *know* how you feel." She stepped in from the terrace, he thought playfully, but when she reached the rounder light by the bed he saw a sharper mood. She said, "You see, I *am* quite fixed on our future. While this war goes on—I had forgotten, disgracefully, how unbearable, how

205

intolerable it is—while the war goes on we must try to understand how it was that it happened in the first place. There are so
many things it is *necessary* to remember now. We must, people
like us, we must never let those people who conceived of this
war, we must never let them have that kind of power again.
*Ever.* That must be the overriding concern of our lives, our
*work*. The one compensation of this war is that it will produce an
enormous sea change. Before I left London, I could see that
already. You've no idea how things have started to seep through
the censorship. It's so big, so awful, that nothing can hide it, not
from even the simplest people. They know, even if only from the
graveyards. You can't hide those.''

Bron swung his reluctant legs to the floor. ''That sounds very
political to me.''

''Political?'' she asked impatiently. ''All I've ever claimed for
myself is the right to see things my way. Is *that* political?''

''You know it is.''

Beyond the terrace, everything in the garden was still; there
was not yet a breath of wind. She came between him and this
lushness like a nanny barring a child from a nursery fantasy until
it had scrubbed its face. His disciplines were not hers. The
firmness he had seen in her body was an extension of the
firmness of her mind and there was no use in trying to humor it.
She looked at him calmly, not contesting what he had said. In
this light, without any makeup, she had the pale certitude of the
nunnery, the vocation she had renounced.

Bron pulled on a pair of red moccasins. ''They're not used to
political women in Cairo.''

''Oh, you needn't worry about that,'' she said, with a tinge of
sarcasm. ''I'll not rock that boat. I'm gathering my strength for
later, for London.''

He walked to the terrace, leaving her in the room. He had the
vague disgruntlement of dissuaded libido, and the scent of
oleanders, palms, and greengages did little to appease it. Somehow the dream was already punctured.

She addressed his back. ''Speaking of things political, do you
notice any change in Owen?''

''Change?''

''I've been watching him. I suppose it began while he was in
India, but I hadn't really noticed until lately. Outwardly, he
seems the same—the old physical clumsiness, like a boy who
has grown his limbs too fast. You always think he's going to trip

over the cat. But underneath that . . . I see something else. It's almost as though he cultivates the awkwardness to conceal the fact that really—really there's nothing hesitant about him at all. He seems sure of himself in a way he never was. That diffidence that they spent so much time instilling into you both at Winchester—he can't quite bring that off anymore. At least, not to me. There's too much ambition there.'' She broke off with a throaty, rather masculine laugh. ''Ambition! The very worst thing for a Winchester man to reveal!'' She came from the bedroom to the terrace, still talking. ''But in what direction *is* that ambition? Who would have thought . . .?'' Alongside Bron, she awaited a reply.

''I think it's obvious, surely. He's shooting for a good wide desk in Whitehall.''

''As straightforward as that?''

''Is careerism so surprising in him?''

''It seems too . . . conventional.''

''Well, I don't see anything odd in it.''

''I think you're too close. You can't see it from that distance.''

The three sleeping figures were entwined with all the ingenuity of an erotic Indian miniature, even the gender of an individual limb hard to discern in the half light of dawn. After Leo Solomon's death, his Persian pavilion had been bought from his estate by the authority on Rameses II, whose name was Dr. Ibrahim Ghazi. Solomon's departure left little disturbance: Ghazi, his Amazonian wife, and Esther Mosseri were able to meet each other's varied needs without introducing a new partner. From her days on the Cairo streets the Amazonian had worked with both dildo and Sappho, and helped by hashish, the trio proved worthy inheritors of the richest of Mediterranean cultures where Western sexual conventions were thought pedestrian. There was also a baser motive for the new ménage: Ghazi directed an activity that was best restricted to as few people as possible, a political activity that increasingly aroused British vigilance. He ran a cell of the Committee for Union and Progress, under whose bland name gathered the most zealous of those who wanted to rid Egypt of all imperialism—whether Turkish, French, or British.

It was Ghazi who stirred first. His head was adjacent to a rump whose identity he could not at first determine. Only when, in a slight turn, he saw his wife's head flanking the rump could he be sure that it was Esther Mosseri whose head was between his own legs. As he drew himself carefully from the damask cushions, the two women, still asleep, drew closer in their invert embrace. Ghazi paused to look down at them. Neither was a delicate figure; his wife's tutelage seemed to have encouraged in Esther Mosseri a Rubenesque bulk that was becoming flaccid in places. He reflected on the anatomical disparities of the two branches of the Semitic family. There was something indelibly Jewish in Esther Mosseri, as there was something indelibly Pharaonic in his wife—the reason why, with the memory of Rameses to uphold, he had rescued her from her tawdry past. But it was Esther Mosseri's brain that had most encouraged his sense of racial tolerance, and it was her future use to him that preoccupied him as he went slowly down shallow steps to the small kitchen and prepared coffee.

"I could smell it," said Esther, coming down the steps a few minutes later. She wore a silk gown carelessly open at the front.

"Please—sit down. I have something to say." Ghazi's look over her shoulder showed that he was not to be distracted by her nakedness.

"It's all right. I think she had too much hashish." She came to squat by the hearth. She pulled the gown around her and looked at him, intelligence supplanting sensuality.

He poured the coffee in the fussy way he had. "You must realize, my dear, that some people are very nervous about having a Jew with us. They notice the company you have been keeping."

"What company?"

"Bron, his wife, Victor Harari . . . and Kippax."

"But *you* know how important it is to watch Kippax. You know *what* he is."

Ghazi became soothing. "Of course, *I* know that. Indeed, it is about Kippax that I want to talk. But I want you to be careful—about the appearance of things. You know, some of the people in the Committee are . . . well, they are ultra-orthodox."

But she was not so easily calmed. She put down the coffee cup and her legs pushed out from under the gown. "You *know* how I feel—I thought you understood. This movement will not work unless it embraces *all* Egyptians—Christians as well as Arabs, Shi'a Muslims as well as Sunni, the Baha'is, the Jews. Egypt was syncretic before Islam."

"I appreciate that. Others are not so tolerant. For example, you should be careful about the Baha'is. They are the real heretics to many Muslims. It's not wise to speak openly on these lines, as you have. They're not opposed to the Jews, particularly, but they are opposed to heresy within Islam. After all, this is not *just* about nationalism. It's about the kind of state that would emerge from it, and how the sacred and secular powers will be balanced."

She subsided a little. "I do see that, but it seems a little utopian to even be talking about what kind of state it will be, when we are nowhere near winning our freedom. I want that freedom—as a Jew *and* as an Egyptian. I despise the consul mentality, this pretense of enlightened imperialism, and all those who flourish by observing it—like the Hararis. We have no rights of our own that matter. We may not be physically enslaved, but we are spiritually and intellectually enslaved, and that is worse. Not even the mummies are our own. There's really no difference for Egypt between living under the British or the Roman empire; it's thralldom."

"It is not I you have to persuade." He smiled, but his paternalism had an incestuous overtone.

"I thought that killing Solomon was proof enough," she blurted, *"and it should have been."*

"But, my dear, it was your carelessness. Once he found the picture of Mazhar in your office, he was bound to see you were involved with us. And he was the kind who would have done something about it. So we were really tidying up a problem that you created."

Still belligerent, she said, "And Kippax—what about him?"

"Ah." He took his time pouring more coffee, then said, "I have received word from London that a very important person, a man who has many enemies here, will be coming shortly to Cairo. We have decided that it is time to make an example, to give a demonstration of how far we can reach. I am to arrange the assassination of this personage. One of the people he is coming to see is Kippax; Kippax is sure to know the details of his movements, and I am depending on you to obtain them—by whatever means possible."

Her laugh was derisive. "The usual means do not present themselves with Kippax."

"To do this would serve you well."

"Don't make it sound like blackmail."

He didn't reply; his wife was coming uncertainly down the steps.

\* \* \*

Sir Cedric Assay spoke in an overwhelming surge, through mint-scented breath: ". . . I find these Egyptian minarets rather . . . well, *coarse*. Islam expresses itself with more sensuality the further east one travels, don't you agree, Owen? In Arabia itself they are still far too aware of the Prophet's shadow to allow anything at all *stirring*. Baghdad may once have been a little less arid, but the Mongols left so little of it one cannot really be sure. It is Persia, I think, where the real sensuality begins—though I think Isfahan too *showy*—but the to my mind *quintessential* blooming of Islamic building and decoration is found only at Herat and Samarkand. India has a few gems, but nothing quite to match those two beacons." Sir Cedric disregarded further aspects of the Cairo skyline. "Don't you agree, Owen?"

"Quite." Kippax noticed that in spite of the heat, Sir Cedric did not perspire. Ten minutes earlier, he had stepped from the train incognito—or as incognito as it was possible to be for a man of six feet two inches under a panama hat and wearing a cream suit that, because of his pear shape, was cut something on the lines of a tent. Kippax had been asked to ensure in advance that no attention should be drawn to him, so the considerable quantity of luggage had been collected discreetly by the army once the train had emptied, with Kippax and Sir Cedric by then well on the way to Shepheard's Hotel.

"Well, I *must* say," said Sir Cedric (whose imperative speech was the cost of a long voyage without compatible conversation), "one does get quite in need of seeing how things really are in the stations, lest one fall into the occupational habit of always believing that the stationmen have lost their balance." He had arranged himself in the upholstery of the official but unmarked Mercedes-Benz in such a way that his knees were level with his eyes, while his head rested on both the side and the rear of the sedan's coachwork. He gave Kippax, from this position, a long and expressionless scrutiny, and then said, "People *do* lose their balance, I fear."

The car had reached a more Europeanized quarter, and was able to pick up speed. Sir Cedric's head was ill-placed for acceleration, and he shifted nearer Kippax, settling the panama hat in his lap. "They say that in a year or two, one will be able to come out by airplane, in two days. That would be *much* more to my taste. As one gets older, one wants more rather than less novelty, and the P & O ships these days are full of the most *lumpen* types, the war having required less selective recruitment than heretofore. Yes, one hopes so much for *novelty*." His left knee had reached Kippax.

At Shepheard's, the request for anonymity had been overlooked. The manager himself, a Swiss who was never seen without tailcoat and white tie, whatever the temperature, intercepted them in the lobby with an all too audible: "Sir Cedric—it is such a great honor to receive you. It has been too long since you were with us."

Years of practice had given Sir Cedric a dexterity of eye that enabled him in the same movement to gleam pleasure, if false, to the fawning manager and glint acute displeasure to Kippax. "Herr Heuer—of course." Sir Cedric took the offered hand but continued to advance, thereby cutting off Kippax from his flank and taking the manager with him, whispering—still without breaking step: "Herr Heuer, I would appreciate it very much if as little fuss is made as possible. In point of fact, I would like the greatest discretion to be maintained. This should have been explained, but it seems that there has been an oversight. As you know, Herr Heuer, these are difficult times and one appreciates tact, the utmost tact."

By this time Sir Cedric had taken the manager clear across the lobby and held him hostage by a large potted palm. Kippax was hovering awkwardly beyond the palm. The manager assumed the air of a man inducted into conspiracy. "Of course, Sir Cedric. You may have every confidence—"

Sir Cedric cut him off. "I knew you would understand." He glared over the manager's shoulder. "Kippax, I wonder if you would be so good as to await the arrival of the luggage, while Herr Heuer shows me to my quarters?"

At that moment the single valise that Sir Cedric had carried from the train—partly to add to the impression of convention and partly because it contained documents—was brought by a porter and deposited at Kippax's feet. Even the porter had assumed now that Kippax's role was, if not servile, subsidiary. The porter waited for Kippax to move his attention from the retreating Sir Cedric, still firmly detaining the manager. As Kippax turned, the porter—a lively Nubian—said, "Pliss, this only bag?"

"No, you bloody fool, it is *not* the only bag."

A thick, henna-stained beard enclosed the mouth so completely that it became vaginal, a feeling enhanced by the way the tongue, like a permanently moistened membrane, obscured the teeth as every word was lubricated. Esther Mosseri could not loosen the hold of this image in her mind—with its voice, lisping Arabic. It was now her inhabiting incubus, the will greater than her own. Ghazi had introduced her to his secret leader; the imam's voice had been the exact opposite of demagogical, and that was its real terror. In the beard-brushed whisper was the essence of that authority peculiar to holy conviction. She was hostage to a whisper, knowingly but not wholly voluntarily. In following her own beliefs, she had become ensnared in more complex intrigues and had left the point where escape was possible. So, though deficient in zeal, she was nonetheless deliberate in action.

Nile water reflected in a dappled, moving stain across a pink-tiled ceiling. Everyone under the ceiling wore a hat, the monotony of khaki interspersed with dyed straw, silk ribbons, and artificial flowers. Esther's veil was a discreet fold of sand-colored silk wound as a turban and then brought down each side of her face to a loose shawl at the neck, the color lighter than her skin. She managed to be radiantly exotic, yet decorous. The gazebo—an enlarged version of an octagonal Victorian bandstand—overhung the river as an abutment of the hotel terrace. At this hour of the afternoon, with governing long since over for the day, officers and their ladies (not all as ladylike as they seemed) took tea as they might have done in Cheltenham or Simla, reinforcing their parochialism with Dundee cake and Lapsang Souchong. In a corner by the water, at a table shadowed by a plaster Aphrodite, sat Tessa Bron. Seeing Esther's arrival, she picked up and waved the small menu card with its gold-leaf deckled edge, its prosaic food described in French in copperplate script. Tessa had defected from the floral motifs of the other Englishwomen. She wore a gray linen suit with a mannish cut to the shoulders, the only "soft" relief a high-collared silk blouse fastened at the neck with a brooch of filigree ivory, in a silver frame. Her hat was of plain gray straw with a gossamer of studded black lace as a veil falling to her brows. Esther came escorted by the maître d' hôtel, a Levantine Greek who seemed to know her.

"I'm sorry to be late. It was the traffic; more military cars every day."

"I know." Tessa smiled and waited for the Greek to see her seated and then said, "The set tea—is that agreeable?"

Esther had already seen the laden silver cake stands. "More than enough."

"I was wondering, after all, whether I chose the right place," said Tessa, looking around them.

"Oh, it's fine; very pleasant."

"It's just that . . . well, I never feel quite comfortable among this set. To me they represent everything I hoped to escape from."

In their young acquaintance Esther had felt an empathy with this often grave woman. Even in the ballroom when her engagement had been celebrated she had seemed in some delicate way to have been holding herself apart. "I know what you mean," Esther said, pleased to be able to encourage the note of dissent— and pleased that the table afforded the chance to be private. "You know, Egypt wasn't always like this. When I was a child here, the English who were here then, they lived differently. People mixed; that generation were linguists, and even if they weren't, they made the effort. But now you hear that awful platitude, 'It's best to keep ourselves to ourselves; the natives don't appreciate visits.' "

"The natives!" Tessa grimaced. "The whole mentality is in that phrase, isn't it?" She arranged a napkin on her lap as a Wedgwood pot of tea arrived, followed by the cakes.

Watching her movements, Esther was intrigued by a sense of contradiction: that the precision of behavior with these appurtenances of English life was at odds with how she spoke—and thought.

Having poured the tea, Tessa resumed: "I was so glad you called. I wanted to thank you for your part in making possible our wedding ceremony."

"It was no trouble. There is not often the opportunity, these days, to use the full Coptic ceremony."

"No—I expect not." Tessa broke off from the tea. "I suppose you must wonder why we wanted it at all."

"I did, I admit."

"It seemed to be necessary—for appearances, at least." They became perceptibly more collusive as she added, "It was for Michael's sake. The army is very conventional about these things. Especially someone called the chaplain general." She laughed. "That title represents a conflict of interests in holy eyes, I would have thought." She looked aside. On the river, a boat slipped through water the shade of cane syrup.

213

To Esther the movement of Tessa's head was that of a caged bird seeing unstinted flight. They were both of them caged here among the prattling, reedy voices and clinking china and silver.

When Tessa turned back to Esther, her eyes were clear of gaiety. "How do *you* bear it here? Women are so *confined*."

"I bear it by thinking of my mother. She has never shown any discontent. Jewish women of her generation have the traditional view. It's not, to them, passiveness. After all, once a Jewish woman becomes a mother, she gains an accepted authority, at least within the family. But, you see, that's what I cannot bear, and by looking at my mother's acceptance of that, I find my own determination. Why should I have to become a mother to get respect?"

"Of course; you have your work."

"Yes, I have that. It was difficult enough; it still is. But I can mark off my own ground there." She drained the tea with uninterested haste. "In Egypt you feel this oppression more than in other places because you see how common it is to all the religions. God was certainly a man . . . and of course, His prophets."

Tessa smiled wryly. "It seems we have common cause, you and I. From my own experience, having tried the frontal assault with Mrs. Pankhurst, I have seen its futility. I believe *infiltration* is the answer. Any confession I make—like the formal nuptials—is based on its future value as a pass into the citadel. I have been dismissed from the greatest of the Christian temples, Rome. It taught me a great lesson."

"You needed Mrs. Pankhurst, though, to light the fire."

"Of course—*of course*. But tactics must change with the times."

"Your husband—how does he feel about this?"

"Michael? Michael has his own conflicts, of background, of culture. I don't think he has yet quite developed the strength for nonconformity, perhaps because he has not yet decided what it is he should be opposing. I think that's often more difficult than deciding what you support."

Esther felt uneasily close to her own turmoil. She chose to retreat. "Well, for the moment the army tells him who the enemy is."

"Oh, yes—he sees that," said Tessa, with an inference of cynicism. "As a matter of fact, when we got back from the honeymoon, he seemed more convinced of it than ever. And now there's quite a flurry of work. An eminence has arrived from London. They all seem in awe of him—even Owen Kippax. It's quite, quite amazing. Michael says this man looks like a cross between a Buddha and a butcher. I knew of him vaguely. . . . One of those names who are known only in the kind of company my father keeps, and I would therefore view him with the greatest caution. An odd name too—Assay.''

"How long will he be here?"

"Not much longer, I'm happy to say. Michael says they are feeding him material from their files in the way an animal is fed at the zoo—in specified quantities at appointed hours—and he consumes it all. I don't know what it is he's after, but it must be important. I shall be glad—for selfish reasons—when next Tuesday arrives. He's on the evening train to Alexandria, thank God.''

The sightless Aphrodite responded no more than did Esther. Carefully she cut a slice of cake, bisecting a flagrantly artificial cherry, so gelatinous that it stained the knife.

Petulance was second only to malice in the armory that Sir Cedric Assay deployed against the world, and an acidic petulance had lacerated Kippax for days until, finally, he was able to retrieve his relationship with his mentor. The healing process began with what Sir Cedric found in the files: Kippax's own work as recorded there. A single nod as he put down Kippax's report on his journey to Riyadh presaged the thaw. "The idea of awarding Ibn Saud a medal was an inspired one—efficacious and yet economical.'' His professional mood was then more privately humored by arrangements made by Kippax in one of Cairo's secret worlds, a world where delicacy, aristocracy, and deviancy met. It proved regenerative. Now, basking amid cushions in his hotel suite, exhaling the finest smoke from Cuban leaf, and intermittently sipping a *digestif*, Sir Cedric looked upon Kippax with replete forgiveness. "It is a pity, Owen, that claret does not travel—at least, not this far south. One has objections of a patriotic nature to Moselle, which otherwise would be about the kind of thing. Still . . .'' He rolled the cognac around his mouth and it flowered in his breath. "Still, Bonaparte set an example which compensates. This is an extraordinarily good cognac, dear boy.''

Kippax wished he didn't feel owned so.

"Allenby seems very slightly disconcerted by Lawrence,''

said Sir Cedric, stubbing his cigar into an ivory bowl. "He turned up at a general headquarters in the wedding vestments of a Bedouin prince."

"Hashemite prince—not Bedouin."

There was the merest flicker of offensive in Sir Cedric's mouth, but it was overtaken by a contemplative relapse.

Then he began speaking in a languorous way, with mandarin lids barely revealing his eyes. "I fear, Owen, that perhaps you do not realize what an asset Lawrence may become. I speak of the diversity of our peril. Not too apparent in Cairo. All too apparent in London. Russia diseased by revolution. French troops in a state of mutiny. Italy just as useless. Deadlock in the trenches. And now America. How unctuous these Americans are. How desultory their effort. Oh, yes, they have joined us against Germany—at a price. America will contribute nothing to winning the war, while actively interfering to ensure that we lose the peace. You are surprised? Then listen to this. Not only have they refused to declare war on Turkey, but there is a pro-Turkish gang around Wilson who have persuaded him that the Turks would accept a separate peace. You see the infamy of that? After everything we have done, are doing out here: the cost of Gallipoli? To leave the Ottoman Empire *intact?*" The final word broke from the surrounding indolence like a rifle shot.

Kippax murmured, "How tiresome."

"Do you know what one of Wilson's men told one of our ministers? He said, 'America has entered the war to exert her influence against greed and the improper distribution of territory.' You see what I mean? They are bent on undermining the British Empire. That mongrel nation is going to be a sore burden to us in the future." Straining to make the effort, Sir Cedric refilled his *ballon*. "However, I think we shall be able to head off this madness about Turkey—with the aid of Lawrence. You know how susceptible the Americans are to the moral fable. Well, there's rather a bright chap involved in our propaganda now, writes rather lurid novels, name of Buchan. He's been very inspired by these escapades of Lawrence's. He sees in them a classic instance of the knight versus the savages—even if in this case it is something of a masquerade, with the Turks as the savages and a fake Bedouin as the knight." Sir Cedric halted, to dare Kippax's correction again, and noted with smug pleasure that it did not come. "So you see, dear boy, Buchan is going to choose an American reporter of suitable gullibility to come out here and join the Lawrence rabble, complete with camera.''

"A reporter?"

"Why not? Drum up a pretty story. A few set pieces, a blown-up train or two. Amateur dramatics—but with real blood. The Americans will lap it up. Of course, I know that Lawrence is not doing anything that others—Newcombe, Garland, Hornby, et al.—are not doing with becoming modesty, but Lawrence does it so absurdly."

"And the Americans will see the Turks as the barbarians they are?"

"Precisely. It has echoes of their own noble struggle against the Indian savages."

*"Where* it is done; *when* it is done; *how* it is done." Dr. Ghazi was being didactic again. A thin yellow finger tapped Esther Mosseri's desk. "Your information suggests an answer to the first two parts of the question. The last has already been decided. We have a man trained in Constantinople. The days of a martyr with revolver"—he made the reference without mercy—"are behind us; we must learn more sophisticated methods. We have a more sophisticated enemy. And we want a more spectacular effect."

"How, then?"

He knew she was stung. The tapping finger stopped; the hand on the desk became proprietorial. "I would like that to be a surprise." The more incensed she became, the more he wanted her. "You did well. There can be no suspicion?"

"She would never remember that she told me."

"The Committee are reassured. I want you to know that."

She took up a pencil from the desk and sucked it like a testy child. He stood up and walked around behind her and put a hand on each shoulder, beginning gently to massage her through her cotton dress. She recoiled, hunching her shoulders. The hands took a tighter, more demanding grip.

"Not now."

"Why not?"

"It's not the time—of the month."

"That never stopped you before."

"It does now."

He caught the gathered hair at the base of her neck, extracting the comb and pulling back her head until it was nearly horizontal, but there was belligerence in her watering eyes that deterred him. He released her and rubbed his palms together, a single gold tooth curiously amplifying his carnivorous appearance. Without saying anything more, he picked up a pair of white silk gloves from the desk and slipped them on slowly, each finger finding its place like a reptile growing a new skin. He fussed over the set of his collar and checked the symmetry of his diamond tie pin, as though about to appear through a door to walk to a lecture podium. He could not quite bring off the effect he intended, of leaving with his vanity intact, of having successfully intimidated her. She knew he was insecure in his authority over her, that he had never had the measure of her in the way that Solomon had. He explained this to himself as an aspect of the racial gulf between them, and it was with the reassurance of this prejudice that he walked from her office.

Kippax was to see Sir Cedric to the train in two hours' time. He had noticed that Sir Cedric liked frequently to wash his hands—indeed, it seemed almost to be a fetish. This and Sir Cedric's inability to perspire were faintly unsettling insights of acquaintance, for at the end of the visit Sir Cedric and Kippax were closer than at its start. Close enough, for example, for Sir Cedric to address Kippax via the mirror of his bathroom. "Tell me—do I detect just a slight faintness of heart in our colleague Hogarth?"

Kippax knew he was being tested. "He does seem to have become perhaps a little wistful."

"Ah!" Sir Cedric held aloft two pink and dripping hands, while Kippax gave him a linen square. "Wistful, you say? I thought as much. Wistfulness can be such a weakness, I think. Surprising, in an Orientalist." The hands were caressing each other in the towel. "And you, Owen. There is something on your mind. You'd better be plain."

Kippax felt isolated in carbolic space, not sufficiently anchored for what now had to be said. He moved slightly, achieving a semblance of poise. "It's the Arabs. We've opened a box that won't be closed again." He was judging how much force was politic as he spoke, and judged uncertainly, his voice hitting an awkward rhythm. "It mayn't be a force that we readily recognize. Indeed, it seems a relic. After all, what are they but a people calcified in the Middle Ages? I think it fatal to take that view—natural, perhaps, from our advantage of time and culture. But Arabia isn't Africa. We're not bringing the Book to pagans and subduing them with piety. The essence of it is in the desert. There, you can feel an extraordinary spiritual strength around you, not the kind that requires cathedrals to consolidate. It has never been domesticated; it's elemental, not having been weakened by our ideas of refinement." He had run up to an abrupt stop, realizing suddenly his energy. "I hope I'm not . . ."

"No—not at all. That was quite *passionately* put, Owen; and necessary to say. However, I would not like to see you carried off by this experience." He put the towel on wet marble and remained expectant.

"My point is, by encouraging them into a sense of their own sovereignty, we had better make sure that we know what we are dealing with."

"And whom?"

"We must be careful with Ibn Saud. In my view, he is the outstanding force."

"You *have* become partisan."

"He will expect constancy."

"Ha!" Sir Cedric's exclamation rattled the mirror in its setting. "*Will* he, indeed? Let me tell you this. Between these walls. I fear there is an awful web of promises that don't all quite fit . . . at least, not if they are ever allowed the light of comparison— which, of course, must not occur. Empathize with them, if you must. I see the value of that, if it reassures them. But be sure of this, if you are sure of anything: History should be disregarded in making policy. It introduces a contaminating element of sentiment."

During the conversation, from somewhere in the caverns of the suite, came dimly the sounds of servile distress—of heavy objects ineptly handled and then of one strident voice transcending others in the cry *"Pis Arabler, pis Arabler!"*

At this, both Kippax and Sir Cedric were forced to take notice. Returning from the bathroom, they saw Sir Cedric's two large cabin trunks standing in the center of his salon, like ceremonial totems, while three porters danced around them, under the direction of a Turkish assistant manager whose appearance and stance gave the impression of ritual priesthood. It was the Turk who, driven to impotent rage, had uttered the double epithet of "Dirty Arabs," to little perceptible effect. In disorder beyond the cabin trunks were curios that Sir Cedric had acquired, or been given—a low, round table with a beaten brass top; a Turkish tribal runner, bound in a roll; a carpetbag of similar source; a small boxwood packing case from which straw seeped and which was labeled "Fragile"—in English, not Arabic. This contained a personal gift from a respected tomb robber.

Icily, Sir Cedric said, "What seems to be the trouble?"

The Turk bowed with shameless subservience. "Sir Assay, Pasha . . . the trunks are heavy. I call another porter."

The porters were temporarily suspended in their agitation, trying to follow the conversation. Sir Cedric pointed to his valise in a corner. "Owen, I wonder if you would take care of that for me; it goes in the car, with us." The Turk continued a series of genuflections as Sir Cedric went to his bedroom and Kippax took the valise down to the Mercedes-Benz, where Baxter, Bron's driver, had been assigned for the journey to the station. Baxter, though adaptable, did not care for Kippax.

"Corporal, secure this valise in the boot, would you?"

"It would be better with me, in the front, sir."

"As you wish." Kippax turned from the car and stood, hands on hips, apparently studying the twilight but in fact preoccupied; intimacy with Sir Cedric, he realized, embraced a number of potentially compromising bonds, both professional and private. It was a mark of his own prowess that so much had been confided; and also a cumulative test of his acumen. His expression lightened and he breathed in the scents of the picaresque alleys in which he was now so much at home.

Somewhere above him, from a stifling, disused boxroom in the eaves of the hotel, vigilant eyes watched Kippax as he came out with the valise. The vigil continued with a calm, psychopathic detachment as the bag was placed alongside the driver. A heavy silver-plated fob watch was consulted. Give or take half a minute, the timing would be felicitous—and recalling with relish the vocabulary of the class he so despised, the observer was glad that they would bag two birds rather than one.

# 12

Koblensky was speaking in Russian, a tongue Sarah did not
know, and his words expressed a personality as strange to her as
the language. They were more deep-throated than his English,
and came like a chant heard from a far greater distance than
between his bed and where she lay, just awakened. The blanket
fell away from her and she went to kneel by his head. His face
turned toward her, remaining on the pillow so she could see only
his right eye clearly. The movement was his most autonomous
since he had been in the bed. She put a hand on his brow. The
melancholy chant still came from him and she noticed that his
lips did not form the words: they came from some inner chamber.
His brow was dry and cool. The eye regarded her through a
half-lowered lid.

Quietly and unsurely, she said, "Asa?"

The flow of Russian faded away and his cracked lips moved.
They were fused at each corner and each took a flake of the other
as the movement parted them. The eye slowly gained the intensity of will. At first, his speech faltered, only a whisper coming.
Then, in a voice much weaker than had issued in Russian, he
said, "Sarah . . . is it . . . Sarah?"

She took the hand from his brow and rested it on his chest,
and pulled a chair to the bed.

"Yes."

"How long?"

"Three days."

The lid closed over the eye for a few seconds, but it was a
rekindling of strength, not a fading of it. His tongue ran along
his lower lip.

"Could I have water?"

She had to raise his head cradled in her right arm while with

221

her left hand she carefully let him sip. The blistered lips adhered to the glass and as much water was spilled as he was able to drink. But when she settled his head back on the pillow, his eyes were clearer and had regained personality.

"You are very weak. You have had a fever, but it seems to have passed."

He smiled weakly with his eyes.

She crossed her hands in her lap and leaned toward him, speaking quietly. "There was good news in the pouch. Aaron is in Cairo. It was an extraordinary journey. He did get an American ship from Copenhagen, but he got word to the British in advance, and they took him off the ship in British waters, making it look like an arrest. He saw the top military people in London, and they sent him out to Cairo. There's a new military commander in Cairo now, called Allenby. It seems that everything will change: a new prime minister in London, and talk of America coming into the war." She stopped and put a hand on his brow again. "I mustn't tire you."

"Aaron, in Cairo?" he said.

"They are trying to get a Jewish brigade formed, for when the British attack." Koblensky's voice was not equal to his hunger for information; she had to wait for him to find the words.

"An attack?"

"They have asked for detailed reports on the Turkish defenses, from Gaza to Beersheba."

"They are coming? When?"

But she didn't answer. She realized that she had no idea of the time. Outside it was dark, cloud cover as low as the peak of Carmel to the northeast. She stood up, becoming the composed nurse again.

"We must get you well. You don't realize how ill you have been. The doctor didn't have much hope."

Koblensky's mouth tightened. "I always cheat the doctors," he said, in a last draining flicker of aggression before his eyes closed. But he was thinking of her three degrees of contact with him in the room: kneeling by his head, sitting by the bed, and standing a step away from him, withholding herself.

In the pull between the urgency of the NILI's new work and his convalescence, Koblensky surprised Sarah by allowing himself time to recover strength; in part it was a sign of his maturity, in part an acknowledgment of how weakened he was—and in part a realization of the value to him of time to watch the others, to think through the dangerous moves ahead of them all. He convalesced at the house in Zichron. His absence from the field left more initiative to Feinberg, and in becoming more decisive Feinberg drew closer to Koblensky. Lishansky was more of a problem. Koblensky had asked Sarah about Lishansky's survival at the beach and her tone then had signaled problems: "It was only his vanity that was wounded, facial scars; it's helped his sense of his own importance." Feinberg had more disturbing news, that Lishansky was parading too openly at the Hotel Fast in Jerusalem as a partisan Scarlet Pimpernel.

But Feinberg's main worry, and Sarah's, was the failure of the British to make regular rendezvous at Athlit. Even though the weather was improving and their information was said to be urgently required in Cairo, the frigates were called away to other work. The last pouch from Cairo suggested training pigeons to carry messages over the Turkish lines to Sinai, and offered a code for the purpose.

"Pigeons?" said Koblensky, sitting in the conservatory at Zichron Jaacov.

Sarah shrugged. "Apparently they've used them before. There are people here who know how to train them."

Koblensky shook his head. "The British treat us like birds. They feed us scraps, hardly enough money to keep us going, a few drugs, and all the while they pour gold into the hands of the Arabs. Pigeons!"

"You met a Captain Lawrence in Cairo, you said."

"Yes. Why?"

"There are stories of an Arab revolt. Lawrence has got his own army in the desert, blowing up Turkish trains on the line to Medina."

"It sounds like Lawrence. Lawrence isn't like the rest of them."

"In what way?"

"He never looked right in uniform; he hated the way they think." Koblensky rubbed his nose speculatively. "I had a feeling he would be forced out by them; he made them nervous. I thought they would send him back to Oxford. He did not seem cut out for action. But with the Arabs, out there? It is strange—I don't understand the English: so conservative, and yet they love an eccentric."

"Blowing up Turkish trains—that's eccentric?" Sarah laughed. "I want you to close your eyes."

Koblensky was puzzled.

*"Close* them," she said, with a playful vehemence that was unusual.

Koblensky obeyed, though bewildered.

She went behind his chair and pulled something wrapped in tissue from a pocket. It was a Star of David pendant on a fine gold chain. She said, "Take your hands from your face, but don't look." He was frowning as she positioned the chain over his head and then dropped it, the star falling on the matted hair under his chin.

He had to push his chin into his chest to see the pendant: It was not gold but finely embossed brass. Fingering it with astonishment, he looked up. "Why?"

She had come round to a few paces in front of him, judging the effect with maternal concern. "Because you don't have a trinket to your name, because you have brought so much to us—and because it's your birthday."

"How did you know that?"

The maternal expression adapted to one of teasing discretion— almost, though not quite, suggesting a sexual game. "We have our ways. After all, we *are* spies."

His right index finger and thumb ran along the chain, around the still-gaunt neck that seemed too burdened by the head. He looked at her with lowered lids, embarrassed and yet all the more aware of her persisting formality under the playfulness. "I have done nothing. You gave me a home."

"No," she said, keeping her distance. "We didn't give you a home; you knew where your home was in a way we didn't, because we were here. I have never had to want it in the way you did, to risk everything for it. *You* showed me that strength; until I knew you I didn't understand that. Not in that way."

He remembered again, with more pain, how gratuitously he had once, in this house, accused her of being featherbedded, and looking at her now, pallid and strained from too much danger and too little food, seeing all her will in relief like implacable bone under drawn skin, Koblensky was forced into emotional insights of himself and could only shake his head slowly. "I had nothing to lose. You have everything."

"It will be all right," she said. "I know that." She seemed for a second to falter, convincing herself, and then she regained her confidence and said, "We used to think here that we could let the rest of the world go by, that we could remain in our haven, that it didn't really matter who governed Palestine." She dipped her head. "It's foolish to believe that, even if many people here still do." She looked at him again and spoke more self-assertively. "Something has changed. We will be caught up in it. Aaron knows that; you know that. We have to *impose* ourselves."

Koblensky got up from the chair, his bare feet feeling the warmth of the sun on the conservatory floor. His right hand took up her left hand and he kissed the red, toughened knuckle, consciously aping the flourish of a Victorian gallant. Looking archly at her, he said, "Yes—that is what we have to do. *Impose* ourselves." They were as close, in this exchange, as he felt they were ever likely to be. He released her hand and she stepped half a pace away, looking through a lacework of plants to the bleached land outside. The land was untilled and the orchards limp from drought. What had burgeoned was now stunted. The land and the people had a common suffering that changed their surface, powdering earth and parching skin. They were down to their last reserves, and she was fearful for the weakest. Little could be done for them. They were either like her father, passively consenting, or rabid with spite. Did Koblensky, with his new maturity, see this danger or was he still too headstrong? At the window, she said, "We can only be as strong as the weakest among us. That is the limit on us."

He saw that she was not challenging him but asking for his tolerance—expecting more humanity from him in return for her own new clarity of purpose.

"The really weak—those I do not mind," he said. "Those who hide behind weakness, who *use* it—they are dangerous."

"That is very Russian," she said, but the half jest became consent; she saw the truth of it.

"To me, life *is* very Russian. Always."

But she was thinking, this time to herself, that the house breathed more substance than they did, that it had permanence beyond them—but an unsatisfying permanence. She had not advanced this thought to him because she resented it. She thought then of her father above them. He had got through the winter and looked at her each morning expectantly, as though she would come through the door with a British soldier at her side, and the survival of the next winter would then be assured.

Koblensky's instincts about her were not even now certain; she seemed to reach out to affirm their empathy and then, as

225

now, to become suddenly distant and unwilling to confide further. All that he could tell, when she turned to him again, was that her view of him was still in the scales, tilting which way he didn't know; perhaps it had reached that fineness of balance when a grain of doubt could make it move again. None of them—he, Sarah, Feinberg—had stable views of each other; such intimacy needed easier times to foster it. They were holding together, but not without effort.

Their lives were not always under acute stress. Indeed, against the monotonous, almost prosaic attrition of their existence, the moments of high risk were a stimulant. The eking out of what food and water there was had settled into a routine and the routine, after a while, assumed the semblance of normality. With his convalescence behind him, Koblensky sometimes felt that while his feet plodded through the quotidian days, his head lived a parallel life of military calculations and unstilled alert. But by early summer, there was still no sign of a British offensive. The longer it was delayed, the more vulnerable the NILI became. Rumor was more pervasive than hard information. They heard that the war in Europe was going so badly that reinforcements would be drawn from Egypt, making the invasion of Palestine impossible. Koblensky knew, from information they had passed to the British, that Turkish officers were disillusioned with the war and hoped that the beleaguered British would make a separate peace with Turkey. The delays weakened the morale of the NILI. Sarah was frustrated by the nonappearance of British warships and the unreliability of the carrier pigeons. One message from Cairo did get back, via an Arab courier. Aaron was still there, and still convinced that the invasion would come, but he warned that it would depend on America's deciding to join the European war. And that, he said within the enigmatic phrasing of the code, hinged on "the Jewish question."

"It means," said Koblensky, as he and Sarah sat with the deciphered message, "that if the British back Zionism, America will send troops to Europe."

"You think so? Aaron used to think that American Jews would never support joining the war on the same side as an ally of Russia."

"Your brother Alexander—he has connections in America?"

She nodded. "The money for Aaron's work came from Chicago. A man called Julius Rosenwald." She saw Koblensky's chain of thought.

"Aaron might be the key to this—himself."

"That frightens me," she said, barely above a whisper.

"Why?"

She looked at him foursquare, with sudden impatience. "He wouldn't understand how many enemies he would make."

"He knows that." He saw that her nerves were near the breaking point. He got up and walked across the room, his back to her. When finally he turned, she was bowed and crying, the deciphered message compressed in her right palm. He knew his own vulnerability—all their vulnerability—was linked to hers. He also knew better than to try to console her, and saw that she needed to be alone. Quietly, he went out into the night to his horse. The suddenness of her breakdown had taken him by surprise. They were nearer to the edge than he had thought.

Improbably, it was Feinberg who met these new tremors with a stoic calm, and who had the look of command when he dealt with Sarah. With mixed feelings, Koblensky realized that the unrequited flame Feinberg carried for Sarah gave him the delicacy needed to rebuild her confidence. Koblensky consciously encouraged him, and by growing closer again to Sarah, Feinberg was able to ward off his bouts of melancholia. More reluctantly, Koblensky conceded to Feinberg in a tactical decision: to use Arabs as agents. At first, Koblensky argued that this was a needless risk, but Feinberg pointed out that the Bedouin (and fake Bedouin) Arabs could move through the Turkish lines with much greater ease than Jews. It was one of Feinberg's couriers who had brought the message from Aaron, and Koblensky had to admit that the Arabs were more naturally clandestine than some of the NILI's Jews, like Lishansky, who courted a reputation for living dangerously.

Feinberg relished his ascendancy; his manner with Koblensky was of tolerant partnership. Koblensky was acknowledged to be the military technician who set the priorities for espionage and who assessed the results, while Feinberg assigned the agents. Feinberg's most skilled agent was a town Arab from Haifa who, in the guise of a shepherd, built a line of informants as far east as the Turkish garrison at Deraa in Syria. And it was this man who came one morning with a message carried directly by him for Koblensky. It was from an old friend in a new role—the Englishman already called by the desert Arabs "El Aurens."

Feinberg took the Arab agent to the Athlit station, and translated for Koblensky from the Arab vernacular:

" 'Most esteemed Koblensky—' " Feinberg broke off with a grim smile. "Merely an Arab courtesy." He resumed: " 'Word must pass between us by the rising of the sun on the tenth day of this month. I shall be in waiting for you at the place of Tel Shahab where the river meets the iron path.' "

Feinberg grimaced and got the Arab slowly to repeat the message, stopping at the date and cross-examining him, explaining to Koblensky: "He says it is the English calendar, not the Arab. That means the tenth of June." He picked up the thread again and, reassured, explained: "The Tel Shahab is a gorge where the railway crosses the river Yarmuk."

"How far?"

"About sixty miles from here." He paused. "You came here on the railway."

Koblensky nodded.

"Then you must have passed over the bridge. It's the only line into Palestine from the east."

"It may be only sixty miles, but it is crawling with Turks. I remember that. The line runs through Affula." Koblensky recalled Jemal, Brusse, and the opulent wagon-lit; it seemed an age away in the past. "And Lawrence wants us to meet him there?"

"He's blown up trains from Arabia to Deraa."

"I know."

"He doesn't need our help to do that. He's got his own army out there—desert cutthroats. This man here"—Feinberg nodded to the courier—"he's terrified of them. The town Arabs hate those people."

"We have three days," said Koblensky flatly.

"I'll come with you."

"I'll need you. If I am going to pass for an Arab."

It took half a day to procure two donkeys and consult the Arab guides on a route. It was safest to cover most of the ground at night, but that meant following difficult trails. The first stage was the least dangerous—through the Samarian hills and down to the plain of Armageddon. From there, even if they skirted Affula to the south, they still had to work around the south of the mountains of Lower Galilee and up into the Jordan valley, the narrowing funnel through which rivers, road, and railway all passed and in which there were numerous Turkish camps and guard posts. The riskiest route was a shortcut taking them north of Affula instead of south, to skirt Nazareth and slip across a shepherd's trail south of Mount Tabor that would bring them within sight of Galilee. Then they could follow the Yarmuk to the rendezvous, less than twenty miles to the east.

They left in the afternoon and by midnight were looking down from the Samarian heights on the town of Abu Shusha and the road from Jenin to Haifa. Beyond the town, in the moonlight, the plain was visible all the way to Affula and beyond. A train was disappearing to the west, where the line left the plain for the last leg to Haifa; Affula itself was ablaze with lights and even from this distance they could hear locomotives in the yards. The clarity of detail and the amplification of sounds made them more aware of their own conspicuousness—exaggerating it, Koblensky suspected, but in the unaccustomed Arab robes he felt as prominent as a blazing beacon anyway.

They wanted to be across the plain by daybreak, but the first light came while they were well short of cover. They were north of the railroad but in flatlands between Affula and the foothills of Tabor. There were no other Arabs in sight and the prescribed route took them under the noses of a guard post, an extension of a walled compound in which stood a low, L-shaped wooden building. By the time they reached the guard post, the tip of Tabor had turned orange and the brief dawn chill had given way to a strange, fetid stillness. The wooden building looked like a barracks, but what a barracks was doing in such a location puzzled Koblensky.

There was no movement in the tower of the guard post, but from a latrine at the back a Turkish soldier appeared. He was obese, and, barely able to reestablish his trousers, was struggling with the buttons when he caught sight of the two men on their donkeys. There was a clearly audible and drawn-out fart as he finally hitched the trousers, and hands still on belt, he came toward them shouting.

Feinberg pulled his donkey to a halt, and Koblensky drew alongside him.

Although he was fluent in Turkish, Feinberg threw up his hands and wailed uncomprehendingly in Arabic.

The Turk, a sergeant, began bellowing in their faces, looking from Feinberg to Koblensky and then—as if hoping to find more response there—to the donkeys. Finally he subsided and called to the guard post. Another soldier, clearly just wakened, came running out, carrying a rifle. The sergeant said something and the soldier approached Feinberg's donkey, poking it in the neck with the muzzle of the rifle and then speaking to Feinberg in rough Arabic.

The prepared alibi was that Feinberg and Koblensky were brothers on their way from a village to a family funeral in Tiberias. Koblensky was able to understand, from the combination of Feinberg's arm-waving and the Turk's response, that the alibi was being put to the test.

The soldier turned to the sergeant, who was relieving himself of another seismic fart, and passed on the story. The sergeant looked at the donkeys again and then barked an instruction. Feinberg had no chance to explain to Koblensky what was happening. He nudged the donkey to follow the soldier to the guard post.

The sergeant went ahead of them, and when they reached the building he was already talking on a phone. Following Feinberg's lead, Koblensky got down and tied his donkey to a rail by the duckboard that led to the latrines. He could not gauge from Feinberg's face what was happening, but Feinberg seemed more bemused than alarmed.

The fetid smell was worse, and at first Koblensky thought it came from the latrines, but he realized that its source was the marshy ground beyond them.

With the soldier standing over them, they watched the sergeant leave the phone and open a gate of the compound. In a few minutes, two more Turks, wearing soiled white coats, appeared pushing a roughly improvised wooden cart over the ruts left by military trucks. As the cart lurched over these ruts, its load shifted and Koblensky saw a naked foot suddenly appear above the sill of the cart. The white-coated men halted at the gate, with a precision that indicated a demarcation of both territory and responsibility. They didn't speak to the sergeant, but turned back into the compound, leaving the cart and rubbing their palms briskly together, but not from cold.

The soldier brought the butt of his rifle swiftly into Feinberg's hip, knocking him forward and giving instructions at the same time. Feinberg muttered in Arabic to Koblensky, who grunted inaudibly and followed.

When Koblensky reached the cart he was sickened by what he saw. Feinberg, less fortified than Koblensky by experience, stepped back and vomited. There were four corpses in the cart, but none of them was complete. There were remnants of crude field dressings around their wounds. One had been emasculated, another had lost his eyes, a third was dismembered. None had been instantly killed. The wounds had festered. The stench of the cart had been inadequately doused in some liquid, probably plain alcohol. Looking from the cart to the wooden building, Koblensky realized that this must be a Turkish military hospital.

The rifle-toting soldier had no patience with two Arabs who were blanching before his eyes. He gave Feinberg another push with the rifle and shouted in Arabic. Feinberg gave Koblensky one glance of distress, wiping his mouth with his cloak, and got behind the cart. He and Koblensky pushed the cart through the gate, and the soldier led them to the rank pasture behind the latrines, where sewage and the waste of the charnel house mingled. They were shown a spot at the end of a recently covered trench, took spades from the cart, and began digging. The effort of the interment supplanted their nausea. In an hour the task was done, the trench extended another six feet and, with the sun already adding its chemistry, they were joined by a shallow cloud of flies that hovered at ankle-height like a turbulent mantle, uninterested in live flesh.

They returned to the donkeys. Feinberg had lost all appetite and was in a cold sweat under the robes. Koblensky untied both donkeys and waited for Feinberg to finish a conversation with the soldier. Feinberg managed to convey supplication and sympathy in the same movements, a feat of mime that in other circumstances Koblensky could have found funny. But now, not following the conversation, he was too tense.

Finally the soldier waved Feinberg away and went back into the guard post.

Not until they were several hundred yards along the track, without daring to look back, did Feinberg explain. "We were lucky that they took us for Palestinian Arabs. The hospital is full of casualties from attacks on the Hijaz Railway. Arabs, led by the British. Those poor creatures we buried had been ambushed by a tribe called the Howeitat. I know of them, they're led by Auda abu Tayi. Barbarians—even the other desert Arabs are terrified of them. You can see what their idea of war is. If the British are employing Auda, they will need a trunkful of gold. And they should watch their backs."

"How many are in that hospital?"

"I couldn't get that out of him. It's not much better than an abattoir. The Turks are not very modern with medicine." Feinberg fell silent, looking ahead to the peak of Tabor. The stench of the field was receding behind them. He gulped in the cleaner air, and then laughed without humor. "We *were* going to a funeral, after all. The guard noticed that you didn't talk. I said you were mentally defective."

"We had better get to those hills," said Koblensky, feeling the donkey wilting beneath him in the heat.

"I have never seen anything like that," said Feinberg. He looked across to Koblensky's impassive and purposeful face. "Can you—do you get so used to it that you don't feel anything anymore?"

"There are different ways of feeling it."

Feinberg's nausea had ebbed into a depletion of spirit in which he knew he was distinct from Koblensky, but whether this represented a difference in their natures or a gulf in their experiences, he couldn't be sure. Koblensky became insistent on finding cover and remaining in it until late afternoon, checking the route map again and recalculating the time needed to reach the rendezvous. Then Koblensky slept without a movement while Feinberg could not shake his mind's eye loose from the vision of the abyss. When Koblensky awoke, Feinberg was mentally as well as physically drained, and still unable to eat.

Koblensky had taken off his outer robe to use as a blanket and he sat now in his loose undershirt, unmistakably not an Arab, his forehead tanned right to the fringe of his closely cropped hair. He looked at Feinberg without mercy, jabbing the air with a date pit. "You should eat. It will be a long night."

This was too close to the Russian arrogance that had first annoyed Feinberg months ago. With the darkness of his skin against the coarse white undershirt, Koblensky had the animal vitality that Feinberg imagined was typical of the hordes from the steppes. The philistine in Koblensky always surfaced under stress—*that* was their real incompatibility—but Feinberg was too weak to pick a quarrel. "I will be all right," he said, and pulled himself up.

Koblensky said, "We have to go over the top of that next range of hills. There is no way around. It is more than twelve hundred feet high. I hope these donkeys are up to it."

The donkeys had been feasting off the grass and then, swollen, had sunk into it, their tails listlessly disturbing flies. Koblensky had to kick them back into life. They began the long gradual ascent to the ridge that lay between them and Galilee. The cool of the night increased with altitude. Climbing crabwise on a track frequently broken by outcrops of rock, they took three and a half hours to crest the ridge, by which time they were both wishing that they were more warmly clothed. The egg-shaped crater that formed the Sea of Galilee encompassed their whole horizon; it took the best part of another three hours to reach the head of the Jordan valley, where they had no alternative to crossing main routes and the Yarmuk River itself.

Koblensky decided to hold back in the foothills until the day brought the regular traffic into which they could infiltrate. Feinberg slipped into a deep sleep. When Koblensky awakened him it was ten in the morning. The roads were a confusion of military vehicles, horse-drawn traffic, and itinerant Arabs. They were able to reach and cross the Yarmuk uneventfully and then follow it as it slipped below into a series of ravines.

The message from Lawrence had failed to specify on which bank of the river he proposed to meet them. Koblensky judged that he was more likely to approach from the south, where he could be relatively unimpeded in a night run from the desert into hills where there were no Turkish camps. This judgment was confirmed when, from their vantage point on the trail above the river, they saw that all the guard posts were on the north bank. River and railway cranked around farther east, and the skyline was now dominated by Mount Hermon to the north of them. As the light faded they heard, faintly at first, the sound of cascading water.

"That's the falls at Tel Shahab," said Feinberg. "No more than a few miles now."

The texture of the air was different. There was no longer the interval of Mediterranean haze in the settling evening sky; the night bore the grip of the desert and though the limestone hills seemed identical to those of Samaria, the villages were different, more pressed into the rock, with fewer trees. The sound of the water increased.

Feinberg said, "We won't get a clear view of the bridge without climbing down. We should leave the donkeys tied up here."

There was a cairn of rocks and a small, grassy plateau. By this time it was so dark that not even the line of Mount Hermon was clear. Until the moon came up, their only guide was the rushing water. The hill below the grass fell sharply away. They edged down cautiously, unable to see more than a few feet ahead and conscious of a blackness below that had no substance at all.

233

Then, above the sound of the falls, they heard a train. It was coming, invisibly, from the east—along the line on their side of the river, before it curved sharply to meet the bridge. They stopped scrambling and waited. They did not see the bridge until the train was on it, giving the eerie impression of crossing on air. In the train's reflected light the skeletal metal of the bridge threw a brief tracery of shadows.

"What a place for blowing up a train!" said Feinberg.

"They must know that. The bridge must be heavily guarded."

The train and the bridge were deep below them, like toys. Slowed to a crawl for the bridge, the train took another curve to the west and within a minute was passing directly opposite them on the north bank of the gorge. The rendezvous with Lawrence was not until dawn. Koblensky wanted to get much nearer the bridge. They began to slip downward again. There was still no moon, but the night had lightened enough to see down to the river. They moved obliquely, finding easy footholds on the firmer rock in the lower ravine, and found the remnant of a road that must have been used when the bridge was constructed. The bridge was clearer now, resting on abutments built out of the rock on each side of the cliffs. There was no guard on the southern side, but across the ravine, about sixty yards away, they picked out the dim flames of a campfire and the outline of a tent.

Koblensky was incredulous. "This bridge could be in pieces in the river before they woke up," he said, picking out soldiers' laughter above the sound of the water.

"But how would you get enough dynamite down here to do it?" asked Feinberg.

"It would be difficult—but it is possible."

By the time they had climbed back to the grass plateau, they were exhausted. They slept in the shelter of the cairn.

It was still dark when Koblensky was disturbed by movement from the donkeys. This was out of character—the donkeys normally needed kicking awake, day or night. They were not on their feet, but their heads were raised and their tails and ears were agitated.

Koblensky shook Feinberg awake. Feinberg watched the donkeys, and pulled himself up. The two of them climbed around the cairn to higher ground and reached the trail they had originally taken. Koblensky beckoned to keep climbing, to where the elevation would give them a wider view and protection from surprise. Before they could reach the summit, they saw, advancing at a walking pace along the trail from the east, three cloaked riders on camels.

"It was the camels. Donkeys and horses—they hate that smell," said Feinberg.

They crouched against the limestone slope. The leading rider was half crouched in his seat, looking down at the trail. The other riders, each with a rifle strapped over his left shoulder, were peering around them, below and above. Koblensky hoped that their own dark cloaks were less conspicuous than these riders' white ones; the leading rider's cloak seemed almost iridescent. The three came to a stop immediately below, spotting the cairn. The leader indicated the rocks and the plateau and they turned the camels off the track, descending in a peculiar, halting stride, the camels obviously unhappy with the angle of the ground. The men exchanged a few muttered words in Arabic.

Feinberg focused on these voices. "One of them—I think it must be the leader—he's speaking very bad Arabic, a desert dialect but not naturally."

"Could he be English?"

Feinberg strained to hear as the men continued with the precariously canted ride. "It's possible," he said.

The rearmost rider lowered his camel to the ground and slipped off it, walking across to the donkeys and then calling back to the leader. This time both Feinberg and Koblensky heard distinctly the leader addressed as "El Aurens."

Koblensky checked Feinberg's impulse to break cover. They waited as Lawrence and the second Arab dismounted and went to the donkeys. Lawrence climbed around the rocks, found the camp, and picked around in the stones. He called the two Arabs over and spoke to them, then on his own climbed to the top of the cairn. He stood, peering about him, and then called out, once, in a birdlike way: *"Yishuv."*

Koblensky stood up.

Lawrence saw the movement and beckoned them down with a wave.

Lawrence was barely recognizable. Koblensky tried to equate this wraith with the ill-at-ease subaltern who had taken him to the polo game in Cairo. Only the eyes, acidic blue in the mask of a weathered face, confirmed the identity.

Lawrence extended a hand and, scrutinizing Koblensky and Feinberg, laughed. "Five of us in Arab dress—and only two are authentic. Welcome to the masquerade."

"How did you know it was us?" said Koblensky.

"Those are Palestine donkeys."

"And *yishuv*?"

"That was desperate—the only Hebrew word that came to mind. It's what you call your settlements, I believe?"

Koblensky nodded.

"I should have been more exact about the meeting place," said Lawrence, looking from Koblensky to Feinberg. "And this is . . .?"

"Feinberg; Absalom Feinberg," said Feinberg, stepping forward and feeling Lawrence's hand fall passively inside his.

"Well . . ." Lawrence broke from the handshake and gave a self-conscious flourish of the arm like a thespian. "We had better talk." He pointed to the gorge. "You see—what a devil of a place for the most spectacular of all train wrecks! But that must wait. Other matters first."

They sat by the rocks, Koblensky and Feinberg with knees bent under their robes, backs against the incline, and Lawrence squatting Arab-style on the grass facing them. Koblensky now saw that Lawrence's robe was of a fine white silk with elaborate gold embroidery, and a gold-hilted dagger hung at his waist.

Lawrence said, "This information could come to you only firsthand. Couldn't risk any other method. No doubt you've been losing faith in our ever coming. Well, there's a new man, Allenby, not a timid general, nor a hasty one. He's preparing carefully. We've looked at your stuff; it's been first-rate. Nothing else of the same quality. However, it's clear that the Turks have a strong line. Do we go for Gaza, or Beersheba? I don't know. Allenby, fortunately, doesn't come from that school who think the only honorable course is to attack the most entrenched positions. We're going to need impeccable information on which to base that decision. I fancy we'll need an element of bluff. Make 'em think we're going for one, and go for the other. You may have to help. But first—and I can't overstress the importance of this—we must have, to the very last minute, the groupings and strengths all along that line from Beersheba to Gaza."

He stopped speaking and studied Koblensky.

"We can do it," said Koblensky.

"But?"

"The pigeons. I do not like it. Can the navy work with us again, if this is so important?"

236

Lawrence frowned. "It's felt that it's too great a risk for the navy. The submarines are becoming a menace."

"Well, we will do it anyway."

"Look," said Lawrence appeasingly. "I'll give you the whole picture. You should understand." He pulled out a piece of paper that had been minutely folded and secreted somewhere within the billows of the gown. He spread it on the grass. It was a map penciled with the same pedantry Koblensky remembered from the trestle tables in Cairo. Lawrence's finger settled on the distended northern prong of the Red Sea, the Gulf of Akaba. "Here's the immediate stroke. Akaba. If we can take that, the way is open for us to move right up the eastern Turkish flank, to draw off more and more of their troops from Palestine."

"Akaba?" said Feinberg, with naked amazement. "You think you can take that?"

"We are going to take it from behind. From the north. The very last place they'll expect us to come from. All their guns are facing out to sea." He was willing the incredulity out of Feinberg's face. "I came here from Nebk—that's southeast of here, in the desert. At this moment, one of the largest Arab armies since the seventh century is gathering there." His finger rose from the map and the hand closed and cut the air. "We'll smash them."

"Nebk?" said Feinberg thoughtfully. "That's Ruwalla country. Are *they* with you?"

Lawrence underwent a rapid transition from advocacy to caution. "You know the tribes?"

But Koblensky interceded. "He grew up with Arabs. They call him Sheikh Salim."

Feinberg said, "I'm familiar only with Palestine Arabs. I've heard them talk of these desert tribes, that's all."

"Ah," said Lawrence, still curious. "As you say, it is the territory of the Ruwalla, under Nuri Shaalan, and old Nuri is indeed jealous of his domain. But while he openly declares his allegiance to the Turks, he has, with the encouragement of a little gold, given us the right of passage to Akaba. My sword is Auda."

"Of the Howeitat?" said Feinberg, looking from Lawrence to Koblensky.

"We shall fall on Akaba," said Lawrence adamantly. "And with that done, move north again. While Allenby prepares."

Feinberg and Koblensky were simultaneously associating this effetely garbed figure with the dismemberments they had shoveled into the maggot-rich earth the previous morning. Koblensky had noticed that the index finger making epic motions on the map had been greatly coarsened, with a chipped and discolored nail.

From the west, echoing along the gorge, came the whistle of an approaching train.

Lawrence jerked around and got to his feet. The train was still at least a mile away, not yet in sight. Without turning back again to Koblensky and Feinberg, Lawrence ran across the grass plateau, with the silk drawn out like a skirt behind him. There was enough light to cast his form into a sharply angled shadow. The robe transfigured Lawrence, masking the awkwardly proportioned body, even suggesting a newly released nature. Koblensky and Feinberg followed him down the rock face, the Arab bodyguards behind them.

Lawrence came to rest at the same level Koblensky and Feinberg had reached the night before, within sight of the bridge. The guard camp on the far bank was now clear. Men were moving about. The train came at a crawl to the curve before the bridge, wheel flanges biting rail. When it was on the bridge, they could see three troop cars full of men and two flatbeds with wooden crates lashed down.

As the train disappeared, Lawrence turned to Koblensky. "There you have it—the whole point of meeting here. This is their weakest link. The only line to Damascus from Palestine—and we'll cut it like a jugular!" His hand chopped the air. "That will be our masterstroke, but it must come at precisely the right time. We could finish this show between us—my desperadoes and you."

Koblensky's expression requested enlightenment. The cumulative effect of Lawrence in this role was unnerving.

"You see they only guard the bridge from the northern bank? I can get enough explosives down there, under cover of darkness, with my people, but we'll need someone to take care of that guard post, to come around behind it. I want *your* people to do that." He hesitated and became transparently sly. *"That* would secure your account."

"When?" said Koblensky.

"Not for a while. Allenby would have to have them on the run, and I would have to be able to synchronize; a much harder thing coming here with a whole party, explosives and all, than with three." Subsiding into a squatting position again, he said,

"We'll give you plenty of notice." Then the exhilaration seemed to drain away; he held his body half backward, with shoulders hunching, and began a monologue addressed to the ground. "I'm as muscularly strong as people twice my size, and more enduring than most, but I'm not going to last out this game if it goes on too long. Nerves going and temper wearing thin, and one needs an unlimited amount of both. Every year in Arabia counts as ten." He moved his eyes slowly from the ground to Koblensky's. "You wonder why I'm in these lordly silks? I love to try and hide my Frankish exterior. So it's a kind of foreign stage on which one plays day and night, in fancy dress, in a strange language. . . . Still, my war is a decent imitation of soldiering—a good fraud."

"I was surprised to see you on a camel," said Feinberg. Arab chiefs usually ride horses."

"The camel is a marvelous gunship. You can use the light automatic guns, Lewis or Hotchkiss, from the saddle of a camel running at eighteen miles an hour. We pounce on the Turks and destroy them in heaps. The dead men look wonderfully beautiful in the night . . . faces softened into new ivory. But sometimes the corpses are flung so pitifully on the ground, huddled anyhow in heaps, that I put them all in order, one by one . . . myself."

Koblensky and Feinberg were silent until Koblensky finally said, neutrally, "Doesn't the killing trouble you?"

Life, but not vigor, came slowly back to Lawrence's head. He turned to one side, gazing down into the gorge. "There are more terrible things than death."

Koblensky began moving to get up, but Lawrence, by speaking, deterred the movement. "Only one man in Cairo really knows my game. I'm his best trick yet. It's such a deception that I think it might be genius, or at least art. Nobody dare keep a true record of accounting in this thing, even for themselves. One deceives even one's diary. This little excursion, for one thing. I can't leave any trace of it." He stopped abruptly, as though in fear of indiscretion, and then, dropping all subjection, said, "I know you're going to take the chance that's coming; I knew that in Cairo. But remember, promises of convenience are good only for the duration of the convenience."

Climbing back to the plateau, with Lawrence ahead of them, Koblensky and Feinberg watched the two bodyguards drop into step with their charge. Once, when Lawrence faltered, the nearmost Arab caught just his left elbow with an extended hand and

239

steadied him with a light yet propelling touch—a physical transference that became lodged in Koblensky's mind as an unresolved speculation. The three camels broke into a light-footed canter toward the east, Lawrence's mount a nose ahead of the others.

"What does 'Frankish' mean?" said Koblensky.

Feinberg had pulled the headpiece of his cloak away, and was wiping perspiration from his brow. He seemed distracted, and only slowly focused on the question. "Frankish? I think it's a medieval term, used by the Orientals about Europeans."

They relapsed into silence again, until the outline of the three camels fused into one undulating form and vanished over the brow of the path.

Feinberg said, "Is this how things are going to be done?"

Koblensky swatted a fly from his face. He was feeling saddle sore and profoundly uneasy in a way he preferred not to confide. "We are too young to grow old," he said, "but I wish, sometimes, I could be old—just for a few minutes." He began to think of his father, involuntarily, and for the first time in a long while.

# 13

## *Cairo ❋ May 1917*

Kippax was still not sure how his future stood with Sir Cedric; even as they drove to the station, the older man behaved as though unaware that the younger looked for and needed some encouragement, some return for his ardent loyalty. Kippax wedged himself into a corner of the car so that Sir Cedric could uncoil over most of the seat without touching thigh to thigh; that would have been too familiar, without first knowing Sir Cedric's mind. Parting the waves of evening congestion, the black Mercedes-Benz was worthy of a viceroy's progress, not this anonymous mandarin's. Kippax imagined Sir Cedric in a viceroy's plumed hat and gilded uniform instead of the creased suit and panama, but knew this to be miscasting. The men in plumed hats were usually mere puppets; real power belonged to the shadows and to the corps in which they both served—though how much of this power Sir Cedric was ready to assign now was the speculation causing Kippax to be so on edge.

"Owen—you don't seem very comfortable."

Kippax ventured closer.

"You know, Owen"—Sir Cedric's knee brushed Kippax's—"the service works with more finality than life. It decrees its allotted span quite inflexibly. I do not complain. Though I feel senility is still some distance away, I do hope I am not sounding already posthumous."

"Surely you are not due yet for retirement?"

"You flatter me, dear boy." Sir Cedric patted Kippax's knee. "Barely three years. And so much seems about to happen." He looked from the car into the polyglot human soup through which they moved. "One wonders how all this can be rendered coherent." His chin sagged into his starched shirt collar and the tilt of the panama took on the same gesture of weariness. "Surrey

241

and Ravenna, roses and frescoes . . . beauty may come to pall, as a companion."

"Surely you'll go to the Lords?"

"Nominally, perhaps. It is expected. But it has too much the quality of a mausoleum, and I fear, with these rather rapacious socialists beginning to be heard . . ." The car came to an imperceptible, expert stop. But Sir Cedric hesitated, and leaned to Kippax again, hand returning to his knee. "It would sustain me greatly, dear boy, to know that things done or about to be done will not lightly be undone."

Though this gesture, this subtle vocational pledge, answered and satisfied Kippax's calculations, it did not for long remain the dominant memory of that day.

The car's arrival at the station, and Sir Cedric's discreet boarding of the train, were the first signs of a miscalculation; by then, according to carefully laid plans, Sir Cedric should have been blown to bits. The miscalculation became by the minute more fateful, though it was not until later that Kippax came to know how it was time itself that had cheated calculation.

Kippax had left the station with a smugness that seemed unlikely to pass in the night. Baxter, the driver, who was an observant man, could explain the reason for Kippax's manner and very quickly did, to another driver: "He was bad enough before, too big for his boots. But I warn you, he's goin' to be a right pain in the arse, that one. You should've seen 'em in the car, thick as bloody thieves. If you ask me, our Mister bleeding Kippax is goin' to be walkin' around here like he owns the place."

"Could've told you that."

Something in the spirit of passage, perhaps leaving behind the protocols of Cairo, relaxed Sir Cedric's prohibition on German wine. Studying the wine list in the dining car, feeling the need of familiar habit, he ordered the Moselle. The evening train to Alexandria was as near in style to the Orient Express as was possible in wartime Egypt. The dinner menu had seven courses, enough to last the entire journey—which, in darkness, was dull enough.

The train had reached the halfway point, and Sir Cedric the *caneton pressé*, when the heavens fell in. Everything in the dining car that was not anchored was convulsed. Simultaneously the lights went out. Sir Cedric, without knowing how, ended up under the table with his legs pinned by a seat half-torn from its moorings. Shattered glass, hot liquids, food, china, and furniture went surging past him and crashed against the opposite wall, where other bodies were. The train began braking; Sir Cedric was conscious enough to realize that this ruled out a collision. The braking worked against the first impact: All the debris took off again. This time a heavy silver tureen narrowly missed Sir Cedric's head and came to rest between him and the buckled bulkhead behind his seat. In the imbecilic clarity of such moments, he had time to observe that the tureen carried the crest of a European royal house—a house already liquidated in the realignments of the war.

The train stopped and for a few seconds there was only the stillness of the delta night. In that interval Sir Cedric detected a pungent, acrid smoke. As voices recovered themselves, he knew the fire was spreading and he could already feel its heat at his back. To release his legs, he had to double up under the table and push away the skewed seat. This took several seconds and all the strength he had. Even before he got on his knees into the aisle, the heat behind him was borne on a mist of sparks and cinders.

Sir Cedric did not remember what followed (later the military doctor said he had suffered a mild concussion in the first fall) until he was out of the train, staggering down a shallow embankment, and coming to rest, face up, in bulrushes. Of those in the dining car at the time, he was the lightest casualty. Six passengers and five staff were consumed in the resulting inferno; eight more passengers and the kitchen staff got out with burns, lung damage, and broken limbs. Accounts of the accident were put through the hands of the military censors. They quickly announced that it had been caused by an explosion in the gas oven of the kitchen car. The surviving kitchen staff were incarcerated, tried in camera by a military court, and not seen again for some years. Within hours of the "accident," Sir Cedric, by then resting in a military hospital in Alexandria, was told that the valise he had left in his compartment had contained an "infernal device."

It was a serious breach of security. The assassination of public officials was familiar enough in Cairo, but the nearly successful assassination of such a clandestine figure as Sir Cedric warned of a different quality of adversary. Sir Cedric was composed enough, when Kippax saw him the next morning, to point out that political assassination—indeed, the very word "assassination"—

was an eleventh-century Oriental innovation, devised to strike down even the most apparently secure vizier. "There is really no defense against a well-informed assassin," Sir Cedric told Kippax, "information being as important as conviction." He assured himself that Kippax had grasped the point. "It is not the first time for me, of course. Twice before, in fact: once in Kandy—the charms of Ceylon do lull one's senses so—at the hands of an inept Portuguese with no apparent affiliation; and once, believe it or not, in Caerphilly, a very methodical advocate of Welsh independence who, alas, blew himself up. The Prince of Wales was most upset—on my behalf, of course." Sir Cedric's black exhilaration was in his eyes. "With two such escapes, one learns to value life; with three one acquires a certain *aura*—would you agree?"

In the circumstances, Kippax did.

And in a different tone, Sir Cedric said, "Have you any idea who?"

"Not yet."

Finding the answer was made more difficult by the location of the offense; it came in the territory administered not from Cairo, but from Alexandria. A cumbrous machine claimed rights, the army's field security. They knew nothing of Kippax's shadowy world. They went by what they called "the book." Very soon their approach was driving Kippax to despair. Their mentality found its quintessence in Major "Bull" Lindquist. It wasn't that Lindquist was a fool, more that he was a type. He had been decently educated, but within a narrow tradition: a minor public school, Sandhurst Military Academy. Since then, he had pursued miscreants in Africa, India, and Mesopotamia. Egypt was too complicated for Lindquist, Kippax soon saw. Lindquist had gray hair cropped to the stiffness of toothbrush bristles and gray brows that knitted in the perplexity of Egypt's treacheries. The problem was that instead of being deterred by his incomprehension, he was made more certain by it. He put this succinctly to Kippax, after detecting toward the end of their first conversation that Kippax appeared to be a victim of hesitation. He said, "You have doubts? Show me a doubt and I'll show you wasted time. We round up all the likely chappies. We know where they are. These people soon rat on each other. It doesn't take much to make that happen, I can tell you—not like those devious Hindu wallahs."

Kippax left Lindquist making what he called his "sweep."

Kippax felt he should be in Cairo, because it was in Cairo that the train had originated, and Kippax was beginning to recall with disturbing suspicions the inept comic dance around Sir Cedric's cabin trunks before they left. He tried to retrieve every face in that scene, their exact dispositions. While Lindquist was "sweeping" the alleys of Alexandria, Port Said, and Cairo, Kippax went in search of the Turkish assistant manager who had supervised Sir Cedric's departure.

When frustrated, Dr. Ibrahim Ghazi acquired a contained rage, like a cat cheated of a bird by only the length of a claw. He was reclining on the ottoman in Esther Mosseri's office. It was early on the morning after the abortive assassination. Ghazi kept the window shaded. He said, "It was the one thing nobody thought to check." He wanted to dampen Esther's misplaced sense of comedy—to make it clear that a ludicrous mistake must not encourage open derision among their accomplices. He tried to silence her with a terminal stare.

She was not so easily cowed. Her sense of farce was too much a part of her mind. Once again she failed to keep a straight face. "Nobody thought to check!" she repeated, already surrendering to a giggle. "There is a kind of poetic justice in it," she continued, not managing at all to be grave, "you must see that. Here we are, making a demonstration of our cultural assurance, that we can kill as efficiently as the British can, and what happens? The bomb goes off at the wrong time because it was set by the *Islamic* clock and not the *English* one! So much for training people in Constantinople!" Only when her final laughter tapered off did she really understand the malignity of his pique.

"Perhaps, if you have recovered, we can consider the consequences."

"Consequences?"

"It will not be long—only a matter of hours—before the British react. It will be dangerous, dangerous for everybody."

"Surely they won't find out?"

"Oh, but they will—they will find out. As a matter of fact, it is essential that they do."

"What do you mean?"

"I'm surprised that I have to explain that, after your last acquaintance with an assassin—another *unsuccessful* assassin."

All trace of her frivolity had gone; she was chilled by her comprehension.

"It will fall to you, of course, to ensure that they do get the right man."

"May I ask how you came by this information?" Kippax was at his most languidly curious. He was enjoying the insubordinate pleasure of sitting in Hogarth's own chair, having selected his office for this impromptu midnight assignation.

Esther Mosseri sat, less relaxed, in a chair at one corner of the desk. "I have old friends at the university. I cannot give their names, you must understand. But they can be trusted. These people, they realize how much damage is done by such things, how the whole Arab cause can be discredited by a few fanatics."

"The whole *Arab* cause?"

"They value the way Britain is supporting the sharif of Mecca in his revolt against the Turks; they see that if Arabs are to prove themselves as reliable allies, they must not give nationalism a bad name . . . that working with Britain is the best policy."

"For a Jew, you seem to have a profound insight into the workings of the Arab mind."

"In Egypt we have always lived easily with the Arabs. And there are Christian Arabs too."

"Yes—that is what puzzles me slightly." Kippax did not like the feeling that he was dealing with a mind as agile as his own. "You say that this man was sent here by an organization called al-Fatat?"

She nodded.

"You see, they are thought to be long extinct. There were Christian *and* Muslim Arabs in that outfit, most of them educated in France. There were other branches with other names; they seem never to agree for very long. At any rate, they were essentially Syrian. And the Turks, with their usual thoroughness, soon rooted them out. As I understood it, al-Fatat had gone the way of all martyrs, nothing but a chest-beating memory. So *why* should they surface here, and even more puzzling, why should they go for such an inconsequential person as Sir Cedric? After all, he's just a bureaucrat, with little interest in this part of the world, and he has certainly never heard of al-Fatat."

In the nocturnal vacuum of the office, the two of them were in a strange affinity, as though only at night did they really harness all their facilities—a kind of animal life that enhanced what otherwise passed for their daylight lives. The office, the hour, their handling of themselves—all gave off the atmosphere of a natural habitat shared between them for the first time. Each by now sensed it, but neither was able to confess it. They were bats from different lairs, not sure whether they were compatible or inimical.

She particularly admired his dismissal of Sir Cedric's power; it was done with the kind of easy conviction that only the British managed when they were lying. "Inconsequential" was so outrageous an adjective, and yet shamelessly used. She tried not to smile, and said, matching the game, "There are always mutations. Sometimes they don't even know where the name comes from."

"But why Sir Cedric?"

"I cannot answer that," she said without any nuance. "I am sure you will be able to find out, eventually. If you catch this man."

"Tag el Din—you say he's being sheltered there?"

"That is what they said."

"Anything more?"

This time she did smile. "Isn't that enough?"

"The name is almost certainly false."

"I imagine so."

"Well . . ." He reluctantly extricated himself from the chair, knocking a knee against the desk. "When first I asked for your help—we must have another of those musical afternoons—I must confess I didn't realize that you would show such *aptitude*. We are all, I fear, amateurs in a world infested with these deranged and hopeless causes, but one can never underestimate the consequences of a bomb. After all, think of Sarajevo. One well-aimed bomb, and we have the war to end all wars. It was right of you to come. And I am glad you came to *me*. It is the kind of thing that should not be left to the locals—or for that matter, to the uniformed people. If what you say is right, it definitely falls into the political sphere, and one must be able to tread delicately there."

Each bat then went its way, to the dark, mossy places where other bats congregate.

Tag el Din Street was in one of the more modern areas of southern Cairo, not an ideal place for refuge since it lacked the labyrinthine escape routes of older districts. It would have been too melodramatic to describe the operation that Kippax planned as a "raid." And too clumsy. Although not wanting to lose the prize, he took his time. A network of informers was tapped in

247

such a way as to imply an unfocused, routine inquiry: Had anyone lately arrived as a refugee from the tyranny of Constantinople? Was there a place where such people knew they could find sympathy? Might it be possible that such people were working as Turkish agents? As always, the catch offered up more than the net wanted, and a number of small fish were let slip through its trawl until, heavy with the appropriate smell, the big one seemed to be there, and not even wary enough to feel the net closing about it. The name—as Kippax expected—did not tally with Esther Mosseri's account, but other circumstantial details did. Kippax's most exacting concern was not to disturb the now accepted fiction of the exploding oven. ''Bull'' Lindquist had come near to doing just that with his abortive but noisy ''sweeps'' and Kippax had had to pull devious wires to have him stopped. It would be galling, therefore, to do something himself now that would draw renewed interest to what was already fading as a topic of conversation.

Kippax used two men—an intelligence corporal trained in Ireland and highly recommended, and a Levantine Cypriot whom Kippax had used, very selectively, before. They waited until three in the morning, having established that their quarry was sleeping alone on the roof, and spirited him off without arousing so much as a dog. An hour later, Ali Hassan (Kippax never knew his real name, or cared) was safely below street level.

Even without the use to which Kippax adapted it, there was a nauseating flavor to the cavern, or more precisely, series of caverns. They were impregnated with a stale vegetable smell; olive oil had once been pressed here on a contraption worked by camels. The camels were harnessed to an arm fixed to a huge grinding stone and they walked, in almost total darkness, around the circular base of the press until they expired from the effort. More efficient (and enlightened) machinery was now crushing olives.

Ali Hassan was no more than twenty, deceptively soft in appearance, with placid, girlish blue eyes. He was stripped and tied down by pegs to a shallow stone trough, part of the runoff from the press. A single oil lantern was suspended from the vaulted roof, not centrally over the trough but to one side, giving Hassan no clear view of his torturers. Kippax stood well behind this light, the detached interrogatory voice, speaking in a classic Arabic. The Levantine Cypriot, called no more than Constantine, was, once Hassan had been staked down, given the redundant task of keeping watch. The specialist was the corporal trained in Ireland, whose name had a certain grim aptness: it was Quail. Quail had a small and very assiduously waxed Gladstone bag made of the finest pigskin by a merchant in Piccadilly. This bag contained Quail's instruments, which he used as selectively as a surgeon might a special set of steels. Quail applied his skills to only three parts of Hassan's body—an ear, one set of fingers, and his genitals. Quail's finesse was a revelation to Kippax, whose experience in India had, by comparison, been in the medieval phase of the art. Ireland, it seemed, called for a far subtler artistry; Kippax had said that, as far as possible, the body should be unmarked, and Quail very nearly obliged.

But Ali Hassan was not an easy man to break. He gave Kippax a new understanding of how close the borderline can be between life and death, and—this was a private interest of Kippax's—how narrow was the line between pleasure and pain.

"It's a pity," said Quail in his fastidious, clucking way, "that we don't have more time. Given a few days, I might be able to prove a few theories of mine about endurance." He looked down on Hassan with something like admiration, and sighed.

"I can't treat it like an experiment," said Kippax testily. "It's quite simple. All I want to know is if he did it, why he did it, and with whom he did it. Your overture has confirmed the first, though I would remind you that it *is* important that he can still hear what I'm asking him."

Quail was confident. "Oh, that's nothing, sir. The loss of one eardrum leaves his hearing almost unimpaired, as far as this side is concerned."

Quail was less confident two hours later. His repertoire had been fully deployed, but Kippax's voice was losing its coolness. He had worked to a preconceived plan, trying to score the interrogation like a piece of music—allegro, andante, presto—relying on Quail to find the appropriate instruments. He was now, in desperation, trying an interlude.

But Hassan, still able to recite with daunting coherence, did so into the darkness: "We have come to know that the world and everything therein is not worth in comparison with Truth the wing of a mosquito."

Quail looked at Kippax with all the impatience of the mind closed to metaphysics.

"Those are wise words," said Kippax, still in the classic

Arabic, but with an edge. Then he nodded to Quail. "Step it up a bit," he said in English.

Even Hassan's scream retained an eloquence. When it subsided and Quail withdrew, Hassan somehow mustered more strength, enough to say, "We will indoctrinate our children with a hatred that is sacred."

"I realize you are Mohammed's apostle, and that those who follow him are ruthless believers. It seems a pity, since we both value the Truth so highly, that we cannot share it. You are earning your place in paradise alongside the dark-eyed houris, but by then you will be able to give them very little pleasure." Kippax nodded again to Quail.

This time the scream was indelibly carnal. Quail had gone further than Kippax intended. They both began to doubt whether Hassan would be able to speak again; the limestone channel of the trough to which he was strapped was discolored with excrement and blood. Quail moved back into the shadows with Kippax and said, "I'm sorry about that."

"No matter," said Kippax, wanting respite.

But Hassan's head moved in a blindly searching way, trying still to pick them out. Then he said to Kippax, "Whose people are you of? What devil wrote your Book?"

Kippax's resentment became tempered by a disturbing respect. "What devil plotted your downfall?"

Hassan's face cracked into a form of triumph. He cried, "Allah is the supreme plotter." And then, as he died, he mumbled in a spasm of delirium, "The dark-eyed houri knows the Truth."

Constantine came from the shadows and flicked cigarette ash on the broken body. "They don't have no sense," he said. Kippax was too self-absorbed to answer. An essence very like bile surged in his throat and soured his mouth. But his only outward emotion was dissatisfaction over the prize that had slipped through his hands. It was more than frustration; it was a feeling of being present at the beginning of something, rather than its end. The still-warm corpse was mocking him.

Hogarth, to whom Kippax's nether world was an unglimpsed and unsuspected warp of duty, was able to see only a starkly formal secret report that listed Ali Hassan as having been killed "while resisting arrest." He pressed Kippax for more, and within the bounds of discretion Kippax was casually obliging. He even confided who his most useful informant had been.

This perplexed Hogarth in the way that his classical mind would fasten on to inconsistency; he stroked his goatee and drawled out the problem: "I confess to having some qualms when a Jew comes to us claiming to be acting in the interests of Arabs."

"You mean, in view of the consequences?"

"Precisely. That the consequences were that an Arab should be hunted down. Yes—one is reluctant to take it as an entirely disinterested act."

Kippax smiled. "The Jews are positively rushing at us with support these days."

"Yes, and getting some very high-level encouragement, from what I hear."

"Lloyd George?"

"Oh, not only the prime minister. Half the cabinet, so I'm told." The hand at the beard reverted to an earlier speculation. He looked again at the official report, not lifting his eyes when he spoke. "This girl Mosseri. Interesting background; the best kind of Jew, I should have thought. Perhaps we shouldn't read too much into it." His voice then took on a finer discretion. "Young Bron is really a *very* steady type, you know. Seems quite above those emotional factions; very useful to have with us in the circumstances."

"Yes," said Kippax. "It's a matter of background."

That morning Kippax drove from Cairo to Port Said, where a recuperated Sir Cedric was boarding a P & O steamship for London. Unlike many of his contemporaries, Kippax had no love for Port Said; it had become a caricature of Arabian voluptuousness, trading its obscene postcards to every passing troopship.

Greeting Kippax, Sir Cedric held the handshake a little longer than Kippax expected. They stood at the rail of the promenade deck in brown shade, gazing south along the first straight cut of the canal through the marshes. Anyone observing them from a distance, the older corpulent man and the younger willowy man with one foot oddly placed at the rail, would have taken them as perhaps uncle and nephew.

"It's a pity, Owen, that our man was not more forthcoming."

"A typical fanatic, I fear."

"Not so typical that he earned his martyrdom, fortunately." Sir Cedric's right hand fell on Kippax's left shoulder. "No matter, the affair is closed."

Three great storks went flapping down the canal, a few feet

above the inert water, keeping to the man-made line as though embraced by it, finally swallowed in its converging perspective. Both men watched in silence, externally focused on the birds but internally weighing the mutual junction in their lives.

Then Kippax said, "In the end, I found I had to respect Hassan—or whatever his name really was. So much for the idea that these people always break easily."

"Did you . . . *did* you?" Sir Cedric looked at Kippax with slightly raised brows. "Yes. I imagine there was quite a lot of pain." He brooded further and then, discarding the gruesome subject with a rub of the palms, he said, "And Hogarth—he has no inkling of what really happened?"

"None. He was a little bothered, though, about the paradox of a Jew claiming to speak for Arabs, the Mosseri girl."

"Yes—Hogarth would pick *that* up."

"Hogarth is saying that Lloyd George has fallen under the spell of the Jews."

"That, I fear, is the case. I, too, have seen the faces of Zion—or at least, one of its faces."

"How far will they get?"

"I don't know. Fortunately, some of the most influential London Jews are anti-Zionist—Edwin Montagu, for example—and that helps in cabinet." Sir Cedric secured his panama more firmly on his brow as he looked over the rail into the water. "The Jews worry me almost more than anything. Their international influence is insidious. They already have more power—anonymous, selective power—than most people understand. American Presidents are hostage to them; European money is largely in their hands, and of course, they will have the German purse in their pockets after the war. They have all the coercive power of the international merchant banks."

"Yes. No one is quite so *holy* with his money as the Jew. It's their holy ambitions that one sees surfacing now."

"Quite." Sir Cedric waved a hand toward the canal. "They will not fail to remind us that, but for Jewish money, the canal would not have been built. Disraeli found Rothschild money when the treasury could not."

"Disraeli had the right personal credentials."

"My point exactly. They've had their finger in things ever since. Frankly, though, I cannot think what they would gain by formalizing their power, in a Jewish state, when they can manage so much more by stealth. The clever Jews see that, of course. That's why they so dislike this man Weizmann. He's the one who seems able to mesmerize Lloyd George.''

''A Jewish state? It could come to that?''

''It had better not. Such a thing would unbalance the regional alignments fatally. Not to mention its effect on our desert kings.''

''It would be disastrous.''

Sir Cedric nodded to a distant horizon. ''No. We simply cannot have it.''

# 14

## *Zichron Jaacov* ✳ *June 1917*

Abu Farid, one of Sarah Aaronsohn's remaining Arab staff, was the first to see the black carriage with cracked mica windows turn into the drive. He realized the ominous novelty of its arrival and ran into the house to find Sarah—but met, instead, Koblensky.

"Mister Asa—" Abu Farid's explanation got no further than a hand wavering at the figure climbing down from the carriage, tilting it like a casket in the hands of feeble pallbearers. Rabbi Dor remained, among a steadily wasting people, one of the bulkiest figures in Zichron Jaacov. His black silk robe girdled him with authority, his waxen face under the beaver *streimel* was already hostile. It was the first time this severely Orthodox figure had crossed the Aaronsohns' threshold.

"You fetch Miss Sarah," said Koblensky, and waited for the rabbi to reach him in the hall.

The rabbi immediately recognized in Koblensky a figure beyond his flock. "I wish to see Miss Aaronsohn."

Without a word, Koblensky led him to the parlor. As he was returning, Feinberg appeared in the hall. Koblensky said, "We cannot leave her with him—we must all three go in there." He heard Sarah coming. "You know what has brought him here."

As it happened, Sarah was in austere black with a high collar and, with her gauntness, looked more reverential than she felt. She went into the parlor flanked by Koblensky and Feinberg, paused to make a perfunctory bow, and said, "I welcome you to my house."

The rabbi looked from her to the men, and glowered.

"I would like Mr. Feinberg and Mr. Koblensky to be present."

"Of course," said the rabbi sonorously. "It is your house and I think they should hear what I have to say."

Koblensky moved a chair to complete a semicircle facing the

rabbi; the rabbi had triggered old memories of other encounters with the Agudath Yisrael, of silks and piety and incense and disdain. The rabbi waited for their combined attention.

"You will know," he began, "that our people are being driven from Tel Aviv and Jaffa, expelled. You will know our situation is desperate everywhere. There is even the disgrace"—he raised his palms in pious despair—"that Jewish girls are giving themselves to Turks in order to survive."

There was another house-deep silence. His voice then rose slightly: "It should not be necessary to tell you these things, because I am sure that there is little that happens in Palestine that does not come to your notice." He seemed to want a response, but all three of his audience were impassive.

"Very well, then. I am not here in only a religious capacity. I realize that would be futile. I represent all opinion, all sections, and the collective feeling. We of Agudath Yisrael have never wanted anything other than to be left in peace to follow our beliefs. But those who are less pious than ourselves also want to be left in peace. We do not want to provoke the Turks into expelling us. And yet this is very possibly going to be our fate. So far, we have convinced them of our absolute neutrality. For some time, Jemal has directed his man Hassan Bey to ensure security in this district, and for that time we have persuaded Hassan Bey—only, I must say, because of the position Meyer Malik enjoys—we have persuaded him of our integrity. *Our integrity*—as a town, and as a people."

Again he paused, and again there was no response. He ran his tongue along his lower lip in a gesture that could have expressed either impatience or puzzlement. "However, there are rumors. There are suspicions pointing to this house, suspicions of activities that would jeopardize us all. I am not here to question it. I am here to say, on behalf of Zichron, that whatever it is you do, it must stop. We cannot protect you, because you threaten all of us. I will not make a judgment on why it is you do what you do. These are things I do not have any interest in. It must stop."

The last sentence was pronounced without any emphasis, with a flat finality.

To Koblensky the black figure was from a gallery of his past and so much familiar, in every minatory breath, that he was inviolate. Koblensky could not strike out at the man, either in word or in action, because the rabbi came from the core of the racial being that bound them all and consigned them to an unbearable affinity. Koblensky feared this impotence as no other because he—alone among the four of them—he knew and had seen how great the cruelty of the weak could be, and would yet be.

Feinberg was the first to answer, after another sepulchral silence. With the composure of the dispirited, he said, "Those with us have chosen to be with us. We ask nothing of anyone else."

The rabbi was implacably still.

Sarah, with a spark of reproach, said, "We brought you medicine. People would have died without it."

The rabbi said, "We do not want your medicine; your medicine will kill us all."

At this, Feinberg became less composed. "And you believe the Turks will *not?*"

The rabbi rose slowly, the folds of the silk too elaborate to show the mechanics of his rising, so he seemed to float from the chair and went past them like a heavy cloud, still gathering intensity. Only at the door did he pause, and then—half in the house and half out of it, half in shadow and half in stark sunlight—he turned and looked across the hall to them and said, "Expect no pity."

Why were they chastened rather than outraged? Each was struck by the thought at the same time; Sarah voiced it first. Turning back into the parlor, she said, "They are frightened. I've seen that in them for months. And so they are angry."

Feinberg, more splenetic now, said, "He disgusts me! What have they ever done, his people? Nothing! Nothing but live off the money sent from Russia and Poland. And make trouble about how butchers slaughter the cows! Well, they won't be so fussy about how the Turks slaughter us."

This grim joke got no endorsement. Koblensky said, "You know why the people are being herded out of Tel Aviv and Jaffa? They do not want any Jews near the front line. They know Allenby is coming and they think they know *where.*"

"The rabbi dares to talk of integrity," said Feinberg. "You know where the headquarters of Agudath Yisrael is? Germany. That's where their integrity comes from!"

"We must not give up, not now," said Koblensky.

The three of them fell silent, until Sarah, as grave as Koblensky had ever seen her, said, "No, we cannot give up; not *now*. We cannot let this moment pass. We have too much to trust to the pigeons. We know there are only thirty-five thousand Turks in the line, and Allenby must be told. What is the point of everything we have already done if we do not complete our work? Allenby will come.''

"We must get through the lines ourselves," said Koblensky.

"Ourselves?" Feinberg looked from Sarah to Koblensky.

"With the help of your Arabs."

Sarah nodded. "It is the only way now."

"But you . . .?" said Feinberg quietly. "It means we must leave you here."

"Yes."

"You will be in great danger," said Koblensky.

"And you?" she said firmly. "And you will not?"

Koblensky and Feinberg had grown perceptibly closer as a result of their journey to the Yarmuk, and at this instant they knew the resolution in Sarah was as ineluctable as their own. The rabbi had rendered them indivisible. There was precious little valor around them; the columns of dispossessed Jews straggled through the country but got scant sympathy. As Koblensky planned with Feinberg the route south, their staging posts were put in the care of Arabs. Arabs! Remembering Lawrence, Koblensky agonized that it was the Arabs who were killing Turks, while Jews accepted humiliation.

For greater safety, the planning was done at Athlit. Poring over the map, they agreed that they could leave within forty-eight hours. Then Abba Laski appeared. Laski had been of only intermittent help to the NILI. Military organization was, for him, uncomfortably close to the ladder of family authority, which he hated. Koblensky knew that Laski's worth was as a hired gun, and this was how he had been used. This time he came unsummoned, and alarmed.

Koblensky took him into Aaronsohn's old laboratory, to keep the map out of sight, but Laski had guessed that a trip was being planned. There were too many signs of preparation, from the horses outside to Koblensky's far too guileless manner.

"What is it?" said Koblensky.

"I heard about Rabbi Dor."

"Well . . ." Koblensky shrugged. "We live with it."

Like the rabbi, Laski seemed not to have withered on the vine; he was still nearly as wide as tall. The strange voice was penetrating. "I hope you do . . . live. I hope you know how many are against you."

"We know."

"I don't think so." Laski took a chair from under a basin and squatted on it. "What you don't know is why I came. You don't know about my old colleagues in Ha Shomer." In a patently Napoleonic gesture, he leaned against the basin and pushed one porcine hand between the buttons of his shirt so that it embraced his left breast. In his eyes was something Koblensky had not seen before, affiliation. He said, "Ha Shomer has changed, changed with Russia. The revolutionary spirit. The difference between theory and practice." He grunted, as though chastising himself. "I did not see it would happen like this, not here. But it has. Anyway, Ha Shomer has changed. They feel the same about you as Rabbi Dor does. Their reasons, of course, are different."

"What do you mean?"

"You are the agents of imperialists, lackeys of the oppressor."

"That is crazy!"

"Dear fellow, you are Russian; the language must be familiar to you."

For the second time in their association the word "fellow" seemed at odds with its user, but Koblensky was too provoked to notice. "What are they going to do?"

"At the moment, it is Lishansky they most object to. You know how it is with him—too much mouth, too little brain."

"He is reckless."

"Well, . . ." Laski stopped and withdrew the hand from the shirt, looking about the laboratory, one end of which was an arched Victorian hothouse for the development of Aaronsohn's exotic plants. "You know the saying: People who live in glass houses . . ." He smiled thinly. "We all came here with dreams. What else do people come here for? I have mine, you have yours—even Rabbi Dor has his. And now the Ha Shomer have theirs. You are going away somewhere?"

Koblensky saw no point in deceiving him. He nodded.

"It must be very important." Laski hoped for more enlightenment, but saw that none was coming. "It will not be a good time to be away from Zichron. You are worried about Miss Sarah?"

Koblensky nodded again, annoyed that everything was so transparent to Laski.

"You should be . . . you *should* be worried." He got up from the chair, which was on casters, and kicked it with a boot so that it went careening across the linoleum between two benches on which stood racks of test tubes. The chair bounced from the pedestal of a bench and the glass rattled like the bells on a distant flock of sheep. "You should be very worried. She is what they hate most in Zichron—a proud woman. So you see, I came here to say, dear fellow, that I will do anything I can: I will keep watch over her. She need not even know about it. But I will do it, because she is a very brave woman, and because you are doing what must be done, and because things have changed in Ha Shomer."

"And Lishansky?" said Koblensky.

"I don't worry about Lishansky," said Laski.

Outside, Koblensky said, "It is good you will be here." He waited for Laski to remount his horse. "I don't know how long this will take. A month; maybe longer."

More equably, Laski said, "I understand . . . but I hope the English are really coming, this time." He rode off, leaving Koblensky with the feeling of not having been forthcoming enough with him. Like them, Laski seemed aware of picking his way across swiftly shifting sand. Telling Feinberg about it afterward, Koblensky said, "I think, for the first time, I really trust him."

"I hope you are right," said Feinberg, and then, having heard his own cynicism, said, "We have no choice anyway."

There were to be no more of the trials with donkeys; they had to cover too much ground too fast. With some trouble, they had picked out two small white Arabian horses from a Bedouin source of Feinberg's. Horses in any condition were scarce, and to find two that had been well littered when most horses were as ill fed as the people was a minor miracle, though Koblensky worried that it might be too conspicuous a miracle. This was one reason for keeping away from large towns and for riding tracks known better to Arabs than to anyone else. They would ride as Arabs, Feinberg the spokesman.

They were traveling as light as possible, and with no incriminating papers: All the intelligence was committed to memory. They waited for darkness to ride from Athlit to Zichron, to see Sarah again before going south. There were few lights in the house now; one came from her father's room upstairs, another from the kitchen, and one more from the hall. Over the months, the house, like the land around it, seemed to have become threadbare. Feinberg remembered it from before the war as the liveliest house in Zichron, echoing not just with the normal family clamor but with the good-natured competitiveness of

Aaron and his brother. Sarah, then, had been overshadowed. Now it was only her spirit that kindled any life at all in the house, and both men, without even voicing it, knew that once they had gone that spirit would be a very precious, vulnerable flame. She met them unemotionally, making them sit down in the kitchen to eat potato soup. She stood over the table with all her concern for them and none for herself. The plain benefaction of the kitchen and her face in an unsteady light from the stove lulled their nerves and provided a deceptive security; in all their lives, kitchens had been the earliest and most easily gained refuge from the outer world, and their contentment now, albeit fleeting, had that same childish quality.

"I don't want Aaron to worry," she said, taking the plates and knowing the spell was about to break. "I don't want him to worry about me. Don't tell him about Rabbi Dor. *That* will make him worry. He has too much to do, things that can only be done by him."

Feinberg got up and wanted to say something, but was inhibited by Koblensky's presence; then he reasoned that it was probably better left unsaid.

Koblensky, too, got up. "If we are going to be south of Nablus by dawn, we must go now."

Sarah looked at him strangely, as though in relief. Feinberg said, with a forced humor, "We will never make an Arab of Asa. He always worries about time." Sarah pressed down her apron as though completing a normal domestic routine. Then her right hand, still pink from the heat of the stove, went to her forehead to press back hair that was already pulled tight to a bun at the back. Her eyebrows rose in another effort to simulate the kind of supervisory maturity with which she was trying to control herself. She said, still firm in voice, "It is right to worry about time, with so far to go." The eyebrows had risen in a bias, with the left eye slightly more widely open than the right. There was the most fugitive of twitches at the corner of the left eye, but both men saw it. She turned away to the door, and—by design—gave them no further chance to see her face in a clear light. As they left, she stood on the steps, expressive only in outline—an outline of stoically collected feeling—assigning its hope to them.

The night ride got them to their first haven without incident; they remained all day in a small house and here Feinberg took little sleep. Feinberg's mood became disconcertingly lighthearted, almost frivolous. He played checkers with the Arab who was his NILI contact, and when Koblensky woke later in the afternoon, he could hear Feinberg's easy laughter among a larger group of Arabs. Feinberg's dialect was indistinguishable from the others'; it was only in his laughter that his normal tone reasserted itself. He was joking in Arabic and laughing in Hebrew.

On the third night they were forced to follow a zigzag course in the foothills west of Jerusalem and then, more exposed on the coastal plain, they stopped to get a bearing. Feinberg watched Koblensky check the compass with his map, and show other aspects of his military lore as he picked out the distant lights of a station on the coastal railroad. There was an instinct for the systematic in Koblensky that Feinberg knew he would never have; watching it reminded him of Koblensky's consistent dependability. Feinberg said, "I could never read a map."

"We are very close to the lines. Those lights are the yards at Gaza."

"What should we do?"

"Not get any nearer. Find some cover, somewhere to keep the horses quiet. When it is light we can have a better look. Then it is up to you. And your Arab friends."

The note of reproof was clear enough. Feinberg didn't contest it. He went looking for a refuge, and found a shallow depression of uncultivated ground where a clump of bushes would offer just enough cover for the horses. As far as they could determine, there was no habitation nearby.

When they were pushing their blankets into a gap between the bushes and preparing to sleep, Feinberg said, "You don't understand the Arabs, do you?"

Koblensky grunted. "Do you mean, what they say?"

"No. How they think."

Koblensky laughed grimly. "I have not studied that—no."

Feinberg gathered the blanket around him. "The first thing to understand is what is common to all Arabs; and then, how many differences there are between them, not to generalize too much."

"I would not generalize about Jews. I ought to make the same allowance for Arabs?"

"If you can. What they have in common is the religion. That is supposed to hold them together. Whether it seems to or not, it does give them a state of mind in common." He was unsure of Koblensky's attention. They were both lying down, and Feinberg was looking up at a sky laced with stars. "I would like—I would like some reason for *elation*. There has been no elation for so long. I need that."

Koblensky laughed ambiguously. "Let's reach Cairo."

"The Arab is supposed to believe—it's what Mohammed promised—that there will be plenty of elation after death. They don't really believe that; they would rather have it now. There's one of their poems I like; it has that honesty. I'm trying to remember it. . . ." Not caring whether Koblensky was still listening or not, Feinberg began reciting, with the same slightly forced humor that had compelled him over the last two days:

> "Opulence, luxurious ease,
> With the lute's soft melodies—
> Such delights hath our brief span.
> Time is Change, Time's fool is Man,
> Wealth or want, great store or small,
> All is one since Death's are all."

He was thankful, at the end, that Koblensky could not see that his eyes were as moist as his voice was dry.

For an hour or so after dawn, the land around them remained concealed in a mist, at first a yellow-white vapor that came from the pores of the ground like breath and then a thickening whiteness that cut off the sun but absorbed its light as a sponge absorbs water—an alchemy converting light into an almost palpable entity, which enclosed them as they moved. There was a rare beauty in this sight that each man experienced in a different way. Sound was deadened and Feinberg felt suspended in an interval between dream and substance, while Koblensky was more aware of what this ethereal light did to Feinberg's features, making him more than ever the disconsolate mystic. But Feinberg was now needed for earthly skills: His linguistic impersonation had to supersede Koblensky's fieldcraft. Very little about Feinberg was consistent. Sarah had asked Koblensky to trust Feinberg, but trust was too simple a relationship; Koblensky knew he was caught, *fait accompli*, with a man who was unpredictable in a situation where too much else was unpredictable. It tipped the odds.

With the mist burning off, Feinberg decided to go off alone in search of Bedouin who might be gathering to cross the lines. The lines were visible now, no more than three miles to the south. Randomly placed mounds indicated artillery positions, a line of poles marked the field telegraph, nearer the coast were the crowns of a tent encampment. Feinberg went on foot in a northwesterly direction, where, he said, the most likely Bedouin route would be. By chance they had chosen an ideal refuge. The horses had adequate cover and yet the land around them was too derelict to attract attention. It also revealed, as Koblensky studied it more carefully, that dichotomy of textures familiar in Palestine: the discontinuity of two worlds, the barren and the cultivated. About a quarter of a mile away, the granular dun changed to a scoured green—scoured and wasted because the irrigation pipe that had brought life to it had been ripped up and the remnant of cultivation was only this strip of land, pressed into the desert like an indicting finger for half a mile or so north and south of the pipeline. The Turks had taken the pipes for their own use, and the desert lost no time reclaiming its territory.

As Koblensky waited, the wind picked up, and it carried intermittently to him the sounds of an army with its nerve ends in the jittery stage that always preceded an assault: desultory, probing gunfire; single vehicles moving between posts; faint voices carried by false bravado. These were sounds and a condition Koblensky knew well, and they were the same whether carried on a warm wind or a cold one. The Turkish lines were far more tangible than they had been when he had come this way before, on his first trek to Cairo; then there was no opponent in the Sinai, none of the linear concentration that comes with defense; instead, there had been a casual, negligent mood that made his passage easy. This time, beyond the staked-out ramparts, there was a force so far invisible but gathering its strength by the day. To get through these lines would need all the nerve, guile, and luck that could be summoned.

Feinberg did not return until late afternoon, and when he did he was again in the state of edgy euphoria that Koblensky most distrusted. A small Bedouin party, no more than a dozen camels and a score of men, was on a trail not far east of Gaza, already equipped with papers for the roadblock. They crossed the lines frequently to pastures in the Negeb, apparently in an area of concern to neither the Turks nor the British. Feinberg claimed to know this area, which he said was dotted with wells and had once tempted Jewish settlement, until it was judged as too vulnerable to marauders among the wilder Arabs in the hinterland. These Bedouin, with whom he had gained assent to travel in return for a few gold coins, were of a milder nature, engaged in coastal trading more than desert raiding. "We could have waited for days for such a chance," he said, as though daring Koblensky to question it. Koblensky agreed.

They waited until dusk and then intersected the migratory trail in open land north of Gaza. In half an hour the camels appeared, some carrying two men and others one, the latter also bearing nondescript cargo. Feinberg had told the Arabs that he would be traveling with a mentally retarded relative, a young man who was virtually incapable of coherent speech. This charade encouraged evil humor from the start. Feinberg effusively greeted the leader of the party, an aged and yellow-eyed man in a black cloak. The old man pointed to Koblensky and other men followed the hand and made a throaty, deriding chorus. Feinberg laughed and embraced the same tone. But Koblensky noticed that the old man's appraising eyes soon lost interest in him and moved to the nimble white Arabian he was riding.

For about three miles—Koblensky could not be sure of the distance—they adhered to the prescribed trail, flanked on each side by camps, artillery emplacements, and ineptly stored supplies. Then, once the military occupation seemed at an end, the caravan left the trail and went, with the confidence of familiarity, diagonally to the east-southeast, into the desert. Leaving the trail they also left a rancid, pervasive smell that Koblensky knew must be of congested latrines and, probably, of contaminated water, a sign of military disorder that Koblensky added to his intelligence. The Arabs kept the camels running at a pace that surprised Koblensky and kept it up for more than two hours. The night was reasonably clear, although there was no moon. There was no sign at all of a British presence. Shortly after midnight, the old man called a halt. The party dismounted and they sat in a semicircle to eat dates.

Feinberg now felt so secure that he began to play the part of a dervish, entertaining the Arabs with histrionic fables. Koblensky sat in the shadows, eating the dates in a watchful, vaguely uneasy way. He became aware that Feinberg's spell had lost its power. The old man was interrogating him, and occasionally motioning to Koblensky. Feinberg was still animated, but his gestures were becoming strained. The old man's voice, until then characterized by a monotonous evenness, broke into a succession of high-pitched complaints, which in turn brought endorsement from his followers. Gradually the whole assembly was arguing and looking in Koblensky's direction and, beyond him, to the two horses.

Feinberg rose, gathering his robes around him in a defensive way, and walked over to Koblensky ahead of the others. Feigning a kind of Arabic doggerel, he muttered in the few seconds available, "They want the horses. We might get away with one. We may have to." He then began cursing Koblensky in Arabic, kicking him off the ground. This brought the temporary distraction he wanted. The Bedouin cackled and pointed. Koblensky played along with this to occupy them while Feinberg got them nearer the tethered horses. Koblensky leered stupidly and dragged a foot to simulate an injury from Feinberg's smothered kick. He wished there were less light. More shadow would have masked Feinberg better, for he was—Koblensky saw—losing his nerve. Koblensky played the idiot with more obtuseness. He stumbled into the old man and, tongue wetting his drying lips, laughed obscenely. The old man faltered and another Arab grabbed at Koblensky, pulling him roughly out of the way. It was a fatal piece of theatrics. As Koblensky recoiled, his cloak fell open. Swinging loosely across his chest, between his chemise and the cloak, was the pendant Star of David, as salient in the mat gray light as if suddenly illuminated by a beacon.

The old man, regaining his balance, stopped speaking. The Arab who had pushed Koblensky pointed to the offensive symbol. All of them seemed to be frozen for a drawn-out pause. Then, simultaneously, they found voice again and closed like a phalanx.

Feinberg had untied one horse and was half on it. The horse was unnerved by the exploding rage of the Arabs and bucked, leaving Feinberg still unbalanced. He threw himself back over the horse and in the same movement kicked it into flight toward Koblensky, who was only a pace ahead of the Arabs. Koblensky knew he had only one chance. He was encumbered by the ungainly robe, but put all his strength into a cat leap, having to judge distance and timing instantly.

He had no clear recollection of that jump later; one second he was kicking off from the ground, the next he had his arms around Feinberg as the horse galloped away with the velocity of terror and no controlled direction. The horse went so fast that within seconds—or so it seemed—the pursuing clamor had faded into a sound like dogs disturbed in a distant village. In fact, the Arabs were not pursuing. They were already disputing ownership of the remaining horse, but neither Feinberg nor

Koblensky realized this. Their horse ran with undiminished frenzy across a flinted plain and headlong into a void. Feinberg bent forward with the movement of flight, head aligned with mane. Koblensky kept grip and balance by putting his weight onto Feinberg's back, not able to grip the horse's flanks with his thighs. Gradually the horse tired, still running in a willful, erratic course. This puzzled Koblensky; they were long out of reach of the Arabs. With the horse slowing to an aimless canter, Koblensky saw that it had not been under rein during the whole gallop. Slowly he withdrew his right arm from Feinberg's waist and reached down for the reins. His left arm then felt the full weight of Feinberg's body pitching forward and was unable to hold it. As the horse came to a standstill, Feinberg's trunk fell along its neck.

Koblensky slid gently down from the horse and then, with a sickening effort, got Feinberg to the ground and laid him out, face up. A knife had gone into his heart—so precisely and so fast that the only blood on his cloak was a small stain where the hilt had fused garments to flesh. In death, Feinberg's face still held surprise—and, Koblensky realized, a trace of elation.

The loss was acute. Hardened as he was to death, Koblensky had never lost anyone as close to him as Feinberg had become. He had barely grasped that Feinberg was that close to him; and now he perceived that not only Feinberg, but part of the tenuous new life he was constructing about himself, had gone. It was a crazy death—a caprice, an avoidable folly. The assailant who had thrown the knife would never know his luck. He remembered the Arabs shouting for the horse. Koblensky gazed at the featureless desert around him, which offered no target for his fury.

The only instrument he could use for digging was a small knife. The gravel was cleared easily enough, but it took him until nearly dawn to scoop out a shallow grave from the sandstone beneath. He used a tin canteen to level the bed of the grave. He moved nothing from the body, not even the handful of dates in a pocket of the robe. Absalom Feinberg, Sheikh Salim, would go to dust in this wilderness without nationality.

# 15

## *Sinai Peninsula ✳ June 1917*

The first English voice that Koblensky heard in the Sinai intercepted him as he came over the southern ridge of the Wadi el Azaria an hour after dawn. '' 'Ere, you bleedin' wog, you ain't no business bein' 'ere.'' The colloquial flavor was enriched by an Australian accent. Koblensky saw a titanic figure, knees virtually black between shorts and socks and a face almost as dark—a sergeant, about thirty paces in front of an overnight camp: two armored cars, one tent, and four other men, eating from cans.

Koblensky was near to exhaustion. After burying Feinberg he had tracked southwest and run right into this patrol. As he cantered up to the sergeant, he could smell heated bully beef. The Australians were readier to accept his story than he expected; within three hours he was at the British advance headquarters in the desert and by dusk he was in Cairo. But in one aspect this accelerated day had been dispiriting: From what he had seen in the Sinai, it was clear that Allenby was still weeks away from being ready to attack.

The army gave him a set of khakis, unmarked by rank or regiment. He had worn no uniform since his flight from Turkey, and the British bush jacket was cut for a more substantial body, but it suited his Spartan nature.

His accommodation was grander than before: a suite—bedroom, bathroom, and a narrow sitting room—with one window overlooking the Nile from the third floor. He was not impressed by it. It was one of those hotels so pervaded by one class, so completely inhabited by their set of values, that without effort it marked out any alien identity. And Koblensky was assuredly alien there, alien to the pastel shades of paint, the plaster cornices, the balanced disposition of the rugs, and—most immediately—

the distinctive mist of polished smells and sounds disseminated through the doors and walls.

The first delegate of his generous host to call on him was Michael Bron. Koblensky was standing at the window when the bell rang. He found Bron at the door, marginally plumper than he recalled, in full evening dress. For half a second Koblensky thought the maître d'hôtel was calling to check on his well-being.

"Well . . ." said Bron, picking up Koblensky's confusion. "I just got word that you had returned."

"Come in."

Bron beamed approval of the room, a transparent effort to cover their awkwardness. "I'm glad to see they've made you comfortable."

It was the one thing they had not done, but Koblensky forgave Bron his optimism. "Yes. I am not used to it."

Bron came to rest with his back to the window and put a finger between his starched wing collar and his neck; the shirt had not adapted to his recent indulgence. "They sent a message from GHQ that you were here. I was at dinner, but I thought I ought to come straightaway."

Koblensky saw that Bron was perhaps embarrassed by the sheen of his appearance, having had time now to see Koblensky's more haggard aspect.

"Actually, the message was from Allenby himself. You've attracted the old man's attention. He wants to see you in the morning." He hesitated, as though doubtful that Koblensky would by then be presentable. "Is that all right?"

"All right?"

"Would you rather rest up a bit first?"

Koblensky checked his first response by walking to the window. Quietly, as though addressing an obtuse child, he said, "A man died so that I could be here. Others may die *because* I am here. What time would the general like to see me?" The rage inside Koblensky hardly touched his words but nonetheless filled the room and assaulted its opulence: it was tangible enough for Bron to recoil from it.

"Yes—of course. I am sorry. I should have known." His voice failed the moment. "Seven-thirty. I'll pick you up at seven." Unable to recover the congeniality he desired, Bron tugged once more at his collar and let himself out. Before the door closed again, from somewhere in the heart of the building Koblensky heard the beat of a waltz.

*      *      *

Koblensky knew enough of armies to believe that competent leadership seldom expressed itself in acts of magnetic personality. It was the gift for impeccable and relentless routine that gave soldiers a faith in their generals, an assurance that they were not being led into a catastrophe by the predominance of vanity over sanity. Soldiers, Koblensky knew, had a predisposition to see the outcome of battle in the delivery of the wrong paperwork, and they were usually right. So, several minutes before he actually looked on the countenance of General Sir Edmund Allenby, Koblensky was assembling a mosaic of incidental detail—a voice over a telephone, a certain alacrity of eye, even the way a file lay on a desk—to judge the temperament of the commander in chief on whom the fate of Palestine depended. And when the judgment was fleshed out by the man, it harmonized: Allenby was tall, martial in stature, and lacking totally in luster.

Allenby signaled Koblensky to a chair, but came around from his desk and paced slowly across a threadbare Afghan rug, knuckles pressed into the small of his back. Given their privacy, Koblensky saw in this very slight tenseness of bearing the mark of some burden, perhaps the accumulation of years.

At first Allenby addressed the rug. "You people have taken great risks for us. When I came here, they overlooked to tell me. It was only yesterday, seeing the signal about your appearance, that I asked for the files." He came to a standstill and placed his hands on his hips. He looked directly at Koblensky. "This is an odd kind of show. We seem to make more progress with free lances than with whole divisions."

Koblensky knew that as Allenby spoke he was also coming to a judgment of character.

"I saw what Lawrence said about you. Do you think you'll be able to pull off that bridge between you?"

"I think so."

"He took Akaba—did you know?"

"Lawrence?"

"And that scoundrel Auda. They fell on the Turks from behind. So that gives us the Red Sea. At a bargain price." He was standing over Koblensky now. "I'm going to make my main thrust at Beersheba. But I want them to think that's a feint, that with our usual lack of imagination we're going for Gaza. The information you brought confirmed me in my intentions. What concerns me now is that they must be deceived. And if that

269

works, we shall need your help again. To join Lawrence if he can get to that bridge.''

"When will it come, the attack?''

Allenby looked steadily at Koblensky, not without calculation. Then, still silent, he walked around the desk and resumed his seat. With a quiet and decent earnestness, he said, "I wish I could move this ponderous beast more quickly. I was brought up as a cavalryman, in the days when it all seemed much simpler. However, so much is at stake here, and we have had setbacks before. To put it plainly, I am not ready. We are already greatly in the debt of your people, but there is nothing I can do for them now. We must pray that they can hold out.''

For a second or two there was a sympathy between the two men that bridged the gulf of age and background—at the least, a shared acquaintance with mortality as part of a professional calculation, at the most, a secrecy of spirit that was no part of any profession. And then it was gone.

"You'll help us, then?''

"Of course.''

"Good . . . *good man*.''

Only when he left Allenby did Koblensky discover that Aaron Aaronsohn had departed for London. Bron said, with a disinterested air, "He went in something of a hurry. I'm not clear why.''

"London?''

"He spent a lot of time communicating with people there, and New York. Then there was Jabotinsky. Several messages from him. He's a very *determined* kind of chap, Aaronsohn, isn't he?''

"So?''

"Rather got people's backs up here.''

Koblensky lapsed into a grim silence. They had reached Bron's office.

"Look here,'' said Bron briskly.''I expect you could use a good meal.'' He grinned. "At any rate, we would love to have you for dinner, Tessa and I. It's not much of an apartment, but you have to take what you can get. At any rate, how about next Monday? I'll see if Owen Kippax is free too.''

"Certainly.''

"Good. Tessa's dying to get to know you.'' He settled at his desk. "You're getting talked about, you know.''

At no time with Koblensky had Bron acted with naturalness. The verbal gaucherie, Koblensky was beginning to realize, was not a true reflection of Bron's intelligence; it was like the limp of a man with a cramp, a tension of some kind impairing his assurance. It was clear that Bron understood *what* Koblensky and Aaronsohn were doing, though apparently not *why*. It was an Olympian *why*, a cause as high as a mountain range to those who pursued it, but to Jews like Bron it was, if noticed at all, little more than a molehill, something they tripped over.

At first sight, Tessa Bron was what Koblensky expected: she seemed to be of the frivolous Cairo world. His prejudice rested on small things; grooming was one, and her hair, drawn tightly back from the tall forehead, the hairline impeccable, skin melting into the glistening roots of the hair, all producing the aura of her being pampered in an expensive salon. Very few women Koblensky had ever seen, and those only from afar, had that aura. He was from places where grooming was subordinate to survival.

Thus it was that Tessa unknowingly (she would have been mortified to know) sustained Koblensky's prejudice for at least another half hour; to the grooming he added her scent and the plain but handmade tailoring. He came in his khakis because they were still all he had, and this heightened his initial unease. Bron and Kippax were already there, formally informal: Bron in a cream linen suit and Kippax in gray flannels and white cotton jacket; both wore ties and both had brown brogues with uppers perforated for the tropics, buffed bright by their batmen.

The apartment was less modest than Bron had implied. It had an airy living room that, partitioned only by a beaded screen, opened into a shaded courtyard walled with vines and bougainvillea. It was more Mediterranean than Egyptian and Tessa had set dinner outside, where a mosaic-tiled patio was covered by an arch of vines. They were served drinks and then dinner by a mute Indian borrowed from the officers' mess.

In spite of himself, Koblensky felt gradually disarmed by the charm of the setting. He realized he needed to relax; why not here? At the same time he became aware of Tessa's earnest intelligence. She questioned him in a solicitous way, having already heard from Bron of his ordeal in the Sinai.

"So," said Kippax, "you saw Lawrence on the Yarmuk?" Koblensky nodded.

"Well," said Kippax, "Lawrence is a celebrity now, after

Akaba. He is no longer seen as a flea on the rump of the Ottoman bull. Akaba was the bite of something bigger—something to be noticed.''

"You don't like Lawrence?" said Tessa with a deadly mildness.

Kippax was not quick enough to avoid being sly. "I don't know why you should think that. . . ."

This was the beginning of Koblensky's perception of Tessa's true mind.

Bron said, "The old man is going to back Lawrence to the hilt. . . ." But then he, too, saw the astringency in Kippax's eye. "More whisky, Owen?"

"The thing about Lawrence," said Tessa, undeflected, "is that whether you like him or not, he wins. There hasn't been enough of that."

"At a price, at a *price,*" said Kippax, holding out his glass as the decanter gurgled. "I would hate to tell you how free Lawrence has been with the gold."

"Better British gold than British lives," said Tessa.

This further impressed Koblensky, and was the death of his prejudice—at least, as far as she was concerned. He thought she looked like a nun who had tentatively taken to fashion: the grooming, the toilet, and the beige poplin blouse, the brooch at her neck, were not sufficient to suppress the immanent gravity. It was she who was the sobering force here; the tartness in her handling of Kippax was the pounce of a frustrated intellect.

They began with a soup strange to him, even more strangely named—mulligatawny. Seeing his curiosity, she explained that it was one of the fruits of the collision between English and Indian cuisine, devised in a kitchen of the raj, bearing the tang of curry.

"Owen," she said, "served there, in India."

Kippax had a delicate care with soup, sucking shallow spoonfuls, and merely nodded confirmation.

"It has always surprised me," said Koblensky, "how the English, wherever they are, seem to be at home—making the soup to their taste."

For the first time Tessa laughed, an endorsing, genteel laugh, moving from Koblensky to Kippax. "Yes," she said. "Owen is a good example. He adapts *so* well."

Kippax smiled tolerantly. "One does, one does. . . ."

Then, with a suddenly gimlet eye, he said, "Our guest also seems to wear several cloaks with apparent ease—the Russian

soldier, the refugee, the farmer, the secret agent, the wandering
. . . Bedouin.''

It was Bron who, strangely, was more openly sensitive to the
averted epithet than Koblensky. He seemed to flush. He said,
''It's fortunate for us, I should have thought.''

''Of *course*,'' said Kippax, as though only then aware of an
ambiguity. ''Fortunate that he is on *our* side.''

Tessa had noticed the chain low on Koblensky's neck, but the
pendant was hidden under his uniform tunic. At first, and, she
realized, foolishly, she had thought of a crucifix. Now she said,
''Where *do* you think of as your home, Mr. Koblensky?''

''Palestine. Palestine is my home.''

''Everybody's Jerusalem,'' said Kippax.

''Well, it's going to be *our* Jerusalem before long,'' said
Bron.

''But is there, I wonder, room for all three deities there? What
do *you* think, Koblensky?'' said Kippax.

''The land has never been properly used. It can support many
more people.''

''Really . . .?'' Kippax drawled. Though not theological,
Koblensky's answer interested him more.

But Koblensky was to be drawn no further into this game. A
chastising memory had returned, of Sarah by the oven in the
feeble light, assigning her hope to him and Feinberg, summoning
the last reserves of her spirit, then the wordless shadow on the
steps. The rest of the dinner floated by him with a fragment of
his attention—until a barely perceptible vibration between Tessa
and Kippax intruded.

Pouring and passing the Turkish coffee, she said, ''I meant to
say, Owen, I didn't much take to your visiting fireman, Sir
Cedric.''

''Oh?''

''It's not just him, it's the *type*—the secular cardinals of this
world.''

''What *do* you mean?''

''I could explain better if I knew which catechism it is that he
follows. But perhaps you know that. He's certainly awesome,
though not in a way that I found reassuring.''

''How strangely you put it. He is what he seems, or at least
should seem—a pillar of the Foreign Office, no more, no less.''

''Well, that's not very helpful.'' She completed the distribution of the coffee. "You know, I thought there was something a bit fishy about that accident on his train."

At this, Bron said, "Fishy, darling? Nothing fishy at all. You've been listening too much to the Polo Club gossip. Isn't that so, Owen?"

"Of course. It was just bad luck he was on that train."

"It was very nearly much worse than bad luck," she said, adamant in her skepticism.

The congeniality of the meal was displaced by palpable wariness. Koblensky had seen beyond the artful surface of Kippax; he was reminded of a certain Russian colonel, though that man had not had to make the effort to filter his innate despotism through the constraints of a democratic world. Kippax would have served a czar well.

In Koblensky, Kippax had found a peculiar problem, partly linguistic. His habit was to build an incremental picture of men by sifting and evaluating conversations, classifying them as for a file. But Koblensky eluded this technique. His English was good—getting better all the time—but Koblensky did not *think* in English. Kippax had, with effort, overcome a similar barrier with the Arabs, crossing the gulf between mechanical literacy and the Arab way of thought. But Koblensky thought in Russian and Kippax knew that even if he had Russian—he didn't have a word of it—he had no aptitude for the cipher of the Russian mind. A less clever man than Kippax would have left it there, that Koblensky was merely cryptic. Kippax, though, already knew better: Koblensky had a different grain and to counter it Kippax would need different skills.

Of Koblensky, Tessa remembered with most speculation one sentence: *Palestine is my home.* The quiet force of this statement was, she thought, flawed. It was a declaration made by someone uncertain of it—a claim that would never have been necessary of someone with confident roots. And yet this was its salient appeal. It settled in her mind, this picture of affirmation, like the ring of a religious vow. Inevitably, she measured Bron against it, and equally inevitably, it became a speculation of his Jewish ties.

She was thinking of it still when Bron was dressing the following morning. She heard the soft crackle of the starched shirt and the brush of his socks on parquet and she knew these movements as part of the change in him. The regularity of his rising, the slight, nervous cough that punctuated the selection of each item of his uniform, the occasional murmur of a thought to

274

himself—these things had become the daily ritual of his moving apart from her, he embracing the routine of imperial Cairo and she, increasingly, holding herself back from it. He stood at the foot of the bed, the long tail of his army shirt coming nearly to his knees.

"I'm sorry," she said. "I simply cannot get up."

"That's all right, darling. No need to stir yourself."

Even the reasonableness of his voice began to irritate her; it contained no criticism and yet his tolerance had become a kind of indifference, older than his years or their marriage. This, too, was, she knew, part of the change the army had made in him. At first, it surprised her, this drift of his into convention, until she realized that because he had cut himself loose from one familiar world, of family and country, he had needed to find security in another, and had improbably done so within the khaki bureaucracy of Cairo. They had both broken from old ties, but while she had been renewed by it, he had needed new anchorages to replace the old. Here, where she felt herself to be an anomaly, he believed himself to have found a niche. It was, she realized, making him smug.

Pulling the silk sheet more closely to her, she knew that she could never fit in this place and that her morning lassitude was a futile fending off of the undirected energy that plagued her in every waking moment. Within earshot, the natural discordant vigor of the city excluded her. Her life seemed a succession of places in which she could not belong—not because they rejected her, but because of her own overwhelming certainty that she could not accept them. As strong as this sense had been, she had never yet been able to redirect it to a place she *could* claim for herself; Bron seemed not to see this in her. The war would, sooner or later, take them from here, she hoped in time to save her marriage. For all its futility and horrors, the war had become an agent that had disrupted and undermined those who fathered it.

She had renewed her old addiction to cigarettes. Leaving the bed, and before bathing she made coffee and sat, naked, drinking it and consuming three cigarettes, finding in this mild delinquency a new determination.

Bron had left her with no more than a faint disgruntlement over her failure again to make his breakfast. They could have had a resident orderly as servant, but she had rejected it as an invasion of privacy, though he suspected a more egalitarian impulse. He had therefore lately taken to breakfasting with Kippax in the officers' mess, and Kippax had, without an indiscreet question, guessed the reason.

On this morning, Kippax appeared incisive of eye and hand; decapitating his boiled egg in one stroke he said, "Koblensky— what do you make of the man?"

"Koblensky? Well, I thought he's not very engaging."

"Hmm." Kippax's response seemed more a reaction to his egg, a watery pool. "He's a headache."

"The old man has taken a shine to him. He's sending him back to the Sinai."

"I know. I know the old man seems to trust him. That's why this might be difficult. The fact is, we have to read the riot act to Mr. Koblensky. And since it will require tact, I thought this something you might handle. He's less likely to see in it some disobliging prejudice. I hope you don't mind."

Bron looked uncomfortable. "What is the trouble?"

"Hogarth is hopping mad. Koblensky has been conducting a private cable traffic with London, with that man Aaronsohn. We were supposed to keep track of all their messages, but somehow he found a way through Alexandria instead of Cairo. The Zionists are having a run at the government right now. Koblensky has passed on stuff to them in London about our arrangements with the Arabs. God knows how he got hold of it, but I want it stopped, and I thought it might come best from you."

Bron was more alert. "You mean, better from another Jew?" Kippax nodded.

"Yes, I see." Bron scraped away at some toast. "I don't know that will make it any easier, you know, but of course I'll have a go."

"I knew you would. You know what's going on with them in London?"

"Not really."

"No . . . well, it's not very clear. But I get the impression that Lloyd George is captivated by a vision of sponsoring the new Israel."

"How far is that likely to get?"

"I'm not sure." Kippax pushed aside his second egg. "Hogarth has a high regard for you, you know. I think he would be very obliged if you could relieve him of this Koblensky problem. Make it absolutely clear to the man that however much use he is

to Allenby, he can't run his own private show at the same time.
It's got to stop."

"It's always the Russian Jews," said Bron, shaking his head.
"They are always the agitators."

"Yes—isn't it!" Kippax wiped his lips and settled back
contentedly.

Instead of summoning Koblensky to his office, Bron chose to
seek him out, feeling that he could be more effective by not
relying on formal authority. Koblensky had moved himself out
of the hotel into a unit kept for men in transit. Waiting until
evening, Bron went there on foot, walking through the hotel
gardens just as the lights came on. Many staff officers had taken
their families to Alexandria and the Mediterranean coast to escape
the summer heat, and the gardens, which usually at this hour
were ringing with English voices, had regained their native
tranquillity. Only a few rooms in the transit unit were occupied.
A Syrian concierge, disturbed by Bron from a nap, indicated a
room at the end of a corridor on the ground floor.

The door of the room was open, in an obvious attempt to
improve ventilation in the stultifying air. Bron knocked lightly,
and coming through the door, found Koblensky stretched on a
bare canvas cot wearing only shorts. Scattered on the floor
around the cot were notes and sketch maps, but it was obvious
that Koblensky had succumbed to the heat and had been on the
brink of dozing. He raised himself slowly on his elbows.

"I wasn't expecting anyone," he said.

"No," said Bron, smiling tentatively. "I thought I would just
drop by. I wonder, would you mind—don't disturb yourself—if I
took a seat for a moment?"

Koblensky waited for Bron to settle on a precarious canvas
chair. Koblensky's bare skin was wet with perspiration; Bron,
having worn full uniform all day, and with his tie still in
place, looked saturated. "I'm sorry," said Koblensky. "I can't
get any more air in here. Don't you want to take off that
tunic?"

"No—it's perfectly all right. I'm getting used to the heat. I
don't think this will take long."

Suddenly Koblensky realized that Bron's formality was an
intended prelude to whatever it was he had come to say. Koblensky
remained on the cot, leaning against a window frame. "As you
like," he said.

*Clive Irving*

Bron settled each hand palm down midway on the top of his thighs. "The fact is, I came here with a warning."

Koblensky's expression, calmly speculative, did not alter.

"It's been discovered that you have been sending your own messages to London, via Alexandria—specifically, that you've failed to use the agreed channels."

Koblensky's only movement was a slight raising of the eyebrows, implying that he, not Bron, was the offended party.

For the first time, in the half light, Bron saw the Star of David pendant at Koblensky's chest. Not able to divine Koblensky's response, he continued: "I'm sure you understand that these are very sensitive issues, that it's quite irregular. . . ." He began to feel annoyed by Koblensky's indifference. "Look—let's not beat about the bush. I know why you did it. But d'you see, you can't mix politics and the army; they just won't have it." Annoyance had added to Bron's discomfort by turning his face scarlet.

Koblensky levered himself more upright against the wall. A twitch of amusement came to the corners of his mouth but then dissolved. "Politics and the army," he repeated slowly, his voice as viscous as the air. "You do not see any connection?" He shook his head. "Only an Englishman could say that."

"You know damned well what I mean," said Bron.

"I understand why you are here," said Koblensky, swiveling himself on the cot and finally putting his bare feet on the floor. "The messages were my business. That is why they went through Alexandria. But the army does not want me doing private business, and the army watches over everyone."

"It wasn't exactly *private* business."

"So . . . you know that too." Koblensky was now hunched forward, looking with concentration at Bron. "You are not a supporter of our claim to Palestine?"

"I'm not involved in it."

"But you are a Jew. You are involved."

Bron's hands tightened on his thighs.

"If you are not with us," insisted Koblensky, "you must be against us."

"No," said Bron, his voice more assertive by being softened. "No—but that's just it, isn't it? That's what's between us. I can't think in that way, not in absolutes like that. I just don't see life like that, and I've seen that in you, almost from the start."

"My friend, life *is* like that."

"No. I can't believe that." Bron's intensity had shed all the coating of the military stricture and, instead, was vehemently personal, no longer intimidated by Koblensky's arrogance. "Look—I think I know how you feel, I know the things that have happened to you, I can see what that has required. But I can't—in spite of that—take this 'If you are not with us you must be against us' stuff; it just defies reason. And *don't* patronize me as a Jew. Just because I don't happen to see things as you do."

Koblensky, for the first time, began to feel an interest in Bron. "You know, when I first saw you, I had no idea you *were* a Jew."

"Should I *wear* it—like you wear that star?" snapped Bron.

Koblensky remained even in his tone. "No. But you should *feel* it."

"Now you tell me what to feel as well as what to think?"

"*I* cannot tell you what to feel. But what kind of Jew are you? Do you believe in Jewish nationality?"

"I have a nationality already; my family has a nationality. We are English. And we are Jews."

Koblensky smiled condescendingly. "That is self-delusion, my friend. You deceive nobody but yourselves. You are more tragic to me than the most persecuted, the most terrorized, the most oppressed Jews of the ghetto; however hard you try to assert this other nationality, you will never be really accepted, you will never really have a home, you will never really be wanted."

Bron tensed and abandoned all effort to be moderate. "But those views are a tyranny in themselves. You know why? *Because you would make us aliens again!* I cannot stand the kind of intolerance you espouse, the intolerance of believing that all Jews everywhere, however completely they are accepted where they live, are part of some vast homeless nationality, incapable of ever belonging anywhere except in this Israel you think you can create again."

Koblensky seemed inexplicably placid; slowly he got up from the cot. The army shorts hung loosely on him, the hipbones showing above slack elastic. In the weak light he would have seemed insubstantial but for something in his eyes which matched the glint of the metal on his chest. He turned his back on Bron to push open the small window for more air, but the air was inert, inside and out. Still not facing Bron, he looked out the window and said, only just audibly, "You know, until we have Israel, we are a people that does not exist."

There was a long silence between them, Koblensky settling again on the cot and Bron getting up from the chair and going halfway to the door and then stopping, leaning against the wall and loosening his tie, aware of how unkempt he had become in the fetid room. But the uniform was more than a physical discomfort to Bron. It compromised him, put him more at a disadvantage with Koblensky than he wanted to be. Finally he said, "You'll have to try to believe me: I'm not *against* you, I'm not trying to *stop* you. I just do not go along with you. I feel that the true well-being of Jews all over the world, their emancipation and their freedom wherever they are, is a thousand times more important than this passion for creating a Jewish homeland. It's a long time since the fall of Judea. I'm not against the idea of more settlements in Palestine. There is a rightful place there for Jews—but not at the expense of anyone else."

Koblensky made no attempt to reply. He looked at Bron momentarily and then began reassembling the papers from the floor. "You can tell your people I will not be sending any more *private* messages to London. They can read what they like. Our business is done. You can believe me."

Bron walked out; until he was outside, he was not really sure of what most agitated him about the encounter, and then—in the listless gardens—he realized what it was: He had fallen under some obligation to Koblensky; just in what form and to what degree, he was unsure, but it was there.

His edginess was immediately clear to Tessa, who was used to seeing him return each evening as composed as he left in the morning. She waited for him to come from the bath, and giving him his routine whisky and soda, folded herself on the floor at the foot of the bed and asked, "What is it?"

He sat in a wicker chair and slipped on Moroccan sandals and didn't answer until he had virtually drained the drink and sunk back into the chair. "A bloody day," he said, hoping that this easy answer would satisfy her.

Her hands pressed the folds of a light cotton dress into the base of her thighs and the skin, still undarkened by the sun, tightened over her knuckles. This posture of hers, partly demure and partly combative, signaled her persistence even before she spoke. "What kind of bloody?" she said.

"*Bloody* bloody." He put down the glass. "Mainly that chap Koblensky."

"Ah. Him."

"Yes. Him."

"You know, his face does keep coming back. I've never seen such *age* in a young man. I don't mean that he looks old, do you understand? It's that when you look at his eyes, they're not the eyes of a young man. . . ." She broke off, comprehending that by some instinct she had located the cause of Bron's agitation.

"I didn't realize you studied him so assiduously."

"Don't be facetious, Michael. You must know what I mean."

"I would say, of his eyes, that they were feral."

"He *has* got under your skin."

"He began to tell me how I should feel as a Jew."

"Oh? How did that come up?"

"I think I need another whisky." He rose and came back into the bedroom with a stiffer drink. "Koblensky's been intriguing with the Zionists in London. It was discovered; I had to warn him off. You know, he's really quite a fanatic. It all came out, suddenly. He described assimilated Jews as tragic. And he said that without Israel, Jews are a people that does not exist."

"Israel? He means Palestine?"

"A Jewish Palestine, to hell with all the others—Arabs, Christians. . . . The man is an absolutist; either you're with him or you're against him."

"I see. Poor Michael. You're not used to zealots, are you?"

"Don't patronize me, Tessa."

"I'm sorry. But it's shaken you, hasn't it?"

He glowered into the whisky. "No, it hasn't shaken me. The devil of it is that I don't *want* to be against him, up to a point. I know what he's been through; there's no doubting his courage. It's just that I distrust anyone who wishes to impose his own experience as a kind of unquestioned logic on everybody else. He believes he should pity all the Jews who don't follow him, and I don't need his bloody pity. I'm quite ready to let him and his kind find a place they can call home, but they're not going to make all other Jews homeless in the process." He gulped more whisky. "No wonder the anti-Semites are always sympathetic to Zionism; it suits their book absolutely."

"You're too reasonable for him."

"Absolutely. Isn't that a terrible sin, being reasonable in the face of adamantine faith."

Clive Irving

"Yes—the definition of sin requires adamantine faith."

Slowly he smiled. "Thank God, you and I don't have that kind of faith."

"Thank whom?"

282

# 16

## Cairo ✳ July 1917

Kippax spent more time out of uniform than in it, a measure of the independence he had won under Sir Cedric's sponsorship, slipping free of the routine of the Arab Bureau and of Hogarth's supervision. He had moved from military quarters to a small villa near the river on the northern edge of the city. Apart from making the summer nights more bearable, the villa gave him more privacy for both professional and sexual intercourse (the two sometimes merged). And yet, despite having so completely embraced Cairo and its deviant ways, he was aware of a developing deadness in his life. The more replete it was, the less it satisfied him, like a drug that lost power with continuous use. Then he realized that the Cairo he had so keenly embraced was an abstraction, an idea of an existence. In the midst of this gregarious city he was, in truth, solitary. The desert had been more companionable.

And then the desert reached out and found him. One morning a note was delivered to him—an elaborately formal address inside a stiff manila envelope bearing a wax seal. Kippax recognized the seal: it was that of the house of Saud. The note was in the elegant Arabic calligraphy of a court scribe, a thing of beauty in itself, and the correspondent Ibn Jiluwi, as Ibn Saud's personal envoy. Having read it twice, Kippax put down the note and picked up the envelope, running it under his nose like a cigar. It still bore the scent of Nawaf's hand, the scent of the eunuch lover, of an oil scented with herb, of cool, cleansing desert night.

Early the following afternoon, Kippax drove himself, in the black Mercedes-Benz, across the bridge to the west bank of the Nile and south beyond Giza, far enough south for the pyramids to be left behind. The road deteriorated into conflicting textures, in one place surfaced with broken stones, in another subsiding gravel, finally becoming sand so fine that the car left a trailing cloud of it behind. Slowing to be sure of direction, he took an even poorer track, winding off toward the river. He picked out his destination—an oasis bordered by date palms and poplars. At the heart of the oasis he found the small palace, walled by high pink stone. Once it had been a retreat for the Egyptian khedive; now it was owned by a rich merchant who used it for hunting parties. Here, through some long-reaching and discreet arrangement, rested Ibn Jiluwi with his closest lieutenants and all his harem.

The palace, originally furnished with the eye of a connoisseur, had been, with the coming of the merchant, vulgarized in a way that was depressingly familiar to Kippax. It was carpeted throughout in white velvet. Against this the tribal guards made a fearsome, incompatible sight. Ibn Jiluwi and two of his subchieftains sat on the velvet against a backdrop of a heavy gold gaselier and crimson flock wallpaper.

Kippax offered the ritual respects and was given a pink velvet cushion on which to squat before them. Ibn Jiluwi was effusive with his own greetings and those, by proxy, of Ibn Saud, and then he verbally repeated the substance of his note: that the canopy of medieval isolation was already, like a tent before the *shimal*, being torn from Arabia by the gusts of war (in Arabic this imagery was rather more sublime). In view of this, Ibn Saud, whose kingdom was destined by God to claim all Arabia, had seen that his people would have to prepare—and be prepared— for change. None of this meant that they would surrender the fiercer values of their faith (Ibn Jiluwi delivered this caution with hard-eyed conviction). Ibn Jiluwi had in his care in Egypt a young man who had already proved himself a religious student without equal after months of study under the guardians of the true faith. Ibn Jiluwi was now charged with introducing this student to the wider world, a world he knew nothing of. In Egypt he would continue his sacred studies, but Ibn Saud wished this to be simultaneous with courses to learn English and certain other secular subjects. For this reason, Ibn Jiluwi was directed to seek the guidance of the greatly respected El Khibeg. This was being requested as a personal favor. The king well understood that the officers of the Great Government were fully extended (and here there was a pained digression on the caprice of the Great Government in continuing to encourage the "profane dreams of the

Hashemite king of Mecca,'' who, as every true Muslim knew, was ''an unworthy keeper of the holiest of shrines''), but the king hoped that nonetheless . . .

This address took, in its uncondensed form, nearly an hour to deliver.

Cups of coffee were intermittently produced, like props carried in from the wings of a theater, but the coffee had been refined for palates other than those of desert princes. Ibn Jiluwi suffered it for a while, but finally spat the dregs onto the white velvet, a defilement that Kippax thought appropriate. The unease, the sheer incongruity, of these lions of men amid such gross furnishings was tragicomic.

Although he never once glimpsed them, Kippax sensed the presence of women. Like the men, the women of the harem had brought with them too much energy for the garish palace to contain, to domesticate. The sexual charge Kippax felt came from plain and ancient roots. Even the Ikhwan, in the bare settlements they called the *hujar*, having renounced all material pleasure, avidly tended the secret gardens of the body. Sex was the first and last anchorage of their replete asceticism; probably the bone of their endurance. Occasionally, as Kippax squatted before the three men, there were murmurs from somewhere under the pink-tiled roof, perhaps a sweet and patient laugh no more audible than a poplar branch brushing a casement, but enough to give these men a reassuring distraction. Kippax, too, was in his way aroused: Nawaf was here somewhere, his grace another fruit of the secret gardens.

It took Kippax a week to prepare for Ibn Jiluwi's formal introduction to Cairo. It might have taken less time, but Kippax was in no hurry. He introduced Nawaf to his villa and diverse other pleasures of the city, for some of which he showed more relish than Kippax thought seemly. An instinct warned him that Nawaf could become a liability; perhaps, after all, with Nawaf, this should be hail and farewell, before grace fell to smut.

The largest car that could be found was a 1915 Rolls-Royce, normally reserved for the high commissioner. Stressing the diplomatic priorities, Kippax gained the use of it, confident that Ibn Jiluwi, though ascetic in both desert and palace, would want to make a regal impression in motion. The appearance of the Rolls at the white palace provoked something near to delirium; a succession of shrouded women had to be given tours of the gardens and when, at last, Kippax was able to head back to Cairo, the car was contaminated by a heavy and none too alluring perfume. Corporal Baxter, who was driving, did not realize that he had come closer to the secrets of the harem than any white man, but Baxter by then was immune to mystery. In the rear, the Rolls had two facing bench seats in studded crimson leather. Kippax sat with his back to the driver, facing Ibn Jiluwi and the main charge of the mission, Khalid Abbas.

It was a critical point in the boy's emancipation. Ibn Jiluwi had already seen the profanities of Cairo, but until now Khalid had remained behind palace walls. The *ulema* were dubious about losing their grip on him, but his head was now overfull of Koranic wisdom and they had to trust that it was therefore bulwarked against all the impending alien traps. Kippax, in two encounters with the boy, had already found a kind of muscular sanctity that both impressed and repelled him; there was none of the softness of Nawaf in him and there was a quickness of mind that owed nothing to tuition. Now, in fresh plain white robes, Khalid was the one person apparently untouched by the luxury of the car, as indifferent as if entering Cairo on a mule.

They came to rest in the densely shaded courtyard of a mansion built of patterned lime-colored brick in a French colonial style. Kippax left Ibn Jiluwi and the boy in the car until he had roused an aged janitor, who then led the three of them through several cool and sparsely furnished lobbies to an inner room which, in contrast, was crowded with sagging armchairs, three or four tables all stacked with books, dark and cracked oils in heavy gilt frames, and in the gloomiest corner, a heavy oak desk from behind which, in a limping step, came a delicately boned man in a black serge suit that seemed to have been slept in. He peered at them with large, spaniel-like eyes.

"I'm sorry we are late," said Kippax.

"Are you? Are you late? One never senses the passing of time, does one, in Cairo?" The man halted with the weak leg still behind the other, giving him the stance of a water bird. He bowed slightly toward Ibn Jiluwi and spoke to him in an impeccable Riyadh dialect.

Visibly impressed, Ibn Jiluwi answered, gesturing to Khalid Abbas.

286

Kippax had sifted through a list of a dozen or more Oriental scholars before settling on Professor Denis Arkwright. Hogarth had consented to the choice with only one reservation: "He's an atheist—but then, that hardly matters in this case." Arkwright was to be the means by which Khalid Abbas would learn English and be given an understanding of Western culture and science. Arkwright had lived in Cairo for thirty years and—it was never clear how—had learned more than twenty Arab dialects without ever once venturing into the desert. As far as anyone knew, he seldom even left this building, an academy usually attended by the children of diplomats. It was closed for the summer, but Arkwright was taking Khalid Abbas under his wing as a private tutor.

The boy was as impervious to the strangeness of this academy as he had been to the opulence of the car. He followed the conversation intently, replied when spoken to, and not a fold of his cloak moved.

Some time later, describing the encounter to Hogarth, Kippax said, "There's something very arid about that boy."

"Arid? I should think, in the circumstances, he's rigid with trepidation."

"No, no—that isn't it. I don't think he is at all fearful. It's that . . . well, he's been so long with the *ulema* that he has that dreadful lack of curiosity that too much dogma creates. It's often called holy, but I never see it like that. I just hope Arkwright can deal with it."

"Well, Arkwright has a high reputation."

"Yes . . . ." said Kippax thoughtfully, fingering his belt. "You know, this is an absolutely fascinating experiment, taking a boy like this, with no knowledge of any modern kind, none at all, completely *sui generis*, so to speak. It's as though one part of his brain, the speculative, wondering part, has never been used. Everything put there so far is unquestioned, all sealed up. If we can open up that other part of his brain, we'll find it quite empty; we can fill it how we choose. It really is an irresistible opportunity."

Hogarth grunted cautiously. "He's not a specimen, you know, Owen. The idea is to enlighten him, not confuse him. I'm not sure how reconcilable these two parts of the brain you describe will prove to be. If you stand the whole idea on its head, look how difficult it is for us to accept their way of thought, not to mention their values and their style of living." He hesitated, looking carefully at Kippax, whose enthusiasm for the experiment was unabated. "After all, even you, Owen, as someone who seems to have embraced the desert ways more adeptly than most—even you must understand the potential damage to the personality that attempts to live at ease in both worlds."

Kippax caught the edge in Hogarth's comment. His chin rose aggressively. "Damage to the personality?"

"Well, look at Lawrence. You can't tell me he's going to hold together."

Kippax was not deceived; he knew Hogarth had been thinking as much of him as of Lawrence. "Well," he said, with a perceptible sneer, "Lawrence wasn't really balanced to begin with, was he? At least, now he *has* a personality, however bizarre."

Hogarth fixed Kippax with his most tutorial eye. "Don't condescend so. You know the dangers of love of desert."

"The desert won't remain as it is. We will see the end of it as a place apart, immune."

"*We* are the end of it, do you mean?"

"Not only us. Its time is running out. This boy, he will be one of the first of them to understand that. So in that sense, what we are doing for him is inevitable. Better we do it than someone else."

"Ah, always the patriot, Owen."

Kippax smiled. "But of course." He didn't like Hogarth's recently developed cynicism, a part of what Kippax felt was a case of innocence lost far too late in life. He was annoyed, too, by the vestigial habit of Hogarth's to be the mentor, and yet he felt unable to sever the present, as he lived it, from the past of their relationship. Even now, Hogarth's eye lingered on him, partly with open misgivings and partly with the old, donnish affection.

"You know, Owen, I do have a high regard for your skills, for your understanding of things here—your *feeling* for it. However, I do sometimes feel that your life is incomplete without fear."

"I don't quite follow."

"I think you do. It is frequently said, now, that the war has destroyed your generation—and so it has. But I remember the initial, tonic effect. War provides a kind of fear which many young men find irresistible—not a tediously punctual fear, but as capricious and impending as the result of a gaming table. It's quite intoxicating, when it takes hold. I'm not sure but that your love of desert might not begin to be like that. It's certainly a part of what has turned Lawrence.'' Hogarth moved away from Kippax and rested a fist on his desk, looking out the window in a doleful way. "We are all of us much changed." He seemed to want to say more, but hesitated, reassessing the words. Then, with more force, he said, "You are certainly not as straight as I once thought you to be." He turned to face Kippax. "Perhaps it's Cairo, perhaps the desert, perhaps the war. All I know is, you represent something I hoped never to see us getting into. Perhaps I can't—shouldn't—blame you for it; you're just an instrument. But I thank God I'm too old ever to go the same way."

Kippax smiled with forced grace. "I'm sorry if I have disappointed you. The fact is, it's not a very straight world. I'm not sure it ever was. Not even at Oxford."

# Part Two

Part Two

# 17

## *Southern England ✳ Late summer 1917*

Hedgerows heavy with layer upon layer of grasses, wild herbs and flowers and bramble—so heavy that nature seemed to have exploded out of the earth in a rush to light. No one prevailing wind had set the line of trees: each tree had taken its own course, bending, arching, or plumb true. Some of the trees were more ancient than any other living thing, and each hill was varied enough in shape and texture to be a universe of its own, and complex enough to engage a botanist for life. Aaron Aaronsohn could not look at this abundance without at the same time thinking of the tenuous crops of Zichron. English skepticism of a Palestine turned green must rest right here before him in the easy cultivation of their shires. England trapped him. How would Sarah understand, being left alone so long on that arid hill?

He slipped the car back into gear and cruised slowly down into the valley, more depressed than enlivened by the summer fragrances. The lane crossed a humped stone bridge and joined a wider road that ran parallel to a stream. Half a mile east along this road, a dozen wooden huts had been rudely imposed on what had until then been a meadow. The huts sat on brick piles and an asphalt bed, and were set around a small square. At a gate in a wire-mesh fence was a sign: ROYAL FUSILIERS, 38TH BATTALION. At the gate, Aaronsohn showed a slip of paper and a corporal affably waved him on: "Sergeant Jug-o-whisky? Second hut on the right." But even before Aaronsohn saw the hut he saw Vladimir Jabotinsky, squatting on the grass at the center of a small group of men. Jabotinsky noticed the car and broke off.

*"Shalom!"*

The Hebrew greeting jarred against Jabotinsky's military bearing. "Am I too early?"

Jabotinsky looked back at the men he had left on the grass.

Clive Irving

"No—I can leave them. They will hardly notice I have gone. They are my Hebraists. We have to work out our own terminology for exercises and commands in Hebrew. You can imagine how long that will take. They are better with semantics than guns." He took Aaronsohn by the arm, fraternally. "You saw the announcement in the *London Gazette*?"

"Who did not? A Jewish regiment! At last! But it worries as many people as it pleases."

"There is an inn about a mile down the road. We could talk there."

In the car Jabotinsky became less the martinet, more philosophical. He said, almost wistfully, "It is beautiful here, green as no other country on earth."

Aaronsohn smiled. " '. . .and we shall build Jerusalem in England's green and pleasant land.' "

"Why is it that they wander the world, these people? They have paradise here, but they have always been looking for something else. *Why?*"

"Because it is all finished here. There is no struggle left."

Jabotinsky didn't seem convinced.

There were only three other people in the inn, but Aaronsohn and Jabotinsky sat away from them in an alcove and spoke in French. Aaronsohn, ruddy and yet somber in a plain suit, and Jabotinsky passionately voluble in his sergeant's uniform—they looked and sounded so alien, drinking the English ale from pewter tankards.

"Suddenly I am getting a lot of volunteers," said Jabotinsky, stressing the irony.

"From Whitechapel?"

"From Whitechapel. The same people who were screaming at me before; the people who thought they could sit out the war on their fat backsides—and *Russians*, most of them."

"They were threatened with deportation if they did not volunteer."

Jabotinsky smiled without humor. The foam of the beer settled on his upper lip until the violence of his reply dispelled it. "So they come to me rather than go back to Russia. What kind of allegiance is that?" He took another draft of the beer and pulled a face as though for the first time realizing its sourness. "But I need as many as I can get. To make it look serious. The British have told me we cannot wear the blue and white insignia, the Star of David. We have to fight as Royal Fusiliers. It seems even the idea of our own flag makes these people very nervous." He banged the tankard on the table. *"One day . . . but not yet."* Then he seemed to recover his humor. "This is a strange conspiracy we make, my friend, a long way from home, in this beautiful country, drinking their terrible beer. I wonder, can anything that begins so small *ever* succeed, ever become what we want? I have about sixty men who know what they are doing. That is all. Sixty."

"Well, it is a beginning."

"It began two thousand years ago."

"Still, we have to be patient."

"And obedient? Who sent you here? Weizmann?"

"He is sure now that the British see the logic, to them, of a Jewish Palestine."

"Weizmann believes too much in British honor."

Aaronsohn eased himself back from the table into a beam of dusty light and shook his head gently in protest. "You should be more generous. Without Weizmann, without his way of handling them, his understanding of them, we could not have come so far. I know that you and he . . . you are together in what you want, but perhaps apart in how best to achieve it. The fact is, he is doing what he does best, and now, my friend—at last—you have the chance to do what you do best. You can put the iron into our dream."

"And Samson said, 'They must get iron'—you know the lines? 'They must give everything they have for iron—their silver and wheat, oil and wine and flocks, even their wives and daughters. All for iron!' " Jabotinsky squinted at Aaronsohn's bright face. "So far, it has been only words, no iron. And you . . . you are sent as the peacemaker? I know how much Weizmann was against this Jewish army. Iron does not appeal to him."

"No," protested Aaronsohn. "No, my friend, not forever. But he worries that you will make the British too nervous of us, at this time when we are so close."

"Close to what?" Jabotinsky unbuttoned one of the deep pockets of the khaki tunic. He brought out a piece of paper and unfolded it on the table by his tankard; it was a page torn from a school exercise book, covered in scrawled signatures. He pressed it carefully flat in a gesture that was, for him, uncommonly delicate, and spoke with a matching restraint. "You see this paper? Three years ago, in the Mafruza barracks in Alexandria, I sat with the refugees the Turks had just uprooted from Palestine;

there were thousands of them. I, the Russian ideologue, and these people whose *real* home was Palestine. Three years ago. At the head of this paper—look at it—is the proposal: 'To form a Jewish Legion and to propose to England to make use of it in Palestine.' There are one hundred signatures on that piece of paper. The first—*there*—is that of a Mr. Ze'ev Gluskin. He snatched the pen from my hand. He said, 'I am old, I am useless as a soldier, but I want to bear the responsibility.' '' Jabotinsky's hand rested half on the paper and half on the dark encrusted oak. "My men march like geese, *but they want to bear the responsibility.*"

This was oratory, even though modulated for an audience of one. It was effective oratory, but Aaronsohn was not in need of it, nor in patience with it. In trying to restrain Jabotinsky he had met the standard Jabotinsky response—beguiling vehemence. But listening to it, Aaronsohn had suddenly seen through Jabotinsky: the oratory was aimed shamelessly at the emotions. From many a platform Jabotinsky had addressed the Jewish emotions and cast his spell—yet it was false. No Jew was probably less emotional. And now in this shaded inglenook he was looking at Aaronsohn, for applause, for endorsement—for pliancy. Jabotinsky was a demagogue . . . a reasonable demagogue, perhaps. Reasonable when sure of prevailing.

"Yes," said Aaronsohn neutrally. "We all bear the responsibility, but Weizmann must not be embarrassed, not now."

For a second it seemed that Jabotinsky would renew his assault, not yet satisfied with the outcome, but then he subsided. He put away the precious paper and adjusted his spectacles, and said, "You can count on that."

When they parted they were less close than when they had met. Both knew it; neither resented it. Aaronsohn was too tired for resentment. He was tired of talking, tired of committee rooms, tired of good manners, almost tired of reason. Reason was taking too long, far too long. Reason required comfort and civility. The whole trouble with London was that it was eminently reasonable; even in war, even when assaulted by fractious Jews, London moved with stately reason, arranging all disputing parties around the green baize tables in the certain belief that if each view had its allotted chair, then order could extend from furniture to men. Meanwhile Sarah was left too long on the arid hill.

High, heavy doors were opened and closed on silent hinges.

As agreement seemed near, the number of men behind the doors diminished, but Aaronsohn's fatigue was in some way made more burdened by the doors; they imposed too much discretion and they oppressed. They were doors he never touched, and he hardly saw the hands that moved them, and this expressed more than anything the remoteness of the will that had kept him here so long, that would keep him here until the thing was settled. "The thing"—what *was* to be achieved here? Three of them left now behind the closed doors. Three of them and one sheet of paper. So many words, so many hours, so many interests had been distilled into this one sheet of paper, the calm and stately residue of so much fury, so calm and so reasoned that it seemed unrelated to its authors—a device made without blood.

" 'The British government accepts the principle that Palestine become the national home of the Jewish people. . . .' "

Weizmann was reading out the phrase slowly, so familiar with it that he ignored the sheet of paper that lay on his knee. "We have conceded a lot—*but not that.*"

"We have conceded enough." Aaronsohn's weariness had the better of his grace. He was swallowed, enclosed, by the room. The room had no place in reality; it seemed not to be earthbound. It was emboweled in a mansion so vast that no sense of day or night existed. He and Weizmann sat side by side before a black lacquered secretaire. Behind the secretaire sat Lionel Walter Rothschild, the second Lord Rothschild.

Rothschild frowned at Aaronsohn's churlishness.

But Aaronsohn did not yield ground. He said, "At the beginning it read: 'Palestine should be reconstituted as the national home of the Jewish people.' The change weakens it."

Rothschild looked to Weizmann impatiently.

Weizmann said, "What matters is to have it agreed."

"Just so." Rothschild became a shade more benign; he looked back to Aaronsohn. "I understand your qualms, but I assure you, this is now a form of words that I can get Balfour to submit to the cabinet. I have had to think of his needs, as well as our own. He has opponents to overcome."

"Montagu," said Weizmann.

"Montagu." Rothschild sighed. "It is deplorable that having come so far along the path of reconciliation, there remains one Jew who opposes us so adamantly. The only Jew in the cabinet. A brilliant man. The problem, I believe, originates with his background. The family was rigidly Orthodox, of the old school.

297

Montagu was stifled by it. He once confided to a friend that he had been striving all his life to ecape the ghetto—figuratively speaking. And now, it seems, he wishes to demonstrate his independence of mind by thwarting Zionism. Because of his prominence he has had to endure much prejudice, in public and private. I am sure you know the kind of talk. He is an ambitious man, and he would rather appease his critics, however bigoted, than endanger his ambitions.''

"Can he stop us?" said Aaronsohn.

Weizmann answered first. "Not now."

Rothschild said, "He will try."

Weizmann said, "Jabotinsky does not help."

Aaronsohn said, "I think he will be kept too busy to embarrass us again."

Weizmann rubbed his eye and then settled a hand on the sheet of paper. "I do not know how Jabotinsky keeps any friends. I could not work as he does, in an atmosphere where everybody is angry with him and can hardly stand him. It would poison my life and kill in me all desire to work."

"Well," said Rothschild, "few have your gift for diplomacy. Without you, we could never have gained the confidence of the British government. Of that I am sure."

Aaronsohn looked at the piece of paper and thought of Jabotinsky's page from the exercise book. "If they accept this proposition, what standing will it have?"

"Standing?" Again there was a vestige of irritation in Rothschild's voice.

"What is its legality?"

Weizmann said, "It will be a binding commitment of policy."

"More than that, I hope," said Rothschild. "I look upon it as a covenant, an irrevocable commitment, a public signal to the whole world that Jews will be reestablished in Palestine—if not at first *de jure*, then at least *de facto*. It is a declaration. A declaration. And to give it substance, enduring substance, I have persuaded Arthur Balfour, as foreign secretary, that he should put his signature to it, make it a lasting monument to his own beliefs and policies. He is not immune to considerations of that kind, to his own place in history."

"A *covenant* . . ." repeated Aaronsohn contemplatively.

"Yes—a covenant," said Weizmann. "If not with God, then with the next greatest power on earth."

"But how will it be enforceable . . . beyond our time?"

"It is a matter of honor," said Rothschild.

"And principle," said Weizmann.

Although unsettled by Aaronsohn, Rothschild persisted in the effort to put him at ease. "May I explain something?" he said, dropping the formality of being the chairman of a quorum. "Some forty years ago, in this house, my grandfather was entertaining the prime minister at dinner. The prime minister was Disraeli. A message arrived that the controlling interest in the Suez Canal Company was for sale. It was owned by the khedive of Egypt, whose own insolvency forced the sale. The French had made an offer, but the khedive thought it too low. For Disraeli it was a tantalizing chance, an opportunity—an opportunity for Britain to gain control of the canal, with all its salience to the sea routes of the empire. You can see it. But it was a weekend, and even the Bank of England could not have moved quickly enough. The price was four million pounds. My grandfather provided the loan, at three percent. We have, as a family and as a bank, an intimate understanding of British interests—and they of ours."

There was nothing imperious in Rothschild's voice, nothing remotely condescending, but Aaronsohn had the impression of being educated by a monarch.

Weizmann said to him, "When this declaration is agreed to, it will be in the form of a letter from Balfour to Lord Rothschild."

"No more is needed," said Rothschild.

Rothschild *did* look like an Edwardian king, full-bearded and replete. "What about Montagu?" said Aaronsohn.

Rothschild leaned forward on the secretaire. "I have arranged for Dr. Weizmann to be in Downing Street on the morning the cabinet considers the draft. If it seems necessary, he will be invited by the prime minister, Mr. Lloyd George, to address them, and particularly to reassure them that Montagu's view is not—as he suggests—the view of the majority of English Jews. That the letter will be addressed to me is, in point of fact, a matter of protocol rather than of justice. I have done very little. You know very well, both of you, how much the Jews of Palestine already owe to Baron Edmond; your own settlement, Aaronsohn, is named after his father, Jacob. Perhaps you know less well how much is owed to my nephew James. He is the *real* Zionist in the family, the invincible force. But, as I say, it falls to me as the head of the English house to represent the Jewish concordat, even though there are still others like Montagu who would rather Zionism were rejected. The people who have been

so bitter towards you, Dr. Weizmann.'' Rothschild stood up and
offered cigars to them both. Only Weizmann took one.

Quietly, looking at Aaronsohn as he cut the cigar, Weizmann
said, ''I am not dismayed by passion. That I am used to. That I
can answer. I have never been intolerant of opposing convictions.
What I cannot stand is fanaticism—and treachery.''

Rothschild settled a hand on Weizmann's shoulder. ''You are
a great man. You cannot despair now. We shall have it.'' He
drew on his own cigar and looked at Aaronsohn. ''After all,
money is not enough; there has to be more. I begin to see that. It
is a matter of feeling. Look—you see there, the cornice?''

Aaronsohn followed Rothschild's finger. Huge embroidered
satin curtains excluded all natural light; the room was lit by a
chandelier and candelabra. The high ceiling reflected the gold
and scarlet patina of the rest of the room as the lid of a jewel box
might shimmer with the brilliance of its contents. In the lofty
corner there was one flaw, one imperfection—a plaster cornice
that seemed scarred.

''When my grandfather built this house, the cornice was left
unfinished—to mark the destruction of Jerusalem. Yes—it is a
matter of feeling.''

Inwardly, Aaronsohn was uncharitable enough to wonder about
the real interests of this patrician who spoke with an English
upper-class voice unblemished by any trace of alien lineage,
whose hands were manicured like his lawns, and who carried his
wealth as if it were as natural as leaves on a tree.

Weizmann said, ''You know, Lord Rothschild, what is peculiar about this document of ours? Neither party to it, Zionists or
British, is actually, at this moment, in possession of the land we
are proposing to occupy. *That* is what is peculiar about it.''

Instantly Aaronsohn saw that Rothschild's humor was too
Anglicized, too refined, to see the point in the same ironic
spirit—the spirit of the shrewd trader making a joke against his
own cunning. It had too much the flavor of the Russian Jew and
had fleetingly exposed an unbreachable distinction between the
two men.

Rothschild's eyes settled on the marble floor, and then rose
again to look at Weizmann. ''The war cannot last much longer.
Everyone is too drained by it. When it ends it will be too late to
submit claims. Arrangements are already being agreed—here, in
Paris, in Washington. The division of the postwar world. Arrangements between ourselves and our allies.''

It was the use of the word "ourselves" that for Aaronsohn brought his final understanding of the world of the doors he had never had to touch.

"Of *course*," said Weizmann, recovering from the slight error of propriety and taste, "of course that is the point, that is the urgency."

*Ha-Nadiv*—the phrase came back to Aaronsohn, the phrase used in Palestine of Baron Edmond, meaning the Benefactor. Aaronsohn was familiar with patronage, but his American backers, for all their generosity, had never known the wealth or the pervasive influence of the Rothschilds. He fancied that this Rothschild was not used to having to explain his actions to anyone, that he had just about exhausted his patience with Aaronsohn; a sense of imminent lese majesty hung with the cigar smoke.

When they were outside again, standing on the mansion's steps, rain had chilled the streets and the drizzle blew into their faces as they waited for a taxi. Free of the stifling mansion, Aaronsohn made no attempt to shelter from the rain. It reaffirmed reality.

Weizmann looked at the weathered face held stubbornly to the wind. He said, "I remember being told once, by a very wise man, that the Jew learns not by way of reason, but from catastrophes. He won't buy an umbrella merely because he sees clouds in the sky; he waits until he is drenched and catching pneumonia—*then* he makes up his mind. You and I, we are running against that philosophy."

Aaronsohn stepped down to the pavement. At the corner of Hyde Park and Piccadilly, the rain had caused confusion to the traffic; motor vehicles, omnibuses, and horse-drawn carriages were tangled and there was no sign of a taxi. "We can walk," he said, not waiting for Weizmann's agreement. "We should walk."

In Whitehall, the real distances between the British dominions of the world shrank finally and conveniently to a few compact acres. Here the empire was run from three adjacent buildings: the Foreign Office, the Colonial Office, and the India Office. Only the India Office had the piratical flavor that was true to the roots of the empire; the other buildings were Victorian monoliths, indelibly clerical. For this reason, Sir Cedric Assay always felt more himself as he crossed the threshold of the India Office from

Clive Irving

a Foreign Office corridor, more in his own time. A pity, he thought, not to have been born two centuries earlier. Then he would have been understood, then he would have been appreciated, then there would have been less hypocrisy, no cant about the morality of statecraft. He would have been among his own kind. Futile musings now. He rearranged his bearing, lest this anachronism betray itself.

He did not like Edwin Montagu. Normally clear and uncomplicated in his prejudices, Sir Cedric was unsure what it was about Montagu that he disliked. It was only partly that Montagu was a Jew. As Jews went, Montagu was tolerable—not too much the tradesman, even something of an aesthete. But there was still a little too much *thrust* about him, too much *ardor*—yes, perhaps that was it. But perhaps not. There was a more professional objection—a glibness. Montagu had come to take charge of the India Office mouthing the phrase "Reform but firm rule." Such fashions; such vanities. India was too volatile to be offered even the hint of leniency. And it would not be made docile by solecisms. Sir Cedric, after all, knew; Sir Cedric had advised; Sir Cedric was ignored. But he had to cultivate Montagu, he had to swallow his dislikes—for now. He was getting like a man who had swallowed too much. He wondered if it was as plain in him as in others. God knows, there were others, and these were hard times for them all. Nothing stable now, damn this war; nothing would hold. There was a coal fire somewhere near. As he went into Montagu's office, the dust of it percolated the hall, a warm and congenial dust that he had loved since childhood.

They greeted each other already as familiars: Montagu taller even than Assay, coming from behind the desk to shake hands, saying, "I am *most* obliged for your note, Sir Cedric, most obliged. It was *very* welcome. Sometimes one feels . . . well, one is hesitant to become an unpopular minority against such a widely supported cause."

There it was again, the ardor, in the handshake; how overdone it was. "I understand, Secretary of State." Despite the formality and despite his instincts, Sir Cedric purred with fellow feeling. "You see," he said, "I do feel strongly, quite strongly, that though our Arab alliances are at risk, plainly enough it is the *entire* Muslim picture one must insist on presenting—and the Muslims of India are rather more our direct charge and so numerous that we must not fail to foresee their sensibilities, lest we unleash a terrible reaction. A *terrible* reaction."

302

Montagu nodded solemnly. "Please—sit down, won't you?" He waited until Sir Cedric was settled, but did not resume his own seat behind the desk. He took short, quick steps back and forth, head down, as he said, "It is reassuring to have resort to someone of your expertise. You will appreciate my personal difficulty, I am sure, as a Jew. I am caught in the middle. The Muslims will suspect me of partiality and the Jews—at least, the alien Jews—they accuse me of betrayal. But it is the empire I will not betray."

"Quite so." Sir Cedric was careful not to sound too unctuous. "Of course, one sees how painful it must be for you. For myself, I trust I am not speaking out of hand when I say that I fear the prime minister is not, perhaps, as aware as he might be of the very serious repercussions of conceding to these Zionist pressures. A Jewish state is what they are after, with us as the midwife. However much it is glossed over in their semantics, *that* is what it leads to."

Finally Montagu sat down. He said, "Yes, of course. If you know anything about Zionism, you know that that is what it exists to achieve. It cannot have any other aim. The prime minister has been misled by Weizmann. Of course, the prime minister is in poor health, and Weizmann takes advantage. He hints that if the Zionists do not get satisfaction in Palestine, they would turn towards Bolshevism, as they have already done in Russia. This has a powerful impact, I fear." Montagu lapsed for a few moments into what seemed an exclusive thought, then continued: "The prime minister, though, will not be at the next cabinet. How much support do I have, at your level?"

"In both offices, the senior people share my own analysis. If the policy had been entrusted to us . . ."

"Yes, I know." For a moment Montagu was more guarded. Then he said, "One does need to carry the *professionals* with one. Policy is not only politics." He shed all formality and leaned forward. "You know, Sir Cedric, it is quite galling to me, after a lifetime of public service, coming from a family that has pledged itself to and fought for this country, to be confronted by this Russian brand of mischief, presented to us as a racial imperative, and to be lectured on one's allegiance. For a family of the distinction of the Rothschilds, for them to support Zionism—it seems so guileless. I cannot for the life of me see how it can have come so far. Of course, the Americans do not help. They have so little understanding, yet so much to say."

"One feels, sometimes, that the Americans see the dismantling of the British Empire as a moral obligation."

"Quite so. Quite so. Of course, with the war going as it is, I fear we shall have at least to *appear* sympathetic to Washington, in order to get them to the battlefield. At any rate, we must not be deflected, not on this. I believe, after what you tell me, I can have this so-called declaration of Balfour's held at bay long enough for the dangers to be understood by Lloyd George. It is not lost yet."

"No, Secretary of State, it is not."

When Sir Cedric left, he felt Montagu to be far more resolved than when he had walked into the room; certainly he had never heard a Jew use the word "Jew" with less sense of affiliation. But he was not sure of Montagu's weight. At least, not against Balfour. The thought of Balfour unsettled Sir Cedric's liver. He had survived seven foreign secretaries, but Arthur James Balfour, after only a few months as foreign secretary, had shown an irritating curiosity in Sir Cedric's activities. Balfour had introduced Scottish rectitude to policy, and it was a rectitude of truly terrible innocence. Sometimes Sir Cedric thought that innocence was the deadliest force in the world, certainly a serious liability in a foreign secretary.

A week after his meeting with Montagu, Sir Cedric was summoned for his fifth encounter with Balfour in as many months, which for a head of department used to autonomy was almost a breach of manners. And he was kept waiting, for twenty minutes. Balfour's secretaries offered no small talk. They regarded Sir Cedric as a delicate and complex piece of machinery that might explode if mishandled. So he sat in solitary fury, looking beyond the deep windows to the tops of the trees in Saint James's Park, trees that had already turned lemon and rust, but there was no poetry in his soul today.

When finally he was ushered into Balfour's room, he had again the uncomfortable impression of finding a man in a country house sitting room, a landed man not too familiar with cities. Balfour's thick and waved white hair was foppishly long, with full sideburns. It was deceptive. He might be dressed and groomed like a gregarious, easygoing man, but Balfour had no gift of intimacy. He made no offer of a seat, and Sir Cedric remained on his feet before the great desk like an errant courtier. Nor were there any preliminaries.

Balfour said, "My attention has been drawn to a telegram

dispatched to you from Cairo. From a young political officer called Kippax. It implies that he has been dealing with a delegation arrived there from King Ibn Saud of Riyadh."

"Yes, Secretary of State."

"It is not clear whom it is that Kippax serves."

"He is attached to the Arab Bureau."

"That does not answer my point."

"Originally, he was assigned by me."

"He reports to you as well as to Hogarth?"

"That is the procedure, Secretary of State."

Balfour's hands rested palms down with judicial stillness on an unblemished blotter. He betrayed no emotion in voice or eye; it was this assiduous impersonality that most unnerved Sir Cedric. After a pause, Balfour said, "Some of his work seems unscrupulous. I imagine *that* is procedure too." It was not a question but a statement of deplored fact.

Sir Cedric moved his weight from one foot to another, trying to conceal his outrage.

Balfour continued, "Well, it is perhaps propitious that we have such an opportunity to make contact with Saud. There is a matter of some delicacy to be explained to all the Arab sovereigns. I think perhaps you are aware of it?"

"Palestine."

"Palestine. We are about to confirm our support for Palestine as the future home of the Jewish people. May we entrust Kippax to deal in this matter with Ibn Saud? Saud is likely to present the most *unpredictable* response, though for myself, it is a peripheral rather than an immediate nuisance."

"Kippax would be an excellent choice."

"Then he should be recalled to London, so that he may be properly instructed."

"As you wish, Secretary of State."

Balfour seemed to expect more, and waited, but there was no glimmer of deference in Sir Cedric, no readiness to elaborate. Balfour picked up a note and scanned it as he spoke. "There is another matter. Tomorrow the War Cabinet has before it the final draft of the Zionist proposal—of which I approve. I wish Dr. Weizmann to be available to us, should we need to call him for background." He looked up suddenly. "You seem surprised, Assay."

"It is . . . rather *unusual*, I should have thought, Secretary of State, for an outsider to speak to cabinet."

Clive Irving

"You may, I think, contentedly leave the protocol to others. The prime minister thought it might be helpful. At any rate, I would like you personally to ensure that Dr. Weizmann is accommodated here in the office, and to be ready if called across to Downing Street."

"Of course."

"Yes." Balfour gave Sir Cedric an arctic smile. "You see, you clearly have such a *personal* interest in this issue, such familiarity with its ramifications, that it seems that you might usefully give Dr. Weizmann a briefing on the Arab point of view, which would serve well for the future."

Over Balfour's head hung a larger-than-life portrait of Lord Palmerston. Outwardly as regal as any monarch, Palmerston had always been one of Sir Cedric's inspirations. Palmerston had cemented the empire with a splendid lack of scruple and now, in the face of this far too pious master, Sir Cedric yearned for another of Palmerston's kind, a realist. Yet Balfour was clever, clever in the sly Scottish way; clever enough—or so it seemed for a moment—to have checkmated Sir Cedric.

He left Balfour, having faced but not conceded apparent defeat. There was little time left to evade it. The one hope was to enlist help from among those others who, with him, had swallowed too much.

And so he went that evening to the Turkish baths in Jermyn Street. In the steam room he sat with his breasts forming a fold like a dowager's carapace. With age, his skin had softened, not coarsened. Moist with steam, his belly shone. He sat alongside a man who was as angular as Sir Cedric was corpulent, who had the hue of bone china. They were alone in the vapors, with towels limp at their loins.

"I must say, Assay, you ask a lot in so short a time."

"It would be such a grievous lapse, to allow this Jew to address cabinet."

"I daresay it would. Tell me—I hear your master is a trifle squeamish about the activities of your department."

"Balfour is insufferably sanctimonious."

"It's a style—but not, my dear, the *entire* man."

"Oh?"

One limp towel was raised as the man dabbed his face and arranged himself on the slatted bench with spread legs. "Yes," he said, "but of course, you are an Oxford man. I was a contemporary of Balfour's at Cambridge. In those days he was

306

known as Pretty Fanny—a term not without the flaw of envy, due to the attraction he seemed to have for young maidens. Behind the Calvinist facade, I fancy, the lust is even now not quite dead, the volcano retains a faint glow.''

"You surprise me.''

"You have not heard of the Countess of Wemyss?''

Sir Cedric shook his head.

"The former Lady Elcho—of the greatly landed Wyndham family. A rather tragic liaison. She married old Elcho in preference to Balfour, but has surreptitiously nourished Balfour's flame ever since.''

Sir Cedric's buttocks slid forward on the slats as his curiosity advanced.

"As far as one knows, this passion has never been consummated—that is, *conventionally* consummated. Though to call it a chaste affair would, I think, diminish its ingenuity.'' He seemed suddenly to tire of prurience. "You need not, therefore, feel chastised by a morally superior force.'' He put the towel back on his loins with a gesture of virginal modesty. "So . . . you would like me to ensure that if there *is* a summons for Weizmann, if that should occur, the messenger will, unhappily, be misdirected? Inadvertently?''

"Can it be done?''

"But of course. You know, this Jewish chorus is becoming a frightful digression. I simply cannot get the prime minister's mind off it, though there are hopeful signs of dwindling patience; Montagu has sorely tried him. To the point, in fact, where this very morning the prime minister was reduced to shouting at me—yes, shouting like the Welsh primitive he can sometimes be. His words were quite revealing, as I recall: 'For God's sake, I will promise them the earth, if it wins surcease.' Alas, surcease is about all we *shall* win. Perhaps we should enlist some Jews as generals. They, at least, seem never to give up.'' He looked at Sir Cedric's roseate brow. "What *is* on your mind, my dear?''

"I was thinking, how fortunate that history is not a matter of record—not *real* history.''

"Ah! But you see, my dear, it is such a flawed word.'' His white skin was, in patches, becoming uncomfortably pink. "Conceptually flawed . . . with as many truths as points of view, and yet no real truths at all. As you say, how fortunate. I thought we might go to the Cavendish. Mrs. Lewis has managed to preserve some especially fine claret—and these days, one finds that that is one of the few remaining joys."

"Oh, *come* now."

By the time Kippax arrived in England, the weather had closed in on London; late October, and Whitehall was a place of unwarmed stone. Shivering under a melton coat, he knew that the East had thinned his blood and taken his heart; the city hit his senses not as a familiar habitat but as a strange one, cloistered for men breathing gray air. But the strings were always gathered here and his ambition lay, in the end, here too. His ambition and his nature were in conflict. His nature was better served in unroofed places than in these clotted rooms smelling of wax and kept too chill.

The truth was that, disgruntled by a hasty and opaque order home, he had become uncertain of his place. The war here was different. There was a bleakness in people's eyes, and tangible signs of shortage: of food, of fuel, and of stamina. In Whitehall, one generation remained in winged collars while another, more casually dressed but more out of patience with the futile conflict, spoke with the hardness of survivors. There was a demarcation, new to him, between rulers and apprentices. Kippax should have known his side of it, but he did not, another symptom of his uncertainty of place. Europe was still the only war to most people here. He was a stray from another theater, of which jokes were made—many of them now jokes at the expense of Lawrence.

Sir Cedric was quick to see this discord in his protégé. The Kippax last seen on the ship's deck in Port Said, accomplished and obedient, now sat with an edgy, mobile eye. Standing over him, Sir Cedric put a hand on the shoulder of his heavy coat. "You feel the cold?"

Kippax nodded.

"Acclimatization can be difficult at this time of the year. I am sorry it was so sudden."

"It's not only that."

"I see." Sir Cedric withdrew the hand slowly and walked back behind his desk, rubbing his palms together and looking at Kippax more carefully. "You have noticed the change, then?"

"It feels like the capital of the *defeated* power."

"Yes." Sir Cedric showed a trace of nervousness. "It must seem like that."

"How true is it?"

"No progress in France. The so-called big push gained nothing. Russia is no longer a force. It's going to be a damned close-run thing, depending now on America."

"I hadn't realized."

Sir Cedric was prepared to confide. "You know, our wits have always been more extensive than our resources as a nation. Alas, we cannot any longer live off our wits, Owen. We are bankrupt, or very nearly. Bust. *Broke*. Henceforth we shall have to get used to doing things on the cheap, as best we can. That is one of the reasons, I fear, for the lamentable concession on Palestine. It is imagined—quite foolishly—that the Jews will serve as the Occidental influence on our behalf."

"I thought you could stop that."

"Alas, not for want of trying. It has been fended off for some time—quite ingeniously, as it happens. But now that Montagu is out of the way, in India, Lloyd George wants to have it settled. One has tried. The original intent has been greatly diluted. A form of words will issue forth in a day or so—nebulous, to an extent. 'Auspices' is such a useful word. But I am under no illusions. It will prove troublesome."

"And that's what I have to try to explain to my Arabs: that you've opened the door of Palestine to the Jews?"

"*Your* Arabs? My dear Owen, you sound as possessive as Lawrence. Yes—that *is* the point of your being here, I'm afraid. The explanation is not something we could commit to a telegram."

Sir Cedric waited as Kippax got up to remove his coat, seeing his restlessness was verging on rebellion. "Look, Owen. I really think you had better understand. This will not be carte blanche for a Hebrew Palestine. We've stopped that, at least. There is a very specific safeguard for the indigenous peoples. As I said, we shall no longer command the resources to garrison every place that is vital to our interests. Our aim is to have Palestine as a secure base of Western influence—*not* to create an unnatural Hebrew enclave in an Oriental land."

"Forgive me, but that sounds like far too elegant a rationalization of a defeat."

"*Damn it, Owen!* You cannot walk into Whitehall with your desert allegiances and behave as though we can do as we please here—as *you* do there." Sir Cedric's face had turned florid.

But what deference Kippax may have had was draining from him. He folded his legs, one over the other, as though to mark a new independence. "But I was led to believe that you would be able to stop this—that the *office* would stop it, in spite of Balfour.''

Sir Cedric was driven to a dangerous point of anger that moderated rather than amplified his voice, easing it into a lapidary clarity. "Let us understand this. I went as far as I could—further, perhaps, than was wise. The original commitment to Zionism has been emasculated. It can in *no sense* be seen as a charter for statehood.'' He rubbed his palms slowly together. "I think you should understand how unbearable it would be for me to have to think that at some time in the future, near or distant, one of my successors, or *anyone* from the office, would find themselves facing across a conference table, on equal terms, the delegates of a Hebrew power. Unbearable. *Impossible.*''

"But it will carry some kind of moral obligation.''

"Moral obligation?'' Sir Cedric was suddenly and bizarrely amused. *"Moral obligation?"* He laughed in a series of mild, epicene convulsions and then, just as quickly, became injured, petulant. "Nobody has given any thought, *none at all,* to moral obligation. Had they done so, there would be no Balfour Declaration.''

# 18

## *Palestine ✻ August 1917*

They watched the frigate until its outline was lost in a featureless sea, one faint smudge of its smoke drifting north on the wind. The ships came rarely now, this one sent because the NILI had found a Turkish deserter with detailed knowledge of the defenses at Gaza, and he had been taken back to Cairo. With the ship's going, their lifeline seemed gone too; Koblensky had sent a note trying to uphold their spirits, but he could give no date for the offensive. Abba Laski sat with Sarah on the cliff, knowing her solitariness.

"You could have gone with them," he said.

"How could I—now?"

"There is little for us to do; you know that."

"There is my father."

Laski was reluctant to challenge her, but the reason was hard to accept. Ephraim Aaronsohn could be taken care of by others and would probably have been safer clear of the NILI than surrounded by them. Laski suspected that a stronger reason was that Sarah, without Feinberg and Koblensky, had become the group's spiritual sustenance. Laski and others filled part of the gap, but it was Sarah who provided what her brother had before her: the force of will and conviction to shield them from the faint hearts and antagonisms of Zichron as well as the Turks. Laski recalled the legend of the Maid of Saragossa and how she had been the steel of a Spanish resistance. Sarah, the sometimes strangely distant and unreachable Sarah—she must know how she bound them together. They needed binding. Lishansky was acting wildly in Jerusalem, and they had lost to the Turks an agent who was carrying documents that, if found, must compromise their security.

The sea had hardly the force to break over the rocks. The

311

night was motionless all along the coast. The land seemed to have lost its own energy. Bearing few crops now and extensively wasted, it had the look of a battlefield once the armies had gone. Yet the battle here was yet to come. Despite the heat, Sarah shivered. Laski helped her up and they went to their horses, she riding ahead. He felt the contradiction in their appearance—her slightness, his bulk—and how it misrepresented their relative strengths. He, as much as anyone, drew spirit from her and he had let her ride ahead as a natural thing. It was impossible to say to her what he felt—that she should have gone, given the chance. His misgivings were made worse because he had at this moment to leave her. He had to ride south to Tel Aviv to know more of the agent captured by the Turks, and to collect new intelligence on the Turkish supply lines. Later, leaving her at the house, he managed a pretense of confidence and hoped that she hadn't seen through it.

Not so long ago, Farouk Pasha had known the contentment of power within a secure empire. He had come from Constantinople to be the police chief, the *mudir*, of the ancient port of Caesarea. Albeit Caesarea was a backwater, but power over a backwater—absolute power—was preferable to the disputed power in the Ottoman capital. Farouk Pasha had also left a shrew of a wife and a disagreeable daughter in Constantinople and found in Caesarea a mistress, a Bedouin girl with the gift of mellowing him with sweet passion. The creases of despotism in his face gradually slackened. Palestine captivated him as a place in which a man could enjoy the last of his seasons in peace. Then, in as short a time as six months, Farouk Pasha saw the essence of his peace slip away. Caesarea was still seldom troubled by the war, but you could not walk the ramparts of that town now without knowing the Ottoman empire was ending its reign. Farouk Pasha closed his own world around him as tightly as he could, but the girl saw the melancholy in him—and saw his hardness reassert itself, and that frightened her. As men often do in such a mood, Farouk Pasha realigned his affections from people to pets, in his case his homing pigeons.

The yard was matted with brittle straw and crusted with pigeon droppings. It was enclosed by three walls that had been part of a Roman cell for the incarceration of zealots at the time of the Jewish revolt. The *mudir*'s home and headquarters had lineage. Successive tyrannies had been conducted on this spot for two thousand years, and the walls, still retaining three rusted iron rings, had absorbed as many screams as stains. Farouk Pasha, mindless of the past, had built his pigeon coops into the south wall. In late afternoon, when the yard still held the accumulated heat of the day, it had a powerful smell of fresh droppings and of those limestone walls. Farouk Pasha did not mind the smell—in fact, it had become a quirkishly soothing touch of an illusory domestic permanence, in a place where he and the birds communed, they with their arcane telepathy and he with his last narrowed affection.

He spread the seed in a random and capricious way, loving to have them beat around him as they fell on it. He spoke softly to them and they answered in a way he imagined to be reciprocal. It was their broken harmony that first drew his eye to the interloper—a less well fed bird than any of his own, pushing its way into their congregation like a lone heretic rising in a prayer meeting. The other birds snapped at it and beat their wings, but there was something obdurate in this bird that frightened them off and they left it to one strand of seed.

Farouk Pasha experienced an irrational outrage which, if inflicted on a human being, would have been lethal. But since the offender was a mere bird, he checked himself. The bird ate greedily, flicked its head round occasionally as though feeling the murderous gaze, and then, apparently sated, flew out of the yard and climbed in a slow circle directly above. Farouk Pasha's heat subsided a little and he gave out more seeds. Then the bird came back, at first flapping around the top of the walls, and Farouk Pasha realized that something had disrupted its sense of direction. It settled on a wall, half raising its wings nervously and bobbing its head. It looked down again into the yard, saw more seed, and rejoined the other birds, who this time did not molest it.

Farouk Pasha was about to swing a boot at the pigeon when he saw, for the first time, a small cylinder tied to one of its legs. The swing of the leg gave way to a quick lunge with his hands and he had the bird. The cylinder was tightly bound to its leg. He put the bird in a coop and went to find help.

What followed was the most bizarre interrogation ever seen in the police post. They took the cylinder, but the slip of onionskin paper it contained was covered in a code which none of them could read, a numerical cipher.

"Without a key, it's useless," said Farouk Pasha.

"Is it British?"

"How can we know?"

Then Farouk Pasha had an inspiration, remembering his own intimacy with birds. "We can talk to it," he said.

For a second, those around him, who knew of his childish communion with his birds, were about to laugh, and then they saw the reason in the idea. They tried giving the bird commands in English, German, Turkish, and Arabic, without result.

"How about Hebrew?"

None among them spoke Hebrew. There was a hiatus until an old Jewish trader, at first terrified and then deeply perplexed, was produced and ordered to address the pigeon. Still it stood, anchored in a sergeant's palm, the least agitated creature in the room, occasionally soiling the sergeant's wrist. Farouk Pasha had now taken the bird's attitude as a kind of insolence and was about to wring its neck. But then the old Jew offered, "What about Yiddish?"

Farouk Pasha checked himself and nodded.

The old man spoke in a low, singsong tongue that the rest of them in the room knew only as something that in the past had excluded them by design.

Immediately the bird began to flick its head and flex its wings.

"Come," said the old man.

The bird tried to leave the sergeant's hand.

"So . . ." breathed Farouk Pasha. "Now we have it."

The old Jew was released and Farouk Pasha went to the telephone. After twenty minutes of bureaucratic entanglement, he finally reached not Jemal Pasha, whom he had demanded, but Jemal Pasha's henchman, Hassan Bey.

Hassan Bey had the tone of a man disturbed from deep comforts. "A pigeon? You call Jemal Pasha about a pigeon?"

But as his mind clarified, Hassan Bey paid more attention, and said, with sudden resolution, "I will be there by morning. The bird is no use to me. I want the message."

Few Jews remained in Tel Aviv. Some of the Arabs from Jaffa had taken advantage of the Turkish persecutions to appropriate Jewish quarters, occupying them to their own convenience and in their own way. Abba Laski looked at these streets with despair: despair that the Arabs were so inflexibly regressive. He could never accept this in the Arabs, their rejection of innovation. It was, he conceded, a perverse strength, but a strength that must ultimately be doomed. He resisted generalized prejudices and, trying to accept the stench as though it were a fragrance, he rode to Rosenfeld's Quarter in the guise of a Levantine trader.

He came to a brick two-story block, the street level a series of arcaded shops, with apartments above. The old craftsmen in the shops had been allowed by the Turks to remain because their skills were irreplaceable. Silversmiths and goldsmiths, a tailor, and several carpenters were there as they had been for more than twenty years, even before the block had existed, when it had been a village. Laski went into a tailor's workroom. Three men, none less than sixty, sat in shade, talking. They gave him a cursory glance and then resumed. The stairs were behind the workroom. Coming to them, he heard from above the melancholic strains of a fiddle.

The fiddler sat in a pool of blanching light by a lace-fringed window. With one eye he saw Laski come into the room, but he continued to play, the rim of the fiddle implanted in his neck and his few remaining strands of black hair falling over his forehead. There was a square of silk cushioning his chin on the fiddle. When he stopped playing he wiped his chin first, then his mouth—the mouth of a sensual man, even though old, with the jowls fallen around it.

His voice had the same melancholia as the music, but in Yiddish was expressive of soul as well as mind. "You don't lose weight," he said.

Laski settled into a sagging leather armchair.

"You should lose weight," persisted the fiddler. "I don't understand, in these times, how you stay fat. Fat we don't have."

"It's glands, Isaac."

"Glands? They tell you it's glands? It's not glands; it's the mind." He laid the fiddle on a small table with the gentleness of a mother putting a child into a crib, and kept two fingers on it, tapping lightly, as he spoke. "Fat is not good. You won't live to see forty."

"Does it matter? It's not likely that I will see forty whatever shape I am."

"*Does it matter?* You shouldn't talk like this." The fingers stopped tapping. "You know about Naaman Belkind?"

Laski nodded.

"He was careless. Like Lishansky. Lishansky will be caught

315

too. Too much mouth, Lishansky. We should never use people with mouth. Naaman had papers.''

"They got the papers?"

"They got the papers, that we know. What we don't know is, can they break the code?"

"*Damn* it."

The fiddler rose and dabbed his forehead with the silk. "How is Sarah?"

"She should leave Zichron."

The fiddler went to a samovar and there was silence between them as he filled two glasses and dropped lemon slices into them.

"No sugar. We don't have sugar for months. . . . You tried to get her to leave?"

Laski grunted.

The fiddler smiled knowingly. "She didn't leave. She won't leave. She is not the kind." But the speculation troubled him. "It's better that she leaves now."

"Because of Belkind?"

The fiddler dipped a finger into the steaming tea and pulled out the lemon to suck it. "Not just Belkind. The rabbi we have to worry about."

"Rabbi Dor?"

"Dor has his back so close to the wall that he cannot see the writing on it. You know how they think. The Agudath Yisrael have warned him. We are a curse." He put the lemon back into the glass and drained the tea. "The Aaronsohns are hated most. Dor will betray us."

"And Malik."

"Malik too. But with Malik there is no art. With Dor it becomes holy." He looked solemnly at Laski. "I want that you get Sarah out. Even if you have to drag her by her hair."

"It's that serious?"

"It's that serious. The British are not coming in time."

Hassan Bey fingered the sliver of paper and held it up to the light as though by transparency it might reveal its secrets. He was a small man, reaching only to the shoulders of Farouk Pasha standing beside him, but he was trim and dauntingly in command. "I have seen this before," he said.

"You can read it?"

"I do not need to read it. At least I know where it comes

from." He spoke in high classical Turkish, and part of the intimidation of his presence was the aristocratic sureness in every one of his movements. Even the grip of his fingers on the paper was almost exaggeratedly fastidious; the hands were white and manicured. "Yes . . . I know the source." He discarded the paper and turned to Farouk Pasha. "Your passion for pigeons is propitious." He brushed the cracked mahogany floor with the point of a boot to detach a crust of the straw from the yard. "It gives you pleasure, the birds?"

Farouk Pasha found the triviality of the question suspicious. "It is interesting."

"Strange, is it not, how they navigate?"

Farouk Pasha nodded.

But Hassan Bey frowned. "Not much else to excite you?"

"Well . . ."

"To be betrayed by a pigeon—would you call it an act of God?"

"Well . . ."

"Do you *like* this place?" This time he lacked the patience for Farouk Pasha's evasions. "Has it ever struck you what an accursed place Palestine is? In particular, how it seems always to destroy its rulers?"

Farouk Pasha was about to reply more affirmatively, but Hassan Bey was already walking away, adjusting his belts and beckoning his two adjutants out of the shadows. Over his shoulder he said, "You had better come with us. At least we can put an end to this nuisance." Then, in the sunlight, surveying the Roman ramparts, he said, "It will break the monotony for you."

Why, wondered Farouk Pasha, did Hassan Bey use cloves on his breath?

Sarah watched the birds clustering in the orchard below as the light broke over the hill. She had been sitting all night with her father. Now he was sleeping and she was too fatigued to sleep. There was no fruit on the trees for the birds to ravage; lack of irrigation had withered the orchard and the few leaves were already a shriveled ocher. Where did the birds find their food? They seemed as numerous as ever, though poor things. She turned away from the light to look again at her father. In what seemed to have become a progressive reduction in family and friends, she had grown closer to her father as he had grown weaker. The thinning thread of his life sustained her, making her

317

more aware of her own resilience. She was more fearful for others than aware of her own jeopardy.

She was distracted by the sound, unusual so early, of a car climbing the hill from the northwest. Looking beyond the orchard to the road, she saw a black sedan and recognized it as Meyer Malik's. While the land withered, Malik had somehow progressed from his horse carriage to a Panhard landau. It changed gear at the top of the hill and did not stop at the Aaronsohn house, coasting down into Zichron. She went downstairs to make breakfast, without any appetite.

Alone in the kitchen, she realized what it was that had reinforced her affection for her father. There was an element of selfishness in it. He embodied their will to hold this land; he had known it as she never had, far more barren even than it was now. That was her obligation, to carry on, made more secure by his presence. She wondered about the past she had never known and about which he seldom spoke, of a ghetto in Rumania and the peculiar claustrophobia that ghettos had—at one and the same time their strength and their curse, the strength of the tight community and the curse of confinement. She tried to imagine what her father's first step onto Palestinian soil must have felt like, how it must have lifted from him the last vestiges of that confinement with its burst of a light that no European city had known, the same light she had seen tint the orchard that morning. If there was such a thing as a holy light, it was here. Religious hyperbole had little appeal for her, but "holy" would serve as an explanation of how the light raised her spirits.

As he had now for weeks, her father would sleep through the morning. She found Abu Farid and he brought her horse around for her. She rode down to the coastal plain on deserted tracks, through a eucalyptus grove and to the banks of a river called the Nahar Ha-Taninim, after the crocodiles supposed to inhabit it. She had swum here often, and encountered nothing more frightening than the sweet water crab. As a child she had looked back up toward Zichron, and the escarpment had been covered in a forest. Now it was blighted, only stumps of the trees left. On the bared land, once deep in fern, the winds had already stripped the topsoil to rock and the hillside was discolored like oxidized iron. The surviving eucalyptuses in the grove were outcrops of trees that her brother had introduced into the salt marshes as a device to drain them: eucalyptus soaked up the brine. The relative scale of one man to this landscape had once seemed to represent an unequal struggle, but Aaron Aaronsohn had not been daunted by it. She was sick at heart to be reminded of how easily his work had been undone, reminded by these trees which were like his handprints. She tethered the horse in the grove and slept until the sun left no shade.

She returned on a track that brought her to the stable at the back of the house. It was not until she got down from the horse that she had a sense of disturbance, not from anything she could see but from an absence of things. None of the boys was in the gardens or stable, nor was Abu Farid. The window of her father's bedroom above, closed when she left, was open and the curtains lifted in a breeze. Borne on the heat of the day there was a new, intrusive smell: of oil and gasoline, of motor vehicles.

She came to the drive from the side of the house. There were three Turkish military cars there, a dilapidated Turkish truck, and a few yards behind them, glinting with mirror-bright metal, Meyer Malik's car. Everything was clear to her in an instant—not just these physical details, nor even their implication, but a sense of something overwhelmingly inevitable. It was as though everything about to happen to her had been already assembled in her subconscious, wanting only the definition of faces. The sudden reality of it induced no fear; the fear had gone before and been a fear of the uncertain, and the fear for others. Uncertainty had gone; the next hours would settle things as they had to be settled.

The house had been ransacked. Any part of it that might have been used for concealment was torn apart. Turkish soldiers were still at work upstairs. The staff had been herded into the kitchen and were being interrogated by two sergeants, one using Turkish and the other Arabic. Hassan Bey, with little interest in this process, had gone on his own into what had been Aaron Aaronsohn's study, and from the things strewn on the floor was picking out items and looking them over in the calm manner of a connoisseur going through objets d'art in an auction room. He was holding and appraising a watercolor of a wild flower, its frame hanging loose, when Farouk Pasha burst into the room.

"We have her!"

Hassan Bey shifted his attention slowly from the painting to Farouk Pasha's enlivened and flushed face. "Bring her."

Sarah came slowly into the room, Farouk Pasha gripping her by one arm. She looked from the devastation to Hassan Bey. Her eyes were moist but her gaze had an iron contempt.

319

Hassan Bey bowed gravely and held out the painting; fragments of glass fell from the frame. "The windflower, I think? *Anemone coronazia,* to a classicist. Your brother is a classicist, I fancy. This is a revelation to me, the perfection of his work. Something I was not prepared for, although Jemal Pasha has often spoken of it." He put the painting on top of other debris on a table and then pressed his palms together as he looked at her, in a gesture more of gravity than of accusation.

With sudden force, she said, "When Jemal Pasha knows what you have done here, he will want an explanation." She spoke in French, which Hassan Bey understood but Farouk Pasha plainly did not.

Hassan Bey's expression did not change. He said to Farouk Pasha, "Leave her with me." Then, in the French of a Paris salon, he said to Sarah, "You really do not suppose that he would do this without Jemal Pasha's direct consent?"

"Then why?"

His gravity changed to a fragile smile. "I am sure you know why."

"There is no possible excuse for—"

He cut her off with a suddenly hardened voice. "First, we have Belkind. Then we were fortunate enough to intercept one of your pigeons. In the last few minutes we located the rest of the pigeons, and the cylinders. I do not understand how you have survived for so long. It is quite inexcusable. Of course, the betrayal of Jemal Pasha has caused him great pain. So I would prefer that you make no further evasions. We are intelligent people, you and I. Civilized people. We do not have to abandon our standards—even if we do find ourselves on different sides."

Sarah heard an altercation from the kitchen and then a man's scream.

"Where is my father?"

"Your father is a sick man. I have not moved him, for the moment."

She tensed and cried out, "You will not move him, you *cannot.*"

"You will be cooperative, then?"

Before she could reply, someone spoke from behind her, coming into the room. "I am sorry to see that you have been left here so defenseless. What has become of your dear friends, Feinberg and Koblensky? I am told they have not been seen for some time."

Even before he spoke she knew the heavy perfume of Meyer Malik. He was at her side now, and looking into the study, sighed and said, "So unnecessary, this distress, after all the advice I gave you."

Hassan Bey echoed Malik. "Where are they, your bold praetorians?" Knowing he would not get an answer, he added, "At least we know where your brother is."

For once, she betrayed herself. "My brother?"

Malik laughed. "Too far to help you now—in London, with the Zionists."

"Yes," said Hassan Bey. "His defection has added to Jemal Pasha's feelings, so much that he was quite unable to come here himself—and your obtuseness has disappointed Mr. Malik, as you can see. We have no quarrel with anyone else in Zichron. The rabbi seems as out of patience with you as we are. You are a woman alone now; what is the point of frustrating me any further?" He maintained the pretense of regret, turning half away from her, shuffling through papers pulled from a rolltop desk. "Of course, you would need little imagination to see what must happen if you cannot help me." He came upon a photograph, an old and slightly yellowed group portrait. His finger settled on a face. "This is Joseph Lishansky, I believe? Malik—can you confirm?"

Malik took the photograph and nodded.

"We have him too," said Hassan Bey. "There were British documents in his room. *They* are your paymasters, of course."

More shouting and screams came from the kitchen. Hassan Bey stepped forward and took Sarah by an arm, lightly, and led her to the kitchen. One of the stableboys was on his back on the floor, pushed so violently to the wall that his head was dipped into his chest. One side of his face was blue and swollen and blood ran from his hair. A Turk stood astride over him with one boot slicing its heel into his chest.

Sarah cried out, "Stop . . . *stop!* He knows nothing. None of them knows anything."

Hassan Bey let his hand fall from her arm and quietly said, "If that is the case, you can save them any more discomfort."

"She will need more encouragement," said Malik.

Hassan Bey nodded. He called Farouk Pasha, who had been appropriating some silver cutlery. "Take her. When you have persuaded her to talk, you can call me." He dusted the hem of his tunic with a brush of the fingertips and adjusted his belts.

321

"Malik, we shall call on the rabbi. Perhaps he can find something for us to eat."

By delegating her torture to Farouk Pasha, he seemed to put a wall between the world in which he could talk to Sarah in French and the world into which she now passed, where her interrogator would demand answers in Turkish and his methods would have no vestige of decency. For a second, watching Hassan Bey pull on white kid gloves before she was dragged away, she saw quite clearly that the wall was self-deceiving. He had the same barbarism in him that in Farouk Pasha was unconcealed; it was simply that for Hassan Bey, the problem involved how much of himself he could reveal to her.

The house subsided into a deceptive peace. The staff were taken off to a Turkish garrison. Farouk Pasha and two sergeants remained, one of them with Farouk Pasha and Sarah in the basement and the other left to roam the house and to keep an eye on Ephraim Aaronsohn upstairs. The air of calm, though, was unnatural in the way that a plague-visited village might seem calm.

North of Tel Aviv, the coastal plain was divided, north from south, by the largest Palestinian river, the Yarkon. For the Turks, the Yarkon was an effective barrier to freedom of travel. The few crossings from the coast to the river's source at the base of mountains in the east were covered by guard posts. Going south, Abba Laski had chosen to cross the Yarkon well to the east, where it was more sparsely populated and the Turks less vigilant, but now on his return to the north he was in too much haste for the detour. The best road out of Tel Aviv kept south of the Yarkon until it reached the oldest Jewish colony in Palestine, Petah Tikva, and from there it curved north to cross the river at an iron bridge. In Petah Tikva, the orange groves were as devastated as Aaronsohn's crops and most of the original settlers had been driven out with the first Turkish purge, ending up in Alexandria. But in a collapsing barn at the corner of an almond orchard was another survivor of the NILI's staging posts.

It was nightfall when Laski reached the barn.

The old man looked pityingly at the horse. "You ride that horse too hard. Like that he will die under you."

"He needs water, that's all."

"And a day in the stable." The old man took the horse and patted its nose. "You kill the horse, where will you be?" He led the animal into a corner of the barn where there was barely enough straw to cover the stone, and much of it had already been fouled. The old man produced a bucket of water and another of alfalfa. The horse's fatigue had the better of its thirst and appetite; it seemed hardly able to dip its head to the bucket, and the old man had to encourage it to drink and then took a handful of the alfalfa to get it to eat. He looked over to where Laski was splashing his face from another bucket. The old man said nothing and continued to feed the horse until half of the alfalfa had gone, then he put it down and the horse was able to finish it.

"You're crossing by the bridge?" said the old man.

Laski nodded.

"By day it's dangerous, by night reckless. The Turks have been replaced by Germans."

"I have papers."

"You have papers." The old man shook his head as he echoed Laski and squatted on a wooden bench. "The Germans, they don't look at papers, they look at people." Suddenly his face cracked into a laugh. "I am German too. Did you know that? I come here in 1888. This colony was ten years old. You want tea?"

Laski nodded.

"Where you come from? Not from Germany."

"England."

"Ah—England." The old man groped myopically in a corner for glasses. "How long you live here?"

"Since I was two years old."

"You have English in your face." The samovar coughed and spluttered as he turned the tap. "The English, they don't usually stay. Where's your family?"

Laski took the glass. "They died. Malaria."

"So." The old man's tone became a shade less critical and a shade more patriarchal. "You take my advice, wait until morning. The best time is between seven and eight. The Turks are moving then."

"I can't wait."

"The river is low. Twenty miles from here, you could ford it."

"Too far."

"Then give the horse an hour." His hands were shaking. A father without sons, a son without a father—their incapacity to connect distressed and defeated him. His ancient long-tailed alpaca coat seemed to hang on him as not merely too large but suddenly too heavy, one shoulder, its seam split, slipping an inch down his arm. His yellowing eyes hung on Laski, but Laski was indifferent, taking up a fistful of straw and dusting off his boots. The old man felt there was too much energy left in Laski for his own good, and more strength than at first appeared possible in so porcine a figure. The frailty of the barn, with its splintered timbers and sundered roof, the exhaustion of the horse, and the disconsolate old man were all of them ill-matched to Laski's momentum. "Give the horse an hour," repeated the old man.

Laski looked at the horse. "An hour," he said, relenting with reluctance.

Watered, the horse did seem to revive. The old man stood, head cocked to one side, as Laski prepared to leave. He said, "The river is difficult. You could ford it about six miles from here. Crazy in the dark, but you are crazy, maybe crazy and lucky. Then you miss the bridge. I feel a lot better if you miss the bridge."

"Six miles east?"

The old man nodded.

"I don't like Germans. Perhaps you are right."

He found the crossing in little more than an hour, but the old man had not exaggerated the problem of an attempt in the dark. The track dipped sharply down to the water, and it was impossible to gauge how deep it was; the far embankment was hard to pick out, and the current showed itself in dark rippled lines moving fast. The horse was reluctant even to take a step beyond the gravel—frightened as much as anything by the noise. Laski's heels urged it forward. The riverbed seemed firm from frequent use, and not as deep as he had thought. He eased up the pressure on the horse and let it find its own confidence. They were two-thirds over when, without warning, the horse's front legs lost their hold in a sudden shift and the current smacked into its flank, pushing them sideways. Laski felt the water to his knees and tried to pull the horse back. By then the animal had had enough of Laski and the river. It kicked at the riverbed with its hind legs and unbalanced him. As Laski fell into the water, the horse swam off on its own, head and mouth just clear of the torrent.

\* \* \*

Rabbi Dor adjusted his *streimel*, looking in a mirror, and then gathered around him his folds of silk like a duchess preparing to enter a ballroom. "Two days . . ." he said, and shook his head in perplexity. "*Two* days. You see, the woman has lost her reason; she is a fanatic. I saw that in her long ago. That, I knew, was what would bring us this trouble."

Behind and to one side of him stood Meyer Malik, tiring of the rabbi's prolonged vanities. "We must go."

The rabbi tried one more arrangement of his garments and then pulled a hair from his nostril. "What is the hurry? I cannot help her now, even if I wanted to."

"Hassan Bey has been waiting half an hour."

"Hassen Bey," repeated the rabbi equivocally. "Hassan Bey . . . How well do you know him?" He turned from the mirror and gave Malik an imperious scrutiny.

"Not all that well."

"Would you say he was a devout man, a good Muslim?"

"Well . . ."

"He is too much of an aristocrat; I know *that* kind. He cannot conceal his profanity."

"We have to go," insisted Malik.

As they drove up the hill through Zichron, they were watched visibly and invisibly. By now the town had a collective knowledge of the terrible event that was taking place and of which the rabbi's journey was the latest sign, Malik's car bearing the aura of one on is way to join a funeral cortege.

"Earthly things," intoned the rabbi as they caught sight of the Aaronsohn house. "I see Hassan Bey as a man who loves earthly things." The car could not get far into the drive because the Turkish army vehicles blocked the way. Malik got down and opened the door for the rabbi. They walked into the house at a pace that the rabbi measured as appropriate to underscore his indifference to punctuality.

It was the morning of the third day after Hassan Bey's arrival and nothing had been done to conceal the initial devastation of the house. In fact, things had grown worse. Farouk Pasha's men had taken up residence, demanding of the staff to be fed in the kitchen, and appropriating rooms to sleep in. Farouk Pasha and Hassan Bey had each taken bedrooms, Farouk Pasha displacing Ephraim Aaronsohn, who had been moved to a servants' dormitory. As well as the disarray, there was a new odor which made both men recoil.

Clive Irving

Hassan Bey greeted the rabbi in the hall, showing no trace of impatience. "I am grateful," he said, bowing and kissing a ring on the rabbi's hand. "It was a lot to expect of you." He led the way from the hall into the rear of the house, finally to the room backing onto the conservatory.

The curtains were closed. Hassan Bey went in first and drew one of the curtains half open.

The odor here was even stronger. As the single filtered shaft of light came across the floor, the rabbi's eyes began to make out the edge of a divan and part of an arm and a hand. The rest of the body on the divan was in brown half-light and seemed inert. Then the clearly visible hand moved away from the light, shrinking from it, and rose to shield a face.

Hassan Bey drew aside another curtain.

The rabbi drew in his breath sharply, unable to keep his composure.

Sarah Aaronsohn's head was on a pillow. The hand was still across her eyes, but her mouth was visible, both lips swollen, dried blood on her chin. She was in a light cotton dress that was gathered at her calves as though in an attempt to seal her in a shroud. The dress had lost all shape. It was ripped across the waist and discolored by bloodstains. The last thing the rabbi saw was her feet—or rather the soles of her feet, with great weals across them.

"How long—how long has she been like this?"

Hassan Bey, as though noting the time of day, said, "Thirty-six hours. You see how stubborn she is."

"Stubborn?" said the rabbi.

Malik looked nervously at Hassan Bey.

"Stubborn?" repeated the rabbi. He went slowly to the divan and looked down at her. The bending of his head was in itself a collapse of his hauteur. He stood like that, silent, shielding her from the intrusive light with his great draped shadow for a full minute before speaking again. "I did not understand. . . ."

The hand moved slowly from her face to her side, but her eyes remained lidded. They were bruised and puffed, and there was a deep scratch just above the bridge of her nose.

The rabbi picked up her hand and pressed it between his. "Can you hear me, my child?"

Her lips broke apart, dry and raw, but no sound came.

"I did not understand," he repeated in a voice that was no longer sonorous. He turned on Malik. "What good can this do?"

326

"You said yourself, she is a fanatic. Only a fanatic would refuse to cooperate."

"What do you want from her?"

Hassan Bey, retaining his immunity to the circumstances, said, "Names. We need names. Then we can leave her."

The rabbi's heavy brows dipped again toward the divan. Sarah's eyes remained closed. He bent and replaced her arm by her side, finally letting go the hand. He walked from the divan to the windows and pulled the curtains closed again. Then, his back to the windows, he said, " ' . . . and for the informer, let there be no hope.' " He looked at Malik. "That is the law of the Torah. She knows it better than you." He walked slowly across to the door and stopped. "I cannot help you. Nor can I help her. There is no fear in her."

"That is the trouble," said Hassan Bey. "Fear must be respected. It is a form of sanity. Your people know that."

Rabbi Dor bowed his head and left the room.

In the dark, Sarah's eyes moved painfully; she heard the rabbi's steps, heavy and slow, cross the hall.

Hassan Bey said, caustically, in French, "So passes God." He looked down at the divan. "We will leave her . . . for the moment." But when Malik had left, driving a silent rabbi back to the town, Hassan Bey returned to her, alone. Leaving the room dark, he moved a chair some feet away from the divan, took out a cigarette and lit it, looking at the shapeless form as he exhaled. For some minutes he sat without speaking, the smell of the cigarette countering the other smell. He could see that her eyes were open now, but she stared up at the ceiling, and no other part of her moved. There existed a form of intimacy between them—a level at which each was revealed to the other in a mute and yet complete knowledge beyond the stalemate of wills. He knew that each of them had been broken in the contest, she bodily and he just as severely, but internally, in parts of him that had no name, or none that had any meaning to him. Her resistance had dislodged his self-esteem in some fateful way, more profoundly than what the crass Farouk Pasha felt was humiliation; Hassan Bey's self-esteem was a refined state of grace now irreparably flawed by this woman, and with no result. Even worse, the injury was an omen he could read all too clearly. She had become part of a dissolution far greater than anything testing his own authority, but she intensified it by personalizing it, bringing it to the dimension of this room and thereby trapping him within it. This was a sickening knowledge and the most offensive part of the feeling in him, laying waste his life while hers—at his hands—had culminated in meaning. Leaving the room, coming again into light, he had the face of a general who knows he has lost a battle before it even begins.

To Farouk Pasha he said, "Leave her until afternoon."

But half an hour later, Farouk Pasha heard her moving. He called Hassan Bey and they went into the room. She was sitting on the divan, hunched forward, unable to keep her feet on the floor because of the bastinado wounds.

"I would like to wash. I cannot reach the bathroom."

Hassan Bey nodded. He gestured to Farouk Pasha and each of them took an arm and lifted her across the room to a door, and through it to a bathroom.

"I'm all right now."

Hassan Bey closed the door and went back into the other room and opened all the curtains, then a window to ventilate the room. Farouk Pasha sensed the other man's tension without divining its cause. Hassan Bey had opened each curtain and tied the sashes with the soulless precision of a drill movement. Now he stood at the open window as though no one else were in the room.

When the single pistol shot rang out, Hassan Bey remained as still as if he had been expecting it. Farouk Pasha, about to leave the room, came running back, but Hassan Bey still gazed out the window, and stayed there while Farouk Pasha burst into the bathroom. Sarah was on the floor, the gun still in her right hand by her head. Blood bubbled from her mouth.

By the time a doctor reached the house from Zichron, she was back on the divan, but the hastily improvised bandaging had not stemmed the bleeding. The doctor removed the dressing and tried to clean up her face. Then he gave her a closer examination.

"The bullet has gone through the mouth and lodged in the spinal column."

Hassan Bey was expressionless.

"She is paralyzed," said the doctor, checking her limbs, "completely paralyzed from the neck down." There was no response from hands or feet. He stood a pace back from the divan, still clinically impersonal. "That will be permanent, the paralysis. But if we got her to a hospital she might be saved."

Farouk Pasha and the doctor waited for Hassan Bey.

He said, "Saved? *What for?*"

\*     \*     \*

For the first time in his life, Abba Laski was lame. It was a trivial injury, the wrenched ankle, but fatal to his journey. He would have had more patience with a serious injury, with anything showing blood, but was enraged by the time the ankle cost him. He had fallen awkwardly into the Yarkon and by the time he was able to swim, the current had carried him well clear of the ford. It was only when he began to climb up the bank that the ankle registered itself and became so painful that his left leg could bear no weight at all.

He dragged himself as far from the river as he was able, unclear of the distance in the darkness. His movement was made easier by an irrigation trench. The pipes were gone, taken up by the Turks to be reused for water lines at the Gaza front. From a derelict orange grove Laski kept trying to work himself northwest, toward the coast. There was no cover until he found the site of a water pump. The pump had been ripped out with the pipes. In its place, where water had formed a pool in the spring, the burnet thorns had sprouted and knitted into a thick cover. Laski was so completely hidden that even when the sun came up, little light got to him. The shattered brickwork was thick with snails and enormous worms.

He left his cover cautiously in the afternoon. He was thirsty, but the pain of the ankle seemed to dull his appetite. Tearing a strip from his shirt sleeve, he drew it in a tight bandage around the ankle. With this support he was able to hobble faster than before. Just before evening he saw the landmark he was making for: a high tower, like a swollen minaret. It was still two miles or more away, but it marked the coast and hoped-for refuge. He stopped moving until after dark.

The tower adorned the tomb of a Muslim saint; within its shadow lived an Arab whom Laski had known only as Ahmed the Fist. Laski had always suspected that Ahmed's Arab blood was mingled with African; his build was more like a Nubian's and his skin had a dense mahogany color. Once, he was a legendary bare-fist fighter in Jaffa. For the last ten years, he had operated smuggling from this ancient port of Apollonia—a place of three legends, beginning with Apollo and then embracing Jews and Arabs. Ahmed the Fist had been one of the NILI's best agents, and the only one who had his own boat.

Laski had to stay with Ahmed for five days, the first three because of his ankle and the final two because Ahmed's boat had other priorities. On the night they finally left, the sea was blowing into a heavy swell with an onshore wind. It was a trip of forty miles to a landing and a rendezvous. Before he reached the shore, Laski was violently sick.

Between the beach and the railway was an abandoned factory, built originally by Baron de Rothschild to produce bottles for local vineyards. The vineyards had failed and the bottle factory with them. Now, in a cellar of the factory, Abu Farid, Sarah's driver, waited for Laski.

In the light of one lamp Abu Farid looked worse than he felt. Farouk Pasha's men had knocked out most of his front teeth, his nose was broken, and his body was scarred in several places. But the physical pain had been secondary to his emotional shock.

As soon as Laski saw Abu Farid, he forgot his own nausea. "What happened?"

Abu Farid told the story of the interrogation and of Sarah's end; she had died three days after she shot herself, the day that Laski had tried to ford the river. As Abu Farid talked, Laski stood quite still, his body stiffening and his eyes half closed. Finally he put a hand on Abu Farid's shoulder. "Where is she?"

"In the cemetery at Zichron."

"Zichron?"

Abu Farid shrugged. "There was no choice."

Laski took his hand from Abu Farid's shoulder and walked away from the lamp. Outside, it was getting light, and the cellar seemed suddenly very cold.

# 19

## *Sinai * October 1917*

Men began to act unnaturally, as men did before battle, forcing confidence into themselves. Allenby had set the attack for dawn, two days hence. His slowness in going to battle had been due to an insistence on massing artillery—far more guns than Koblensky had ever seen. Koblensky knew enough of war to know that a battle very quickly had a life of its own—or rather, a will of its own, the fusion of wills. Defeat was planned more easily than victory. Allenby was careful; the slaughter in France had made him determined not to squander lives. Russian generals had not been so squeamish; Koblensky hoped that the careful general would win. At least he had used his brain. His plan rested on deception: False papers had been "lost" near the Turkish lines, designed to confirm that Allenby's movement toward Beersheba was a feint, that his main thrust would be at Gaza. Beersheba was only lightly defended—and Beersheba was still, in truth, Allenby's main target.

Koblensky had heard people say that Allenby wanted his guns to be heard in London—meaning that this was a remote war that would be noticed only with a victory. If Allenby took Jerusalem, the disasters of France might, for once, fade from attention. Looking at this seemingly unblemished landscape, Koblensky felt unattached to these devious calculations and the juggernaut that was about to roll.

His mind was beyond the armies, to the fragile enclave of Sarah, about which there was no word.

Then Bron arrived at the field headquarters from Cairo. He called Koblensky to the map tent. As usual, he was brisk and yet nervous.

"When you and Feinberg last saw Lawrence, at the bridge, he discussed how it might be blown up?"

"Yes."

"And you—do *you* think it possible?"

"As long as there is surprise—total surprise."

"Surprise . . ." Bron unrolled a map which had been so tightly wound that it kept rolling back on itself until he pressed hard on it. "Luck too, I should think." He nodded to the snaking line of the Yarmuk south of Galilee. "You see what it would achieve for us? At the right time. If that bridge went, the Turks and the Huns would be cut off from Damascus in a decisive way. No heavy stuff, no big troop movements, could happen."

"When?"

"Allenby wants it done on November five or the two succeeding nights. The timing is crucial."

"But that's next week."

"Lawrence is already moving, from Azrak. He has sappers, Indian machine gunners, and a lot of Arabs. We can get you on a destroyer tonight, to Athlit before dawn. The rest is up to you, and your people. Lawrence wants you to cut off the guards on the north side, to cut the telephone between them and their headquarters. But you can't cut the telephone until you see the bridge blown; it would alert them."

"Athlit?" Koblensky's mind leaped from these map rooms with the crayon lines and clustered flag pins, from the drilled and massive army. "We can do it."

The captain of the destroyer was a dour, uncommunicative man, consumed in his charts and asking no questions of Koblensky. As they headed north past Gaza, even though they were fifteen miles out to the west, the flares illuminating the town and the military positions were starkly clear: The Turks had built a deeply layered defense in response to what they imagined was Allenby's own orthodoxy. It was not until the destroyer was abreast of Caesarea, after midnight with a disturbing clarity to the sky, that the captain began to alter course to get closer to the shore, and all the time he had the sharpened senses of a man expecting discovery at any moment. Koblensky sat alongside him on the bridge, recognizing the profile of the distant hills, even the summit on which stood Zichron. The ship's radioman came to the bridge, looking anxious.

"I can't get any answer, sir. No response to the usual signals."

Distracted from a different anxiety, the captain said nothing and then looked at Koblensky.

Koblensky said, "How long have you tried?"

But it was the captain who answered. "We were warned this might happen, but they insisted we come." He looked out into the sea and then back at Koblensky. "Apparently there have been no messages from your people for over a week. We couldn't raise the man in Tel Aviv."

"I've tried all three wavelengths," said the radio operator. "There's nothing."

"Do you want to go?" said the captain.

Koblensky could see that the captain would be glad to turn back. "I have to," he said.

The captain frowned. "It's bloody tricky. I can't take the ship too close. You'll have to row yourself ashore. The dinghy doesn't matter."

The captain, Koblensky saw, was for some reason near to losing his nerve.

The dinghy dropped into the water from the davits with deft control, shipping not one drop of water. Koblensky jumped into it from a lowered companionway. The sea was virtually motionless. He threw the bow rope to a seaman, and without looking up to the bridge, pulled out the oars and turned the dinghy toward the shore, about half a mile away. His first impression of the sea had been deceptive. Closer to the shore there was a strong current running, which he could not fight. He had to push obliquely and all the time was slipping farther south of the Athlit creek, coming to beach instead by the salt marshes, where there was no cover. The destroyer had gone. Forgivingly, Koblensky realized that it must have seemed reckless to the captain to put so many men at risk for this stray dog of the night. The surf was now a brilliant white and about to lift the dinghy with it. He took in the oars and sat low to try to keep the boat as stable as possible as it was caught. The beach was fringed by a shallow rock shelf. The dinghy's bow hit the rock and reared up, tearing at the wood, but with enough force to beach itself, ending portside on at a steep tilt.

Koblensky was hardly wet. He picked his waterproof pouch and his sandals from the dinghy and felt the sharp, cool flint under his feet. The dinghy was hit by another surge of water and began to become bedded in the wet gravel. Ahead of Koblensky was a line of low dunes; mingled with the tart air of the beach he could smell the sourness of the marshes behind the dunes. These were the sensations of acquaintance, of returning. The current had brought him well to the south of Athlit, nearer to Zichron, but there was no cover between the dunes and the railway. Something here had changed; something more than the desolation of once fertile land. There was a new deterioration, some deeper neglect that had its own look, more pervasive than the others—the look of subjection and defeat. He knew it because as a Russian he was no stranger to it. A land could die as easily as people. He reached the railway. Down the line to the south there were no lights at the station. The telephone line overhead seemed the only live element of the night, sighing in the light wind. There were no lights anywhere on the hillside.

There had been no rain for months; the track he climbed had horse prints embossed in it as hard as rock, but no trace of recent horse droppings. He reached the boundary of the Aaronsohn land as the dawn came, but there was no chorus in the orchards, not a thread of nourishment in them. When he saw the house, its darkness was uniform; windows were shuttered and nothing moved in the breeze. He reached the stables. The stalls were as dry and unsoiled as the path had been, and stripped of straw. The most ominous sight was the conservatory. Its door was locked, but through the glass he saw that the vines and plants, though all in place, were withered into parched and brittle effigies; like the specimens that Aaronsohn had once dried for his albums, but in a broken mass with just a few shriveled colors, pepper-tinted buds, fallen to the floor.

The lock of the conservatory was feeble and he forced the door easily. As it cracked open he was repelled by the blast of stale, rank air. Once he was through the conservatory, his eyes had trouble adjusting to the pitch darkness of the house. The air here, too, was stale. It had the faintly putrid scent that he associated with military hospitals, of airless rooms with failing bodies and bad food. As his eyes got used to the gloom he saw that some things were out of position, and that other furniture had been rearranged, apparently in haste. Pictures had been taken from a wall; there were pieces of glass on the floor. Someone had tried ineffectively to clean up after a ransacking. Now there was no doubt in his mind what had happened.

He could bear to be in the house no longer. He left the way he had come, and went to the stables. The sun was up and in the stables one fly began circling Koblensky in a frenetic aerial dance; Koblensky realized he was probably the first edible thing the insect had seen in days. After several lunges he smashed it on the wall of a stall in a blow that seemed suddenly to break his control.

The violation of the house kept attacking his imagination with premonitions of Sarah's fate, more terrible because it was imprecise, suggesting unbearable possibilities. He went outside and found a standpipe that still functioned. He doused his head, mindless of the water spilling over his shirt. Turning off the flow, he heard a train moving up the line. The singularity of the noise, its intrusiveness and identity, reimposed his immediate reality. He then realized again his own danger, which gave him a strange sense of smallness, of his insignificance in what seemed the onset of a titanic struggle and in which he now appeared to be alone. The train was a prelude, one piece moving into place.

He broke into Abu Farid's quarters, as ravaged as the house had been, and cleared debris from a mattress. He was suddenly exhausted. The wooden hut, an extension of the stables, was dark and cool, and he was asleep within five minutes.

He slept so deeply that he did not hear the door open, or feel the sudden shaft of light. All his old reflexes failed him and even when he realized that someone stood over him he was sluggish, blinking and moving his body with the indifference of a man who wanted to be left undisturbed. He didn't even know where he was.

"Mister Asa," said the shadow.

Koblensky cranked his head up and shaded his eyes. It was Abu Farid. Abu Farid's English was as feeble as Koblensky's Arabic. Once he came to his senses, Koblensky began an urgent but stumbling interrogation.

"Miss Sarah dead," curtailed the questions.

Koblensky sank back on the mattress. Abu Farid rubbed his eyes and then picked around in the wreck of his room for something to sit on, settling on a box, then saying only, "Hassan Bey."

Koblensky did not respond. He pulled himself up and groped by the mattress for the pouch he had brought from the dinghy. The outer canvas was lined inside with rubber for waterproofing; all the contents smelled now of the lining. He found a small container of army iron rations and offered Abu Farid a biscuit, then took another for himself.

"Mister Laski here," said Abu Farid.

"Where?"

"I take you."

Outside it was midafternoon and still brightly lit, but the air had an autumnal softness, something Koblensky had forgotten after weeks in Egypt and the Sinai, another twist of memory he would rather have done without. Abu Farid took him back exactly the way he had come in the night. The Arab moved incautiously, reassuring Koblensky: "Turks all gone." They went to the old glassworks.

The shuttered and sealed factory was stifling.

Laski, lying on a bunk in a corner of the basement, was startled to see Koblensky behind Abu Farid. Laski was wearing a dirty Arab shirt that was too large even for his girth, and it tangled around his feet as he jumped from the bunk.

"Asa!"

Koblensky came to a halt and stood with no purpose in him.

Laski, looking in the shirt like a slovenly woman, went slowly to him, realizing that Koblensky already knew about Sarah. Koblensky's spiritless posture seemed to make him smaller and vulnerable, something Laski had never before seen in him. Laski embraced him, sinking his head onto Koblensky's left shoulder and clasping him at the waist. They were silent for a minute and when Laski broke away, both of them had moist eyes.

"Too late," muttered Koblensky. "We were *too late.*"

"I wanted to get her out," said Laski.

"Who was it, in the end? Who gave them away?"

Laski sank to a small stool, enveloping it in the shirt. "No one thing. They picked up Belkind; he had papers. Then it was one of the pigeons. A pigeon. I never liked that idea. A pigeon was caught at Caesarea; they traced it."

"How did she die?" Koblensky remained on his feet.

"She wouldn't talk."

"Who—who did it?"

"The police chief from Caesarea, the Turk who caught the bird—Farouk Pasha."

Koblensky tilted his head toward Abu Farid, who had settled on a bunk. "He said Hassan Bey."

"Hassan Bey directed it, but he never gets blood on his own hands; he's not that kind of Turk." Laski pushed a foot clear of the shirt's hem and looked hard at Koblensky. "Malik was there."

Slowly resolution seemed to come back into Koblensky's body. He unstrapped the pouch from his belt and put it on a table, then unbuttoned his khaki tunic. The star medallion hung over a white undershirt. He sat at the table and in a clockwork way unpacked the pouch, making two stacks, one of his personal effects and the other of equipment: first a map, on top of that a notebook, then small field glasses, a small sheathed knife, a clip of ammunition, and finally a British Webley revolver in a holster, which he placed between the two stacks. He said nothing as he did this until he was finished, and then, speaking in a remote way that matched his movements, he said, "The invasion begins at dawn tomorrow. We have a part to play. Within five days from now we must be at the Tel Shahab bridge on the Yarmuk. On the north bank. Major Lawrence is making for the south bank. His party is blowing up the bridge. We have to cut the telegraph to the guard post."

Laski straightened himself, the foot retracting again under the shirt. After a pause, he said, "I tried to get here in time, but I lost my horse, and an injury slowed me down."

Koblensky took up the holster and unbuttoned it to slip out the revolver. He removed the chamber and began loading it, inserting each bullet precisely, with an unwavering hand, then spinning the chamber. In the cavernous basement, each click of metal was resonant. Holding the gun level and looking along the sight, he said, "Five days. We have five days. Can we do it?"

Laski rubbed the dark bristle on his chin and stood up, the shirt outlining his sagging gut. "We could do it on foot in that time, but we should get mules. The Turks have drawn all their forces to Gaza. There are only skeleton garrisons up here now. If we keep clear of the railway and the main routes and move at night, there's nothing to worry about. You did it before. You know the way."

But Koblensky remembered Feinberg and realized that Laski didn't know of his death, and that Sarah had died without knowing. "Can you get mules?" he said, not ready to say more.

Allenby's guns were more than eighty miles away, but when his dawn barrage opened, it was audible in Zichron; it drew people from their beds, a rolling, repeated percussion like the beat of drums coming obliquely from hillside to hillside, dying away for a moment and then returning, too weak to shake houses or even to stir the trees but more unsettling because of that. Once its source was clear, people clustered in agitation: the barrage finally broke their illusion of immunity. Even the most cloistered and pious knew that their doors could no longer shut out the

337

sound of another empire following all the others that had laid claim to this land. Rabbi Dor knew it better than any of them.

Had they been there to see Allenby's assault, Koblensky and Laski would not have been consoled by it; their own clandestine army was destroyed. The barrage was a ponderous and tardy ceremony reminding them of a ponderous and tardy army too far away and too late to be of use. To them, the power of the guns was empty and immaterial. They sat at the table looking at the map in the light of an oil lamp. Abu Farid brewed coffee. Laski had discarded the robe, shaved, and put on boots, breeches, and a shirt. Koblensky wore just trousers and undershirt. He was raw in the eye and gulped the first mug of coffee without pause.

"You called him Major Lawrence," said Laski. "He's been promoted?"

"I do not think he cares."

"Can we depend on him?"

Koblensky looked sharply at Laski. "*Depend* on him? We depend on ourselves."

Laski had given Koblensky, as far as he knew it himself, and as impersonally as he was able, a detailed account of Hassan Bey's destruction of the NILI, of Malik's part, and of the rabbi's exit. Much of this story depended on Abu Farid, who had been badly battered by the Bey's men. Koblensky and Laski now had the bond of survivors, but it was a bond with limits. Laski suspected something new in Koblensky, a carelessness for his own fate. It worried Laski, though he realized its cause. Laski had his own grief, but he retained a sharp concern for his continued survival. Some people had never seen this in him. He had done dangerous things, but he had always calculated the risk with finesse; it was a part of knowing himself (and of being able, because of his bulk, to seem highly improbable as a man of action). Until now, Koblensky had never seemed reckless. Laski hoped his suspicion was wrong; there were enough risks ahead of them.

Skirting the junction of Affula on the first night, they could see the supplies and reinforcements coming south from Damascus, but the single track from there to Gaza made Affula into a bottleneck. By now, Koblensky realized, the Turks must have seen Allenby's trick, and be desperately trying to move their defenses east to cover Beersheba. That would make them even more dependent on the rail artery, which in turn would make

Lawrence's destruction of the bridge that much more devastating. Koblensky craved the means to paralyze the railway himself, and raged within at his impotence.

Reaching the Tel Shahab from the northern bank of the Yarmuk instead of the southern, where he had gone before with Feinberg, proved simpler than Koblensky anticipated. All the Turkish effort was concentrated on the southern front and the Jordan valley seemed unpatrolled except for main routes, which were easily avoided. Their Arab costume began to seem redundant, but Laski insisted on keeping it. On the third night they were in the foothills of Mount Hermon, able to look northeast across the top of the gorge where the Yarmuk ran and to hear water in the falls. They were at least a day early; more if Lawrence was late. Half a mile up a slope of Hermon, they found an underwood of sage, where the mules could be left in cover. In the afternoon, while there was still enough light, they went down on foot to check their map against the terrain. The Turkish garrison that supplied guards for the post at the bridge was in a camp at the edge of a village about a mile from the gorge. This garrison appeared still to be fully manned. The telephone line from the camp to the bridge was strung between low poles, conspicuous and vulnerable. But the fact that the garrison was not depleted showed that the Turks knew how crucial a target the bridge made.

Koblensky scanned the village and the camp with his glasses. "About a hundred men," he announced. "Before, with Lawrence, I saw one Maxim on a tripod at the bridge post, and there would be about twenty men there. A good position. They have a clear line of fire to the whole bridge. If they see anything, it would be over, very quickly."

"Is there no cover on the other bank?" said Laski.

"Nothing."

"I hope Lawrence has machine guns of his own."

"I hope Lawrence arrives."

That night they got to the gorge, to a plateau of rock west of the bridge and guard post.

Looking at the bridge for the first time, Laski drew in his breath. "It's *irresistible*. Just imagine . . ."

Koblensky had imagined it many times.

The next night, the first of the appointed dates, they were in position, with a good view of the opposite bank and above the post, where they could cut the telephone line in half a minute.

But there was no Lawrence. Nor was there the next night,

when the weather seemed on the point of breaking. High cloud obscured the moon and the wind had gone round to the northeast. Their Arab gowns were not warm enough.

Laski had no trouble sleeping the next day, but was wakened several times by Koblensky's restlessness. At the third disturbance, Laski saw Koblensky hunched on a rock and brooding.

"What is it?"

"If he doesn't come, it will have been for nothing."

"There is still tonight."

"He could have been caught. He had a long way to come."

"Well, we can't help that." Laski's sharpness gave way to perception. "What is it? What are you thinking?"

"The bridge is safe from us. We have no explosives. But the garrison . . . Did you notice where they keep their ammunition? I saw them getting belts for the Maxim. There is a large arms dump there, in the hut at the end of the village."

"So?"

"They are cooking with kerosene—kept in drums."

Laski comprehended. "I don't see how . . ."

Koblensky stood up. "No? Are you sure?" He turned away to look down the hill. "One more night."

By midafternoon the sun had gone; the change in the air that woke them foretold rain. By the time they were ready, the gorge was out of sight, masked by the curtain of a steady drizzle. The hill, dry for months, was suddenly slick and their Bedouin sandals useless. They went down barefooted.

Their position over the gorge, bare rock on the previous nights, was now covered in a slime of topsoil sliding from above. They could barely see to the other side, and the bridge was distinct for only half its span. For three hours they lay there, the chill reaching their bones. Then the drizzle petered out, and the opposite bank grew lighter at the top, where it caught a faint shaft of moonlight from over the summit of Hermon. The bridge, too, was restored to clarity.

It was the strange, halo-like silver light at the opposite horizon that first caught what they had waited for: a long line of camels, heavily laden.

Laski said, "Is it them?"

Koblensky nodded. "Look—at the head."

The first camel, picking its way tentatively because of the mud, bore a rider in a robe that in the moonlight, even from this distance, was spectral. The camels had come from the north. For a minute or more they disappeared behind an outcrop, and then, when they reappeared, slowed down to begin descending below the line of the ridge.

"How many are there?" said Laski.

Koblensky had his glasses on them. He picked out Lawrence and then moved along the line. Some of the riders were in army uniforms, but the majority were in Bedouin robes. "Enough to take a city—seventy or eighty of them." He looked back to the Turkish post. There was no watch being kept from there.

Once Lawrence's force went down toward the river they were harder to see. It was more than an hour before Koblensky was able to observe that the force had divided. At least half of them were held back, with the camels, on a plateau. Koblensky watched six of the uniformed men assemble a Lewis machine gun, screwing its body to a tripod, and then clipping the circular magazine on top. They manhandled it across rocks to find a firm position with a clear field of fire.

"All those men, and only one machine gun," said Koblensky. "I hope they never have to use it." He moved his glasses to another group of men, who were beginning to clamber down toward the bridge, taking a path that Koblensky remembered. "He has Arab porters carrying the explosives—a lot of explosives." He panned the glasses from the embankment to the bridge. On the northern end of the bridge, directly below Laski and Koblensky, the single sentry was asleep on the ground by a small brazier. The rest of the Turks were in their tents, and the Maxim stood unattended, its fat fluted barrel dipped to the ground; nothing better symbolized their complacency. Panning back again, Koblensky saw Lawrence, scrambling ahead of the porters, with the impetuosity of a schoolboy, making for the abutment. Then, rising above the steady beat of the water, he heard a train's whistle, one blast and then its echo bouncing through the gorge. Lawrence was waving wildly at the porters. The porters appeared on the verge of dropping the explosives and running, but then they scrambled together under Lawrence's direction, taking cover while the train came down the south bank and began the long curve before the bridge. The moon was now clear of Hermon and the last strands of cloud gone. Lawrence's position seemed dangerously exposed.

Laski, crouching by Koblensky, watched the train reach their side of the bridge, and the one sentry wave to the driver. "If

341

they had been any closer they would have been seen, from the train."

Koblensky nodded. "Lawrence is lucky."

The train was packed with troops, some leaning out the windows to see the spectacle of the gorge, unaware of the crouched party in the rocks.

With the train only a reverberating and receding sound, Lawrence came out from his cover and led the porters to the abutment. Then Lawrence and one of the Arabs broke away and began crawling across the concrete to reach the first span of metal. Koblensky saw Lawrence swing himself onto the seat of the bridge, astride a girder, calling the Arab to join him. Koblensky's glasses moved away to the sentry, but despite the train, he dozed on. The glasses panned the bridge, settled on Lawrence for a moment, then moved back up the rock face. A man in a British officer's uniform was supervising the moving of the Lewis gun. Dissatisfied with its position, he was directing the six men to another ledge, nearer to the path taken by Lawrence and the porters. The move was difficult; the rocks were still wet. As Koblensky watched, one of the gunners slipped. The tripod canted over and another gunner lost his grip on it. Very slowly, the tripod slid away from them across the moss, and then over a rock and down into the path. Falling several feet to flint, the gun bounced and with each impact set off a noise as sudden and sharp as gunfire, ringing up out of the gorge.

Laski and Koblensky froze. They saw the sentry leap up from behind the brazier and begin to fire blindly, and futilely, across the bridge. This aroused the rest of the guard. Men ran from the tents and the dipped nose of the Maxim rose and was cranked around. Once it began firing, although with no more precision than the sentry, its bullets raked the opposite bank. At first, in his anxiety, Koblensky lost his focus with the glasses, then he saw the porters hurling their sacks into the ravine and clawing their way back up the gorge. Lawrence and the Arab on the bridge, with stone splintering all around them, jumped back to the abutment and climbed in the wake of the scattering porters. Without the Lewis gun, they had no covering fire.

The initial horror of the scene gave way to a sense of tragic farce: The Turks had no idea what they were firing at, probably imagining no more than a few Arab bandits. Had they been on the heights of the gorge, where Koblensky and Laski were, the Turks would have been able to see the truth. As it was, though they fired into the shadows, one bullet into that much dynamite would have atomized Lawrence's men. But the fiasco was galling—all chance of blowing the bridge had gone. Within minutes the men were back to where the camels were tethered, apparently without one of them being hit. Koblensky watched Lawrence with the officer who had been in charge of the machine gun, both men waving their arms. Then the white cloak broke away from the khaki and Lawrence went to his camel, his dejection clear even at this distance in the way he remained slumped in his saddle while the rest of his men assembled. Keeping below the horizon this time, they filed away around the bend of the gorge to the northeast.

"Blowing that bridge could have won the war," said Koblensky, laying down his glasses and realizing how cold he was. There had been no point in cutting the telephone; by this time the Maxim had exhausted itself and a small squad of Turks was being led by a sergeant across the catwalk that flanked the rail bridge to the far abutment. They moved cautiously, still in ignorance of their adversary, and not sure that the adversary had gone.

As Laski and Koblensky worked their way back up the hill, they nearly ran into more Turks going to the gorge from the garrison, six men on horses followed by a platoon on foot. Laski and Koblensky rolled into a gulley and lay there in mud until the Turks passed. Laski could sense that Koblensky was about to explode with the frustration of the night.

But frustration became assertiveness. "It's the perfect time," he said, getting up and climbing back across the rocks to the track. "While they are concerned about the bridge . . . the perfect time to get that kerosene."

Laski was reluctant. The plan had not properly been discussed or rehearsed. He saw that Koblensky, barefooted in the mud-encrusted robe, was impossible to deter. Even on the track he stood like a tethered panther, eyes bright in the shadow. Laski swallowed his misgivings, but was determined to be as cautious as Koblensky was impatient.

Koblensky had been too optimistic; at least half the Turks were still in the camp. The kerosene drums were guarded by two soldiers, who were stamping their feet for warmth and talking. Then one of these guards went off to complete a circuit of the camp. The remaining guard leaned against a stack of drums, put down his rifle, and rubbed his hands together.

"Wait here," said Koblensky. "Cover me." Almost before Laski could answer, Koblensky was gone.

The guard, having brought the life back to his hands, picked up the rifle but remained leaning against the drums, waiting for the other guard to return. Laski saw or heard nothing of Koblensky until, after two minutes, a shadow fell fleetingly between two lines of the drums. The guard, too, appeared to grow uneasy. He moved a step away from the drums and became more alert, peering into the darkness and moving the rifle from his shoulder. Laski heard the steps of the other guard crossing gravel between the arms dump and the fuel stores. A laugh came from somewhere farther away, and then another. Hearing the steps, the guard in the fuel dump relaxed. The strap of his rifle went back to his shoulder. In the same movement, or so it seemed, he leaned back against the drums. But his leaning became a sideways fall, his upper body jerking one way while his legs folded another. Suddenly Koblensky was bent over the guard, stopping his rifle from clattering into the drums. The man had not made a sound.

Laski realized that any second, the other guard would be rounding a stack of drums and would then see what had happened. Koblensky was still arranging the guard's body, and pulling a knife from his back. All Laski's caution was abandoned in an instant; he had no choice. He was too far away for his pistol to be effective. He broke cover and started to run across the open stretch of rutted gravel, his feet slipping as he drew his gun. The patrolling guard appeared at the end of the stack of drums, still ambling along, unconcerned. He heard Laski running before he saw him, and peered into the darkness, lifting his rifle. Laski came out of shadow, a lumbering improbable apparition, cloak flapping about his ankles. The guard froze, his rifle wavering. Laski fired, on the run, without the chance of more than rudimentary aim. The bullet went through the guard's neck, just above his collar. His trigger finger gripped and locked, but the rifle did not go off.

Koblensky had watched this duel impotently. The body of the other guard had preoccupied him and he couldn't pull his own revolver from under the tangle of his cloak. Now both Laski and Koblensky were rooted to the ground, waiting for the sound of the pistol to arouse others. Laski's victim was still alive, but blood was pumping from his neck. The silence was paralyzing them. Then came another, distant laugh, and no more.

Laski's fear, which had parched his mouth in an instant, turned to a lubricating rage; only now did he fully take in how Koblensky had trapped him in his own recklessness. Hitting the guard in the throat had been pure chance. And yet here was Koblensky walking toward him, grinning madly, as though there were no one else around for miles. Laski, nearly as deranged, had to check himself from shouting.

Koblensky had no perception of Laski's fury. He nodded at the Turk. "Fine shooting, my friend."

"Fine shooting?" hissed Laski. "Fine shooting? It was a thousand-to-one chance." His short, layered neck was stretched in the effort of checking his urge to shout, and half swallowing, he muttered, "Let's get out of here."

Very slowly, with a petulant reluctance, Koblensky saw Laski's anger. "Get out? We have not finished. Here—help me." He turned away and went to the stack of drums, turning over one that stood a little apart from the others.

Laski looked around the dump and to the camp beyond. Unaccountably, no one had appeared. Shaking his head, he put away his revolver and joined Koblensky. They had to get the drum across the gravel between the fuel stores and the arms dump. It was heavy enough to leave a deep rut where they rolled it, but there was a slight gradient in their favor. When they reached the dump, Koblensky took the cap from the drum. Kerosene gushed out and lapped around the wooden shack. He let the drum drain until the level fell below the spout. By then it was light enough for them to lift it together and they edged backward, away from the dump, leaving a strand of kerosene in the rut they had made. The kerosene ran out when they were no more than twenty yards clear.

"It's too close," said Laski.

"No. It's all right," said Koblensky. He grinned again at Laski. "You can't run as fast as me. You go now. Leave it to me."

Laski hesitated, but was too sick of Koblensky's obsession to argue. He walked off into the darkness, looking back several times. Koblensky was dabbing a strip torn from his cloak in the kerosene. He stood back a pace, and struck a match. The rag flared. He threw it forward and began running. For a few seconds the flame seemed to have died; then a low band of blue, more like an attenuated bubble, danced across the gravel. It reached the shack before Koblensky was halfway to where Laski crouched. The blue ran around the foundation of the shack like a liquid girdle, still not breaking into flame. The smell was of scorched air. Blue turned to orange, orange to pale pink, and—so sharply that both men blinked in the flash—the flame bloomed into one engulfing sheet of fire, the wood already cracking.

"Now we get out," said Koblensky.

The ignition of the shack brought the Turks running—running imprudently before they realized what it was that was burning. Laski and Koblensky saw the first Turks arrive at the perimeter and stop, staring across the gravel. As they fixed on what had happened, others came up behind them. While the first wave began to comprehend what would follow, the second wave, still rushing forward, blocked their escape. Even more men were spilling out of the barracks behind.

Laski and Koblensky lay behind a low embankment at the edge of the road. They watched one line of Turks trying to turn back the next, and heard desperate shouts. One or two men on the fringe had broken from the mass and were running in a half crouch into the clear ground.

The detonation was as orderly and rhythmic as the firing of the Maxim. A tracery of brilliant scarlet flashes jetted into the sky. The first victims fell while the tracery was still high in the sky, from shrapnel erupting on them from above. But these were random chances. Once the stream of incandescent lead reached body height, the entire tangled front rank of men was eviscerated, their screams surmounting the explosions. Behind them, those who were still untouched had managed to reverse direction and were scattering. But the elegant tracery was only an overture. There was a deeper detonation that seemed to have impacted into the ground. Laski and Koblensky felt it beneath them. Though deflected by something above it, the explosion was the first of a chain reaction.

"Shells!" cried Koblensky.

Laski slipped back lower behind the embankment, but Koblensky remained, his face raw in the glare.

Three explosions occurred almost simultaneously, the last lifting the remains of the shack as high as the first fountain of machine-gun ammunition had gone, dissolving into a shower of white-hot cinders. Underneath this, a swollen cushion of flame spread in a perfectly symmetrical curve, consuming air and earth and anything detachable. It overlapped and swallowed the running Turks, the sound of its galloping combustion eliminating all other sounds. It became a fire storm, and the fire storm reached the remaining kerosene. Laski and Koblensky felt the air being drawn out of them, their lungs burning. Koblensky rolled down the embankment. Hot debris rained around them. As the main explosion subsided, more ammunition, inside cases that had melted around it, renewed the illusion of gunfire, this time reaching the pitch of a barrage. The layer of mud in the road had already been singed dry and cracked; strands of grass curled crisp and burned.

Laski was gulping for air, crawling away from the embankment, unable to see clearly. He realized that he was breathing more smoke than air, and smoke tainted with cordite. He crawled into Koblensky. Koblensky was lying face-down, the back of his cloak scorched from the waist to the neck, and his hair black with ash. Laski coughed and tried to clear his mouth and then, kneeling by Koblensky, managed to turn him over to his side. Koblensky's right cheek was resting in the dried mud. He began to cough, then convulsed. The left side of his face was singed scarlet. His eyes opened and he took in Laski as he bent over him.

Laski coughed again, and then retched.

With his face still in the mud, Koblensky began laughing, hoarsely, painfully, uncontrollably. Then, as the laugh appeared to exhaust him, he muttered, ''Your face . . . *your face* . . . It is like a great black dog's.''

Laski was still doubled up, the pain in his lungs and mouth getting worse.

Koblensky pushed himself off the ground and sat up. Beyond the embankment it was still almost as light as day, and sporadic explosions were followed by more flashes, but the conflagration was dying.

Laski's weight, like a dislodged cargo, had gone out of balance. There was no life in his legs; they folded under him, invisible beneath the cloak, which had only the outline of his hips and seat. Immobile, rooted, and grotesquely transfigured, he resembled a pagan idea of man chastised by thunderbolt. His breath, as he recovered it, failed to restore movement, though it did clear his head.

''*Crazy*,'' said Laski. ''We were crazy to do it.''

At first Koblensky was not diverted. He got to his feet, the raw face staring ahead over the embankment. Without turning, he finally answered. "Crazy? What is crazy? We *defeated* them."

"You cannot go on like this. Not if you want to live long. Maybe that is the idea."

"What?" Koblensky turned on Laski.

"You cannot blame yourself for her death—and you cannot make up for it this way."

With Laski still fixed where he was, Koblensky overshadowed him, and became belligerent. "What has that to do with it?"

"Maybe you can fool yourself, but you cannot fool me. Maybe you should have made it plainer to Sarah, what she meant to you. Then, maybe, she would have got out in time." Laski knew that if he had been on his feet, Koblensky would have struck him; as it was, he barely checked himself.

"You tell me—you tell me my own feelings? *Get out?* She should not have been left there."

"No. You do not see it. What did you think? That to show what you felt for her was a weakness? The weakness was not to show it. You are so fearful of weakness that you lose all sense of what is weakness and what is human. The feelings you had for her were a strength—a strength you never tapped, never used. She knew that. But she had to show her strength alone—without you. Because you would not be honest with yourself. She understood you. But she could not tell you what you could not tell yourself. Weakness. You turn it into a curse, my friend."

The wound in Koblensky's eyes was more salient than the scorched face. No fight in him now, he watched Laski struggle to stand, but did nothing to help him.

Laski did not mind having so spoken. He knew he was the only person who could have said it. If Koblensky was to be saved from himself—and if others were to be saved from Koblensky—there really had been no choice.

# 20

## *Jerusalem* ❋ *December 10, 1917*

On one side of a thin plaster wall, a corporal wearing only shorts, socks, and boots was shoveling wooden chips into the furnace of a small boiler; on the other side of the wall, in a room serving several functions, General Allenby sat in a tin bath mounted on griffin's feet. The efforts of the corporal and the boiler had raised the water temperature to little more than tepid. Allenby was lathering himself in haste, and talking at the same speed. "I am being discouraged, Hogarth, from making my entry on horseback. This advice seems to have originated with you."

Hogarth was seated some discreet feet away, at a table covered in green baize. "I think it would show respect, sir—that we come to Jerusalem as liberators, not conquerors. Moreover, there is an unhappy precedent for entries on horseback."

"Oh? What is that?"

"Kaiser Wilhelm II, sir. He visited Jerusalem in 1898. The authorities were ordered to cut a large hole in the walls of the Old City, and to erect a triumphal arch around it. The Kaiser rode through the hole, in full regalia, on a horse that was similarly decked. It has never been forgotten. Very deep offense was caused in holy circles. After all, sir, the arrival of One Greater was far more modest."

Allenby grunted. "Liberators and not conquerors—that will be the theme of my address. No horse, then." He rose from the bath, the water too cool to have turned his white skin pink. "Throw me a towel, there's a good man." Wrapped in the towel like a Roman emperor, a role that he felt was impending, Allenby rubbed himself down and continued: "I can see we shall need all the diplomatic subtlety we can muster—greater, I fear, than can be provided by the army. As a rule, my officers are not

349

happy in such situations. That is why I sent for you, Hogarth. Political dexterity and, above all, some understanding of the ghastly religious complexity—I'm looking for people who can get us through with a minimum of embarrassment. This is not the shining beacon at the end of the road. The city faces famine. The Turks kept it half starved; now it is cut off from the grain supplies, such as they were, from the other side of the Jordan. The Jews once had grain ships from Odessa, but no more.'' Allenby pulled the towel around him and seemed to want to unburden all his problems in one outpouring. ''Then there is the water. I have two divisions here. The only water comes from a cistern built by the Romans. The place is so high most of the rainwater drains away.'' The already weak light in the room flickered uncertainly. ''Yes—then there is the electricity. It comes, fitfully at best, from decrepit motors. There is also the problem of the currency. Turkish piasters are worthless. Paper money of any kind, even pounds, is looked on with suspicion. As usual, the Jews have cornered all the small change, for which they extort a commission of five or six percent. That filthiness has to be stopped.''

''My people will be of whatever help they can.''

''Has Lawrence turned up?''

''He's on his way from Gaza now.''

''I want him with me when we make the entry in the morning—but *not* in those diaphanous robes of his. He must appear as the major, as impeccably as he can manage. He won't be a mere major for much longer.''

Hogarth averted his eyes as Allenby stepped from the towel to reclaim his underwear. ''Promotion again?''

''I'm making him a lieutenant colonel; he's become too illustrious for anything less. You heard the French have given him the Croix de Guerre, for Akaba?''

''I wrote to tell his mother. Lawrence won't discuss such things.''

''No,'' said Allenby, betraying testiness. ''He's a CB, but won't wear the ribbons. There was talk, you know, of giving him the VC. In view of this perverse modesty he exhibits, better that we did not. Tell me, Hogarth, the man is such an exhibitionist in one sense—this affectation of the princely Arab—and yet he will not honor his own decorations. Tell me, how much is he the genuine performer, and how much the charlatan?'' Allenby paused in his dressing, standing in shirttails awaiting Hogarth's reply.

"He's a man of great complexity—and a man under strain."

Allenby smiled dubiously. "I thought you might say something of the kind." He picked up his tie. "I am beginning to think that the only tolerable places in Jerusalem will be bath and bed."

The small room was damp and nearly as bare as a cell. Its uneven whitewashed walls, in wavering candlelight, were moist with evaporation produced by the press of bodies. At one end of the room, space had been made for a small table, which was draped in a lace cloth; the fineness of the cloth emphasized the utility of everything else. On the table stood the menorah candelabra, eight branches at one level, with the ninth and central branch inches higher. The menorah was of poorer origin than the cloth. It was beaten out of tin and each branch had been crudely welded to the central stalk, and that to a bronze base that had once served, the other way up, as an ashtray. In the light of the candles, an old man wearing an embroidered skullcap bent over a prayerbook. The prayerbook's binding was shredding and its cover bore evidence of having been repeatedly repaired.

The ill matching of the instruments of the ceremony was noticed by Koblensky, who saw in them a reflection of the ill matching of those in the room. Around him, the Jews, men and women, were Ashkenazi and Sephardim, orthodox and casual, pious and profane, Russian, Balkan, German, Spanish, Egyptian, Palestinian. Men wore wide-brimmed black hats, astrakhan caps, yarmulkes; all the women wore scarves over their heads, some as fine as the lace on the table, others threadbare strips of cotton or silk. They had come together not just for the ancient ritual of Hanukkah, the Feast of Lights, but to celebrate the coincidental arrival of the British in Jerusalem. It was a moment of rare unity among them; Koblensky knew it was unlikely to survive the eight days of Hanukkah.

There was a pause in the prayers for glasses of tea to be passed from a samovar.

Abba Laski, standing next to Koblensky against the wall, said quietly, "You seem familiar with this ceremony. I've never seen you as a believer in prayer."

Koblensky smiled. "Hanukkah was always important in Russia. For me, there was a good reason. Or two good reasons. I liked potato pancakes, and I used to get fifty kopecks as Hanukkah *gelt.*''

''No potato pancakes now.''

''No.'' Koblensky took a glass of tea to pass to Laski, then one for himself. Then came cubes of sugar, stained light brown. Koblensky sniffed the sugar. ''No potatoes, but sugar, and brandy from Richon le-Zion. A strange famine, when the rabbis have almonds, sugar, and brandy.''

Lighted tapers were passed, and teaspoons. At a signal from the prayer leader, the sugar cubes were ignited and dropped, sizzling, into the tea. Then, in a discordant variety of accents and dialects, the thirty or so people broke into song. Koblensky was torn by violently disparate feelings. He could not help but feel the binding tie of community, nor—in spite of his cynicism to Laski—was he immune to the power of the Hanukkah legend, since it marked one of the rare occasions in which oppressed Jews had rebelled and, though vastly outnumbered, humiliated a Syrian tyrant. But that had been more than two thousand years earlier, and in the faces around him he saw no similar resolve. Many of these people had complied with the Turks, some even collaborated. However great their indignities, they passively endured them. Now they were falsely euphoric about liberation; he had already overheard some of them discussing the commercial advantages of British rule.

With the ceremony over, Koblensky and Laski hung back. The old man by the menorah also waited, until only the three of them were left. From behind the table, fussing over the disintegrating prayerbook, he said in Russian, ''It is good that you come, Asa. Sometimes you should remember.''

''Sometimes I remember too much, Misha.''

The old man put down the book. ''Pieces . . . pieces. We must begin to put the pieces together.''

''These people won't help us, Misha. They don't believe in us. How can we make them believe?''

''*Believe?* They should believe that what you want will last. To them, what lasts is what does not attract attention. *You* attract too much attention.''

''*You* were with us.''

''I?'' The old man's hand rested on the prayerbook as though pressing it back into wholeness. ''You want to make them believe? You will need a lot of time. Time I don't have.''

\*     \*     \*

A huge portrait of the Kaiser and Kaiserin, so heavy that it was anchored to the wall by chain and hook, hung over Kippax's bed. The bed itself was similarly massive, its mahogany posts crowned with lions' heads. Kippax sat on the edge of the bed, struggling to put on cavalry boots. Bron, already in full uniform, rested an arm on one of the rampant lions.

"How I detest this full regalia," said Kippax, kicking a heel into the boot. "Allenby wants everything done like a parade at Sandhurst."

Bron was amused by Kippax's discomfort. Nothing suited Kippax less than cavalry boots, and the pair he had been given were so pristine that they had no suppleness. "Well," said Bron, "you can't really blame him. This is a day for the history books, probably his greatest moment."

"It wasn't exactly an historic conquest, surrender of the city without a battle. It took the mayor of Jerusalem half the day to find somebody to surrender to. The first soldiers he encountered were two privates sent out by a cook to look for water."

"Better that there was no battle. Jerusalem is supposed to enjoy a divine immunity."

Finally Kippax secured the boots. Pink in the face, he stood up uncertainly and tried a few steps. "Not me, really, do you think? Or perhaps . . ." He examined himself in a full-length mirror.

Bron saw the feline vanity, and mischievously encouraged it. "Very imposing, I would have said. Altogether transforming."

Kippax saw through the teasing and became irritated, moving away from the mirror to get his cap. "The worst of it is the hour," he said. "It's only just light."

In the corridor outside, they nearly collided with Lawrence. He, too, had scrubbed himself, had clipped his hair and buckled himself into a major's full dress, with red staff officer tabs on his lapels. The three of them broke out in laughter at their mutual discomfort.

"One fears contamination, if dressed for too long like this," said Lawrence.

All about them in the Hotel Fast were the sounds of an assembling brotherhood of arms, some of the voices garrulous and excited, others irritable, few of the men able to look on with the detachment of the three paused on the landing, each of whom, in his different way, was no natural part of the regimented spirit. From the drawing room, to one side of the lobby below them, came the sound of a piano and then of its player, singing with a grotesquely mock-German accent, "*Hurrah! Es kommt der Kaiser* . . ." This was drowned by derisive cheers and then laughter and the sound of a piano lid being snapped shut. As quickly as it had come, the ribald note was gone and men began moving out to the street, stamping boots on the hotel's mosaic steps to get their circulation moving in the dawn cold.

On the steps, Lawrence looked out toward the Judean hills, tipped orange by the rising sun. "I've never been quite sure about Jerusalem," he said wistfully. "Is it the last foothold of the West in the East—or the first step of the East into the West? Certainly, to go even a mile east of here is to know that one has left the West. Christianity has no relevance there and beyond, *none at all*."

Kippax followed Lawrence's gaze. Standing next to him, with an advantage in height, Kippax felt the man's physical paradox: He had no stature in the conventional sense, and yet could be picked out among this brisk fraternity as having a presence greater than anyone's. Looking at the line of Lawrence's face, the too-broad chin and the too-high forehead, he saw that the man's power lay in a subtle kind of deformity, of a marriage of the soft and the hard in his face, cruelty at the corners of the mouth, but also a weakness somewhere, perhaps no more evident than a grimace, but there if you looked. The phalanx on the steps began to break up as men crossed the street to go in search of their units, being shepherded for a processional route leading to the Jaffa Gate. The preceding days had been wet, but the morning was breaking clear, with the sweet air that followed rain. Allenby's luck again.

His army was barely bruised; in six weeks they had overwhelmed the enemy and now held a line from Jaffa to Jerusalem. But with Jerusalem as a gift, Allenby had decided to pause for the winter. In the streets outside the walls of the Old City, the guardsmen marched and drilled with that tautness of calf and thigh that had dazzled many a parade ground and now brought British pomp to this strangely exotic dawn. Boots snapped into dirt; muezzins called: the city took up a murmur; somewhere, not far off, large guns exchanged fire.

Allenby's car drew up outside the Jaffa Gate just before seven-thirty. There were spurs on his boots; the boots were topped by leather gaiters to his knees, each stud bright. At the knee, jodhpurs were buttoned tight in a bias; above the knee they flared out and, ballooning under the hem of his tunic, gave him the outline of a broad-hipped, saddle-buttocked cavalry general slightly out of his true element. Above his left breast pocket were three rows of battle ribbons, a modest contrast to the French and Italian generals who joined him, their breasts plated with ribbons. Allenby had measured out national egos: the French had an honor guard of twenty men inside the Jaffa Gate, on the right; and the Italians twenty on the left. Outside the gate, snapping to attention as Allenby prepared to go in, was a guard of thirty, fifteen from the English regiments and fifteen drawn from Australians and New Zealanders. The French and Italians, whose plumage was the most vivid, had been disarmed by Allenby's gesture of inviting them to enter the gate ahead of the British.

Gathering behind Allenby were his staff officers, but he glanced beyond them to confirm that Lawrence was there. He looked up at the clock tower above the gate, and precisely on the half hour led the way through. On the castellated ramparts above the gate and below the clock tower were assorted clergy, turbaned, mitered, and black-capped. In this city it was the headgear that most clearly marked out race and rank.

Allenby came out unblinking from the shadow of the gate and went down toward the citadel, where dignitaries were gathered: Jews, Arabs, Christians, Syrians, Abyssinians, Copts, Greeks, Armenians, Austrians, and even Turks.

Hogarth, Kippax, and Bron were fifteen or twenty feet in Allenby's wake, Hogarth distinctive in the only naval uniform. "It's hard, *very* hard, *not* to feel like a conqueror," said Kippax.

Hogarth nodded; for all the restraint of the parade, he knew they were being looked on as a victorious army.

Bron, falling a pace behind the other two and seeing the Old City for the first time, suffered a confusion of impressions. The people on the sidelines seemed haggard and fearful, and too many eyes seemed to be on him, an illusion he could not shake off. Where had he come from? What could they know of him? What did they expect? All these faces seemed more alien than any others he had known. And the place—this was not the Orient of Cairo, ineffably not. In an instant of comparison, the Orientalism of Cairo was a charade. Next to Jerusalem, even the pyramids seemed ornamental, for here was an archaism invested not only in stone but in people. It *lived*. A contradiction in terms?

355

Contradiction abounded before his every step: the false modesty of the parade, the muezzins and the gunfire, the corpulence of priests and the wasting of children. There was also a more personal distress—a state of severance. He remembered what Lawrence had said on the hotel step: *the last foothold of the West* . . . Bron had lost his foothold, left the West. It was in the air and the light: the air of Jerusalem's high plateau and what the light did to everything.

"*What* a bloody rabble," said Kippax, then, looking more closely at Bron, "You all right, old chap? Look a bit dazed."

"Quite all right. Not quite awake yet, that's all."

"You sure? Can't say I enjoy this too much myself. Bit of a fake. Whatever Allenby says. They know it. After all, it *is* Jerusalem. Once we're installed, it seems to me we're stuck with it, willy-nilly. Be here forever, I shouldn't be surprised." He smirked. "Beat the Frogs to it, and that's a fact. Old Picot is livid; he can see the game already, in spite of his intriguing. Look at him, hobbling along on that cane and thinking of Napoleon."

Georges Picot, gnomelike against Allenby's bulk, did have a face formed in pique.

"I'm sure *he* knows," continued Kippax quietly. "It's when the English are claiming to be magnanimous that they are at their most dangerous."

"I should be careful, lest we take you at your word," snapped Hogarth, catching Kippax by surprise, out of patience with his humor.

"Onward, Christian Soldiers," mused Kippax to himself, but Allenby was supposedly divested of bias at this moment, essentially the temporal power daring to oblige each and every faith gathered in Jerusalem, not only each faith but each sect of each faith, the palpable disharmony of which now confronted him. Skirts, gowns, surplices; miters, crucifixes, stars, beads; Torah scrolls, gold-caked Bibles; Kufic-scribed Korans; beards long and short, jet and white, and smooth pink chins. The crisp sun was not enough to have dried the dust under their feet; the citadel reeked of a holy dankness, incense mingling with dawn-brewed coffee, dung, cheese, leather, sugar, spices, and drains. Allenby produced his piece of paper, the proclamation of British reason. Kippax thought of another soldier, greater than any, who had also combined conquest with declarations of the syncretic ideal: Alexander the Macedonian, precocious god. Kippax would have followed Alexander to his conceived ends of the earth, flawed only by the deviance that the Orient seemed to encourage in its invaders, the deviance that Kippax also relished. But Kippax could not think of Allenby and Alexander in the same frame—not without rendering the present absurd in comparison with the past. These dead bureaucratic words issuing from Allenby—"To the inhabitants of Jerusalem, the blessed and the people dwelling in its vicinity . . . the object of war in the East on the part of Great Britain is the complete and final liberation of all peoples"—fell to the dust as expedient dross. Alexander had carried the high-mindedness of the *polis* east and farther east; all Allenby proffered was administrative cant. From Whitehall, not Athens. When Allenby stopped, the proclamation was then read in diverse tongues. Kippax watched each group perceive the message; ideas were *not* the same in any language, the West did not translate to the East in anything more than the verbal mechanics; when Allenby said, "authority will come from the free will of the people," he was—Kippax knew—being gratuitous to more than one divinity. *Allah Akbar*—God is Great . . . and indivisible in authority. Cairo had come to Jerusalem, and was already lost.

Hovering distractedly between the external and the internal, Kippax was settled finally to reality by the appearance of a face. At first, not even a face, more a movement of one face among others and impinging only gradually its familiar identity. It was Koblensky. Even on this occasion, when Lawrence had managed the semblance of military finesse, Koblensky was notable as a man whose uniform had been forced on him and was worn with disregard. He must have been some way behind Kippax when the entourage passed through the Jaffa Gate, but as the oration echoed from one throat to another, Koblensky infiltrated the mingling mass. Kippax saw him first among the gathered Jews, one flash of khaki among black; minutes later Koblensky rematerialized with the army cavalcade and was seen by Lawrence.

Lawrence seemed glad of the diversion. He put out a hand. "You are safe, then! I couldn't find out."

Koblensky took the hand with a hint of ill grace.

"I saw you, you know," said Lawrence. "Before we went down with the explosives. I'm sorry. We were inept. My Serahin lost their nerve. They know what happens when a bullet hits gelatin."

"I realized that."

There was a second of mutual assessment, concentrated enough to be oblivious of the tumult around them.

"Well," said Lawrence, "the chance was lost. However, on the way back, we caught Jemal's train and I blasted it to pieces. Too well, as it happened: got a piece of boiler plate in my own foot. There were four hundred men on the train, and forty of us. We shot it up end to end."

"And Jemal?"

"Escaped, I fear. There was a fat ecclesiastic with him, a pro-Turk Arab pimp. I blazed at him until he dropped."

Koblensky had seen this in Lawrence before: He always depicted his battles in a language peculiar to English schoolboys, though now he was really covering two failures, the bridge and Jemal's survival. But it was not a moment to carp. Koblensky said, "We might try again—somewhere else."

"We *must*," said Lawrence. He turned to scan the dissolving multitude. "Christmas in Jerusalem, and then back to it. One can't let the Arabs run out of steam."

"You can always fire them with more gold," said Kippax, who had moved to their side.

"Well . . . as a matter of fact, Kippax," said Lawrence serenely, "at the moment, that is a lesser problem. I need to talk to you. Your Arabs are unsettling my Arabs. Allenby has had a complaint from Hussein. Tell me—who or what is the Ikhwan?"

Kippax was supercilious. "Surely, they can't be in Mecca already?"

"Of course not. But I hear they have the effrontery to proselytize among Hussein's tribes, saying the sharif is unfit to preside over Mecca. What *is* their game?"

Kippax noticed Koblensky's interest. "I think, perhaps, we ought to discuss this somewhere a little more tranquil." He acknowledged Koblensky with only a cursory nod, and steered Lawrence away.

Koblensky watched them disappear, and wondered which of them was the greater dissembler. Their backs were more revealing than their faces—more obviously androgynous in the misalliance of uniforms and anatomy.

Bron spoke from behind Koblensky. "Sometimes I think we are all misfits here."

Koblensky had until then not even noticed Bron. Of all of them, and ironically in view of his remark, it was Bron who was the most convincing in uniform, the most fitted—but more than ever the cipher, as though willing himself to be null.

"I'm sorry," said Bron. "I heard about your people . . . Aaronsohn's sister. It must have been . . ." Something in Koblensky's composure checked him, leaving him uncertain.

"Today, you would think the war was already won."

"A battle, not the war . . .?" Bron groped for better rapport. "You cannot deny the historic importance . . ."

"Jemal still has half of Palestine."

"Yes . . . well, when Allenby has got his breath . . ."

"He does not move very fast, this general."

"He makes sure." Bron was disinclined to indulge Koblensky further. "He does not throw lives away."

"No. Not British lives."

"Look," said Bron, holding his temper. "Why don't you come and have a drink—a bit later, when all this pomp and ceremony is over. I'm at the Fast. We should talk."

Koblensky remembered Tessa and wondered about her part in the production of this military mannequin. "The Fast? Yes, perhaps I should come."

The French army band, brassiest of the assembled tribunes, broke into a deafening march. Koblensky slipped away, leaving Bron feeling more than ever lost in alien currents.

Kippax had been stung by Lawrence's complaint about the Ikhwan, and by his pretense of not knowing what they were. It was clear warning that Lawrence would intrigue for his own Arab alliance against any other, and Lawrence was, for the moment, Allenby's star. Kippax, in contrast, had almost no backing; Hogarth was no longer a dependable ally and Sir Cedric was too far away to offer solace. Without even a thank you, Kippax had done the most burdensome things without complaint. The whining note of these grievances, however, made him uncomfortable. He would need to pull himself together, to be patient. There were fashions in policy, as in all things. His time would come. After all, he had to his credit one personal feat of diplomacy that would look better the more that time passed. It was he who had soothed Ibn Saud's complaints about the Balfour Declaration: Ibn Jiluwi had gone back to Riyadh assured that there would be no sudden Jewish colonization of Palestine, and the king had apparently taken Kippax at his word, though ultimately he would look for more than that. No—for the moment it would be enough to keep his wits on Lawrence, the immediate nuisance.

As soon as he was able to get Hogarth to himself, Kippax casually said, on the heels of routine business, "Lawrence doesn't seem too well."

"His foot still bothers him."

"I didn't mean physically."

Hogarth was careful, knowing that little Kippax said was as innocent as it seemed. "He has horrendous burdens. Can you imagine, trying to coordinate his tribes with our armies? They've never been constant in battle, even on their own behalf. But then you know them as well as I—or Lawrence."

"I realize the scale of what he's trying," said Kippax, pouring tea from a Wedgwood pot that had been left behind by a German officer. "It may be too much, don't you think?" He stopped to put two lumps of sugar into each cup. "We're lucky with the sugar; it's a gift from Cardinal Bourne. No, what I mean is, with all due respect, can he carry it?"

Hogarth was annoyed not that Kippax was intriguing but that Kippax had settled on something he was already himself troubled by. "I don't know if he'll last. But that's not *all* you're implying, is it?"

"Well, no. It's something I've heard. Something he's been telling people."

"You mean . . . about the incident at Deraa?"

"Is it true?"

"You needn't be so delicate about it, as though you dare hardly raise it. In you, that's cant."

Kippax's brows rose in exaggerated offense.

"Sodomized by the military governor of Deraa—that's it, isn't it?" said Hogarth.

"That is the story."

"Well, is that so incredible? You know what they are. It's a wonder he got away with his life. As he tells it, quite appalling. I think it had better be kept out of the records, don't you agree?"

"Oh, of *course*. And since he has confided in you, I wouldn't dream of raising it again—to anyone." Then he said, "The scars must be *very* painful."

Hogarth looked across the teapot to Kippax and felt more murderous than it was politic for him to seem. "Yes, I'm sure he has *your* sympathy."

It was raining, cold enough for London in December. Leaving

Hogarth in comfort, Kippax found a trenchcoat and walked to the Mosque of Omar, the rain dripping into his face from the peak of his cap. The building was in bad disrepair, but in the rain the surviving tilework seemed molten, the colors even more luminous than in sun. Tiles were the only indulgence of mosques, the cladding of otherwise plain buildings. Kippax thought of the nearby Church of the Holy Sepulcher and judged it, against the mosque, as little better than a tourist trap. No graven images or idols here; he could focus on one corner of the tilework until it became detached, its radiant surface filling his eye and mind until substance dematerialized and he touched the ecstasy of an art that left its surface behind. No images, no idols. Cast out the idols.

A Muslim cleric watched the intrusive figure, the cap and raincoat turning gradually from khaki to ink in the rain, the figure transfixed, oblivious. The city had fallen to infidels.

The old Russian who had led the prayers of Hanukkah had locked his hands in his lap, a ruby ring on one index finger pushed slightly askew by the pressure, its slackness showing how shrunken the hands were. He had finished talking, but his eyes remained fixed on Koblensky. The rain on the roof and walls outside added to the claustrophobic sense of the small, windowless room. A single lamp burning on the floor gave the lower fringe of the old man's beard a ginger tint.

"There is nothing we can do ourselves," said Koblensky. "We have no medicines left. I would have to go to the British."

"Then go."

Koblensky looked into the old man's eyes. "It may not do any good. There are many sick."

"You think I don't know?"

The old man's obduracy was a cover for his being on the edge of tears.

"I'll try, Misha."

Koblensky felt weaker himself; oddly, the life behind the Turkish lines with Laski, for all its risks, had fully engaged his energies and even the food shortage didn't seem to matter. But since he had been here in Jerusalem, the inactivity and formality of being attached to Allenby's staff were wearing him down. He had never liked the city, and its raw winter climate repelled him more. He trudged rather than walked through the rain, the rubber raincoat giving him a cold sweat, and shortening his patience even more.

In the lobby of the Hotel Fast, someone had mounted a small Christmas tree, a threadbare pine sapling still mud-smeared around its root, now decked with paper chains and topped with a Dresden cherub that had previously sat on the drawing room piano, alongside the sheets of German martial music. The bar had been resupplied from Cairo and rang with the boorish humor Koblensky knew from there. He found Bron alone in the drawing room, reading a month-old London newspaper.

Bron looked up. "You're soaked. You need a drink."

Koblensky put the raincoat on an umbrella stand, where it drained onto a Turkish rug. He asked for brandy, and while Bron found an orderly, stood by a feeble fire.

Bron was surprised to see Koblensky drain the brandy in one swig. "You all right?"

Koblensky didn't like the brandy much, but it seemed to make an instant impression. "I will survive," he said, still standing as Bron resumed his seat.

"We've been trying to cheer the place up a bit."

"I can hear that."

"What's on your mind?" Under Koblensky's cold eye again, he was irritated by the old feeling of being in some way on probation.

The brandy reached Koblensky's knees. He said, "Have you been to the Jewish Quarter?"

"Not yet."

"I see."

"My dear chap, we have a lot to do."

"There is something I would like you to see."

"*Now?*" Bron had detected insistence.

"Yes."

"In the Jewish Quarter?"

Koblensky nodded.

"Well . . ." Bron cast a conspicious look at the clock. "There is a staff meeting tonight to prepare for. Are you sure it can't wait? You look in need of a rest yourself."

"It will not wait."

"Well, I can give you an hour." Bron didn't relish the idea of making an excursion into the Jewish Quarter on a wet afternoon. And what he liked even less than that was something in himself—an inexplicable anxiety that Koblensky should be

362

appeased. Koblensky seemed to know this and to stand over him like a visitation from a dark, intimidating will.

The city now bore little resemblance to the one that had so recently welcomed Allenby. It was more than a difference between early morning sun and afternoon deluge. They went east into the alleys, deep into the Old City. The rain emphasized the lack of sanitation. Even in the cold, the air became rancid. Few people were visible, and most of them were huddled in shadow around fires, ovens, or lamps. The only shops with any stocks were those with useless curios. An Armenian butcher displayed one gutted rabbit. Everywhere there was evidence of prolonged neglect: crumbling gutters, collapsing roofs, desperate improvisations to provide shelter. Koblensky had not spoken since they went through the Jaffa Gate. He could see the shock in Bron's face. Turning into an even more decrepit alley, seeking what little cover it gave, he said, "You have heard of Herzl?"

Bron resented the sarcastic imputation. "The father of Zionism."

"Herzl came here, a long time ago. You know what he wrote afterwards?" Koblensky pressed ahead, shouting the rest of his words as though addressing not only Bron but the whole alley. " 'Should the day come when Jerusalem is once more ours, my first act will be to cleanse thee.' That's what Herzl said. Is Jerusalem ours?"

Bron knew no answer was expected from him. Koblensky's rhetoric had its answer in the sullen, enveloping alley and the way in which the scintillating facade of Jerusalem, the Jerusalem of legend and the Jerusalem gazed at in awe from distant hilltops, had, in this dark interior, crumbled and rotted. Koblensky stopped, wiping the rain from his face, and beckoned Bron to follow through a low arch in a wall. Beyond the wall was a small paved courtyard; in the center of it, what had once been a circular pool was now little more than cracked stone with the rainwater caught in the remnant of a bowl. On three sides of the courtyard were three-story galleried houses, with wooden outside staircases. In one corner, a haggard mule was standing without evident movement, indifferent to the rain.

They went up one of the staircases to a second-floor gallery. Not until they went through the door did Bron see or hear anyone. Then, though the room was half in darkness, he saw its occupants: three women, one very old, one middle-aged, and the other little more than a child, all of them in a vast bed covered by several rugs. The girl was in the center, lying back. The other

Clive Irving

two women, on either side of her, were propped on bolsters. The older woman peered out of the darkness at Koblensky and spoke in Russian.

Bron held back a pace behind Koblensky. There was the odor of fever in the room, as well as of urine and mildew.

Koblensky answered the woman and nodded perfunctorily at Bron, then said to Bron, "These are the family of a man who worked for us. He has disappeared; we don't know what happened. This is his mother and his wife—and the girl is his daughter. She has pneumonia; I think that is what it is. Look at her. She needs help. In here she will die."

"When you say worked for *us*, you mean the NILI?"

"Of course."

Bron went forward to the bed, taking off his dripping cap. He smiled a strangled smile, the barrier of language adding to one of experience. He looked at the girl. In the shadow she seemed to have no color at all. To have called her pale or even white would have been inadequate; her skin was almost without life. She had thick, dark hair, parted in the center and framing each cheek, increasing the recessiveness of the face. She followed Bron's movements with impersonal curiosity. Bron reached over the mother and felt the girl's forehead. Belying its pallor, it burned, and his hand came away sticky.

"It *is* a fever," he said, redundantly. "She is bad." He could smell the bodies of the other women, a fearful smell. They watched him differently: the old woman with a misty-eyed serenity, the mother with skepticism and a protective movement, not wanting him to touch the girl again. "We must get her out of here," said Bron, his mind recoiling from trepidation to determination. "Yes, we must get her out, as soon as possible."

Koblensky was surprised by Bron's decisiveness. He spoke for a last time to the women in Russian and followed Bron out to the small gallery. Bron was looking down into the courtyard, still hatless. "These are all Russian Jews here?"

"Most of them from Bukhara."

"Bukhara? Islamic Russia, persecuted by both the Czar and the Muslims, then."

"Yes," said Koblensky, impressed by Bron's unsuspected knowledge.

"These are appalling conditions in which to live."

"There are twenty thousand of them in Jerusalem."

"You were right to bring me here. I didn't know. One has no

idea, just no idea. . . ." Again, his will recovered abruptly from despondency. "We must save that girl, if we can." He wondered how twenty thousand people could be swallowed up in such a place.

Through the floor of Hogarth's room they could hear the din from the bar, now pervading the whole hotel. Kippax had folded himself into a chair that was too small for him, too intent to care. He waved an arm and splashed his whisky in doing so. "Allenby must be told, and he must be made to understand. It's absolutely disastrous, and there is no time to lose."

"He might feel there are other priorities," said Hogarth, seated at a table, his face almost invisible above a small desk light, as he shuffled papers and listened to Kippax, whose wet bootprints still marked the rug.

"It's a matter of life or death."

"Come now, Owen." The use of his Christian name was patronizing.

"Allenby said—I distinctly recall the words—'Every sacred building will be maintained and protected.' "

"And so it will—in time. I must say, one afternoon at the mosque and you seem to have lost your balance."

"But you must see it. You remember how Chelebi described it? A heavenly palace. I was hard put to find one piece of tilework that was intact. *Really.* The Turks are Muslims, after all, but this, more than anything I have seen, marks the wretched, ruinous negligence of the Ottomans. Do you know, there's mildew on the dome. *Mildew.* It's a slimy gray, not gold. The lead is leaking. Rain was pouring in. Mosaic is falling off the plaster. And the patching up that's been done—horrendous. They don't seem able to make tiles any longer. The glaze is fading. They've actually painted over gaps—painted! We shall need to go afar for the tilework. Allenby must call in someone. There is a chap in London, Richmond . . ."

"Yes, yes—I know him. You imagine the Muslims are going to allow an infidel to restore the Dome of the Rock?"

"They'll have no say in it."

Hogarth laughed, but not warmly. "I see." He pulled out a clip of papers, holding them under the light. "There's something here I think you ought to look at; it's your kind of stuff."

Kippax was annoyed. "Oh . . . what?"

"It's called the Protocols of the Elders of Zion. Originates in

365

Russia. Recently come to light. This is a copy, circulated to all senior officers. Quite why I don't understand, but someone in Whitehall thought it a good idea. It may even have been Assay.'' Hogarth enjoyed seeing Kippax's diligence return at the dropping of that name.

"Elders of Zion?"

"If one can believe it, this presents a detailed, extensive scheme for the gradual Jewish domination of the world. Farfetched, but just credible enough to appeal to a number of people. Here— you can make it your bedtime reading.''

"What's *your* opinion of it?'' said Kippax suspiciously, getting up to take the papers.

"Oh, I have no opinion. One does wonder, though. Look at events in Russia. The Bolsheviks wasted very little time; it was all carried out quite ruthlessly. And one must remember the origins of Bolshevism. Born of a rabid Jewish mind.'' He watched Kippax flip the pages. "I'm sorry, Owen, if I was rather dismissive of your aesthetic concerns. You are quite right. There is so much fakery in Jerusalem, so many ersatz masterpieces, that one must discriminate from the beginning. We should show ourselves at least to be the equal of Sulemain. I shall talk to Allenby.''

The Medical Corps captain was irritated at having been called from the bar. He came into the lobby still carrying his pink gin and breathing a wave of juniper. The messenger took him to Bron and Koblensky.

"What *is* it?"

Bron said, "I'm sorry to have to call you out. We tried the field hospital, but they couldn't do anything and so I came to you. It's a very serious case, a young girl with pneumonia, on the verge of death.''

"A girl? You mean a civilian?"

"It's serious. I think we should take her.''

"Have you any idea what the public health situation in this city is like?'' The captain was turning the same hue as his drink. "We can't start getting involved with civilians. We've plenty on our plate, as it is. No decent sanitary conditions, not enough water. And you come here expecting me to take a girl off the streets?''

Koblensky stepped forward, but Bron restrained him. "There

are reasons, in this case, for an exception to be made, I can assure you.''

The captain looked from Bron to Koblensky. "Where is this girl, exactly?''

"In the Jewish Quarter.''

"Ha. The Jewish Quarter. Tonight, take in a Jew. Tomorrow, take in a Muslim. The day after—''

A shadow fell between him and Bron, someone moving out from a corner of the lobby.

"Captain,'' said a voice couched in almost excessive reasonableness. "Have you empty beds?''

The captain's face swiveled with an expression of redoubled irritation and he began to speak. "As a matter of—'' Then he stopped. "Major Lawrence?'' His face and drink came to rest at the same moment. "It *is* Major Lawrence?''

Still almost graciously diffident, Lawrence said, "You do have empty beds, do you?''

"In point of fact, yes. But I—''

"Then be so good as to find out where this sick girl is, send some nurses, and get her to your hospital as soon as possible.''

The captain looked from Lawrence to Bron and Koblensky, began nodding in a spastic way, and said, "Where can she be found?''

"I'll take the nurses there,'' said Bron.

"Good,'' said Lawrence, and touched Koblensky on the arm. "I wonder, could we have a word?''

They watched Bron disappear with the captain. "It was lucky you were here,'' said Koblensky.

"No—not lucky,'' said Lawrence solemnly. "Not lucky at all. I was waiting for you.'' He stood awkwardly. "Is one of your people called Lishansky—Joseph Lishansky?''

"Yes.''

"I'm afraid he's dead. He was hanged publicly in Damascus yesterday. *Pour encourager les autres.*''

"Lishansky was dangerous—to himself, to others.''

Koblensky's response surprised Lawrence. "I see. And Belkind, Nathan Belkind. Was he careless too?''

"Naaman—Naaman Belkind. They hanged him?''

"Yes. They did. Perhaps you can explain. The report bothers me. Belkind was not caught with Lishansky. He was shot first—by Jews. He was betrayed to the Turks.''

Koblensky had turned white. "Belkind was a brave man, a good agent. Betrayed? Not the first."

"Before Lishansky died, he cried out the name of the NILI." Lawrence took Koblensky by the arm. "I am going to buy you a drink. You look finished."

In the drawing room, the pianist who had parodied the Kaiser's march was now playing Chopin with absorbed skill—and with no audience. Lawrence nodded to him as the fingers paused, the man awed by recognizing Lawrence. "Please—carry on."

Koblensky had his second large brandy of the day, but this time sipped it. Lawrence, drinking a plain lemonade, was silent until reassured that Koblensky was over the shock of the two executions. Then he said, "Do you know about this declaration of Mr. Balfour's?"

"No more than I read in the newspaper."

"It must be reassuring to you."

"It's a piece of paper."

"Yes, it is." Lawrence paused, uneasy. "It is a piece of paper . . . and there have been others." He put down his drink. "Look, it will be essential—it matters a great deal to me personally—that the Jews and the Arabs live peaceably together, where they share the same territory. Balfour's declaration makes that intention clear. I support your ambitions. I'm sure you realize that. But I do want a bridge built between Jew and Arab, one that will last. Now that we have Jerusalem, we must begin that work. Weizmann will be coming here in a month or so. They are putting together some kind of commission, which he will lead. When he comes here, I am going to try to arrange that he sees my Arab prince, Faisal. Faisal has a future with us. After the war, he will be the Arab most concerned with Palestine: That is my hope. His father is now old, and Faisal is a wise and farsighted son. I think he and Dr. Weizmann would understand each other."

"Why are you telling *me* this?" Koblensky put down his brandy. "I don't have any influence with Dr. Weizmann."

Lawrence leaned back and pressed together his fingers to his chin, looking at Koblensky with sharp, insistent eyes. "I always look for the sons of the fathers—in any tribe. I can always pick them out."

"And so to Calvary," breathed Kippax in a parody of veneration.
Hogarth said, "A pity . . . a pity." They had walked the Via

Dolorosa, nearly missing their way where it cranked among the alleys, following the fourteen stations of the Cross. The Ninth Station, "Jesus falls for the third time," marked by a Coptic church, swarmed with desperate souvenir hawkers. Hogarth pushed his way through, and then they were at the threshold of the Church of the Holy Sepulcher. The capricious weather had turned again; an Oriental sun suffused the European Gothic. Hogarth and Kippax ignored the remaining stations of the pilgrims' trail and went before the red limestone slab of Jesus' tomb. "I think it is required," said Hogarth, bending to kiss the stone. Kippax arched his brows, unsure whether protocol, piety, or hypocrisy had been demonstrated. He did not kiss the stone.

"When it comes to authenticity, one cannot be too particular," said Hogarth. "There may be little to choose between the hawker's version of the crucifixion and this, but it is, at least, testament to the power of apostasy. You realize that every sacred Christian mark in Jerusalem was the product of a convert's decision? Constantine's empress—she was born of an innkeeper, a pagan, by the way—came here at the age of eighty and determined everything."

Kippax stood back from the marble, bareheaded and distastefully aloof. "Meretricious," he said, "*ineffably* meretricious." Here he was of a divided mind, the disappointed aesthete and the secular pilgrim. Under the dome of Omar, all the parts of him had been momentarily resolved, he had become one. Between these marble columns were as many dissonances as sects, ranging from Syrian incense to Latin rose water. Rome had to cohabit with Byzantium, Byzantium with Damascus, Damascus with Athens, and each gave off its vapors. Kippax much preferred the untainted absolutism of a truly Roman church and the dogmatic assurance of a high Latin mass in unadulterated cadences. *There* was the equal, perhaps, of Omar's theocracy, not in this mongrel pastiche. But Hogarth was no philistine, and yet had been touched by something here. In way of explanation, Kippax murmured, " 'How beautiful, if sorrow had not made sorrow more beautiful than beauty's self.' "

"Quite so," said Hogarth. "Then we might agree; might we, that aesthetic death can be swallowed in spiritual victory?"

"We might." Kippax smiled, but he was thinking that will rather than spirit was the greater force.

A priest, unmistakably Latin, appeared between vaulted marble, his face managing to be resistantly white in the shaft of roseate light.

"Commander Hogarth?"

Hogarth turned, and nodded.

"Please—follow me."

They were led past two side chapels and along a suddenly plain, flagstoned pathway to a recess of the church and finally into a narrow but high-vaulted room. Rising from behind a desk was a man in the robes of a cardinal, but bareheaded.

Hogarth was uncertain of his stance, and bowed slightly.

"So good of you to come with such celerity," said the cardinal, disposing of the bow with an offered shaking of the hand. "And this is . . .?"

"One of my political officers, Captain Kippax."

Kippax took the cardinal's soft, moist hand.

"General Allenby was concerned that we should reassure you," said Hogarth.

"Please," said the cardinal, waving them to chairs flanking his desk. With them seated, he resumed his own seat, a brocaded armchair, which over time had rearranged its contours in exact duplication of the cardinal's, so that once settled, he and the chair seemed organically united. His breath was short, carrying the strain of his considerable bulk. But despite the slackness of his physique there was a flash of iron in his eyes. "Now," he said, "may I repeat my concern, as briefly as possible? Great though our joy is at this deliverance—and of course, it is a most moving thing, to so nearly coincide with the birth of our Lord— great though our thanks must be, a jarring note has also been struck. People have come to me—some of them humble, some from the finest families among our congregation—to report that the British soldiers are telling everyone that they have liberated Jerusalem so that it may be regained by the Jews. And then there is Mr. Balfour's statement as to the future policy permitting Jewish settlement. A very vague statement, if I may say so. Both Christians and Muslims have approached me on the subject. They feel that they are being handed over to the Zionists—whom they dislike more than their late Turkish oppressors. Unfortunately, for some unaccountable reason, Balfour seems to be favoring this movement."

"Well," said Hogarth, "I think I can reassure you. Inevitably passions are running high. As you say yourself, it is a deliverance, for people of all faiths. However, there are zealots in every denomination, as I am sure you must realize, Cardinal." Hogarth's attempted levity was not responded to; the cardinal's eye was unrelenting, and waiting. "What I mean is, you must not take anyone's word other than that of His Majesty's government, and let me make that quite plain: There is no question of Jewish primacy. It is our intention that, under British protection, Palestine will enjoy a high degree of self-determination—and that authority will be evenhanded as to each group."

"But what about Jewish immigration?"

"The object of Balfour was to encourage Jewish immigration as far as that is practicable. It is, of course, far too early to talk of numbers."

"Commander—the whole Zionist movement appears to me to be quite contrary to Christian sentiment and tradition. Let Jews live here, by all means, but that they should ever again dominate and rule the country would be an outrage to Christianity and its divine founder. I need not tell you, nor your young *political* officer, that the controlling influence of Zionism is German, German finance. Is this what England really desires after this war?"

"I think you will find, Cardinal, that we have drawn the teeth of Zionism, by our giving what is a very limited, specifically limited, concession."

"One looks no further than Saint Petersburg, and one wonders." The cardinal was far from appeased.

"We must let passions cool," said Hogarth.

"You may have noticed, as you came here, how sad is the fabric of the church. I was hoping, if you might bear this in mind for some future discussion, that His Majesty's government would assist in the refurbishment and restoration of our holy places."

"We already have that in mind," said Hogarth, thankful of safer ground. "As a matter of fact, Kippax here was himself saying, only minutes ago, how extraordinarily moving it is, to be reminded of the architectural magnificence of the Holy Sepulcher, and how vital it is to ensure its condition." Hogarth carefully avoided Kippax's eye.

The cardinal mellowed slightly, and his breath became more regular. "Really? That is most gratifying. You must permit me to show you round. It needs to be taken at leisure."

The hotel's kitchens and cellar had been resupplied from Cairo by the French, who were gratefully allowed to organize the

Christmas banquet. Since before dawn, the bedrooms were permeated by the smell of roasting turkeys, and not long after dawn the bar was echoing with the detonation of bottles of Bollinger. Many officers had gone to a Nativity Mass at Bethlehem, and returned vocally complaining that the presiding abbot confused the ceremony and had continually to be prompted. Bron, who in other circumstances would have been swept along in the secular rites, slept late and disliked the mood intruding through the walls. He tried to find a telephone, to call Tessa in Cairo, but there were no private phones in the whole of Jerusalem and the military telephonists would not oblige. Cairo seemed an age away, as far away as a lost innocence and now, to his mind, taking on a curious offensiveness. He ached for, and needed, Tessa.

Koblensky found him staring blankly from a window of the drawing room into the garden. It was raining again, a wet Christmas, and the sodden garden had somehow detached itself and become an English one, abundant with disconsolate possibilities.

"She will be all right," said Koblensky.

Momentarily startled, Bron turned.

"I have come from the hospital. The fever is going. She talked."

Suddenly Bron was impatient with his own maudlin behavior. "That's marvelous—absolutely bloody marvelous!"

More completely than Bron could remember, Koblensky smiled. "Yes. Yes, it is. We should thank Major Lawrence for that."

"No, not altogether. I would say there is a lot to thank you for. I've been wanting to talk to you. Can we get out of this ghastly place? Somewhere . . . anywhere."

With its warmth and its electric light, the Hotel Fast was an island of bacchanalia amid a city that seemed otherwise sullen; it was still an occupied city, though the color of its occupation had changed. Without design, the celebration of Christmas so soon after occupation emphasized the ascendancy of Christian over Muslim, an innocent but perceptible bias; as Bron and Koblensky left the hotel, from somewhere a single bell rang, deadened by the rain. All sound was, like the horizon, attenuated.

Koblensky, who usually walked briskly, seemed content to drift. In the gray oilskin he looked anonymous and not easy to attach to any nationality; a gypsy. Bron, in trenchcoat and cap, appeared more substantial than he felt. Neither spoke. They were converging in thought, this each of them knew. Koblensky led the way through the Damascus Gate; Bron found himself hardly aware of having left the outside until hands reached out for him and beggars called. The alley, dark and wet, became a tunnel of a fireless hell: cripples, mutants, toothless women, and children as hostile as they were imploring. Koblensky pushed through, brutal against obstruction, but the gauntlet closed again on Bron, who had no brutality left for defense. And then the hands were gone, with the alley.

Bron knew what it was; at least he knew it as a name. But there seemed no proper aspect to it. As massive as it was, the Wailing Wall seemed to be fighting for space like a monolith in quicksand, neither consumed nor released. It was, he knew, a fragment—dispassionately the fragment of the Temple or emotionally a fragment of the lost estate of the Jews. With the houses of the Muslim Quarter pressing in on it, the impression to Bron was more of a redoubt, an impression increased by the way only a handful of Jews huddled with their prayerbooks in the rain, their yarmulkes glistening. The Wall was said itself to weep, but in the rain it seemed oddly impermeable, to be unweathered and to have been never wet. Bron thought it pitiless, above abjection, while the men at prayer were pitiable.

"You see," said Koblensky, "they come here for hope. A wall . . . and hope." From under the hood of the oilskin his eyes met Bron's. "Twenty centuries of hope."

The prayers were like cries caught in the crevices of the wall.

"I heard about the two men hanged in Damascus," said Bron. "Lawrence told me."

Koblensky did not look away; he barely blinked.

Bron wiped rain from his chin, and said, "I'm aware of something changing in me—no, of having already changed. Today it was becoming plain what it is. In one way—in one way I suppose it's a kind of desolation. But in another it might be a beginning." Koblensky's unremitting, expressionless concentration on him forced Bron to look away, and he hesitated, and then continued: "In Cairo, when we argued, I could not relate what you said to my own condition. I could understand its appeal to others, but it didn't appear that it could ever have any meaning for me. I was mistaken. I was deceived by my own condition. I thought I could draw a line between my life, its security, its *Englishness*, and the lives of other Jews. What has happened is that when I saw the girl, and then the place . . . What has happened is that I can now see that that line does not exist, never really did exist, *can* never exist. Not in the way I imagined. I wish it did. To tell you the honest truth, I yearn for it, I shall go on looking backwards for it, but I can't restore the deception, I know that. It's not a religious feeling; nothing like that. Religion doesn't feed or heal—not here, at any rate. Ironic, that, isn't it? In Jerusalem?'' He shrugged and then looked at Koblensky again. ''These people are *my* people, I am of them. I see it and I can't turn away from it. I never *have* turned away from it, you know—do you understand that? I never *did* turn away. It's just that I never saw it at all until now. Once I did see, I knew, I understood. I understood about you.''

The strain of the moment had made Bron feel feverish. He took off his service cap and let the rain run through his hair. ''I'm sorry; I wish I could thank you for it, but I don't. I wish I had never come here. *I wish I could forget it.* Most of all, I don't want to become like you. As a matter of fact, I'm sure I never can. Do you see? But at least I understand you, and because I understand, I'm going to do more to support you. I want to try to make sure that in the future every Jew knows, wherever he is, that if he chooses he can live as a Jew in a Jewish state, that he can have that nationality in the same way that, wherever *he* is, an Englishman knows he can live in England. The Jew's claim to that is every bit as legitimate as the Englishman's. But I don't want them living here, like this, in *this* place. I've thought about it. I'm convinced Aaronsohn is right: With proper farming, there's room for all who want to come.''

''Be careful,'' said Koblensky, more guarded than intimate. ''The man who becomes my ally collects my enemies. Have you thought of that?''

Bron nodded, the rain spilling through his brows.

Koblensky looked away to the wall. ''I don't want to live like this, either. And I don't like the name of this place—I don't like wailing. The wailing is over.''

# 21

## *Palestine \* March 1919*

The bus reached the high plateau south of Jerusalem, the spine giving a view, to the west, of the coastal plain and, to the east, of the epic escarpments that bordered the Dead Sea. In the laboring climb, the bus had carried with it the city's smell of clustered bodies; now a plateau wind began to ventilate the vehicle and, holding her head to a half-open window, Esther Mosseri let the air press on her, headscarf flapping against the wooden frame. To be able to take this untainted breeze was to be able to break at last from the mass. The bus was a microcosm of the mass, a shipment of the assorted souls of Palestine: of Arabs, Jews, and Christians; of peasants, tradesmen, and wanderers; of the innocent young and the burdened old. They were all passengers in an uneasy, unresolved cohabitation. The bus, like the country, seemed more improvised than designed—an insecure frame under British power. The warm, clean wind, in contrast, had no clear provenance; it gave her a few moments of freedom and she would have liked to be able to follow an impulse to escape the bus and be left on the plateau, with the mass gone far from her. But she was riding to Hebron.

Hebron, and the partitioned allegiances of Jew and Arab: a Hebrew shrine topped with a Muslim mosque—and embellished by Byzantines and crusaders. The children of Ishmael and the children of Abraham filled separate chambers with their prayers. She was not given to touring the sacred landmarks and came more from a new confusion than a new devotion. Her scholar's head wanted to see the Machpelah cave and the tombs of Abraham, Isaac, and Jacob and of Sarah, Rebecca, and Leah. As the bus lumbered into Hebron, this was how she explained the pilgrimage to herself, knowing still that it needed explanation. But she was confused.

375

Up the great stone stairway, into the congestion of pilgrims and tourists, she was of neither one nor the other. The shrines touched no ancestral nerve, yet she could not stand off from them consulting the Baedeker with agnostic detachment. She read the Arabic legend on Abraham's cenotaph: "This is the tomb of the prophet Abraham, may he rest in peace." Rest in peace; she was as entrapped here as in Jerusalem or Cairo. These shrines were, as simple masonry, banal to her. There were tricks of sound and light; she walked through sudden light and sudden darkness, and a wind on the stone carried voices as insubstantial as dust from wall to wall and through pillars and grilles. Palestine had lessened, not strengthened, her sense of tribe. The tricks of sound and light were part of a sectarian confusion, a disunity of voices and faces—and of gods. Rest in peace. She knew there could be no syncretic peace in the new Jerusalem.

Palestine was a colony still. With the end of the war and the collapse of Ottoman Turkey, it had become another British possession; the regime issued its coercions in English, Hebrew, and Arabic; the British citadel was one of paper, built on the belief that order was the ultimate deity. And victory already had its icons: The Hotel Fast had become the Hotel Allenby. When she returned to the Allenby that afternoon, it was oddly quiet. Normally at this hour the bar would have been taking its prescribed place in the social rites of empire (she had imagined how the path of the sun, like a pagan signal, must summon these khaki assemblies from Malaya to Gibraltar), but there was no lubricated chatter from it today. She went to the lounge. It was similarly deserted. An Indian orderly, a slight, dark hopping figure in virginal whites, followed her.

"Tea, miss?"

"Thank you. Tell me, where *is* everyone?"

"Something is going on, miss. Big flap, miss."

"Big flap?"

"Everyone called to headquarters."

She sank into an armchair of brocade worn thin. The emptied hotel isolated her in the drab chair and dried up her sensuality as years dried up women into old maids. Sipping the tea from the fussy German china, she seemed to be in suspense, the lounge an antechamber, she a displaced person awaiting assignment. She was still brooding on this when Kippax came through the door.

He looked illicit. It was the midnight Kippax of Cairo; the bat, not in uniform but in cream linen, the jacket too short.

He waved aside the orderly and sat opposite her, with a low butler's table between them. "So . . . I hear you've been to Hebron. Via Bethlehem. An epiphany? No. I think not." His laugh was short and piping. "No, of course not. You see, we have to keep our eyes on you—eyes and ears. You must know how satraps work, I'm sure, as a student of history—and empires." Within the winged chair back he looked less intimidating than his voice wanted to imply; the suit impaired the sought-after effect. "There is serious trouble in Egypt—quite serious trouble."

"In Egypt?"

"An uprising. They may call themselves nationalists, but they are really the fanatics. We had to get them out, deport them. It might have been handled better, before it got out of hand. You needn't seem so surprised. We're having to dispatch as many troops from here as we can manage. It's going to leave us with little more than the ragtag gang of the Jewish Legion. *Not* good timing. This is not the placid pool it seems, and with a predominantly Jewish garrison, God knows. . . . But that is not my point. Look, I think we understand each other. I had thought that here, at least, you would be clear of mischief. But this thing has changed all that. Once this so-called bug of nationalism takes hold, it could spread anywhere, and specially here. The Jews have done enough already to incite the Arabs." He leaned forward clear of the chair wings and modulated his voice as though whispering an endearment. "I know your bloody game. I know your associates. You're only at large on sufferance—*my* sufferance. That's because my view as to your use, tentative as it is, has prevailed. So far. My feeling is—no, my *wish* is that you be of better service to us here. I'm being considerate. After all, were you to find yourself in Cairo at this time, your survival might be infinitely more dubious. I make my point?"

A casual observer, such as the incautious orderly, would have been titillated: following this intense address, she settled back into the chair like a yielding lover. Only in the way one hand clenched was there a trace of tension. She looked at the hand and moved it from her lap and then said, as quietly as he, "Once, I thought of the English—it was before I went to Oxford—I thought, if we *must* have empires, let them be at least in the hands of a civilized people." Her smile was that of an assignation. "But Oxford taught me better—and that was the best of its lessons. You really should remain in uniform. The suit does not do you justice."

He leaned back into the chair again and unbuttoned the jacket, then looked around for the orderly. "I think I will take tea, after all. I'm so glad you got my point."

In a matter of minutes, the hotel was repopulated. The officers returned in a tide, all lassitude gone. Few of them went to the bar. Most were directing their batmen to pack their kits. The galvanic spirit revived the old jingoism in their faces, and old epithets in their talk of "bints" and "wogs" and the newer coinage, "Bolshies" and "anarchists." This was more repellent to her than even Kippax's venom. That, at least, was now particular and overt, while the other had the stealthy virulence of bigotry.

She had come to Palestine through a connection of Dr. Ibrahim Ghazi's; the end of the war had made possible a renewal of old links between the museums of Cairo and Jerusalem. She had a legitimate interest in the Coptic collections, but what Ghazi had wanted was to reconnect the underground of nationalist groups. Kippax must have known this all along. She had underrated him. He was, indeed, the all-seeing satrap, thriving in a new Byzantium through the use of ancient tyrannies.

Fear had become a creeping anemia settled in her until death. Its attrition robbed her of feeling; she lived her desiccated life in a zone of indifference between love and hate. Sometimes she thought Koblensky lived in the dead zone too—until she remembered how ardently Koblensky hated. She would always fail him in that.

Koblensky . . . A distance had grown between them since Cairo. His allegiance had become as clear as a proclamation; hers was buried in decay. At least, antipathy was less complex for both of them: She knew how little she could ask of him and he had never asked anything of her. Would he take it if offered? She doubted so, but the satrap had driven her to Koblensky.

He lived in the northeast of the city in a street with a view of Mount Scopus. She had been there before, but only in daylight. His rooms were above a tailor's workshop. Now the workshop was in darkness. Alongside it was a narrow passage, at the end of the passage a small courtyard, and to one side an iron stairway. There was a lamp burning in the courtyard and another in a room at the top of the stairway. The eyes of a tethered goat looked up from under the stairway as she climbed it. Despite the coolness of dusk, the door was ajar. The room was little more than a cupboard, with a washbasin, an ancient wood stove, and a small table. Standing on the table was an old pair of British army boots, an open tin of black wax, and a brush. The boots were pitted, but under the lamp shone bright like new tar. The smell of the wax was curiously pleasant and domestic.

She walked through another door. This room was as large as the other was small; it matched the size of the workshop below, and had deep windows onto the street. There was no light, but some weak illumination from the windows. The foot of the right-hand wall was lined, end to end, with books, as though just unpacked but not sorted. By the window there was a small desk and a chair. Against the left-hand wall was a bed, covered simply with a tribal *kelim*. The bed, more than anything else, signaled the intention of settlement. It was solid and baroque, a remnant of old Russia. Otherwise—apart from two chairs of the same simplicity as the one at the desk—there was nothing else. The floor was bare boards.

"I saw you go down the passage."

The sudden voice nearly broke her nerve. Koblensky was behind her in the doorway.

"In the dark, I wasn't sure it was the right place."

"Is it—is it the right place?" Against the light his face was unclear, but his hard, sarcastic voice was perversely reassuring. In outline he had the same constancy, in the way he stood and held his head with none of the gestures of greeting, and then in the way he walked past her to a lamp on the desk and lit it. It was like the natural impersonality of a doctor.

"May I sit down?"

He nodded, and then looked at her more carefully, sensing distress. "Were you followed here?"

"Why do you ask that?"

He moved round from the desk, looking down at her as she settled. "When you came down the street and into the passage, it was in a god of a hurry. I was getting milk. I saw you pass the dairy. A god of a hurry."

She had not heard him come up the stairway because his feet were bare, bare and hardened like a peasant's. She was calmer now. She smiled, not wanting him to think her at all in need of care. He would only take advantage of that. "It was dark and I thought I was lost."

"Yes." He remained on his feet. "I am surprised you are not in Egypt. Isn't it what you wanted—revolution?"

"It's too soon. You know that."

379

"I don't care about it. I care about other things. I care about a report from Jaffa that the Arabs have somehow got thousands of rifles. I care about these people who call themselves the Black Hand, who want to exterminate Jews. I care about generals who will not let us play our national anthem, about stopping Jews from immigrating here, about not recognizing Hebrew as an official language in a country which is supposed to be a national home for Jews. These things I care about. Egypt I do not care about." He seemed to embrace her in these accusations, and then stopped for a second. "I am making coffee," he said finally. "You would like some? Russian coffee, not Turkish."

"Thank you."

While he was making it, she walked to the wall and looked over the books. Some were in Russian, many in English, and a few in Arabic. He was rounding himself. She was surprised. Despite the feet, he was a gypsy no more. It was too much to expect grace as well.

As he brought the coffee in enameled tin mugs, she pulled the shawl from her shoulders. The coffee was sour but welcome. He glanced at the books and then back at her, making her feel that she had intruded. To hell with him. "You read Arabic?" she said.

"Slowly. Very slowly."

"You should read their poetry. They understand poetry."

"Why did you come here?"

So much for the soul. "Partly—partly out of respect."

"Respect?" As intended, this had at last caught him off guard.

"Yes—out of respect. I wanted to see the man Michael Bron calls his inspiration."

Koblensky seemed to recoil into shadow. She could not determine his mood. "It *is* a compliment," she said.

"You said partly—*partly* out of respect."

"So I did." She had never known embarrassment in him before. It seemed like a wound. She didn't realize what she was going to say until it was said: "*Please*. I know you don't trust me. You've never trusted me, I know that. Perhaps that was inevitable. Perhaps you will never trust me. But my cause has not changed. It is the same. You don't care about it, and I understand. But my cause does not conflict with yours, just because it involves the Arabs. What we want is very similar. And you must remember—*I* am a Jew too."

"Oh, I remember." He stepped forward again. "Being a Jew isn't enough—not nearly enough."

She noticed that some of the boot wax was under his fingernails—blunted nails that were part of his brutishness. "I wanted to say only this: that—*believe* me, please—we have enemies in common, so that we should have interests in common."

"And that I should trust you. You are asking that."

"I know things that you should know. You mentioned the Black Hand. I know names."

"You worked for Kippax."

"That was in Cairo."

He was standing over her again. "Kippax is like the Pope. Once he has you, he has you for life."

"He may think that." Her voice went down an octave, losing some of its Englishness.

"The only terms open to you are one-sided. I will listen to you. You will get nothing from me."

With the snap of a rupture, she laughed—she laughed coarsely and abusively. And as she laughed she also cried.

"What did you expect?" he said, but with a trace of uncertainty that she picked up.

Her voice was still a subsiding wake of the laugh. "I wish your side was my side. One-sided! Do you think I *expected* more? Of *you?* Why does poor Michael Bron follow you? Do you know that? He's still very English, and to him a single-minded man like you is as rare as a palm tree in England. Don't you see how fortunate you are—to be so clear in your mind? My God, I wish I could be!"

"I tell you one thing. One thing I am clear about. One thing I can see—I tell you only what I see. I see the closer we come to the Arabs, the less chance there is of living with them. This I know."

All in one day: so much belligerence in these men, so little reason. He was waiting for a response but already impervious to it. She said, "I cannot believe that," and at least he seemed to see that she was truthful. She stood up, putting the coffee mug on his desk and moving to retrieve her shawl.

"No," he said, gripping her left arm where the shawl would have covered it. "You *can* help us. As long as you understand."

"I know what the risks are."

"Do you?" He released the arm and there was a trace of concern in his eyes. "I hope so. I'm not interested in your

Arabs. We know about them. Our British lords worry me more. You, of course, are closer to them than we can ever be. Too close, perhaps.''

Looking at him, she felt as chaste as he was aloof; the grip of his hand on her arm had aroused nothing between them. When she left, the boots remained on the table. He had never worn boots before, always those wretched sandals—or nothing, as now. The boots were a clear, militant declaration, a sign of a line being drawn.

The withdrawal of so many troops gave the appearance of a less occupied place, but Koblensky knew it was false. Palestine was occupied in all places where power was exercised, military rule *de facto*. It suited the British that the surface seemed so tranquil, and they so benign. Palestine was still an orphan being disputed by the victors of the war, and to world opinion the most seemly parent could not look like an unreformed warlord. Although Koblensky was not fooled, he felt increasingly in the company of fools. The most painful incidence of this was the return of Aaron Aaronsohn.

It was not the Aaronsohn he remembered. They greeted each other as divided personalities, at one level renewing an unbreakable intimacy, but at another level with no intimacy of attitude or experience. Almost immediately, Aaronsohn was autocratic. If challenged, he would, more often than not, rebuff the challenge as disloyal. He had come from the faraway councils of which Koblensky had only a dim perception, and he seemed to have come simply to announce an already made-up mind.

Aaronsohn brought with him a benefactor, an American called Reuben Fine. The three of them met in Fine's room at the Allenby. Fine looked at Koblensky with eyes of impersonal assessment—a banker's eyes settled on a risky prospective investment.

"Aaron tells me you have plans for a settlement."

"Yes," said Koblensky. "In the north."

"I haven't seen the north. Most of the settlers would be from Europe, right?"

"Yes."

"What could it grow, this place?"

Aaronsohn imposed himself. "Wheat, olives, vines, figs—"

Fine cut him off. "Figs? Who eats dates and figs? Olives would be crazy. Wheat . . . well, you know that business.

Everybody needs bread, but from what I hear, you'll never have enough. Vines? You want vines instead of bread? What you don't want is crops you can't store. You won't have refrigeration—or damned much else needing power; not for quite a while. Beans and lentils, maybe. Winter storage. Oranges only later.''

The elements of Fine's face were contrapuntal: flabby cheeks, hard nose; weak mouth, firm chin; tangled gray hair, exactly trimmed black mustache. Yet as Koblensky grew used to Fine, the face, like the onrushing monologue, had a refreshing straightforwardness.

Aaronsohn was drawing breath, caught between ego and need. Managing mildness, he said, "Well . . . we have surveying to do yet; we have a man up there now." He looked at Koblensky. "Asa, your priority is funds?"

"The money would be from America?"

Aaronsohn nodded.

"That is better," said Koblensky.

"Better than what?" said Fine sharply.

"We are not going to build any more feudal colonies. No more Jewish barons coming here in their yachts—no more Zichron Jaacovs."

Aaronsohn flushed. "There would be no Israel now without people like the Rothschilds."

"No Israel?" said Koblensky. "There is no Israel yet. We have a different kind of settler now." He was as cool as Aaronsohn was inflamed.

"Yes," snapped Aaronsohn. "Yes—I know them. I know about those hotheads Jabotinsky has recruited—Ben-Gurion, Ben-Zvi, Eshkol. I didn't realize *you* were one of them."

"Gentlemen!" intervened Fine. "Is this a cause, or a Talmudic debate? Mr. Koblensky . . ." He looked at Koblensky with firmness. "Young man, I don't think you know what is going on in Paris, what Aaron is doing for you there. They call it a peace conference. Peace? Britain and France are carving up the world again, those old men, as though nothing has altered. Palestine is just a little piece in their game. I can tell you, this Jew isn't going to play cat's-paw to the British Empire—but we have to be careful. We have to disappoint a lot of people who expect Zionism to come at them with a gun."

Aaronsohn had calmed a little, and tried to reason. "I know how frustrated Jabotinsky must be, over Allenby's treatment of his legion. But Weizmann doesn't want those disaffected corporals becoming another private army. That would only turn the British Army against us.''

Koblensky shed all deference. "The British Army? The British Army is led by anti-Semites.''

The charge hung in the air, in the room decorated with British watercolors and cushioned in chintz.

"Goddamn it!'' erupted Fine. "I know all about anti-Semites. Don't tell me about anti-Semites. Are you so sensitive that you can't see how we have to play this? There's an American commission coming here soon—I know the people. One of them is an academic, the other makes bathtubs and washbasins. They are no lovers of Zionism. In trying to head off the British, they will fall into the arms of the Arabs. We have to be smarter than that.''

"We stick by Weizmann,'' said Aaronsohn, glaring with open condescension at Koblensky. "Our worst enemy is a man with a map in one hand and the Bible in the other. *That* idea of Israel has nothing to do with reality. I deal in reality, every day I deal in reality—in London, in Paris. I don't want an Old Testament Israel—and you should know me better, Asa—*nor* do I want an Old Testament vassal state.''

Koblensky stood up. "Then you don't understand the British. In their hearts they may be evangelists, but in their heads they are Romans.''

There was a flicker of regret in Aaronsohn's eyes, but his body seemed to subsume his emotions; it was a body dressed in the clothes of the salon and conference room, suited for compromise. Even the heavy-boned frame of Aaronsohn the farmer had softened into this sedentary, magisterial carriage. There was no one to whom Koblensky would more readily have deferred than Aaronsohn, no one he less wanted to offend. But they were now in different worlds.

Koblensky turned to Fine, and was wearily dismissive. "You can't grow Israel, like a crop. It is going to be much harder than that.'' Fine, he saw, was listening where Aaronsohn had not. "If you want to know what I mean, what we face, listen to the people you will find in the bar of this hotel.'' He made no conciliatory gesture to Aaronsohn, and left without shaking hands.

The door closed and Fine said, "*That* man is a Bolshevik.''

"He's a Russian. A Bolshevik? I don't know. . . . Sometimes I suspected it.''

*　　*　　*

Tessa Bron regarded the two images of her companion: the sensual, predatory face composing itself in the mirror, and her substance, from the back demure in the full-length white poplin dress, slightly rucked where her derriere was too full. Tessa kept quiet about the ruck. She said, "We had better not be late."

"No." But Esther Mosseri lingered at the mirror, dissatisfied.

Tessa picked up her evening bag. "Kippax has a fetish for punctuality."

Kippax awaited them in the lobby of the Allenby, his major's crown sewn in gold thread on a black dress tunic, a red-banded cap tucked between arm and chest, hair longer, falling over his face—a wilder, darker Kippax, thought Tessa, who had not seen him for six months. He stepped forward with a conceited formality, playing too much the consul. Tessa was wary without knowing why. His eyes moved from her to Esther, and the word for him was, Tessa decided, "correct." What on earth had got into him? He bowed; his scalp, where there was now one oval of thinning hair, was as pale as chalk and made the tanned face seem suddenly fake, a mask.

The mask smiled. "Tessa—welcome. Welcome to Jerusalem."

"Owen." Tessa obliged the formality by extending a gloved hand for Kippax to kiss; the Edwardian manners were a joke to be played and enjoyed.

"Yes," said Kippax, between the two hands, as Esther stepped forward. "Such a pleasure—except, of course, for Michael's failure to arrive." He caught the musky scent of Esther as he kissed her hand—bare, not gloved. Tessa was trussed and carbolic, the Jew was voluptuous and tainted. He was uneasy touching either of them, but the bare hand repelled him.

"Yes—it is too much," said Tessa, "to come all the way from London and not find him here. Now I am told he will be here tomorrow."

"Ah," purred Kippax. "I fear Michael is increasingly elusive; he's been wandering the hills of Galilee like some aspiring Moses." He led them across the lobby as he spoke. "No matter; I've been able to make up a four for dinner anyway. I wanted your return to be properly celebrated."

Rising from a chair was a young man wearing one of the crispest linen suits Tessa could remember; for a moment the suit seemed to stiffen the man. He was short and unmistakably Semitic, had a strong aquiline nose, dark, closely cut beard, and an attitude of measured deference that, like the suit, seemed bespoke.

Kippax was almost possessive as he introduced Khalid Abbas.

The Arab bowed as Kippax had bowed. "It is such a great pleasure," he said, and the voice was as English as the wardrobe, though a touch too mechanical.

"You are from Riyadh?" said Esther pertly. "From the royal family?"

Kippax answered. "Closely connected." And then, in a sudden confusion of the avuncular and the formal, he added, "Khalid is here as a guest of His Majesty's government. Yes, a *guest*. But I fear that until now we've been dull hosts, so I thought . . ."

Tessa forgot the grievance of Bron's absence; this was yet another piece of the Kippax puzzle, the magician producing a rabbit from his hat. Quite a striking rabbit. She said, "Well, let's not *be* dull, Owen."

But it took time. The hotel's kitchens had surrendered without a struggle to the bland palates of their new clientele and a wretched soup was followed by tasteless lamb and overcooked vegetables. Wine, though, loosened Kippax; he seemed in need of it, drinking most of a bottle of hock before the lamb arrived. And then, having tasted the meat, he speared an orb of gristle and held it aloft, dripping gravy on the cloth. "You may find it hard to believe," he drawled, "but the lamb I have eaten in tents with nothing more than an open hearth tastes, alongside this, like the work of Escoffier himself."

People at neighboring tables were beginning to notice, to shift uneasily with disapproval.

The promise of Kippax making a scene enlivened Tessa. She said, "Owen, you do seem nowadays to spend a lot of your time eating lamb in tents."

"Duty, my dear Tessa, duty."

She turned to her left. "Mr. Abbas, do you not find it strange how the English take to your desert? For a certain kind of Englishman"—she nodded facetiously at Kippax—"for them, it seems to have an irresistible attraction. Doughty, Burton, Lawrence . . . and now Kippax."

Almost in a whisper, Khalid said, "There have always been travelers—even women."

Esther said, "I don't think that's what Tessa means." She saw Kippax's discomfort. "Not travelers. More than that . . ."

"Yes," joined Tessa, wanting to corner Kippax, "*exactly*.

386

More than that." She was watching Kippax detach the gristle from his fork and very deliberately place it in the center of the table so that a congealing stain spread around it on the linen. "I mean, those who really *love* the desert."

With more vigor this time, Khalid said, "Why should that be strange? The desert is not a place to fear. If you love it, it returns your love."

"Absolutely . . . *absolutely*," said Kippax.

Esther said, "It must be unusual, not to say difficult, when the journey is made the other way: for a desert Arab to adapt to our world—to all this."

"Excuse me," said Khalid in his tutored way, "but I do not see why. Why should that be?"

His sudden intensity disconcerted Esther, who was worried that she had given offense, and it was Tessa who said, "*You* seem to have managed the change rather well, Mr. Abbas, if I may say so. Your English is impeccable. May I ask . . . where did you learn it?"

Kippax answered. "Cairo. Professor Arkwright; good chap, And soon, perhaps, Khalid will be going to Oxford."

"*Really?*" said Esther with too much astonishment.

"You are a Jew?" said Khalid.

"Yes."

"It is interesting, how you talk of the desert. We are both Semitic peoples. Once, the Jews, too, were of the desert. We seemed to be the same people. The strength of the Jews was like our strength—it came from the desert. But you are different, you are a different people now. You have become people of the city. I can see that here, in Jerusalem. You have forgotten the desert. We never forgot that we came from the desert. From what I have read, it is cities that bring down their own people, always . . . Persia, Greece, Rome."

His polemic sobered them all; even Kippax was still.

Tessa said, "I can see Professor Arkwright has had an attentive student."

But Khalid's eyes remained on Esther. Her one careless, patronizing word had brought retaliation, and he wanted her to concede the error. He wanted more than that, she suspected, because her offense was more to him than just a breach of European table manners, but this was a setting that limited his powers.

The occasion played itself out over Turkish coffee. They

moved from the restaurant to a small lounge and sat with enough false grace to deceive an onlooker, to merge into the bathos of expatriate talk, but this had been a joyless supper. Yet Kippax seemed not to want to let them go. Finally it was Tessa who stood up.

"You look pale," said Kippax. "Are you all right? It's not this ghastly food, I hope."

"No—thank you. Just tired. So much traveling. Thank you, Owen." She looked at Esther, but Esther seemed to want to stay. "If you will excuse me . . ."

"Of course." Kippax gave a display of solicitude, and Khalid gave a robotlike bow.

She had lied. The camisole under her bodice was already wet with fever. Once in bed, flannel sheets, two blankets, and a counterpane failed to keep the warmth in her. Tightness in the stomach became nausea. The bathroom was at the end of a corridor. She reached it only just in time and crouched wretchedly over the bowl.

Esther found her there. She brought a gown and covered her until she was purged, then helped her back to bed.

Tessa gained the peculiar acuity that follows fever; she could smell the tobacco on Esther's breath and even in the half light seemed to see the whole person there in naked clarity by the bed. "Thank you," she said. "I'm sorry."

"Are you all right?"

"I seem to be warm again. It felt so cold."

"Terrible food."

"It wasn't the food."

Esther sat on the bed. "No. How long have you known Kippax?"

"Why do you ask that?"

"He's frightened of you."

"Of me? Of *me?* That's ridiculous."

"I could see that. I have never seen him frightened of anyone before."

"Why should . . .?"

"Because he has no claim on you."

"No *claim* on me?" Tessa was too weak to laugh, but she wanted Esther to know the full irony of her perception. "Well . . ." she said, managing a smile. "The truth is, all my life I have been evading being claimed. There are so many claims to be evaded . . . claims of the soul, claims of the mind, claims of

388

the heart. You see, I've never had any gift for fealty. That, it seems, is my cardinal sin. I can never surrender to a claim, not even from Michael. And yet sometimes—sometimes my *nerve* just goes. . . ."

"I understand."

"Yes, I think you do. Does Kippax have a claim on *you?*"

"He believes so."

"Is he right?"

Esther did not answer for a full minute, and then she put a hand on the counterpane, a movement that seemed abridged. "I am a friend," she said, and then withdrew the hand and left.

Tessa did not sleep until the muezzins called the rising of the sun, and then she slept so deeply that at noon Bron had to knock with increasing anxiety on the door before she heard him. Still in darkness, she unlocked the door.

They were strange in embrace: he travel-soiled in khakis, she in the shapeless camisole.

"I saw Esther Mosseri," he said. "She told me you were sick." Already he could feel an unusual passivity in her body, but was unsure if it was physical weakness or something else. "I'm sorry, darling, not to have got back when I promised." One of her hands found his tunic belt and clutched it. "What is it?" he said. "What's wrong?" And then he remembered where they were, and took her inside, closing the door. Her fever remained in the air of the room. He took her to the bed and then pulled up a blind and opened the window. In the light she was bloodless and yet, looking at him from the bed, not weak— gathered in a resolve independent of the sickness, brittle in the eye. She did not want sympathy, and the light was more searching of him than of her.

"Do you have a cigarette—not Turkish?" she said.

"Are you sure you should?" But he saw his mistake and found a packet in his tunic, of a cheap English brand.

She waited for him to light it, took one deep breath of it, then said, "I'm all right . . . at least I'm all right now you are here. Where have you been?"

He settled on the end of the bed, still uncertain of the tenor of the question, of her mood—and feeling overdressed for the occasion. "We found a place . . . a valley; it's absolutely—"

"We?"

"Koblensky. Asa Koblensky—and a chap called Laski. We were tracking the water sources. You've no idea how much water there is. Water is the great scandal of Palestine. You can hear plenty of people say there is no water. It's rubbish. Immense quantities are wasted from the Jordan tributaries. The coastal marshes have hardly been—'' He stopped, curtailing his enthusiasm. "What *did* happen last night, Tessa?"

"I don't like it here, Michael. Nothing is what it seems to be, *nobody* is what they seem to be." She drew hard on the cigarette.

"You mean Owen."

"He looks so improperly *black* these days, really quite peculiar. Last night I got under his skin, somehow. I suddenly saw what's happened to him, Michael. What *drives* him so. He's been admitted to the kingdom of the wild, like a man—do you know what I mean?—like a man who's gone up a long river and come back changed; only his river is the desert. He's one of those who discover they can thrive in the wild, unruled places. . . . Your hair, Michael. It's not military length. And you've put on weight." She seemed to make up her mind about him. "Owen says you're wandering around like some latter-day Moses."

"I should have been here. I'm sorry. Owen is a bastard."

"Oh, Michael!" She put aside the cigarette, and with it all composure. He held her, but knew as in their first embrace that he could give her no real solace. Weak as she seemed, there was no malleability in her; she had withdrawn into herself.

"Six whole months without you," she said. "It seems so much longer, far too long. I hate Jerusalem. I don't know why I came back."

"Jerusalem isn't Palestine. There's so much that can be done here, Tessa. And they are just beginning."

Sharply, she said, "What has that to do with us?"

"I wish you could see it."

She drew halfway from the embrace and surveyed him. "The valley you found. The valley that *detained* you. What are you planning?"

"There's nothing more for me to do in the army. Not here. Have you seen the immigrants from Europe? It's all there, in their faces. This is the first time, this is the first place, where they've been able to regard themselves as *free*."

"And when you leave the army?"

"We can build something here, a unique opportunity to—"

"Michael. *My* work is not here."

"You haven't seen it yet."

"I have no work here. I married you, not Palestine." But she knew that he had found something within himself that neither he nor she had known was there. It was like discovering an adversary that could not be overcome with any of the skills she had, and her will rose uselessly against it.

Over the following days she seemed plagued by a perplexing oratorio: Jerusalem, *Yerushalayim, Allah Akbar, Shma Yisrael*—tangled tongues all asking devotion, and the distant one calling her again: *Sanctus, sanctus, sanctus, Dominus Deus . . . Dona nobis pacem . . .* Grant us peace. Ringing and exultant and possessing. It was not her Jerusalem.

There was another draft of troops to Cairo, and this time Bron was ordered there. She wanted to go too, but he discouraged her. The army had its hands full; there was even a sudden report that Allenby had been assassinated, but this turned out to be false. Kippax had also gone to Egypt. Tessa was making inquiries about a steamship passage from Alexandria to London when she encountered Koblensky. She had just left an agent's office near the Mandelbaum Gate when she saw him—Koblensky, the influence she so resented, the embodiment of what it was that Bron had been drawn to. And yet, as soon as she saw Koblensky again, she was struck by a change in him. In her memory he had always been the resolute alien, the outsider. But here, walking on the shaded side of the street, nearly lost in the crowd, he *fitted*. Obviously, and she saw it instantly. Was it that the street was so polyglot, that it had no homogeneity—or that he was, at last, the native? She began to comprehend the alchemy that Bron had succumbed to, despite her own aversion to it. She could not reasonably blame Koblensky for it. She had to cross the street; the impulse to conciliate put her off balance. She ran to catch up, headscarf flowing behind her, and when she called out she sounded almost distraught.

"Asa!"

He turned without knowing the voice.

"Asa . . ." Realizing her appearance, she took a breath. "Asa, I saw you . . ." Face to face, the Koblensky of Cairo had gone; he seemed older. It was enough to sober her.

"Mrs. Bron."

"Tessa—please. Have you been avoiding me? It's been so long."

"Yes—a long time." He seemed uncomfortable on the defensive. "I knew you were here, of course."

"But you thought it better not to appear?"

"Michael has told me that you do not want to live in Palestine."

His directness increased her sense of having been unreasonable. There was no evasion for the sake of her feelings. With people moving all the time around them, he seemed ready to talk as though alone. She became as intense as he. "No. I cannot live here. My work is in London. But I am trying to understand what it is that makes this so important for Michael. I *have* tried, Asa. I thought perhaps it was some deficiency on my part, but I know now that that is not true. I suppose I have to accept that we have separate ambitions. Do you see?"

"It is a pity—a pity that they should be separate. Together you would be . . . but you could not know this would happen. So much has happened. So . . . here we are. I am glad we met again."

She was calmer now. "So am I, Asa, so am I. It is funny. I began to feel towards you as I would another woman—that you had taken Michael." Someone passing jolted her and apologized in a strange tongue. She smiled and returned her gaze to Koblensky. "I was wrong—and unfair. *This* took him. Palestine."

"It is more complicated." He looked at her in silence for a few seconds, then said, "I would like to talk about it. You should understand. And I would like to know, to know what this work of yours is. Perhaps you would come to my home? I am a poor cook, but I would like to return the hospitality you gave me in Cairo. I am in debt to you for it."

"Of course." His solemnity made the invitation sound too formal. "I would love that."

The following evening he collected her from the Allenby in a taxi. He had made an effort: He wore a gray jacket over a white shirt and khaki trousers, but still sandals. He provided cold chicken and coleslaw, served at the plain kitchen table, adorned for the occasion by two candles in ashtrays (Allenby ashtrays, she noticed, freshly garlanded in Union Jacks), and he produced a bottle of native red wine. The table smelled of wax—the candle wax and the boot wax between its slats.

"I'm sorry; it is very simple."

She had walked around the two rooms before they sat down. "It's delightful."

He knew she was sincere. Watching her inspect the large room over the tailor's workshop, he had seen, unerringly, a harmony of identities; his Spartan quarters were better matched to her spirit than her appearance suggested. She had come wearing a high-necked taffeta dress and one string of pearls. The finesse of grooming that had misled him about her in Cairo still bemused him. Vainly he tried to find the answer in her eyes, but she was steadfastly prim.

"So . . . ." he said, still awkward with her, "what is this work that makes you want to leave?"

The candlelight emphasized her fine bones and gave her a glacial gravity. "The war has changed so many things, Asa. Politically. Socially. Women are going into politics."

"*You* are going into politics?"

"Don't make it sound indecent." She looked at him combatively. "You have your grievances to rectify, I have mine."

"You said Palestine has taken Michael. Have you lost him?"

"He isn't the same. *You* know that."

"Are any of us the same? When so much changes?"

"Michael will never be the same. I know that."

"Are *you* the same?"

"Sometimes, Asa, your eyes are as Russian as your voice, do you know that? Your voice is *very* Russian . . . it's something to do with the nose. Russians have a tragic disposition; it always seems to be expressed through the nose."

He was undeflected.

She smiled. "Am I the same? What would *you* say?"

He refilled his glass. "I would say that we are very much alike, at least tonight. We *seem* to be different . . ." He sipped the wine and half smiled. "And of course, I *am* Russian. But we are cut from the same kind of metal."

"Could you fill my glass too?" she said with mischievous complaint. "Michael admires you so. Did you realize that?"

"He should be more careful with his admiration."

"Oh?"

"I do not want to be responsible for anyone else."

"That sounds selfish."

He flared. "I'm trying to tell you how dangerous it is, what we are facing."

"I'm sorry. It's just that, like it or not, you are an influence on Michael. He's not very worldly."

"No. You did not tell me: *Have* you lost him?"

"Yes."

"That will be hard on him."

"I can't help it. Just as you have your cause, I have mine— several causes, as a matter of fact."

"You see," he said, "that is what I meant. We are cut from the same metal."

"I don't know what that means. If it means *stubborn*—then, yes, perhaps I am."

At first they had been sparring, engaging and disengaging as they took measure of each other, finding out what could be said and would not be said. The small, plain room had concentrated the conversation into a communion, and now neither could evade the other. Even the way they ate, as they were silent for a minute, had ascetic overtones.

"It's odd," she said. "I don't know where the stubborn streak comes from. I was the cuckoo in the nest. My family are the most *contented* Catholics I know. It's not a religion that, as a rule, induces contentment, but in my family it does—in all except me."

"Maybe you reacted against that, against the contentment. You could not help that, if you had that kind if mind. A child can feel things like that. It is a sense you cannot change."

"Asa, to hear you talking of childhood surprises me."

"Sometimes a child sees more clearly than his parents. Children are not so blind." It was as subjective as he was ready to be. "Are they disappointed in you—your family?"

"In me? I'm sure they pray for me. I have a brother who is a priest. He has enormous reserves of hope. He hopes prayer will save me, even now."

"A priest? You do not seem to have much respect for that."

"I do regard it as unnatural to want the holy robes; unnatural. It isn't natural; it's a rejection of the natural, a repression really. That side of nature that wants to turn away from self. It doesn't feel able to be trusted with self. So, unable to cope with the full urge of life, they want the holy robes to sort out the problem, channel the urge before it gets out of control. Then they feel ready to gather in the souls of others—once they've tucked away their own dark things. That's how I saw it; it's never seemed any other way. I was, of course, alone in that view." She smiled in a stoic way, a perishable humor.

"Are you good at being alone?"

She fingered the pearls, and in doing so seemed to tire of virtue: The hand was independently lascivious. "We are all born alone. We die alone." She looked down, conceding to the incitement of the hand. "I would rather not be alone tonight."

She had initiated it and he could have refused her. But their candor would then have been curtailed; they had completely to resolve their curiosity in each other now, whatever the consequences. Koblensky accepted this outcome with less serenity than she.

In the bed she was as explicit and naked as she had been elusive in the kitchen. Before he had undressed she stood over him, hands running through his hair, her bodice and taffeta cast off like another nature. When he hesitated, she said, "It's all right. Birth control is the first of my causes—and of my heresies."

Her movements seemed at first curiously formal. She stepped toward him, embraced and then gently drew away to hold him at arms' length, and repeated this several times with minor variations, waiting for him to become erect. This facade of constraint was betrayed only by her eyes. She was strong enough, to his surprise, to lock him where he stood as she ended the dance. Face pressed to face, allowing him slowly into her, she said, "If the mind isn't interested, the body isn't willing."

On the Russian bed he contested her initiative, not using all his strength but asserting himself to strike a balance with hers. She neither yielded nor dominated. For the first time in lovemaking, he found himself unselfconsciously at peace. It was a transient peace; once he remembered Bron it evaporated.

"What's the matter?" she said, for they were in every way too close for concealment. "You're not worrying about betraying Michael?"

"Doesn't that worry you?"

Her laugh was harsh. "I was damned long ago."

"Do you really believe in being damned?"

"Another *Russian* question. Rationally, no. Emotionally, often." She laughed the same way again. "*Too* often."

He thought of Esther Mosseri and the paradox of comparison: Esther was irredeemably amoral, whereas by any reasoning Tessa was compulsively moral; it was Esther's intellect that was corrupted while Tessa's intellect had an incisive purity. Esther was self-abusively carnal while craving eloquence; Tessa was innately eloquent while courting carnality.

She took his testicles in her hand as she had caressed the pearls and said, "It is only tonight. It's probably the only night we'll have. You mustn't mind."

"If *you* don't . . . ."

"We are both against oppression. I'm against oppression presented as sexual morality. That's *quite* an oppression." The hand moved from his testicles slowly up to the pendant star. "And you—you are up against a pretty mendacious kind of oppression yourself. Michael doesn't see that." She examined the star. "If you make enemies of the British, you'll tear Michael apart."

She was too perceptive for his comfort. For once, he lied. "I hope we can avoid that."

"I hope so too." But she was not deceived. It was said to spare her feelings, and he was never convincing when making such a gesture. Had she been less close to him, he would have been more honest. In that sense they were already too close—beyond what was the safe boundary between them. As they had converged, now they perceptibly eased back, without dissatisfaction. They knew the limits. The renewal of lovemaking was that much more sensually complete, in itself an acknowledgment of their disengaged interests. They were each left with their solitariness unimpaired—unimpaired to meet the divergent trials it caused them. If there was, at the end of the night, one splinter of their composure, it was that Tessa felt she had disturbed some scruple in Koblensky that, though he could never confess it, would not easily settle again.

He saw her once more before she left for England. She came to the flat without warning one evening a week later.

"I've had this telegraph from Cairo," she said, standing at the door with a buff envelope. "It's from Michael. There's been an accident. Aaron Aaronsohn is dead. His airplane crashed."

He looked at the envelope as he got up from the small table.

"He was flying from London to Paris. It seems they came down in the harbor at Boulogne. I'm sorry. I knew you would want to know at once. *Michael* wanted you to know."

Taking the envelope but not opening it, Koblensky recalled the acrimony of his last meeting with Aaronsohn. This pain fused with others, a telescopic flash of experience, already enough for a life, lives shared, lives gone. He looked desolately at Tessa. "Yes. Thank you." Some things lived and died in one night, and were the more merciful for it.

# 22

## Akaba ✳ April 1919

Riderless horses, running together, more than a dozen finding their full stride. A clay-colored mare was in front by a neck, her mouth slightly open, eyes protruding with the effort. They were circling a corral attached to army stables. A British staff car was parked in the center of the corral, with its convertible top folded down. Kippax and Khalid Abbas sat on one side of the car, feet on the running board. Kippax had field glasses, panning the horses. They were hard to follow; the ground was baked dry and broke into a heavy yellow dust. Khalid rejected glasses. He could see better without them. Halfway through the third circuit, the horses flagged. Following the mare's lead, they slowed down and a few broke away.

"I would have thought the mare, for certain," said Kippax. "And the chestnut—d'you see him?"

"No. The mare goes too fast, and the chestnut is too big."

"Too fast? Too big?"

"Big horses are no good. They eat too much. We do not want speed; we want strength. Smaller horses are better. What your army needs in a horse is not what we need." Khalid stepped down from the car and walked toward a paddock. "I show you, El Khibeg."

There was always an embarrassment to Kippax in being called "El Khibeg" in places other than the desert.

They were joined at the paddock by the horsemaster, an immense Scot with a deep scar across one cheek, who smelled of whisky and horses in equal measure. "Did you find what you were looking for, sir?" he said to Kippax.

"Not yet, apparently, Sergeant."

The horses returned at random and it was some minutes before they were nosing into their feed. The three men walked along

397

their flanks, giving each a careful scrutiny. Finally Khalid picked out a medium-sized young black stallion and an older but smaller piebald mare. "They would be best," he said.

The sergeant, standing several paces behind and ostentatiously glancing along the whole line of horses, said, "The stallion ran at the back . . . *sir*."

Kippax flicked his swagger stick. "No matter, Sergeant."

Khalid tapped the rump of a horse, not one of those he had selected. "You feed them well, Sergeant. Better than many people."

The sergeant emitted a strangled grunt.

"In the desert, it is enough for the horse to carry the rider, as weight."

"Thank you, Sergeant," said Kippax quickly. "See that the two animals are ready for us tomorrow. We shall leave in the evening." And once they were out of the sergeant's earshot, going back to the car, he said, "You mustn't mind the sergeant. He knows only the army."

"I do not mind." Khalid climbed into the front passenger seat as Kippax sat behind the wheel. "El Khibeg, I am getting used to knowing that many people think we Arabs are ignorant. Tell me, is the sky not blue in your world, El Khibeg?"

"I'm sorry?"

"If I go to Oxford, I am told that in your world the sky is not the same. I know the god is not the same—is that why the sky is not the same?"

Kippax laughed nervously. "It is the same sky, Khalid, but no, it is not the same color." He had an uneasy sense of their respective roles being subtly reversed: that the once pliant pupil, behind his disingenuous questions, had taken the initiative. The horses were the start of it. In the next weeks he would be increasingly dependent on Khalid, but was not sure of his readiness to yield. "You need not worry about Oxford," he said, putting a hand on Khalid's right knee. "Oxford will understand you."

Akaba, Lawrence's trophy, was too arid for British colonization. The garrison was never more than a foothold, and visiting officials preferred to remain offshore aboard the light cruisers of the Red Sea squadron, where both the sanitation and the amenities were more to their taste. Kippax and Khalid had come to Akaba on H.M.S. *Dufferin*, and it was to the *Dufferin* that Kippax had to return for his final instructions from Sir Ronald Storrs. To escape the heat of the wardroom, Storrs had arranged his court on deck. An Indian carpet was rolled out, armchairs brought up, with a table for drinks, and an upright piano from the mess deck.

Kippax always felt that behind Storrs's aesthetic manner was a reservation toward him personally, a glint of moral reproof. Yet why, God knows; Storrs, in Egypt since 1904, the archetype vizier, must have had enough perfidy interred in his discretion. Storrs sat at the piano playing Puccini with a final andante, in pace with his mind. Kippax sat to one side, drinking iced lime juice. There was a dusk breeze off the water; the music seemed an overture to innocence, rather than part of their political labyrinth.

Finished, Storrs stared down at the keyboard and said, almost to himself, "After Jerusalem, there is no promotion." Then he turned to Kippax. "I suppose, at this time of the year, the heat is not quite at its worst. My only attempt to navigate the desert was an unmitigated misery."

"Fortunately, sir, it's not too far—two or three hundred miles at most."

"But desert miles." Storrs left the piano and took the armchair opposite Kippax. "You're quite sure what has to be done, if you can manage it? We rely on your rather unique relationship with these people. We simply cannot have these wild men—"

"The *Ikhwan*," interposed Kippax.

"The Brotherhood—whatever they are—Bedouin with bees in their bonnets . . . We cannot have them snapping at the gates of Mecca. Especially not *now*."

"I do see that, sir."

"Yes. You know, Kippax, I fancy too much is made of the Ikhwan phenomenon, but Prince Abdullah frets so about them." Storrs settled more reflectively into the chair. "You know, Abdullah was the first of the Hashemite princes I met, back in 1914. With his father so erratic, much depends on Abdullah now. We have invested much time in him, not to say gold. Much depends on him, perhaps whether they can keep Mecca, even the whole Hijaz. I'm just not sure of him—Abdullah. How consequential he will prove to be. However, make no mistake." Storrs cast an imperative eye at Kippax. "Make no mistake—on no account must the Ikhwan give Abdullah a bloody nose. That would unsettle everything. That you *must* avert."

"I think we can depend on Ibn Saud to restrain them."

"Do you? *Do* you? You've always been a Saud man, have you not? Well, I suppose you can take a view of it better than I.

399

You know, I've been reading Turgenev. *Fumée*. Russian books are always a slight effort to me, I suppose by reason of the leakage of style in translation." The eyes expected a response.

"Language can be a barrier . . . to feeling."

"Quite. This young Arab of yours, Abbas. He *looks* right. A most interesting experiment. It would be consoling to believe that at some point in the future, men of that refinement will lead these people—lead them out of their dark age."

"*Dark age?*" For a second Kippax forgot himself, reacting too sharply. Then he covered himself with a just plausible deference. "Yes. That would be consoling—in the long run." Storrs, he realized, had no more love of the Bedouin than had the horsemaster. Storrs absolving himself with fingers dancing to Puccini . . . well, bugger Storrs (the unvoiced curse amused him). Let Storrs and his like keep their distance from trouble. How could they understand what they had never felt? Later, leaving the cruiser in a cutter for the harbor, he severed all sense of obligation. It was his game now.

Akaba's lights were nothing against the sharp, metallic brilliance of the night; this sky was the desert's bedfellow. The Gulf of Akaba was a finger of water between great deserts, Sinai to the west and Arabia to the east, water hemmed by grim escarpments. To reach their objective, Kippax and Khalid had to go southeast from Akaba, climbing passes through a massif to the inner Arabian plateau. There was no exact rendezvous, they did not know where at that moment Ibn Saud was, nor where the Ikhwan were—only that the Ikhwan's ultimate target was probably Prince Abdullah's camp at an oasis town called Sabara. Could they find Ibn Saud before the Ikhwan found Abdullah? It was unknown ground to Kippax, but not to Khalid. The Arab needed no maps. He was riding back to what had once been the only world he knew: he wore again the red and white checkered headcloth and camel hair cloak. Kippax's turban was plain brown, as was his cloak.

Because of the heat, they made the arduous climb at night, but the loose flint of the tracks slowed down the horses and by the evening of the second day they had reached only the mouth of a high pass that crossed the massif. The plateau was still at least three days away. The transition from Major Kippax to El Khibeg came less easily than it once had; as Khalid built a small fire within a hearth of loose rocks, Kippax rested, trying to appease new saddle sores. Khalid suspended a canteen of water over the fire and went off foraging. When he came back, Kippax was asleep. He awoke later to a sweet, unfamiliar smell. Khalid was stirring something in the boiling water.

"We are lucky," said Khalid. "None of your bully beef tonight."

Kippax pulled himself up and looked into the canteen.

"Locusts," said Khalid. "You have not eaten locusts?"

"No."

"You do not like the idea?" Khalid enjoyed Kippax's discomfort. "El Khibeg—I have seen you eat lobster. Is a locust so different? You see, you boil them with much salt. And then you shell them, like a shrimp."

El Khibeg composed himself. "I will try it."

The meat was the color of an egg yolk, and tasted similar.

"Well?" said Khalid, watching.

"Certainly edible. A little bland. One would not have much success with them in the kitchens of Europe."

"El Khibeg—not their cup of tea?"

Kippax laughed. "No. *Not* their cup of tea." The joke, and the meal, finally disposed of Major Kippax. He was at one with this land again.

When finally they cleared the mountains, two days later, it was an hour before sunrise and they looked down on the Pilgrims' Railway, a single track on a shallow embankment. Arbitrary where everything else was random, precise in age where everything else was timeless, it jarred Kippax from his elemental mood. It reinstated the memory of Lawrence, whose rabble had left the line derelict. It was also—despite its fate—the first and immutable sign of trespassing change. But he was alone in this sensibility: Khalid rode ahead keenly and cantered up the embankment. The metal already had a skin of caked rust.

"We could ride this path all the way to Medina," called Khalid with childish speculation, as though marveling at it.

But they were not going south. The eastern horizon was already lightly silvered with the coming dawn. It was there, somewhere on the engulfing plateau, that they had to look for Ibn Saud—and the Ikhwan. Nearby the railway crossed a dry wadi. Four small arches had been built to make a viaduct. They made camp under one of these arches and slept until late in the afternoon. And then they rode east.

To Kippax, it seemed that Khalid followed an invisible thread. There were no apparent landmarks, they had no more than a

401

compass and the stars, and yet Khalid led with apparent precision—led through the night to nowhere. This went on for three days and two nights. Each afternoon before they rode on again, Khalid would walk for a while, occasionally squatting in the gravel beds looking at the shrubs and lichen, then return and put out his prayer mat, directed south to Mecca, and submit himself to Allah. There seemed an exclusive relationship between the navigation and the prayers in which mortal and spiritual problems were fused. Kippax was awed by it, and unsure whether to intrude. But on the third dawn after crossing the railway, he said, "How can you be so sure . . . so *certain* that we are right?"

Under the headcloth, Khalid's beard had darkened and his features were altered. Urbane wisdoms had been supplanted by older wisdoms; he was the sage and Kippax the deferring novice. "When I was a boy, El Khibeg, I learned how to track—how to track animals, how to track people." He looked down and one sandaled foot turned over a stone so that the lichen shone yellow and moist in the light. "The desert has millions of eyes, El Khibeg. A good tracker can tell a woman's tracks from a man's." He looked up again at Kippax with a companionable smile. "He can even tell whether or not the woman is a virgin. It is in the way women walk."

This indelicacy deterred Kippax from further inquiry. He said, "Really? I had no idea." He wondered why such a thing should matter; it was too profane for him.

That morning, instead of making camp, they rode on. Khalid explained that they were within two hours of a small oasis. They and the horses needed fresh water and this would be the first inhabited place they had seen since Akaba. Riding in the heat, Kippax became progressively more uncomfortable. His sores were inflamed and his lips blistered. But the oasis ended all uncertainty about their course: From the headman Khalid learned that a large Ikhwan force had been seen some thirty miles to the south, going toward the oasis of Sabara. They were apparently roaming independently of Ibn Saud's own royal squadron, of which there was no word. Kippax saw that his only course now was also to head for Sabara, with as little pause as possible. They took just enough water and supplies for a short, fast ride, and left in the early afternoon, hoping that the horses would hold out.

They rested after dusk for two hours, and continued across

open desert under another brilliantly clear night. At intervals, Khalid stopped to follow tracks. By midnight he was perplexed. For the first time, his voice was uncertain. "El Khibeg—there is no trace of one camel here, nothing of the Ikhwan."

Had they been misled? They were within a few miles of Sabara, where Abdullah was said to be camped. Kippax suspected an inexplicable treachery in the headman. The horses were run out. They slept until dawn. An hour later, they crested a lava ridge and there ahead of them, curiously inert in the low sun, was an extensive and elaborate military camp ringing the northern boundary of the oasis. The garrison was far larger than Kippax had expected, at least ten thousand men. Unlike traditional Arab positions, it had been planned with some heed of modern ideas. Its main innovation was an artillery battery, dug in behind barricades.

The town of Sabara lay south of the river that fed the oasis. Just beyond the lava ridge, the track that Kippax and Khalid had followed joined the north-south pilgrim route. Sabara was as ancient as the road; all caravans from Syria to Medina and Mecca had to pass through it. Before him, Kippax saw two military decisions had been taken: the fortification of the oasis— and a calculated provocation of Ibn Saud. He knew that in Sabara was a sizable minority of the Wahhabi sect, who were loyal not to the Hashemites but to Saud, a large enough minority for Saud already to have complained that if persecution of the Wahhabis continued, Sabara would need to be "liberated." By choosing to put his camp here, Abdullah was marking the frontier, *de facto*, between the house of Hashem and the house of Saud.

Kippax leaned down to his bags and pulled out his field glasses. The artillery had stirred a suspicion: Turkish guns. So there would be Turkish prisoners manning them. But his glasses were diverted from the artillery by the glint of ostentation. In the center of the camp was one dominating tent, resplendently white and fringed with gold. Abdullah. Sharif Abdullah would yield no comforts for battle. How typical. For all its formidable visage, there was something about the garrison, a clue as delicate as the gold skirts of the royal tent, that showed weakness. The heat played tricks with the focus of the glasses, transmuting substance to mirage, making solid things fluid and men ephemeral. Abdullah was taunting the Ikhwan. And what chance would the Ikhwan have against such a fortress?

"They will not be long in coming, El Khibeg."

"They cannot know—about *this*."

"They know. They always know, El Khibeg. There are always spies."

"It will be a massacre." Kippax waved the glasses in an arc that stressed the size of the defenses. "No tribe can ride against those guns."

"Then you do not know the Ikhwan, El Khibeg."

"It doesn't matter *who* they are," said Kippax irritably. "Camels against cannon? A massacre."

Khalid fell silent, his own survey of the vista leaving him placid, although he had assimilated every detail as sharply as Kippax. "They chain their own men to the guns, El Khibeg," he said finally.

Kippax lifted his glasses again and refocused on the cannon. Then he saw it, the men sitting under canvas by their guns. They *were* chained to them.

"An army that uses chains cannot even *buy* loyalty, El Khibeg."

"We cannot enter Sabara."

Khalid did not answer.

"We would probably be taken as spies."

Khalid regarded Kippax with penetrating intelligence. "And so . . . which side are we on, El Khibeg?"

"I think—I think we had better find some safe cover."

Sabara gave off no sounds, not even of a dog; all flesh cowered from the coming heat.

To the right of the bluff on which they stood ran a sandstone ridge that ended with the river feeding the oasis; about a quarter of a mile behind them, this ridge became more substantial, slanting upward in a series of rifts. There were caves there and Khalid found an easy track to the lowest of them, the track partly concealed by bushes. The cave entrance was like a partly opened mouth, its lower lip gently indented and the upper one arching more at the center, high enough for them to ride inside without dismounting. At the front of the cave was a small chamber, its floor scarred from numerous campfires. This small chamber gave onto a larger one, more a grotto, with moist, flaking walls. The horses would not venture beyond the front chamber and—after cursory inspection—neither did Kippax and Khalid. They slept intermittently for the rest of the day and, after a meal of the last of their bully beef, through the night. In sleep Kippax reached a familiar nocturnal levitation. It was his normal habitat, when so batlike, to peer down at the white-shrouded figures in a Winchester dormitory, but this time the public school had dissolved and he was ectoplasmic, rising under an iridescent rose-red dome. Issuing from the dome's surface was a chanting that expanded gradually in intensity as he came nearer and nearer to its source. The subconscious yielded to the conscious. The egg-smooth dome gave way to the pitted dome of the cave chamber, underlit by a faint bloom of dawn, and the ethereal litany took human voice—a congregation of voices: " . . . *la ilah illa Allah; la ilah illa Allah; la ilah illa Allah . . .*"

There is no God but Allah.

The words rose to the cave and were swallowed in it, reverberating, one wave devouring another.

In the center of the cave's lips Khalid was bent in prayer toward Mecca, his voice joining the invisible assembly's. The swathed head rose and fell, breaking the beams of light as Kippax squinted into them to full consciousness. He slipped from under his blanket and crawled to the cave mouth. Below, over the ground before the bluff, were the Ikhwan. Farthest away, immediately under the last summit of the bluff, were massed camels—the cavalry. The camels were on their bellies as their riders prayed by their sides. In the middle distance were a smaller number of horse cavalry. Nearest the cave were more camels, some laden with light baggage and others with tents. Around them were hundreds more men. The apex of the prayers was distant, but Kippax could see that in both prayer and formation, the army was without hierarchy. It did not taper, it squared. Its only division was into three balanced groups: the camel cavalry, the horse cavalry, and their camel-borne support, judged by their numbers at least three men to each beast.

Consciousness had not robbed the spectacle of its transcendental quality, nor Kippax of his divided sensibility. One part of his mind was burning with the ardor of the novitiate, the other with the alarming calculation that there could be no more than fifteen hundred men bowed in prayer. Beyond the bluff, and no doubt waking to sacred voices borne on the stirring dawn wind, were more than six times that number.

The sun had not yet cleared the eastern ridges. There was a valedictory surge of the prayers and then, with no directed movement, the camels rose and the horses were mounted. The earth had no sooner swallowed the last prayer than a cry was taken up, first from the camels along the line of the bluff and then rippling back through the rest of the men, endorsed by raised rifles and drawn swords:

> "I am a Knight of Unity
> Brother of He who obeys God.
> Show your head, O enemy!"

And with that, the first camels broke the divide of bluff and sky and raised a yellow, rolling dust that the following horses rode into. The camels swung left, the horses right. The raiding camels, ridden with ragged formation, held back until the dust settled and then went straight ahead over the bluff. No cannon had fired. The cries of the Ikhwan were deflected and lost by the bluff. All that could be heard now from the cave was an imprecise, faraway trembling of the air.

"God help them," said Kippax.

The cave had lightened. For the first time, Khalid saw how unbalanced Kippax was. "*No.*" He motioned Kippax away from the horses. "No—we cannot follow. Not yet. When it is decided, then it will be safe for us." Khalid despised the rapture in Kippax's eyes, and turned away from it to the metal of the day.

At first they heard but did not see. It was a dubious mercy. The full seismic prelude gave way to harsher sounds, ragged waves of gunfire, and then to a more relentless and rising rhythm, like a beach facing surf—assault and repulsion, the outcome at first in the balance and then, suddenly, one prevailing. The settlement was more rending than the contest. Pigeons rose above the visible horizon, beating their way into an aimless, dispossessed flight. And above them, serenely waiting, were kites and vultures. Rising into the cave came a cry that did not die but tapered and rose again, a cry only half human, from a diminishing congregation.

"*Now*," said Khalid. "Now we can go."

They had waited in the cave for hours. They held back once more, at the crest of the bluff. All the coherence of the camp had gone; the sight of it was paralyzing, but also compelling. There was no turning away from it. A terrible force had concentrated itself here, a blow as complete and as localized in its result as though one shaft of devastation had come from the heavens. They were both struck by this precision. From where they were, the battlefield was a darkness within an encompassing brilliance, one violent blemish in the allure of the oasis.

Abdullah's lines had disappeared. Barricades had been over-run and thrown awry. Tents pitched drunkenly and some burned. Cannon were overturned or lying broken. But these were impersonal, physical things that formed what frame survived. Within this dissolution was another. Until Kippax used his glasses, it seemed no more distinct than undergrowth. Pulled into focus, it became a rearrangement of familiar forms: random deposits of human carcasses, few of them intact. He slowly moved from this to the tents. The royal tent, almost alone, was untouched. The battlefield was deserted except for the dead—and any injured who had been overlooked. The Ikhwan had ridden over the river into the town of Sabara itself, through the main gate.

"It is finished," said Khalid.

Kippax lowered his glasses. Already and evidently trembling, he moved his horse forward.

Both of them adjusted their headdresses as masks against the rising stench. Dismembered and disemboweled bodies were often blessedly featureless. Their horses occasionally bridled and Kippax tried to find the least gruesome path. Khalid's masked face was almost motionless, contained to the movement of the horse, looking to neither side. Kippax had imagined no horror like this and had never been prepared for reality to surpass imagination. His mind left him without a discipline in which to accept what he was seeing. Where his physical relief was to vomit recurrently into the cloth about his face, there was no device of the mind that could, with the naturalness of the stomach, purge him.

His eyes were avid captives of this torment; they fixed on things and would not move, as the flies were already settled on the same things. Colors mingled. In one place the blossoms and bulbs of flowers were blasted into the bodies. Colors. Colors he did not know the human body contained arrested him and fed his morbidity. He had not known what foulness the body contained. How fragile was the semblance of human purity when each body held such a measure of putrefaction and when within minutes of death tissues turned to rotting filth. It was more than the fragility, the deception of bodily integrity. Revealed to him was the slender hold of another, higher purity on these creatures. *Revealed*. It was revealed. His eyes were not drinking in the horrors of a battlefield. These events transcended human agency. It was a religious experience. The revelation was that it was Good that must be merciless. Evil was not merciless; it was altogether too lenient. Good could not be lenient if it was truly pure. The purity of this force before him was indeed terrible, but it was the true and rare terror of Good—of Good not only purging Evil *but proving itself to be the greater terror*. Let *terror* deliver us from Evil; the Christian litany had it wrong. That was the answer: That was the Answer and the Mystery. No longer did he have any doubt why these men—they had been *these* men of the dawn prayers: their ancestors, but the same—could have overwhelmed the antique world and gone from the desert to the heart of France, from Arabia to Indonesia. European conceits upheld the pagan Alexander as Emperor of the World, but he and his empire carried no enduring Truth and died. It had been Omar who delivered half the world to Islam: *the deliverer*. This, too, was deliverance and he had seen it. Nothing had changed. This was a king! Oh, this was a king! This was an Omar risen! Again, from the desert.

A shot. A bullet parted the mane of his horse and rudely drew his eyes from abstractions to fix on one offensive reality. They had reached the redundant cannons. Still chained to one of them—manacled to a wheel—was a Turkish officer. He had not been spared in the attack; he had been cut down and left for dead. The error was understandable. His tunic was caked with blood and his face barely recognizable. But he had moved again, and held a Mauser in his hand, trying to steady his arm on the cannon wheel. The gun seemed to be sensing its way toward Kippax as a snake's head would waver before striking. The man was blind. His eyes were unmoving within a comprehensive wound. This realization killed Kippax's reflexes. He gaped like an imbecilic thing as the Turk again attempted to find his aim from the sound of the horses. Kippax was still paralyzed when Khalid wheeled round and swept down on the Turk. The Turk's aim was diverted by the rush of the horse. The gun fired clear of them both. Khalid had drawn his sword. He made one arcing cut, leaning out from the saddle. The Turk was decapitated; his blood-belching torso hung from the cannon wheel with gun still grasped in a clamped hand and the chains whipping in the wheel spokes like an inanimate extension of the death dance.

Only then did Kippax regain control.

Angrily, Khalid called from behind his headcloth: "*He could have killed you, El Khibeg.*"

Kippax looked at the corpse until the chains were still. The shock had broken his trance. His mind composed itself with mundane things. Military training asserted itself. Military words. Field of fire. Uncovered flank. Static defense. Fluid attack. Cavalry feint. Alexander's genius at Gaugamela, emulated by Marlborough: the advantage of an inferior but mobile force over a superior but entrenched one. Twelve-pounder guns. The chains were still about the wheel, the head lay with unfired shot. Solid round shot. The charge of powder one-eighth the weight of the shot. The handle of the breech lever only half turned, and bloody. Sponge and rammer. Good to remember these things. Good for the report.

"Brilliant tactics." He looked across to Khalid. "Speed, and surprise. Only one chance."

Khalid leveled his wet sword at the town ahead of them. "It is dangerous here. We must go to the town."

Between the battleground and the town was a palm grove. As they rode through it, Khalid pulled the headcloth clear of his face. With the carnage behind them, the palms seemed to cleanse the air, although a few bodies cut down in flight lay in the grass. For the first time Kippax was aware of the pungent sediment of his own vomit and the foulness of his mouth. He, too, cleared his face and tried to conceal the stained fold of headcloth.

"Thank you, Khalid. I'm sorry. . . ."

"It is well, El Khibeg."

Another deliverance, thought Kippax. And realized that as well as vomiting he had urinated.

The town was unnaturally peaceful. They rode through the main gate and into a wide, grit-layered street. Ikhwan camels had been gathered in shade along one side of the street but left with only a few grooms. The peacefulness was one of suspense. The people of the town had withdrawn to their homes. As Kippax and Khalid rode slowly down the street, they could hear an occasional dog nervously barking and women murmuring, but nothing of men. These random sounds were suddenly lost in a tumult: The Ikhwan were praying again, but this time their voices were concentrated by the resonance of a mosque. The prayers of victory were no more exultant than the anticipation of it. Their certitude, their will as it was asserted through prayer, was coupled with abject humility to the force they served. The will could not be spent or satisfied by one victory.

"We must take care, El Khibeg."

"I must talk with them."

"Not yet."

409

"That is why we came."

Khalid deferred with reluctance. "Then I go first. It is best that way."

Kippax dismounted and stayed with his horse in the gateway to a deserted bazaar. Khalid rode off toward the mosque. The prayers were reaching their climax.

Fifty or sixty horses were tethered in a small square outside the mosque. Planted in the center of the square were several of the green *bayraqs*, the Ikhwan war banners. They were perforated by bullets and one was streaked with blood. Under awnings, a score or so of the Ikhwan wounded were being given water. There was no more solace for them than that—and the sound of prayer. The few Ikhwan who remained with the wounded watched Khalid ride into the square and assumed, from his garments, that he was one of them.

Immediately before the portico of the mosque was a squadron of camels. Ikhwan leaders were not ostentatious, but Khalid recognized, without surprise, the vestments of two of the camels— one was that of Ibn Saud's shrewdest battle commander, Sultan Ibn Bijad, and the other of Ibn 'Aqil. As the prayers died in one final "*la ilah illa Allah*," the mosque and the square were like the eye of a storm, wherein power was paradoxically more terrible in silence than in fury. The forecourt of the mosque had only one decoration, a ribbon of tiles at its borders, cobalt blue with Koranic inscriptions in white Kufic script. In the virtually shadowless sun of noon, the blue tiles burned with an intense radiance, not surface light but light of an infinite depth. The dust within the frame of these tiles, as dull as they were brilliant, was sacred ground, the threshold barred to none who knew their way to this God who was everywhere and yet nowhere. Khalid fell to his knees at the axis of the mosque.

" . . . *la ilah illa Allah* . . ."

Sultan Ibn Bijad, his cloak still thick with dust, came out first, flanked by his retinue. He put up a hand to shade his eyes as he saw the prostrated figure.

Khalid lifted his face. "People of Unity! People of Awja! It is a great victory for the Knights of Unity. God joined us together, he joined our hearts together, and we became by the grace of God brothers."

Ibn 'Aqil had stepped alongside Ibn Bijad. He, too, squinted in the sun, and then he recognized the supplicant. "It is the boy with the Book! The boy I delivered!"

Ibn Bijad looked from Khalid to Ibn 'Aqil. "*You* delivered him? Ibn Jiluwi delivered him." He stepped forward to Khalid. "Rise, my son."

Khalid stood up and kissed Ibn Bijad on each cheek and then on the tip of the nose, and the embrace was reciprocated. The contagions of death hung in the sultan's garments.

"What brings you to us, Khalid Abbas?"

As the sultan's retinue formed a crescent around them, Khalid explained his journey.

Ibn Bijad stopped him with a wave of the hand. "Our work is not done. Our Wahhabi people here have suffered much at the hands of the ignorant. The town is cursed by those who do not know the oneness of God. We must make an example of them, so that all the ignorant people of the Hijaz will see who is the true king and servant of God. We will hear more of your purpose, and then you must take the infidel from this place and remain outside until Abdul Aziz is here. He must decide if he should receive the infidel at his court."

Kippax, meantime, had watched rats foraging in the bazaar and now he squatted in an alcove to defecate. His bowels were not as loose as his bladder. He had developed more saddle sores, and the stench of his body, focused in the airlessness of the bazaar, attracted flies. He moved listlessly. It was not his body that was drained but his emotions. He wanted to bathe, but every time he thought of water it turned to blood. Yet somewhere in the core of him, lassitude became serenity, a voluntary submission. *Submission . . . Islam.* He had passed through darkness, but it was the shadow of God on earth.

He did not realize how long Khalid had been gone. Then he heard the horse, still the only open movement in the street.

"El Khibeg, we must leave. We must return to our camp. We cannot stay."

"Who has decided this?"

"We must leave."

"What is going to happen?"

"There will be much killing here."

Kippax realized that Khalid's concern was not for himself. "Who has ordered this?"

"Sultan Ibn Bijad."

"Sultan Ibn Bijad . . ." Kippax repeated the name recitatively. "But not with the king's knowledge?"

"The king is not here."

"More's the pity. I presume they will slaughter all the males
. . . of any age?"

Impatient with the questions, Khalid snapped, "Not only males;
all the ignorant."

"The *ignorant?*" Something snapped in Kippax. He glared up
at Khalid. "Women and children? *They must be stopped.* They
have their victory. That is enough. It will ruin everything, to
have a massacre here. It would be politically disastrous. And it
would be barbaric—uncivilized and *barbaric*. Do you hear me?"
His eyes glared wildly.

Khalid broke from Arabic into English. "Uncivilized? You
use words we do not have. What is your civilization? Do you
know?" The prodigy was screaming. "*Civilization?* How many
millions have been slaughtered in your Great War? You try to
trick us with words we do not have: politics, democracy, law,
republic, civilization. *Do you know where you are?*"

Kippax stepped a pace back. Khalid's black stallion reared its
head as the reins were jerked back. Both heads, the horse's and
the Arab's, had teeth bared. Khalid pulled the horse out into a
dust-kicking traverse of the street and then broke into a gallop
toward the distant gate.

Kippax was left transfixed. The dust settled on him, but he
stared rigidly into the distance until Khalid disappeared in the
palm grove. A dog came from an alley, sniffed, and then licked
Kippax's feet. The touch of tongue and saliva brought him out of
the miasma. He kicked the dog aside and it went howling into
the bazaar. Kippax untethered his horse and painfully climbed
into the saddle. From the direction of the mosque he could hear
the sounds of assembly. He rode unhurriedly out of the town, but
instead of following the path back to the cave, he avoided the
battleground by skirting the palm grove to the north and following the river to the mouth of a ravine. He left the horse free to
drink and took off his cloak and shirt and bathed, then lay back
on the bank. Even from more than a mile away he could hear the
rattle of death. The water and the shaded air balmed his festered
skin. In a while he put on a clean shirt, rinsed the soiled
headdress in the river, beat the dirt from his cloak on the rocks,
and rode back to the ridge and the cave.

Khalid had caught a sand grouse and was kindling a fire over
the ashes of the last one. The gray ash on his fingers was moist
with the blood of the gutted bird. He didn't look up as Kippax
rode in.

Kippax came to the fire. "Twice today you have saved my life."

"It is written," said Khalid, with a trace of humor.

"Perhaps we have the same God."

Khalid blew into the ashes beneath the fresh bed of thornwood, and as the embers sparked into life he settled his eyes on Kippax. "There is one difference between my Book and your Book, El Khibeg. Our God is the same God—without Mary."

It was so: The terror visited on Sabara was uncompromised by that maternal taint found in Christian holiness. Unwittingly Khalid had helped Kippax confirm his apostasy. Kippax watched the fire take hold and felt its warmth displace the mildewed air. His body was repaired and his appetite returned. He left the fire and stood at the cave mouth. The sun was low enough so that its movement could be seen against the line of the bluff; scarlet intercepted by ribbons of smoke rising from the invisible town.

Later, as they ate, Khalid told him, "The Sharif Abdullah escaped. When the battle began he fled in his nightclothes, with his officers. The night before, a man had gone to him and told him the Ikhwan would attack at dawn. He had that man beheaded."

"The Hijazis are finished."

"Tomorrow, El Khibeg, the king will come."

"Then I must see him."

"That also is written."

Kippax laughed and the juice of the bird spilled from his lower lip. But he was careless now, with his new ease of mind.

Just after dawn, they heard sheep passing below. When Kippax looked out, he thought, in the half light, that a shepherd must, unawares, be bringing a large flock to Sabara. Then he heard the cry "al-Saud." A squadron of camels flanked the sheep, keeping them on course, and it was the camel riders who called the approach of the royal caravan. Behind the sheep came baggage camels, some carrying pots and caldrons that clanked like assorted bells. Others were laden with tents and carpets. Then came the caravan's main column, led by Ibn Saud himself—the tallest man on the tallest camel. Kippax gasped at the scale of the caravan and the sight of the majestic warrior at the heart of it; he had forgotten Saud's bearing in the saddle. Behind Saud's camel came the sheikhs and captains of his guard and then, fifteen or twenty abreast, his cavalry, followed by his slaves in scarlet cloaks "al-Saud." The caravan passed on and began to descend to Sabara, green banners streaming in the breeze.

413

Kippax was frustrated by protocol that kept him at bay until noon a day later, when one of Saud's captains came with an invitation to a banquet that evening.

Saud made his camp clear of the flyblown town and battlefield. Sheep were killed for the banquet, but it was not one of the unstinting feasts of Riyadh. The tent was dressed more plainly and the Falstaffian note was missing. With the Ikhwan, even Saud needed to show constraint. Kippax's presence had presented a problem, requiring careful argument. Sultan Ibn Bijad's eyes were nakedly hostile as Kippax entered the tent, but nothing more lethal was possible in the wake of the king's decree. Saud was, however, formal and more wary of Kippax than before.

Kippax extended a long and fluted greeting on behalf of the Great Government, to which Saud responded with reserve. In the way of the court, it took more than an hour for the reserve to be explained. Kippax, squatting next to the king and rolling a ball of greased rice in his palm, had completed a fulsome salute to the military skill of the Ikhwan, citing historical parallels.

Saud inclined his head toward Ibn Bijad and said, "The Ikhwan is the soldier of God. He does not ask anything from us. He will march for three days without food. A man knows he can take a date and freshen his mouth with it. A handful of dates will last him a month. He has a strong camel, his gun or his sword, some bread and a little water, sometimes coffee. Can there ever have been an army that asked for less and gave more?" He ranged the men encircling the gutted feast and they all intoned their agreement. Then he directed his beard at Kippax's chest. "A little with us takes the place of much with others."

Kippax understood.

Saud studied him silently and resumed, "El Khibeg, the Great Government puzzles us. There was another like you, the one called El Aurens. He gave gold and guns to these worthless princes of the Hijaz. You see what befalls them. Gold gets you nothing. The Great Government, and the government of France, both assure us that we have their support. What does that mean? The Sharif Faisal is in Paris. I do not know what you have undertaken with him. I am not there. I have not been asked. I would not go. I will send a message to the Great Government, El Khibeg. You will take it. It is a simple message. Do not give up your friend for your enemy."

All eyes in the tent were on Kippax, most intently Saud's, and from the other side of the food, Khalid's.

"You may trust in me, Your Majesty."

Saud nodded slowly. "I think so, El Khibeg. Tell me, El Khibeg, my brothers here have won a great victory. They wish to continue into the Hijaz. The Hijaz could be ours. It is a good moment for us. What would you advise?"

Ibn Bijad and Ibn 'Aqil were predatory in their attention.

Deferentially, Kippax answered, "I have learned from history, Your Majesty. Very often a decisive battle is not seen as such at the time, only later. What has happened here, Your Majesty, is such a battle. You may have to fight others, but this one is signal. Words will now do greater work than swords. Many men will know in their hearts what banner to follow, what future will come to pass. They have seen the sword of God. It would be my advice, with respect to your own infinite wisdom, Your Majesty, to let this magnificent victory do its work."

The tent was chill with silence.

Saud's right hand stroked his beard; the gold silk threads in his headdress had more luster than his eyes. Then, reflectively, he said, "Three years ago, the Great Government invited me to Basrah. I saw many things there, many things new to me of the world in which we must now live. There was a machine there. I placed my hand inside it, and later I was given a picture which was of my hand without its skin. I could see my bones, the parts of my fingers." He rubbed one hand on top of another, confirming their substance, and looked with asperity at Kippax. "El Khibeg sees like that into my skull."

It was not unalloyed flattery: they understood each other too well. But it was the cementing of an allegiance—a temporal allegiance to take Kippax closer to the spiritual one that now had its breath at his ear.

# 23

## *Jerusalem* ✳ *June 1919*

"Beersheba to Dan!" said Vladimir Jabotinsky. "Beersheba to Dan—*nothing* less!"

"You know where Dan is?" said Koblensky, disliking Jabotinsky's italicized style in conversation. "I have been there. I can tell you where it is. It has Mount Hermon on one side, Upper Galilee to the west—and a swamp between them. A swamp. Impossible to defend, not worth defending. We have to forget about it, for now. And for that matter, the French have taken Dan. I do not want to deal with them. The British are enough."

Jabotinsky glowered and repeated, "Beersheba to Dan. *Nothing less is Israel.*"

What infuriated Koblensky about Jabotinsky was that his will so often got the better of his intellect. Why did he go in for these bouts of bullying? Koblensky and Jabotinsky believed in the same things, and were in many ways similar in nature, but Koblensky had never won Jabotinsky's confidence. Even worse, Jabotinsky drove Koblensky to insolence. He stood up and they were eye to eye, wasting wills on each other again. Very quietly, but adamantly, Koblensky said, "You worry about the map, and I will worry about the guns."

"Guns? We are getting the guns."

"For Jerusalem, maybe. Not for the *really* dangerous places."

"Your place is in Jerusalem."

"No. Not anymore." Koblensky looked away, to the map they had been haggling over, spread on a billiard table. "Not anymore."

"Then you will have to find your own guns."

The room's walls bore several public notices, each in the four languages: English, French, Arabic, and Hebrew. They ranged from a prohibition against demolishing ''any building within a radius of 2500 meters from the Damascus Gate'' to a warning against illegal firearms. The floor began to vibrate: Beneath it was a garage used by Jabotinsky's Jewish Legion.

Suddenly Jabotinsky changed his tone. ''At least the good doctor Weizmann has not turned you into one of his tame dogs. All right, I can help you with the guns. There is a man in Haifa, an Armenian. . . .''

Koblensky knew how much it must have cost Jabotinsky to relent. Even then, he did not wholly trust him because, after all, they were both Russians. But it was best to patch things up before he left. ''Yes, I know that Armenian,'' he said, ''but it would help if you paid him.''

''You didn't get the American money after all? Weizmann thinks the money is for seed corn.'' Jabotinsky's fellowship stretched to a short laugh. ''And in a way it is. *Guns* will be our seed corn.'' He watched Koblensky fold up the map. ''You are calling this place Emek Sarai?''

Koblensky nodded.

''She was a true mother of Israel, Sarah Aaronsohn.''

Koblensky nodded again, this time with a curt, military movement of token politeness before turning to leave. Emotion was the Jewish maggot and he didn't want Jabotinsky to suspect that he was susceptible to it. Emotion compromised the will, they both knew that, but there remained this one agony in Koblensky. Not much was settled in this promised land, not much was clear. Amid all the suspicions, all the doubts, all the aspiration and disillusion, Koblensky had grasped one certainty: He was a soldier again. It had become a vocation.

There were distractions. On the surface it was a beguiling June—hard to set the mind against it, everyone around him seemed softened by it—and Jews were arriving who were patently prosperous, who had come by choice, who were not poor, and who were not fugitives. They reciprocated British manners, they wore British clothes and spoke in British cadences, and sometimes they looked disparagingly at the likes of Koblensky as though, already, he was an anachronism, the surly face in the contented throng. There were discreet glances of that kind when he went to a lawn party on the Mount of Olives. Bron, back from Cairo, had persuaded him to go. It was important, Bron insisted, that when Sir Ronald Storrs gave a party *all* Jewish interests should be represented there, to match all the others.

Tables were set amid the trees, a small garlanded platform had been prepared for a military band, there was a buffet and drinks. The tablecloths were of damask, the twilled linen that tricked the eye with its patterns changing according to light, the damask occasionally caught by a breeze and lifted at the table corners but anchored by heavy Victorian silver. There was the scent of the trees and the sounds of the Jerusalem hills and chairs around the tables that seemed too delicate for officers with the seats of cavalrymen. Koblensky was sorry he had come there, and drifted from the crowd.

Esther Mosseri saw him; he was standing alone under a tree, drinking a glass of lemonade. She saw that at least he had put sandals on; as for the rest, he was making no concessions to style: khaki trousers, not pressed, and a white shirt with rolled-up sleeves. She saw in the rumple of the shirt at his neck one strand of the chain he always wore, a stronger allegiance than any uniform—armor and weakness in one, she thought, with the mean side of her wits.

As he saw her walking to him, he remained morose.

"Why come, if you don't mix?"

He pointed the glass to a distant table, where Bron was engrossed happily. "I came to please Bron. It was a mistake."

"You *could* make an effort, for once." She, too, looked across at Bron in his summer uniform with polished belts. "After all, you should realize, if you do not, how committed Michael is. You know how much he has had to give up for this."

"Perhaps he has not given up enough."

"What do you mean? He's given up a marriage for it."

"Some things are stronger than marriage, and not so easily broken. You said once—it is still true—he is very English."

"What do you want? How much?" Her pertinacity flared up. "You cannot have it both ways. *You* are the reason he has given himself to this. You cannot then turn round and accuse him of not giving enough. Are you asking him to reject his whole past, his whole background? Give him time." She became openly sarcastic. "In time, he will be what you want—your creature."

"I do not think we have the time. He will realize that. I hope so. He is a good man."

"He will miss Tessa."

"It would be better, perhaps, if he missed her more."

"But he does not. You know that." She hesitated, and looked away at Bron again. "Tessa will take care of herself. You know,

418

I expected her to blame you for what has happened. The strange thing is . . .'' She confronted Koblensky again. "It seems that, instead, she admires you. I had a letter from her."

Koblensky looked at her sharply, but her response was to appear disinterestedly conversational. "*Everybody* seems to be here. You would think it was one big happy family. You see that young man over there, in the gray suit—the bearded man? I must introduce you. He's one of Owen Kippax's successes. He's an Arab—I mean, a *real* Arab. Don't be misled by the suit; under that he's still a Bedouin, from far Arabia. Come along. . . . "

She took Koblensky's elbow and steered him back through the trees. He wondered what she meant by "one of Owen Kippax's successes." What had Tessa written? He was compromised, and loathed the feeling.

From some thirty feet away, under shade, Colonel "Bull" Lindquist watched Koblensky led through the groups of people. "That's the chappie—with the Egyptian tart."

Sergeant Quail said, "Not much like the picture we have in the file."

"They never are. Anyway, it's him. Russian."

"He looks as black as a wog."

"More dangerous than a wog. But just give him enough rope . . .''

Khalid Abbas had just broken from the company of two Muslim clerics when Esther reached him. She could not tell, from his expression, whether he was pleased to see her again. He stood on the grass with feet rigidly set, as impassive as a mannequin. Not even as she introduced Koblensky did he show any more life.

Khalid wore glistening brogues; they reminded Koblensky of Meyer Malik. For a minute they struggled through small talk. Koblensky had never heard pure English from the mouth of an Arab and was disconcerted by it.

Then Esther said, "I think you should tell Mr. Koblensky what you once told me—about the great Jewish weakness, cities. He would be interested."

Khalid seemed more grave than provoked, anxious to remain polite in a strained way. "I am sure Mr. Koblensky has better things to do than listen to my theories."

"Our weakness . . .?" said Koblensky quietly.

Esther said, "Khalid—Mr. Abbas—believes that cities emasculate empires—Rome, Athens—and that we have become too much people of the cities . . . while he, in Arabia, is free of corruption."

Koblensky could see the Arab's reluctance and he could equally see Esther's intention. He said, "I think it would be difficult to have a serious conversation on anything here."

"Yes." Khalid nodded, suddenly more natural. "Exactly. Not the place." He looked at Esther. "This is not my place. Not Palestine."

Koblensky laughed. "Not your place—and not ours. Not yet. But we do have one thing in common, Mr. Abbas."

"Oh? What is that?"

Koblensky nodded toward the people beginning to carry buffet plates to their tables. "Our masters. The British. After all, they have us both speaking their language. You know, when I first came here, a few years ago, I came on a train from Damascus. It was the only time I have seen where you come from—and then it was only a glance. I have never seen it properly, but I think I understand what it is like. Not like this. I listen to your voice. They have taught you well. You listen to my voice? I do not speak it as well."

Khalid frowned. "Our masters? I have no masters. You make a mistake. And since you do not understand, I will have to say it, after all. There *is* one very great difference between my people and yours. We never left. We never left what was truly ours. But *you* come back here, after two thousand years, and you think you can reclaim it. You should never have left."

To Esther's astonishment, Koblensky answered with benignity. "That is interesting. You know, I think if we knew each other's tongues, if you spoke Hebrew and I spoke better Arabic than I do, I think even then we could not understand each other more clearly than we do now. At least we can thank the English for *that*."

Khalid's brogues had been planted so firmly in the grass that he seemed a fixture. He searched Koblensky's face as though completely oblivious of their surroundings, and then said, "Yes, we can agree on that, at least."

Koblensky had seen some kind of dissatisfaction in the Arab's eyes—a hunter's eyes they were now, as severe as his barbered beard. It was disappointment at not being able to gauge the caliber of a quarry. Koblensky saw now what Esther had meant by "one of Kippax's successes." He had never known an Arab like this. He maintained his holy facade and said, "*Shalom,*" and then took Esther firmly by an arm and led her free of the crowd as the band began playing its medley of digestive marches.

It was Bron who, months earlier, had led the way through the ravine into the valley. He, Laski, and Koblensky had been scouting the hills of Lower Galilee. He had tracked a stream, a tributary of the Qishon that reached the Mediterranean at Acre Bay, and the stream had taken them to the ravine. Beyond the ravine the valley seemed a secret place. Its northern slope was thick with Tabor oak, descending to the bank of the stream. South of the stream, the valley bed was a shallow, slowly ascending bowl, that part nearest the stream strewn with moss-covered rock and the higher ground covered by scrub and broken rock until the southern slope ended abruptly in a sheer limestone cliff. Bron seemed to see it as a fated gift, a natural end to their quest and the beginning of their new lives. Water was the resource of the valley, and it was this argument that had prevailed with Koblensky, that there was ample water for a settlement. But Koblensky had misgivings—then, when they had first ridden into the valley, and now, each time they came back to it in a truck. The place was as vulnerable as it was entrancing.

The only habitation so far was a long barrack hut, removed from a derelict Turkish camp and reassembled. It served as temporary living quarters, workshop, and storehouse. In one corner was Bron's office, where he was designing a small dam that would irrigate the valley bed. Bron attacked this project with an almost innocent zeal. "Water before everything," he kept telling them, but that was not their priority.

The summer heat seemed too oppressive for even the birds. One lone pied kingfisher skimmed the water. Koblensky and Laski sat on the south bank wearing only shorts, with their legs in the water. Bron remained with his blueprints.

The metal of his pendant chain was hot against Koblensky's chest, but he did not move it. "One way in, one way out," he said, looking back to the ravine.

"That's always bothered me," said Laski.

"Yes," said Koblensky, slipping down the bank into the water. "Either a trap or a fortress—our Masada." His hard feet pushed off flint and he swam in a crawl out to the north bank and the shade of the oaks, and lay with only his head clear of the water. Laski's belly hung over his shorts. Koblensky remembered his first glimpse of that deceptive gut. There was not a

slack muscle in Laski, not a negligent sense, no weakness at all.
Laski was the only true confederate he had.

The ravine funneled sound like a horn; they heard the truck
coming long before they saw it. By the time it reached the hut,
they had walked back.

Bron was the last to hear it. He came out like a disturbed
professor, a hand shading his eyes as he saw the truck bouncing
in its own dust. "Your cossacks," he said.

Koblensky nodded. "But do not let them hear you call them
that."

Two figures, hardly more than boys, jumped from the cab and
spoke to Koblensky in Russian. The vehicle was an old British
Ford, badly down on its springs and smelling of scorched rubber.
Bron walked to the side of the truck, where gray sacks bulged
through gaps in the boards. He felt one of the sacks and turned to
Koblensky. "Cement? Where did you find cement?"

"In Haifa."

"Cement is scarcer than timber."

Laski put a hand on Bron's shoulder. "Everything has its
price."

Koblensky said, "You said you would need cement."

"Yes . . ." said Bron, still tethered by Laski's grip, "but
hardly yet."

"Take what you can *when* you can," said Laski, looking
ambiguously at Koblensky.

Koblensky spoke again in Russian to the youths. They climbed
back into the truck, and driving it around to the storeroom at the
rear, began to unload the sacks. Each one was carried with care,
and stacked with the precision of fruit in a window display. At
the end, the youths were dripping wet. They rejoined Koblensky
in the dormitory and he gave them tea from a samovar—hot
sugared tea with lemon in heavy British china—and the three of
them reached a loud conviviality that Bron had never heard in
Koblensky. He heard it from the other side of a door, and had an
uncomfortable sense of being excluded.

Laski, sitting next to Bron's table with his bare feet resting on
the sill of an open window, said, "Good boys, those two. We
need another score like them."

"Yes." Bron nodded, feeling his annoyance to have been
petty. "Yes, anything that can make Asa laugh."

*   *   *

422

Once, in Cairo, Esther Mosseri had found herself at a dinner table where the conversation was regularly punctuated by a man whose larynx lost its grip on certain words; each time this happened he had to pump the word clear with a strident, gusting breath. This comical distress was less comical when she realized that the man was the old khedive, puppet monarch of Egypt, intended victim of her first lover, and that the affliction was the result of his bullet. She had looked at the khedive then with the dread of failed conspiracy. Alive, he was more fearful to her than the memory of Professor Leo Solomon dead with his lungs full of rose water. The rattle in the throat was death's complaint at being mocked, as the old despot's survival had mocked and haunted her.

She had the same dread now, looking into the face of ''Bull'' Lindquist, His Majesty's interrogator. The guttural harshness of Lindquist's voice was a reminder of the khedive and a nightmare in substance; Lindquist was a name remembered from Cairo, but an enemy never before confronted.

''You have no legitimate employment here,'' he said.

''I hoped to work at the Museum of Antiquities, now that it is open again.''

''Let's not waste time, shall we?''

''I worked with Major Kippax.''

''Ah, yes.'' Lindquist held up a manila file but kept it closed. ''He passed this on to me. I've read it very carefully. It goes back a long way—*quite* a long way.''

''I came here at your request. You speak as though I am accused of something.''

''Major Kippax asked me to deal with this matter. I'm sure he would have done so personally, but you see, he's still in London. Miss Mosseri, you realize how many people there are here who think they can take the law into their own hands? We have a thankless task, I can tell you. But we intend to be the *only* army here. The same people who are asking for our protection are busy arming themselves behind our backs. Now . . .'' Lindquist put the file to rest and leaned across the desk. ''There was a meeting at Petah Tikva.'' He hesitated and looked down to refer to a note. ''The Jews formed an organization—Acdut, something or other. Ostensibly a trade union. What were *you* doing there?''

''There was nothing illegal about that meeting. Nothing was done to conceal it.''

"Jabotinsky spoke—Vladimir Jabotinsky. I understand that even among Jews he is considered an extremist."

"He believes there will be pogroms here against the Jews, as do other Russians. And that your army will not lift a finger to stop it."

"There will be no pogroms in Palestine. And we are not the Russian Army. I think you know what concerns me. Not only Jabotinsky. You know Koblensky, another Russian. I believe, as a matter of fact, that you know him quite well."

Lindquist, she saw, had a mind as vulgar as his voice. She did not respond.

Lindquist sighed and settled back into his chair. It was an ancient swivel chair on casters, which complained with every movement. "You have no legitimate status here. I believe Major Kippax made it clear to you that your continued residence here is at our discretion. The fact is, Miss Mosseri, I believe you are more a liability than an asset to us. I believe you would be better in Cairo; they know how to handle your kind there."

"My *kind?*"

"Whores. Whatever else you are, you are a whore. A whore—and a Jew."

The specter of the khedive dissolved, losing its intimidation. She stood up, leaned across the table, and spat into his face. Tension had concentrated her saliva. It left a sour tincture from his hairline to his cheek. He made no move to wipe it. One droplet disappeared into his gray mustache. He seemed to want to wait to taste it; then his upper lip tightened and nothing of her reached it. The chair squealed before he spoke. He looked up—she was still braced with aggression over the desk—and he said quietly, as though to himself, "Jew juice . . . goat juice would be sweeter." Then he laughed the rattling khedive laugh and the chair squealed again. Terminally he said, "Of course, if there is something you would like to tell us, something that might encourage a change of heart . . ." Only then did he pull out a handkerchief.

Each evening Koblensky sat with the two Russians, drinking tea and exchanging tales. It was a side of Koblensky that Bron had never seen—a nostalgia for his youth, his place, his tongue. It reassured Bron; the valley's magic was taking hold. Bron dreamed clearly in his head what he was beginning to draw on his plans. At the moment it might be just a rude foothold, but with crops developed, the place could become virtually self-sufficient, and beyond that, with power tapped from the water, a sizable town, a showpiece that would prove that where there was water there could be not only life but a populous civilization. Perhaps, after all, it was a dream above politics. It seemed so. They had pulled out a trestle from his office and sat under a porch that the youths had put up in one afternoon. Laski and Koblensky were in shorts, the Russians in undershirts and pajamalike trousers from the sook in Haifa, and Bron in his army tropicals—still believing (Koblensky joked) that neatness was the first condition of civilization. They ate bread, goat's cheese, and radishes: it was a banquet.

Laski was the first to be distracted. He leaned away from the table, looking over a shoulder to the water and the ravine. Koblensky followed his movement. The Russians were still laughing and Bron was slicing cheese into neat cubes.

"Listen," said Laski.

The Russians subsided and they all fell quiet.

Then Koblensky looked at Laski. "Trucks—more than one."

Koblensky and Laski stood up at the same time and jumped from the duckboards to the dust. In the evening light the ravine was already in shadow; it was another half minute before the trucks crossed into clear ground, and then they were indistinct in driven dust.

"At least three," said Laski.

"More cement?" said Bron, as flippant as he was curious.

"No," said Laski, "no more cement." He had lost all his congeniality. He looked at Koblensky.

Koblensky spoke quickly in Russian to the youths. They ran to the rear, to their own truck and the storeroom.

At last alert, Bron said, "Our trucks—*army* trucks. What on earth . . .?" But one look at Koblensky stilled the question.

The trucks closed on them with more than casual speed. When they braked, it was abrasive enough to shower the hut with grit.

Koblensky and Laski stood their ground impassively. Bron dusted his shoulders, reaffirming his captain's crests on the epaulets.

The first figure to materialize from the inundation was "Bull" Lindquist, with swagger stick, followed by Sergeant Quail and then a phalanx of troopers. Lindquist ignored Koblensky and Laski and said, "Captain Bron? I'm sorry to come in this manner. But under the circumstances . . ."

425

"Colonel?"

"I would like your permission to search the premises."

"The *premises?*" Bron was terse. "Not very extensive, Colonel." He looked aside. Koblensky and Laski made no response. "I have no idea what this can be about, Colonel. Of course, it's an intrusion, but go ahead. I can't imagine . . ."

Koblensky laughed. "Go ahead, Colonel."

"*Bayonets?*" said Bron suddenly. "Are you out of your mind, Colonel?" More troopers had descended from the second and third trucks, carrying Lee Enfields with fixed bayonets. "What did you expect to find here—an organized insurgency?"

Lindquist was annoyed. "I think it better, Captain, if you reserve comment. I'm sure these two gentlemen here—Koblensky and Laski, isn't it?—I'm sure they can enlighten you."

There was shouting from the rear of the hut, and a squad of troopers appeared, pushing ahead of them the two Russians. "These blokes were in the storeroom, sir."

Lindquist nodded to Quail. "Take care of Koblensky and Laski." He directed other soldiers to the storeroom, then said, "Captain Bron, I think you and I should take a look at this together."

Inside the storeroom a corporal was jabbing sacks of cement with a bayonet. The cement spilled from ruptures, all over the floor.

"What on earth do you think—" said Bron, but his protest was cut short by the sound of metal on metal.

"Here, sir—I think we have it."

"Tell the sergeant to bring Koblensky and Laski here," said Lindquist. "Just as I thought." He waited for the corporal to pull the sack clear of the others. The bayonet cleaved it from top to bottom. As the cement ran out, it left exposed something bulky wrapped in oiled rags. The corporal bent down and prized apart the rags, as Koblensky and Laski were brought through the door.

Bron looked down on three rifles—two Lee Enfields and an older Turkish model. He turned on Koblensky. "Guns! *Why?* What business have we with guns?"

Koblensky spoke with stretched patience. "Who else will arm us if we do not arm ourselves?"

Laski, in his faint English accent, said, "Your colonel here, he's a Jew-baiter. He knows why we want the guns, don't you, Colonel? We know all about you, Colonel."

426

Before Laski could say another word, Lindquist raised his swagger stick and cut it across Laski's face. Koblensky lunged at Lindquist, but Quail and two troopers jumped on him and held him.

Lindquist hit Laski again, this time cutting his brow. Then, moving as though in a drill, he put the swagger stick under his left arm and turned to Bron, speaking with consoling mildness. "It's all right, Captain. I'm quite sure that you are not personally implicated."

"Not *implicated?*" Bron stared beyond Lindquist at Laski's bloody face. "Not implicated? I am damned well implicated—by *this.*" He tore at the neck of his tunic and ripped it from him, popping the gilt buttons.

"Have it as you wish, Captain. I understand you are soon to be released from the army. Better to go that way, I should have thought. I'm sure Major Kippax would prefer it that way, Captain."

"Kippax?" Bron spoke as though waking. "Kippax is behind this?"

Koblensky said, "Of course."

"As I said, Captain," persisted Lindquist, "shall we stick to the formalities?"

Bron threw his tunic into the dust. "*To hell with your formalities!*" He looked at Koblensky. "I'm sorry. I should have . . . ." But then he turned on Lindquist again. "You are a disgrace to the uniform. I shall make a full report on you, Colonel, you can be sure."

Lindquist nodded contemptuously. "I am sure you will, *Captain.* I am sure you will."

More sacks were being ripped open, and more guns being found. Lindquist directed the removal of Koblensky and Laski. Bron followed them, kicking the tunic away as he went.

The two Russian youths had been put into a truck. They were the least animated of anyone. They sat looking out on the troopers with the resignation of seasoned delinquents. Koblensky, being pushed along by Quail, was the only one to understand why his "cossacks" had fallen so passive. There was grim humor in it, as personal to the three of them as a reminiscence. This was a tyranny of sorts. It seemed malign, at least in the persons of Lindquist and Quail. But as tyrannies went, to those acquainted with tyrannies, it was unconvincing. It had the defect of reluctance. Though directed with purpose, the troopers had about them an almost apologetic manner, an underlying decency that Lindquist could never eradicate. Koblensky saw that his protégés knew that. Laski and Bron did not. A greater tyranny would have made a better enemy; even so, Koblensky knew now that before they faced any other enemy, they would have to defeat this one.

In what little light was left, Bron stood apart, looking down to the river. At some time lost in the past, the valley had been inhabited; in the gorge Bron had found traces of a paved road from a few quartered stones dispersed in the gravel, others in the riverbed. As well as by the erosion of time and weather, the stones had one surface burnished by the passage of feet and wheels. There was no other evidence so far that could fix the life span of the valley's settlement. The stones were a superficial clue, but the only clue there was; the valley had covered all other traces. Had Romans fallen on Jews, or Jews on Romans? Crusaders on Arabs? Bron could not know. The river was separate, coming from a place above and going untapped to the bay beyond, and yet it carried the valley's promise of renewal. The sound of the water began to prevail over the martial voices in Bron's mind, and steadied him. Turning back to the herded men, he knew that he, too, was a fugitive now. It gave him an unfamiliar strength: He was a fugitive, but he had stopped running. That was the point of being here. Nothing had ended; it was just beginning. There could never be any refuge for any of them but this land. That was the point. He retained the image of the valley in the dying light, as it was, the better to know how it would be.

All three of them—Koblensky, Laski, and Bron—sat side by side flanked by guards in the back of Lindquist's truck going into the night. Bron had insisted on bathing Laski's face before they left. The wordless complicity among them affected even Koblensky. He was confirmed in his ruling instinct, the instinct that had brought him so far, that had guided his passage from Russia to this valley they had named for Sarah: A land had to be taken. It was never given.

# Historical Note

This novel is enacted over the few years that largely determined today's map of the Middle East. At this time—1916 to 1919—the oil wealth of Saudi Arabia was undiscovered. Western interests in the Middle East's oil played a negligible part in how the post-World War I map was arranged. Far more decisive was control of the Suez Canal, crucial artery of the British Empire. In 1917, through the Balfour Declaration, the British agreed with leading Zionists that a new national home for the Jews should be established in Palestine, though Palestine was then still a part of the Turkish Ottoman Empire. Earlier and secret pledges given to the Arabs were incompatible with the promise made to the Jews.

The defeat of Turkey (along with her ally Germany) in 1918 was the end of the Ottoman Empire. The British and French then attempted to satisfy their own interests, as victors in the war, while obligated by the territorial promises made to the Jews and Arabs. The modern states of Syria, Iraq, Saudi Arabia, and Israel were conceived from a tangle of diplomatic expediency, deception, improvisation, and aggression. In the end, all four were established independently, not from honored promises but after bloodshed. In history books, Europe dominates accounts of the First World War—except for the legendary diversion of Lawrence of Arabia, much embroidered. Yet no part of the past more critically disturbs the present than the years of this story.

Here is a brief chronology of the principal events that form the background:

**Basel, Switzerland, August 1903:** At the sixth Zionist Congress, the "father" of Zionism, Theodor Herzl, advances a British proposal for Jewish settlement in Uganda, then a part of British East Africa. In May, a savage pogrom had destroyed more than 1,500 Jewish homes in Kishinev, southern Russia. With this pressure to find a refuge for persecuted Jews, Herzl favors the Ugandan idea as an expedient, though not as an alternative to a Jewish home in Palestine. A majority of Zionists oppose Herzl and the Ugandan idea quietly dies.

**Manchester, England, January 1906:** Chaim Weizmann, a Russian-born Zionist working in Manchester as a university chemist, meets Arthur James Balfour, parliamentary leader of the British Conservative party, and explains the Jewish claim to Palestine.

**Cairo, April 1914:** The Amir Abdullah, second son of Hussein, the grand sharif of Mecca and king of the Hashemite tribe, meets British officials who seek assurance that if Turkey, then the imperial power in the Hashemite lands, declares war on Great Britain, Hussein will join the British cause. As well as including the holy cities of Mecca and Medina, the Hashemites' ancestral domain covered most of the strategically critical eastern coast of the Red Sea, the area known as the Hijaz, which overlooks the access to the Suez Canal. This proposal is consummated in a secret meeting in October—one month before Turkey joins the side of Germany in World War I.

**Cairo, December 1914:** "Temporary Lieutenant-Interpreter" T. E. Lawrence, former archaeologist and British spy, arrives to work for the British military command in Egypt.

**Riyadh, Arabia, January 1915:** Captain William Henry Shakespear concludes an agreement with King Ibn Saud, recognizing Saud's sovereignty over central and eastern Arabia, under tacit British protection. Shakespear is subsequently killed while with Saud's army in a battle with Ibn Rashid, whose tribe disputed Saud's territory and was backed by the Turks.

**Gallipoli, April 1915:** Australian, New Zealand, and other Allied forces land on this Turkish peninsula, hoping to cut off Turkish access to the Mediterranean and draw Turkish troops from Syria. The landings gain the barest of footholds and after heavy losses are abandoned in December.

**Cairo, February 1916:** The Arab Bureau, a political and military intelligence agency with wide-ranging scope, begins operations under the direction of Commander David Hogarth, a former Oxford academic, Orientalist, and mentor of Lawrence, who also joins the bureau.

**The Hijaz (Red Sea littoral), August 1916:** The British promise of Arab independence (free of thralldom to either the Turkish, British, or French empire) is tied to Grand Sharif Hussein's uprising against the Turks, which now gets under way, to be supported by Arab partisans under British command, including those led by Lawrence. Hussein's inclination to become "King of the Arabs" antagonizes, among others, Ibn Saud.

**London, November 1916:** British military intelligence assesses a detailed report on Turkish dispositions in Palestine brought to London by a Jewish agronomist named Aaron Aaronsohn, whose "NILI" spy network is enlisted by the British—the first and only Jewish-Palestinian collaboration with British Intelligence during the war. A note on Aaronsohn in the files of the Foreign Office says: "He belongs to a class of Jews who are mostly very intelligent."

**Akaba, July 1917:** This vital Red Sea port falls to Arab forces led by Lawrence; the Turks are driven from virtually the entire Hijaz.

**Zichron Jaacov, September–October 1917:** The Turks discover and wipe out the "NILI" network at its source. Aaronsohn's sister Sarah attempts suicide after torture, and subsequently dies.

**Sinai, October 1917:** General Allenby's army launches its invasion of Palestine.

**London, November 1917:** The Balfour Declaration pledges the establishment of a "Jewish national home" in Palestine.

**The Yarmuk River gorge, Palestine, November 1917:** Lawrence fails to blow up a vital rail bridge linking Damascus with the Turkish front in Palestine. Days later, at one of his desert bases, Azrak, Lawrence, depressed by failure, probably devises masochistic punishment for himself at the hands of an Arab accomplice, later elevates this into a mythical capture and torture by Turks at the town of Deraa.

**Jerusalem, December 1917:** Allenby occupies Jerusalem without a battle, but with only part of Palestine under British control, halts his campaign for the winter. British control of Palestine begins, to endure until 1948.

**Damascus, October 1918:** Lawrence, with his Arab mercenaries, enters Damascus, followed three days later by Allenby. This marks the end of Ottoman rule over the Arabs. (A month later, World War I ends.) Faisal, Lawrence's Hashemite companion in war, believes the occupation of Damascus to be the dawn of Arab independence. Syria was occupied and ruled by France until 1946.

**Palestine, April–October 1919:** For the first time, Palestine Jews demand the right to bear arms "for the defense of the Land and the Hebrew community in it." Instead, the British insist on Jewish *dis*armament. The 5,000-strong Jewish Legion, recruited by the Zionist Vladimir Jabotinsky to fight in Palestine alongside the British, is kept from defending Jewish communities against threatened attacks by Arabs. (In 1920, Jabotinsky is sentenced to fifteen years imprisonment for organizing armed Jewish resistance; a year later he is released and subsequently leads the extremist Zionist Revisionist party—from exile. During the 1940s, armed Jewish resistance against the British in Palestine by the Stern Gang and the Irgun followed the militant inspiration of Jabotinsky.)

**Turaba, Arabia, May 1919:** An elaborately armed and British-trained Hashemite army of 5,000 is virtually liquidated by little more than a thousand primitively equipped members of the Ikhwan, Ibn Saud's religious enforcers. Hashemite prestige and security never recover. (By 1926, Ibn Saud has driven the Hashemites from their homeland, including Mecca, and becomes king of the new nation, Saudi Arabia.)

## ABOUT THE AUTHOR

Clive Irving has had an illustrious career in journalism. He was formerly the Managing Editor of the London Sunday Times, head of Public Affairs for ITV's (commercial television) London Weekend Television, an editorial consultant for McCalls Magazine, and founding editor of Newsday's Sunday Magazine.

Writing a series of television documentaries and a book about the history of Persia led Clive Irving to his interest in British colonialism in the Middle East. He chose this period as the setting for PROMISE THE EARTH because it was so crucial to his understanding of the struggle to establish a Jewish homeland and, ultimately, to an understanding of the current complexities in the Middle East. PROMISE THE EARTH is his second novel. Mr. Irving divides his time between Toronto and Sag Harbor, New York.